WICKED!

ume 1

Bagley Hall, an independent school crammed
h the children of the rich and famous,
ırismatic headmaster, Hengist Brett-Taylor,
tches a plan to share his well-funded facilities
h Larkminster comprehensive. His reasons for
ing so are purely financial, but he is also
couraged by the opportunities the scheme gives
n for frequent meetings with Janna Curtis, the
namic new head of Larks, who has been drafted
to save the fast-sinking school from closure.

nna is young, pretty, enthusiastic and vastly
ave—and she will do anything to rescue her
:moralized, run-down and cash-strapped school.
either parents nor staff of either school are too
:en on this radical move. For the students,
)wever, it offers great opportunities for further
yous mayhem.

nna, meanwhile, finds herself fatally drawn to
Hengist. Will she emerge with her heart and her
school intact?

WICKED!

Volume 1

Jilly Cooper

WINDSOR
PARAGON

First published 2006
by
Bantam Press
This Large Print edition published 2007
by
BBC Audiobooks Ltd by arrangement with
Transworld Publishers

Hardcover ISBN: 978 1 405 61648 5
Softcover   ISBN: 978 1 405 61649 2

The author and publishers are grateful for permission to quote
from 'Three Little Birds', Words and music by Bob Marley. ©
Copyright 1977 Blue Mountain Music Limited. Used by
permission of Music Sales Limited. All Rights Reserved.
International Copyright Secured.
British Library Cataloguing in Publication Data available

Printed and bound in Great Britain by
Antony Rowe Ltd., Chippenham, Wiltshire

This book is dedicated with love and admiration to
two great headmistresses, Virginia Frayer and
Katherine Eckersley, and also in loving memory of
the Angel School, Islington, and
Village High School, Derby

CAST OF CHARACTERS

ADELE   Single mother who teaches geography at Larkminster Comprehensive (otherwise known as Larks).

PARIS ALVASTON   Larks pupil and icon. Founder member of the notorious Wolf Pack.

ANATOLE   Bagley Hall pupil and beguiling son of the Russian Minister of Affaires.

RUFUS ANDERSON   Brilliant and eccentric head of geography at Bagley Hall. Henpecked father of two, liable to leave coursework on trains.

SHEENA ANDERSON   Rufus's concupiscent careerist wife—the main reason Rufus hasn't been given a house at Bagley Hall.

MRS AXFORD   Chief caterer at Bagley Hall.

MISS BASKET   A menopausal misfit who teaches geography at Larks.

BEA FROM THE BEEB	A researcher at the Teaching Awards.
DORA BELVEDON	Bagley Hall new girl. Determined to support her pony and her chocolate Labrador by flogging school scandal to the tabloids.
DICKY BELVEDON	Dora's equally resourceful twin brother who runs his own school shop at Bagley Hall selling booze and fags.
LADY BELVEDON (ANTHEA)	Dicky and Dora's young, very pretty, very spoilt mother. A Violet Elizabeth Bottox, drastically impoverished by widowhood, and determined to hunt for a rich new husband, unobserved by her beady son and daughter.
JUPITER BELVEDON	Dora and Dicky's machiavellian eldest brother, chairman of the governors at Bagley Hall, Tory MP for Larkminster, and tipped to take over the party leadership.

HANNA BELVEDON	Jupiter's lovely and loving wife, a painter.
SOPHY BELVEDON	An English teacher of splendid proportions and great charm. Ian and Patience Cartwright's daughter, and wife of Jupiter Belvedon's younger brother, Alizarin.
DULCIE BELVEDON	Adorable and self-willed daughter of Sophy and Alizarin.
SIR HUGO BETTS	Governor of Larks who sleeps through most meetings.
JAMES BENSON	An extremely smooth private doctor.
THE BISHOP OF LARKMINSTER	A governor of Bagley Hall.
GORDON BLENCHLEY	The unsavoury care manager of Oaktree Court, Paris Alvaston's children's home.
HENGIST BRETT-TAYLOR	Hugely charismatic headmaster of Bagley Hall.
SALLY BRETT-TAYLOR	Hengist's wife, classic beauty and jolly good sort, hugely

	contributory towards Hengist's success.
ORIANA BRETT-TAYLOR	Hengist and Sally's daughter, a much admired BBC foreign correspondent.
WALLY BRISTOW	Stalwart site manager at Larks.
GENERAL BROADSTAIRS	Lord Lieutenant of Larkshire and governor of Bagley Hall.
'BOFFIN' BROOKS	The cleverest boy at Bagley Hall, a humourless prig.
SIR GORDON BROOKS	Boffin's father, a thrusting captain of industry.
ALEX BRUCE	Deputy head of Bagley Hall, nicknamed Mr Fussy.
POPPET BRUCE	His dreadful wife, who teaches RE. An acronymphomaniac, determined to impose total political correctness on Bagley Hall.
CHARISMA BRUCE	Alex and Poppet's severely gifted daughter.
MARIA CAMBOLA	Larks's splendidly flamboyant head of music.

RUPERT CAMPBELL-BLACK	Former showjumping champion and Tory Minister for Sport. Now leading owner/trainer, and director of Venturer, the local ITV station. Despite being as bloody-minded as he is beautiful, Rupert is still Nirvana for most women.
TAGGIE CAMPBELL-BLACK	His adored wife—an angel.
XAVIER CAMPBELL-BLACK	Bagley Hall pupil and Rupert and Taggie's adopted Colombian son, who has hit moody adolescence head-on.
BIANCA CAMPBELL-BLACK	Xavier's ravishingly pretty, sunny-natured younger sister, also adopted and Colombian.
IAN CARTWRIGHT	Former commanding officer of a tank regiment, now bursar at Bagley Hall.
PATIENCE CARTWRIGHT	Ian's loyal wife—a trooper who teaches riding and runs the stables at Bagley.
MRS CHALFORD	Head of history at Larks. A

self-important bossy boots who likes to be referred to as 'Chally'.

TARQUIN COURTNEY	Charismatic captain of rugger at Bagley Hall.
ALISON COX	Sally Brett-Taylor's housekeeper, known as 'Coxie'.
JANNA CURTIS	Larks's very young, Yorkshire-born headmistress.
P.C. CUTHBERT	A zero-tolerant police constable, determined to impose order on Larks.
DANIJELA	Larks pupil from Bosnia.
DANNY	Larks pupil from Ireland.
EMLYN DAVIES	A former Welsh rugby international, known as Attila the Hunk, who teaches history at Bagley Hall and coaches the rugger fifteens to serial victory.
DEBBIE	Ace cook at Larks.
ARTIE DEVERELL	Head of modern languages at Bagley Hall.

ASHTON DOUGLAS The sinister, lisping Chief Executive Officer of S and C Services, the private company brought in by the Government to supervise education in Larkshire.

ENID Lachrymose librarian at Larks.

PRIMROSE DUDDON Earnest, noble-browed, ample-breasted form prefect at Bagley Hall.

VICKY FAIRCHILD Two-faced but both of them extremely pretty. Cures truancy at Larks overnight when Janna Curtis appoints her as head of drama.

JASON FENTON Larks's deputy head of drama, known as Goldilocks.

PIERS FLEMING Wayward head of English at Bagley Hall.

JOHNNIE FOWLER Good-looking Larks hellraiser; BNP supporter; persistent truant.

LANDO FRANCE-LYNCH Master of the Bagley Beagles, whose sparse intellect is compensated for by dazzling all-round athletic and equestrian ability.

DAISY
FRANCE-LYNCH   His sweet mother, a painter,
                      wife of Ricky France-Lynch,
                      former England polo
                      captain.

FREDDIE   A waiter at La Perdrix d'Or
                      restaurant.

CHIEF INSPECTOR
TIMOTHY GABLECROSS
                      A wise, kind and extremely
                      clever
                      policeman.

MAGS GABLECROSS   The wise, kind wife of the
                      Chief Inspector, part-time
                      modern languages teacher at
                      Larks.

GLORIA   PE teacher at Larks not
                      given to hiding her physical
                      lights under bushels.

THEO GRAHAM   Head of classics at Bagley
                      Hall, an outwardly crusty old
                      bachelor with a heart of gold.
                      Takes out his hearing aid on
                      Speech Day.

GILLIAN GRIMSTON   Head of Searston Abbey, an
                      extremely successful
                      Larkminster grant-

maintained school for girls.

LILY HAMILTON — Aunt of Jupiter, Dicky and Dora Belvedon. A merry, very youthful octogenarian and Janna Curtis's next-door neighbour in the village of Wilmington.

DAME HERMIONE HAREFIELD — World famous diva, seriously tiresome, brings out the Crippen in all.

WADE HARGREAVES — An unexpectedly humane Ofsted Inspector.

DENZIL HARPER — Head of PE at Bagley Hall.

UNCLE HARLEY — Jamaican drugs dealer, lives on and off with Feral Jackson's mother.

SIR DAVID 'HATCHET' HAWKLEY — Headmaster of Fleetley, illustrious classical scholar. Later Lord Hawkley.

LADY HAWKLEY (HELEN) — A nervy beauty. Having numbered Rupert Campbell-Black and Roberto Rannaldini among her former husbands, Helen hopes marriage to David

	Hawkley means calmer waters.
Rod Hyde	An awful autocrat, headmaster of St James's, a highly successful Larkminster grant-maintained school, known as St Jimmy's.
'Skunk' Illingworth	Deputy head of science at Larks.
'Feral' Jackson	Larks's leading truant, Paris Alvaston's best friend and founder member of the Wolf Pack. Afro-Caribbean, beautiful beyond belief, seriously dyslexic, and a natural athlete.
Nancy Jackson	Feral's mother, a heroin addict.
Jessamy	A teaching assistant at Larks.
Jessica	Hengist Brett-Taylor's stunning second secretary, a typomaniac.
Joan Johnson	Head of science at Bagley Hall, also in charge of Boudicca, the only girls' house. Nicknamed 'No-Joke

Joan' because of a total lack of humour.

MRS KAMANI	Long-suffering owner of Larks's nearest newsagent's.
KATA	Larks pupil and wistful asylum-seeker from Kosovo.
AYSHA KHAN	One of Larks's few achievers. Destined for an arranged marriage in Pakistan.
RASCHID KHAN	Aysha's bullying father.
MRS KHAN	Aysha's bullied but surprisingly brave mother.
RUSSELL LAMBERT	Ponderous chairman both of Larks's governors and Larkminster planning committee.
LANCE	An understandably terrified newly qualified Larks history teacher.
AMBER LLOYD-FOXE	Minxy founder member of the 'Bagley Babes', otherwise known as the 'Three Disgraces'.
BILLY LLOYD-FOXE	Amber's father, an ex-Olympic showjumper, now a presenter for the BBC.

JANEY LLOYD-FOXE	His unprincipled journalist wife.
JUNIOR LLOYD-FOXE	Amber's merry, racing-mad twin brother.
LYDIA	Another understandably terrified newly qualified Larks English teacher.
LUBEMIR	Albanian asylum-seeker and safe-breaker, which makes him an extremely useful partner-in-crime to Cosmo Rannaldini.
MR MATES	Larks science master, almost as old as Archimedes.
KITTEN MEADOWS	Larks pupil and sassy, hell-cat girlfriend of Johnnie Fowler.
JOE MEAKIN	Under-master in Alex Bruce's house at Bagley Hall.
ROWAN MERTON	School secretary at Larks.
MRS MILLS	A jolly member of Ofsted.
MISS MISERDEN	Old biddy endlessly complaining about Larks misbehaviour.

TEDDY MURRAY	Randal Stancombe's foreman.
NADINE	Paris Alvaston's social worker.
MARTIN 'MONSTER' NORMAN	Larks pupil. Overweight bully and coward.
'STORMIN'' NORMAN	Larks parent governor and Monster's mother, given to storming into Larks and punching anyone who crosses her ewe lamb.
MISS PAINSWICK	Hengist Brett-Taylor's besotted and ferociously efficient secretary.
CINDY PAYNE	Deceptively cosy New Labour county councillor in charge of education.
KYLIE ROSE PECK	Sweet-natured Larks pupil and member of the Wolf Pack. So eternally up the duff, she'll soon qualify for a free tower block.
CHANTAL PECK	Kylie Rose's mother and also a parent governor at Larks.
CAMERON PECK	Kylie Rose's baby son.

GANYMEDE	Another baby son of Kylie Rose.
COLIN 'COL' PETERS	Editor of the *Larkminster Gazette*. A big, nasty toad in a small pond.
PHIL PIERCE	Head of science at Larks, loved by the children and a great supporter of Janna Curtis.
MIKE PITTS	Larks's deputy head, furious the head's job has been given to Janna Curtis.
COSMO RANNALDINI	Dame Hermione's son and Bagley Hall warlord, with a pop group called the Cosmonaughties and the same lethal sex appeal as his father, the great conductor Roberto Rannaldini.
DESMOND REYNOLDS	Smooth Larkminster estate agent known as 'Des Res'.
ROCKY	Larks pupil and ungentle giant until the Ritalin kicks in.
BIFFO RUDGE	Head of maths at Bagley Hall, ex-rowing Blue, who frequently rides his bike into

the River Fleet while coaching the school eight.

ROBBIE RUSHTON   Larks's incurably lazy, left-wing head of geography.

CARA SHARPE   Larks's fearsome head of English and drama.

'SATAN' SIMMONS   Larks bully and best friend of Monster Norman.

SMART   Stalwart Bagley Hall rugger player.

PEARL SMITH   Another Larks hell-cat, member of the Wolf Pack.

MISS SPICER   An unfazed member of Ofsted.

SAM SPINK   Bossy-boots union representative at Larks.

SOLLY
THE UNDERTAKER   Governor at Larks.

RANDAL STANCOMBE   Handsome Randal, definitely Mr Dicey rather than Mr Darcy, a wildly successful property developer. One of his private estates of desirable residences, Cavendish Plaza, sits uncomfortably close to

Larks.

JADE STANCOMBE — Randal's daughter, sharp-clawed glamourpuss and Bagley Babe.

MISS SWEET — Beleaguered under-matron at Boudicca, reluctantly put in charge of Bagley's sex education.

CRISPIN THOMAS — Incurably greedy deputy director of S and C Services.

TRAFFORD — An unspeakably scrofulous but highly successful artist.

GRANT TYLER — An electronics giant.

MISS UGLOW — Larks RE teacher.

PETE WAINWRIGHT — Genial under-manager at Larkminster Rovers, the local second division football club.

BERTIE WALLACE — Raffish co-owner of Gafellyn Castle in Wales.

RUTH WALTON — A ravishing adventuress, voted on to Bagley Hall's board of governors to ensure full houses at meetings.

MILLY WALTON — The third Bagley Babe,

charming and emollient but overshadowed by her gorgeous mother.

THE HON.
JACK WATERLANE   Bagley Hall thicko, captain of the Chinless Wanderers.

LORD WATERLANE   Jack's father, who shares his son's fondness for rough trade.

STEWART
'STEW' WILBY   Powerful and visionary headmaster of Redfords, Janna Curtis's former school in the West Riding. Also Janna's former lover.

SPOTTY WILKINS   Bagley Hall pupil.

DAFYDD WILLIAMS   Sometime builder and piss artist.

'GRAFFI' WILLIAMS   Dafydd's son, and captivating, conniving fifth member of the Wolf Pack. Nicknamed 'Graffi' for his skill at spraying luminous paint on buildings.

BRIGADIER
CHRISTIAN
WOODFORD   A delightful octogenarian, hugely interested in matters

military and his beautiful neighbour, Lily Hamilton.

MISS WORMLEY   English mistress at Bagley Hall—poor thing.

THE ANIMALS

CADBURY   Dora Belvedon's chocolate
                          Labrador.

LOOFAH   Dora Belvedon's delinquent
                          pony.

PARTNER   Janna Curtis's ginger and
                          white mongrel.

NORTHCLIFFE   Patience Cartwright's golden
                          retriever.

ELAINE   Hengist Brett-Taylor's white
                          greyhound.

GENERAL   Lily Hamilton's white and
                          black Persian cat.

VERLAINE AND
RIMBAUD   Artie Deverell's Jack
                          Russells.

BOGOTA   Xavier Campbell-Black's
                          black Labrador.

HINDSIGHT   Theo Graham's marmalade
                          cat.

FAST	One of Rupert Campbell-Black's horses. Aptly named.
PENSCOMBE PETERKIN	Another of Rupert Campbell-Black's star horses.
BELUGA	An extremely kind horse who teaches Paris Alvaston to ride.
PLOVER	Patience Cartwright's grey mare, doted on by Beluga.

1

Larkminster, county town of Larkshire, has long been considered the most precious jewel in the Cotswolds' crown. Throughout the year, its streets are paved with tourists, admiring the glorious pale gold twelfth-century cathedral, the Queen Anne courthouse and the ancient castle, whose battlements descend into the River Fleet as it idles its way round the town.

Larkminster, famous for its splendid beeches and limes and designated England's Town of Trees at the Millennium, was anticipating further fame because its newly elected Conservative MP, Jupiter Belvedon, was hotly tipped to take over the Tory party and oust Tony Blair at the next election.

In his Larkminster constituency, the machiavellian Jupiter was frustrated by a hung Labour and Lib-Dem county council who always voted tactically to keep out the Tories. But in January 2001, to the county council's horror, central government decided to take the running of Larkshire's schools away from the local education authority, who they felt was mismanaging its finances and not adhering sufficiently to the national curriculum. They then handed this task to a private company called S and C Services, the 'S' and the 'C' standing for 'Support' and 'Challenge'.

Larkminster itself boasted a famous public school, Bagley Hall, some five miles outside the town; a choir school attached to the cathedral; two excellent state schools: Searston Abbey and St James's, known as St Jimmy's; and a perfectly

1

frightful sink school, Larkminster Comprehensive, which was situated on the edge of the town's black spot, the notorious Shakespeare Estate.

Like many outwardly serene and elegant West Country towns, Larkminster was greatly exercised by the increase in violent crime, for which it believed the Shakespeare Estate and Larkminster Comprehensive, or 'Larks' as it was known, were entirely responsible.

Randal Stancombe, a Rich List property developer and a hugely influential local player with a manicured finger in every pie, was particularly concerned. Cavendish Plaza, one of his private estates of desirable residences newly built above the flood plain of the River Fleet, was constantly troubled by Larks delinquents mugging, nicking car radios and knocking fairies off Rolls-Royces on their way to school. Randal Stancombe was putting increasing pressure on the police and the county council to clean up the area.

Larkminster Comp had for some years been a candidate for closure. It was at the bottom of the league tables and could only muster five hundred children rattling around in a building large enough for twelve hundred. Taxpayers' money should not be squandered heating empty schools.

Reading the graffiti on the wall, and not liking the prospect of bullying interference from a private company like S and C Services, the then headmaster, Ted Mitchell, had immediately resigned in February 2001. Larks Comp should have been shut down then, but the county council and S and C Services, nervous of the local uproar, the petitions, the poster campaigns, the marches on County Hall and even Westminster and the inevitable loss of seats that occur whenever a school is threatened with closure, dodged the issue.

They should have handed the job to Larks's deputy head, Mike Pitts, a seedy alcoholic who would have killed off the place in a few months. Instead they decided to give Larks a last chance and in April advertised in *The Times Educational Supplement* for a new head. This was why on a hot sunny day in early May, Janna Curtis, head of English at Redfords Comprehensive in West Yorkshire, caught the Intercity from Leeds to Larkminster.

On any journey, Janna overloaded herself with work which she truly intended to do. Aware that Year Eleven would be taking their first English exam in less than three weeks, she should have reread her GCSE revision notes. She should also have checked the English department's activities for the rest of term. Even more important, she should have tackled the pile of information about Larks Comp and the area that she had downloaded from the internet.

But after registering that Larks was underachieving disastrously and those 'right-wing bastards' Randal Stancombe and S and C Services were putting the boot in, she was sidetracked by a *Daily Mail* abandoned by a passenger getting off at Birmingham. Despite her horror at its right-wing views, she soon became engrossed in a story about Posh and Becks, followed by Lynda Lee-Potter's much too enthusiastic comments about 'another right-wing bastard': Rupert Campbell-Black.

The train was stiflingly hot. Even if she'd had the money, Janna would never have done anything so

3

revoltingly elitist as travel first class, but she wished air conditioning extended into standard class as well, so she didn't go scarlet before her interview. She was gagging for a large vodka and tonic to steady her nerves, but, on no breakfast, she'd become garrulous. Not that she was going to get the job; they'd think her much too young and inexperienced and she wasn't even sure she wanted it.

Gazing at a cloud of pink and white apple blossom clashing with bilious yellow fields of rape as the train trundled through Worcestershire, Janna reflected that the past three years at Redfords had been the most thrilling of her life. The cheers must have been heard in Westminster the day she and the other staff were told their school had finally struggled out of special measures (the euphemism for a dangerously failing school).

The fight to save Redfords had been unrelenting, but who minded working until midnight, week in, week out, when you were in love with the headmaster, Stew Wilby, who had made you head of English before you were thirty and who frequently put down his magic wand to shag you on the office carpet?

In the end Stew couldn't bring himself to leave his wife, Beth, and had retreated into a marriage far more intact than he had made out. People were beginning to gossip and the warmth of the reference Stew had sent to the governing board at Larks—which he had showed her yesterday: 'I shall be devastated to lose an outstanding teacher, but I cannot stand in Janna Curtis's way'—gave Janna the feeling that he might be relieved to see the back of her.

'Staying with Beth, staying with Beth,' mocked the wheels as the train rattled over the border into the wooded valleys of Larkshire. In her positive moments, all Janna wanted was to escape as far as possible from Stew into a challenge that would give her no time to mourn. Larkminster Comp seemed the answer.

She was met at the station by Phil Pierce, Larks's head of science. Bony-faced, bespectacled, mousy-haired, he wore a creased sand-coloured suit, obviously dragged out of a back drawer in honour of the heat wave and jazzed up by a blue silk tie covered in leaping red frogs.

Phil didn't drive Janna to Larks via the Shakespeare Estate to bump over litter-strewn roads and breathe in the stench of bins dustmen were too scared to empty. Instead he took her on the longer scenic route where she could enjoy the River Fleet sparkling, the white cherry blossom in the Town of Trees dancing against ominously rain-filled navy-blue clouds and the lichen blazing like little suns on the ancient buildings.

'How beautiful,' sighed Janna, then bristled with disapproval as she noticed, hanging overhead like birds of prey, a number of huge cranes bearing the name of Randal Stancombe.

'That capitalist monster's doing a lot of work,' she stormed, 'and I didn't realize that fascist bast— I mean fiend was MP here,' as she caught sight of posters of pale, patrician Jupiter Belvedon in the window of the Conservative Club. 'I bet he's in league with S and C Services,' she added furiously. 'Private companies only take over education to make a fat profit.'

'Representatives of S and C Services will certainly be at your interview later,' said Phil Pierce gently, 'so perhaps . . .'

'I'd better button my lip,' sighed Janna, 'and my clothes,' she added, doing up the buttons of the crocus-yellow dress she had bought from Jigsaw after school yesterday.

Looking at the terrace houses painted in neat pastels, their front gardens bright with wallflowers and forget-me-nots, Janna wondered if Larkminster might be too smug, rich and middle class.

As if reading her thoughts, Phil Pierce said: 'This may seem a prosperous county, but there's a very high level of socio-economic deprivation. Eighty per cent of our children are on free school dinners. Many have special educational needs.'

'I hope you receive sufficient funding.'

'Does anyone?' sighed Phil. 'This is Larks.'

Janna was agreeably charmed by the tawny, romantically rambling Victorian building perched on the side of a hill, its turrets and battlements swathed in pink clematis and amethyst wisteria, its parkland crowded with rare trees and with cow parsley and wild garlic advancing in waves on wildly daisied lawns.

Phil kicked off by giving her a quick tour of the school, which was conveniently empty of challenging children because it was polling day at the local elections.

All one needed for outside, reflected Janna, were a pair of secateurs and a mowing machine. The windows could also be mended and unboarded, the graffiti painted over and the chains, taps and locks replaced in the lavatories. The corridors and

6

classroom walls were also badly lacking in posters, paintings and written work by the children. Redfords, her school in Yorkshire, was like walking into a rainbow.

She was disappointed that there were no children around, so no one could watch her taking a lesson. This had always secured her jobs in the past. Instead she was given post to deal with, to show off her management skills, and made a good impression by immediately tackling anything involving media and parents. She was also handed two budgets and quickly identified why one was good, the other bad.

She was aware of being beadily scrutinized by the school secretary, Rowan Merton, who was conventionally pretty: lovely skin, grey eyes, dark brown bob; but who simultaneously radiated smugness and disapproval, like the cat who'd got the cream and found it off.

Still too nervous to eat, Janna refused the quick bite of lunch offered her by Phil Pierce. She was then whisked away to an off-site interview because the governors were equally nervous of the Larks deputy head, Mike Pitts, who, livid he hadn't been offered the job, was likely to grow nasty when sobering up after lunch.

Only as Janna was leaving the Larks building did the heavens open, so she didn't appreciate in how many places rain normally poured in through the roof.

2

Janna was interviewed round the corner, past a row of boarded-up shops, in a pub called the Ghost and Castle, which was of the same tawny, turreted architecture as the school. The landlord was clearly a joker. A skeleton propped up the public bar, which was adorned with etchings of ghosts draped in sheets terrorizing maidens or old men in nightcaps. Rooms off were entitled Spook-Easy and Spirits Bar. The plat du jour chalked up on a blackboard was Ghoulash at £4.50.

Janna giggled and wondered how many Larks pupils were regulars here. At least they could mug up for GCSE in the Macbeth room, whose blood-red walls were decorated with lurid oils of Banquo's ghost, Duncan's murder and a sleepwalking Lady Macbeth. Here Larks's governors, a semi-circle of the Great and the Good, mostly councillors and educationalists, awaited her.

Think before you speak and remember eye contact at all times, Janna told herself as, beaming at everyone, she swivelled round like a searchlight.

The chairman of the governors, Russell Lambert, had tiny eyes, sticking-out ears, a long nose like King Babar and loved the sound of his pompous, very put-on voice. A big elephant in a small watering hole, thought Janna.

Like most good teachers, she of necessity picked up names quickly. As Russell Lambert introduced her, she clocked first Brett Scott, a board member of Larkminster Rovers, who had an appropriately roving eye and looked game for a great night on the tiles, and secondly Crispin Thomas, deputy educational director of S and C Services, who did not.

Crispin, a petulant, pig-faced blond, had a snuffling voice, and from his tan and the spare tyre billowing over the waistband of his off-white suit, had recently returned from a self-indulgent holiday.

Under a painting of the Weird Sisters and infinitely more terrifying, like a crow who'd been made over by Trinny and Susannah, quivered a woman with black, straight hair and a twitching scarlet mouth. Appropriately named Cara Sharpe, she was a teacher governor, supposed to present the concerns of the staff to the governing body.

And I bet she sneaks to both sides, thought Janna.

'Cara is our immensely effective head of English and drama,' said Russell sycophantically.

So she won't welcome any interference on the English front from me, Janna surmised, squaring her little shoulders. At the end of the row, the vice-chairman, Sir Hugo Betts, who resembled a camel on Prozac, fought sleep.

Russell Lambert made no bones about the state of the school: 'Larks is at rock bottom.'

'Then it can only go up,' said Janna cheerfully.

Her audience knew from her impressive CV that she had been a crucial part of the high-flying team that had turned around disastrously failing Redfords. But then she had been led by a charismatic head, Stew Wilby. If she took on Larks, she would be on her own.

She also seemed terrifyingly young. She had lots

of dark freckles and wild, rippling dark red hair, a big mouth (which she seldom kept shut), merry onyx-brown eyes and a snub nose. She was not beautiful—her jaw was too square—but she had a face of great sweetness, humour and friendliness. She was small, about five feet one, and after the drenching of rain, her crocus-yellow dress clung enticingly to a very pretty figure. A teardrop of mascara on her cheekbone gave a look of Pierrot.

Phil Pierce, who was very taken, asked her how she would deal with an underachieving teacher.

'I'd immediately involve the head of department,' replied Janna in her soft Yorkshire accent, 'and tactfully find out what's wrong. Is it discipline? Are the children trampling all over him? Is it poor teaching? Academically has he got what it takes, or is he presenting material wrongly? And then, gently, because if he's underachieving he'll have no confidence, try and work it through. After this,' she went on, 'he would either succeed or fail. If the latter, he's not right for teaching, because the education of children is all that matters.'

The semi-circle—except for scowling Cara Sharpe, Rowan Merton, who was taking the minutes, and Sir Hugo Betts, who was asleep—smiled approvingly.

'What are your weaknesses?' snuffled Crispin Thomas from S and C.

Janna laughed. 'Short legs and an even shorter fuse. But my strengths are that I adore children and I thrive on hard work. Are the parents involved here?'

'Well, we get the odd troublemaker,' said Russell heartily, failing to add that a large proportion of Larks parents were too out of it from drugs to

10

register. 'The children can be challenging.'

'I don't mind challenging children,' said Janna. 'You couldn't find more sad and demoralized kids than the ones at Redfords, but in a few months—'

'Yes, we read about that in the *Guardian*,' interrupted Crispin rudely.

Janna bit her lip; they didn't seem interested in her past.

'I want to give every child and teacher the chance to shine and for them to leave my school with their confidence boosted to enable them to survive and enjoy the world.'

She paused hopefully. A loud snore rent the air followed by an even more thunderous rumble from her own tummy, which woke Sir Hugo with a start.

'What, what, what?' He groped for his flies.

Janna caught Phil Pierce's eye and burst out laughing, so everyone else laughed except Cara and Rowan.

Janna had expected the board to get in touch in a week or so, but Russell Lambert, at a nod from Crispin Thomas, asked her to wait in an ante-room entitled Your Favourite Haunt. Phil Pierce brought her a cup of tea and some egg sandwiches, at which she was still too nervous to do more than nibble. Phil was such a sweet man; she'd love working with him.

Breathing in dark purple lilac, she gazed out of the window at buildings darkened to the colour of toffee by the rain and trees as various in their greenness as kids in any school. Beyond lay the deep blue undulation of the Malvern Hills. Surely she could find fulfilment and happiness here?

She was summoned back by Rowan, looking beadier than ever.

11

'We've decided not to waste your time asking you to come for a second interview,' announced Russell Lambert.

Janna's face fell.

'It was good of you all to see me,' she muttered. 'I know I look young . . .'

'We'd like to offer you the job,' said Russell.

Janna burst into tears, her mascara mingling with her freckles as she babbled, 'That's wicked! Fantastic! Are you sure? I'm going to be a head, such an honour, I promise to justify your faith, that's really wicked.'

The half-circle smiled indulgently.

'Can I buy you all a drink to celebrate?' stammered Janna, reaching for her briefcase. 'On me, I mean.'

'Should be on us,' said the director of Larkminster Rovers. 'What'll you have, love?'

'Not if she's going to catch the fast train home,' said Russell, looking at his watch, 'and Crispin and I have to talk salaries and technicalities with . . . may I call you Janna?'

*   *   *

Half an hour later on the Ghost and Castle steps, Janna was still thanking them.

'I'd like to walk to the station,' she confessed. 'I want to drink in my new town. Doesn't matter if I get the later train. I'm so excited, I'll float home.'

But as she hadn't yet signed the contract, Russell, not risking Janna anywhere near the Shakespeare Estate, steered her towards his very clean Rover. Despite the stifling heat of the day, he pulled on thick brown leather driving gloves as though he didn't want to leave fingerprints on anything. As he settled in the driving seat, she noticed how his spreading thighs filled his grey flannel trousers.

As they passed the offices of the *Larkminster Gazette*, a billboard announced Randal Stancombe's latest plans for the area.

'That greedy fat cat's got a stranglehold on everything,' spat Janna.

'Wearing my other hat,' reproved Russell, 'as chair of the local planning committee, I can assure you Randal is a very good friend indeed to Larkminster, not least because of the thousands of people he employs.'

Feeling he'd been squashing, he then suggested Janna might like to ring her parents with news of her job.

'Mum passed away at Christmas.' Janna paused. 'She would have been right proud. I wish I could text her in heaven. We came from a very poor family; Mum scrubbed floors to pay for my school uniform, but she loved books and always encouraged us to read. She used to take me to see the Brontës' house in Haworth. I read English because of her.'

'And your father?'

'Dad was a steelworker. He used to take me to Headingly and Old Trafford. Then he left home; he couldn't cope with Mum being ill.' Her voice faltered. She wasn't going to add that her father had been violent and had drunk the family penniless.

She wished she could ring Stew but he'd be taking a staff meeting. Yorkshire was so full of painful memories; she'd be glad to get down south and make a fresh start.

13

Nothing, however, had prepared her for the anguish of leaving Redfords. Parents and children, who'd thought she'd be with them for ever, seemed equally devastated.

'Why are you living us?' wrote one eleven-year-old. 'I don't want you to live.'

'Are your new children better than us?' wrote another. 'Please change your mind.'

Almost harder to bear was the despair of the older pupils, including some of the roughest, toughest boys, whom she was abandoning in the middle of their GCSE course.

'How will we ever understand *Much Ado* without you? We're going to miss you, miss.'

They all gave her good-luck presents and cards they could ill afford and Janna couldn't look them in the eye and tell them the truth: 'I'm leaving because your headmaster broke my heart and now it's breaking twice.'

Then Stew had done the sweetest thing: he'd had framed a group photograph of the entire school, which every teacher and child had signed. Janna cried every time she looked at it.

Some teachers were very sad she was leaving and wished her well. Others, jealous of her closeness to Stew, expressed their incredulity at her getting the job.

'You'd better cut your hair, you'll never have time to wash that mane every morning. And do buy some sensible clothes.'

'And you'll have to curb that temper and you won't be able to swan into meetings twenty minutes late if you're taking them.'

Waylaid by a sobbing child, Janna would forget about time.

There had also been the hell of seeing Stew interview and appoint her successor: a willowy brunette with large, serious, hazel eyes behind her spectacles—the bloody cow—and everyone getting excited about a Christmas production of *Oliver!* of which Janna would be no part.

Stew had taken her out for a discreet farewell dinner and, because she was moving to the country, given her a little Staffordshire cow as a leaving present.

'I'm so proud of you, Janny. You've probably got eighteen months to try and turn round that school. Don't lose your rag and antagonize people unnecessarily and go easy on the "boogers", "bluddies" and "basstards", they just show off your Yorkshire accent.' Then, pinching her cheek when she looked sulky: 'I don't want anything to wreck your lovely, generous, spontaneous nature.'

'Yeah, yeah. "The only failure is not to have tried",' Janna quoted one of Redfords's mantras back at him.

After a second bottle they had both cried and Stew had quoted: ' "So, we'll go no more a-roving",' but when he got to the bit about the sword outwearing its sheath and the heart wearing out the breast, Janna remembered how they'd worn out the carpet in his office.

I've given him my Bridget Jones years, she thought bitterly. Sometimes she wondered why she loved him so much: his hair was thinning, his body thickening and, apart from the penetrating dark brown eyes, his square face lacked beauty, but

15

whenever he spoke, everyone listened and his powers of persuasion were infinite.

'Little Jannie, I cannot believe you're going to be a headmistress.' His fingers edged over her breast. 'We can still meet. Can I come home this evening?'

'No,' snapped Janna. 'I'm a head, but no longer a mistress.'

*   *   *

Janna, however, was never cast down for long. At half-term, she had come south and found herself a minute but adorable eighteenth-century house called Jubilee Cottage. Like a child's drawing, it had a path spilling over with catmint and lavender leading up to a gabled porch with 'Jubilate' engraved above the door and mullioned windows on either side. It was the last house in the small village of Wilmington, which had a pub, a shop and a watercress-choked stream dawdling along the edge of the High Street.

Janna could easily afford the mortgage on her splendid new salary. She couldn't believe she'd be earning so much.

Wilmington thankfully was three miles from Larkminster Comp. However much you loved kids, it was a mistake to live over your school. When she grew tired of telling her children they were all stars, she could escape home, wander on her own lawn in bare feet and gaze up at her own stars.

All the same, missing Stew, it was terribly easy to go through a bottle of wine of an evening.

'I shall buy a new car and get a dog,' vowed Janna.

3

From the middle of August, Janna was in and out of her new school familiarizing herself with everything, palling up with Wally Bristow, the site manager, who like most site managers was the fountain of all wisdom.

Wally had short, slicked-back brown hair and wise grey eyes in a round, smiling face as dependable and reassuring as a digestive biscuit. Living but three minutes from Larks, he was always on call except on Thursday evening, when he and a team of bell-ringers rehearsed for Sunday's service in St Mary's Church next door, or on Saturday afternoons when Larkminster Rovers played at home. He was inordinately proud of a good-looking son, Ben, who'd risen to sergeant in the Royal Engineers.

Janna's heart swelled when she saw Wally had repainted the board outside the school in dark blue gloss and written in gold letters: 'LARKMINSTER COMPREHENSIVE SCHOOL. Head Teacher: Janna Curtis'.

'Oh Wally, I've got to make every child feel they're the greatest and discover each one's special talents.'

'Smokin', spittin', swearin', runnin' away, fightin' and urinatin' in phone boxes,' intoned Wally. 'As we can't fill the places, we get all the dropouts that get sacked or rejected by other schools.'

Wally showed her Smokers', a steep, grassy bank down which the children vanished so they could smoke, do drugs, drink and even shag unobserved by the staffroom.

'I don't want to frighten you, Janna,' he went on as they lunched on cans of lager and Marks and Spencer's prawn sandwiches, 'but the kids are running wild. Most of them only come in to trash the place and play football. The rest are off havin' babies or appearin' in court. They're demoralized by the staff, who are either off sick from "stress" '—Wally gave a snort of disbelief—'old dinosaurs hanging on for retirement, or commies who grumble at everything and threaten strike action if you keep them a minute late.'

Wally also warned her of tricky teachers: Mike Pitts, the deputy head, who taught maths, did the timetable and who was always burning joss sticks and scented candles to disguise the drink fumes; and Cara Sharpe, who'd glared at Janna at her interview.

'Everyone hates Cara, but humours her. She wanted Mike as head, and her to get deputy head to look good on her CV. She and Mike are thick as thieves. Don't trust them. Cara's a bitch to the kids.'

'Not any more she won't be. Where are the playing fields?'

'Don't have any: they were sold off by the council. The rest of the land is on too much of a slope and you can't swing a gerbil in the playground.'

The playground was indeed awful: a square of tarmac surrounded by broken rusty railings with no basketball nets and two overhanging sycamores, whose leaves, curling and covered in sinister black spots, provided the only shade.

Everything had deteriorated since Janna's

18

interview in May. A lower-angled sun revealed damp patches and peeling plaster in every classroom. The once lovely garden and parkland were choked with thistles and nettles. Pale phlox and red-hot pokers were broken or bent double by bindweed which seemed to symbolize the red tape threatening to strangle Janna's hopes. An in-tray of forms to be filled in nearly hit the ceiling.

The GCSE results out in late August had dropped to four per cent of the pupils gaining A–C grades in five subjects. Only these gave Larks points in the league tables, and only Cara Sharpe and Phil Pierce, the gentle head of science who'd met Janna at the station, had got most of their children through.

'Phil's a good bloke,' said Wally, 'firm, but very fair. He's always online to answer pupils' homework questions. The kids love him.'

'Why's he still here?' asked Janna gloomily.

'He's very loyal. Trouble with kids here, they leave at sixteen so they don't have to come back and face the music of terrible GCSE results.'

'Where do they go on to?'

'The dole queue or the nick.'

*   *   *

Janna kicked off by tackling her office, which was full of the presence of Mike Pitts, who'd done her job for the spring and summer terms and who clearly hadn't wanted people to follow his movements. The door had a security lock and a heavy dark blind pulled down over the big window hiding a view over the playground to houses, the River Fleet and grey-green woods beyond.

19

Janna insisted a doubtful Wally remove both lock and blind.

'I want to be accessible to both children and staff.'

Shaking his head, Wally got out his screwdriver.

'It really ain't surprising [he sang in a rich
    baritone],
That we're rising, rising, rising,
Soon we'll reach Division One.
Premier, Wembley, here we come.'

'What's that song?' demanded Janna.

'Larkminster Rovers's battle hymn. We got to the second division last season. Now we've got to stay there.'

'Larks is going up the league tables too [sang
    Janna],
Soon we'll reach Division One.
Premier, Wembley, here we come.'

Wally nearly dropped his screwdriver as her sweet soaring voice rattled the window panes.

*   *   *

Having scraped scented candle wax off the furniture and scrubbed the room from top to toe, Janna and Wally painted her office white, hung cherry-red curtains and laid rush matting on the floor.

'I need a settee and a couple of armchairs so people can relax when they come in here.'

'The kids'll trash them, the settee'll be an

20

incitement to rape or teachers grumbling and those white walls won't last a minute,' sighed Wally.

'Then we'll cover them with pictures.'

Up went *Desiderata* and *Hold the Dream* embroidered by Janna's Auntie Glad, followed by big photographs of Wharfedale, Fountains Abbey and Stew's photograph of all the children and teachers at Redfords waving goodbye in front of a square grey school building.

On a side table Janna put Stew's Staffordshire cow and a big bunch of Michaelmas daisies and late roses rescued from Larks's flower beds.

'My goodness, you have been working hard,' mocked Rowan Merton when she looked in a week before term started.

As a working wife and mother with photographs of her husband and two little girls all over her office, on the door of which was printed 'Assistant to the Head', Rowan prided herself on juggling. She had wound Mike Pitts round her little finger and clearly didn't fancy extending herself for a woman—particularly one in a denim mini, with a smudged face and her red curls in a ponytail.

'Have you flown in to rescue us?' she mocked. 'Like Red Adair in a skirt?'

'No, I've come to show you how to save yourselves,' retorted Janna tartly, then, remembering Stew's advice about not antagonizing people, added, 'How are Scarlet and Meagan? They must have loved having you to themselves in the holidays.'

Rowan relented fractionally and said they had, then launched into a list of staff requests for broken chairs, desks, leaking windows and computers to be mended.

'And Mrs Sharpe wants a blind. The sun casts such a glare, no one can read the whiteboard in the afternoon.'

Cara Sharpe's own glare, Janna would have thought, would see off any competition.

'And my anglepoise lamp collapses without the aid of two bulldog clips and the angle being wedged open by the last *Education Year Book*,' went on Rowan. 'If Wally could sort all those things out before term begins?'

'Wally's flat out,' snapped Janna.

Rowan glanced round the office. 'Yes, I can see. Nice settee. We have to watch the budget now S and C hold the purse strings.'

*   *   *

Slowly, Janna familiarized herself with classrooms, halls, gym and labyrinthine adjoining corridors in the main building, which was known as School House. Fifty yards away, the annexe, known as Appletree because it had been built on the site of an old orchard, housed the labs, music, design and technology and food technology departments.

Then she pored over the children's personal files, counting the asylum-seekers, Indians, Pakistanis and Afro-Caribbeans—far fewer than at Redfords. She had also noticed lots of BNPs and swastikas amongst the graffiti: she would have to watch out for racist bullying. She was now frantically trying to memorize the names before term began.

'The ones you have to watch are those going into Year Nine and particularly the Wolf Pack,' said Wally as he carried in a mini-fridge for milk, butter and orange juice, and put jam, marmalade, coffee, tea bags, lots of biscuits, two packs of Mars and Twix bars and a tin of Quality Street in the cupboard. 'These won't last a minute.'

'Oh, shut up,' said Janna, who was gazing down at a photograph of a beautiful black boy with long dark eyelashes and a smile of utter innocence.

Wally glanced over her shoulder. 'He's Wolf Pack. Feral Jackson. Comes into school to play football and start fights. Very druggy background; mother's an addict, off her face all day. Feral went inside at the beginning of the holidays for mugging some women shoppers. His brother Joey was stabbed to death last year. Uncle Harley, his mum's boyfriend, is a mega pusher. That's Feral's best mate, Paris Alvaston.'

Janna looked at the boy's ghostly face, the wonderful bone structure, the watchful pale grey eyes of a merle collie.

'Paris has been in different care homes since he was two,' added Wally. 'Goes AWOL from time to time on trains all over the country searching for his mother. Advertised for a home in the local paper last year, but there were no takers. Shame really.'

'That's terrible.' Janna reached out and switched on the kettle. 'Poor boy.'

'Looks too spooky. Teachers say he's very clever, writes wonderful stories one day, then just puts his name at the top of the paper the next. Everything goes inside. He and Feral are joined at the very narrow hip. Give them a detention and they jump out of the window, climb down the wisteria and run away.

'That's Griffith Williams, known as "Graffi".' Wally pointed to a thickset boy with black curls and wicked sliding dark eyes. 'Graffi was a Welshman, Graffi was a thief . . . But he's a good laugh. Don't stand anywhere near him or he'll graffiti you. That's Pearl Smith: she's got a temper on her, scratch the eyes out of any girl who tries to get off with her boys, particularly Feral. She's trouble. Cuts herself. Got arms like ladders.'

'Well, she's not wearing make-up and having hair that colour in my school,' said Janna firmly as she broke open a packet and dropped tea bags into two mugs. 'That one's pretty.'

'Kylie Rose. Already had one kid at twelve—wanted something to love. Time she spends on her back, she'll have another any minute. Anything to avoid SATs. Those five make up the Wolf Pack.'

'Feral, Paris, Graffi, Pearl and Kylie Rose,' intoned Janna as she poured boiling water over the tea bags and added milk and two sugars for Wally, who carried on with her lesson.

'There are three more you want to watch from Year Nine. One's Rocky; he's autistic. Attention Deficit Disorder they call it these days,' he added scornfully. 'Nice kid, but violent if he don't get his Ritalin. More serious are "Satan" Simmons—a racist bully, excluded last term for carrying a gun, overturned on appeal because his father's a councillor—and "Monster" Norman. Monster's mixed race'—Wally stirred his tea thoughtfully—'in that his dad, who keeps walking out, is a quarter black, which Monster denies, which makes him even more of a racist bully. He's also a great snivelling toad, really spiteful, but his mother's a governor, so you can't touch him.'

Janna put her hand over the names: Freddie 'Feral' Jackson, such a beautiful face; Paris

24

Alvaston: no one could forget him either, he looked so hauntingly sad; Griffith 'Graffi' Williams; Pearl; Kylie Rose; 'Satan' Simmons; Rocky; 'Monster' Norman.'

'What's that?' she demanded, noticing a switch inside the well of her desk.

'Your panic button,' said Wally, then, when Janna looked mutinous: 'You don't know what you're up against. Most of our kids come from the Shakespeare Estate. Their parents are crazy people who respect no one. From the beginning of term you're wearing a radio mike, and if there's any trouble, you summon back-up. Someone's always on call on the internal radio link.'

'I'm not bothering with any of that junk. This is going to be a happy school.'

*   *   *

Before the teachers came back, Wally also gave her a sneak preview of the staffroom.

'Why do they need a security lock?' she asked as Wally punched out the code to enter.

'To keep out violent kids and parents.'

'And me too, presumably. God, it's awful! Who'd want to break in here?'

Walls the luminous olive green of a child about to be sick were not enhanced by brown and yellow check curtains. Mock leather chairs in the dingiest browns and beiges huddled dispiritedly round low tables. Staff pigeonholes overflowed, clearly untackled since last term. Three potted plants had baked to death on the window sill. A Hoover, weak from underwork, was slumped against an ancient television set. Health and safety laws and union posters promising significant reductions in workload shared the noticeboard with details of half-price Calvin Klein button-fly boxers and Winnie-the-Pooh character socks. Also pinned up was a letter from Cotchester University announcing that a former pupil Marilyn Finch had attained a second in maths.

'For those who remember Marilyn,' Mike Pitts had scribbled across the bottom, 'all our efforts were worthwhile.'

'Only graduate Larks ever had,' volunteered Wally. 'Pittsy taught her.'

'I'm going to have to tackle him on the timetable,' sighed Janna. 'It's covered with drink rings and Year Seven A and Year Eight B are having English with the same teacher in the same classroom at the same time on Tuesday morning— and it gets worse. God, look at that.'

On the breakfast bar, untouched since the end-of-term party, sink and draining board were crowded with dirty wine glasses, moth-filled cups and orange-juice cartons. Scrumpy, beer and vegetable-juice cans littered the floor.

Debbie the cleaner, said Wally disapprovingly, would blitz the place before the first staff meeting tomorrow.

'None of this lot can wash up a cup.'

'We'd better buy them a dishwasher.'

'They'd never load it.'

To the right of the door, imperilling entry, hung a dartboard with two scarlet-feathered darts plunged deep into the bull's eye. Last year's Christmas decorations had been chucked into a far corner between a ping-pong table with one leg supported by a German dictionary and a billiard table with a

26

badly ripped cloth.

'Don't matter,' said Wally philosophically. 'Table's mostly used for late-night nooky.'

'Anyone I know?' asked Janna, who'd moved to examine a big picture frame, which contained cigarette-card-sized photographs of all the staff in order of seniority. Heading these were the Dinosaurs who'd been at Larks for ever. To memorize them, Janna had made an acronym—P.U.B.I.C.—out of the first letters of their names. 'P' for Pitts, 'U' for Uglow (Miss) who taught RE, 'B' for Basket (Miss) who taught geography, 'I' for Illingworth (Mr) who taught science and 'C' for Chalford (Mrs) who taught history.

'That's one I haven't memorized,' mused Janna, 'with the piled-up dark hair and operatic make-up. She must be Miss Cambola, head of music.'

Wally, however, had noticed that into Janna's photograph on the far top left someone had plunged the missing red-feathered dart between the eyes. Hastily Wally whipped it out. Fortunately, Janna had been distracted by the photograph of a good-looking blond man, affectedly cupping his face between long fingers.

'He's not bad.'

'Jason Fenton. Kids call him Goldilocks. Cara Sharpe's toyboy, so hands off. He wanted her job as head of drama and English, and believes in constantly switching schools to jack up his status and his salary. Claims you go stale if you stay more than a year, which upsets the Dinosaurs, who've been here for ever.'

'And him?' Janna pointed to a black-eyed, black-browed, bearded man with dishevelled black hair.

'Robbie Rushton, chief leftie, rabble-rouser and

27

has-bin. Spends his time plotting and telling you what you can't do. Longs for a strike so he can appear on TV again. He and Jason both have the hots for Gloria, deputy head of PE.' Wally pointed to a pouting strawberry blonde. 'Gloria prefers Jason because he's posher and washes more. "Soon we'll reach Division One. Premier, Wembley, here we come," ' sang Wally.

Who the hell had plunged that dart into Janna's photograph, he wondered? She was such a sweet kid. He was determined to protect her.

' "P" for Pitts, "U" for Uglow, "B" for Basket, "I" for Illingworth, "C" for Chalford,' intoned Janna.

4

On 3 September, all the staff came into school for a full day to prepare work and classrooms for the children, whose first day of term was the fourth. New staff were also initiated into school practice: which included what coloured exercise books to use, pupil data files, playground rotas, policy towards parents and bullying, and what was laughingly known as the golden rules of behaviour management.

Janna had decided to break the ice and tradition by scheduling her first staff meeting at five o'clock, rather than first thing. Desperate for it to go well, she had not only memorized names and achievements until her head was bursting, but also ordered in three large quiches and a couple of crates of red and white to jolly things along.

Her day running up to the meeting was frantic: coping with endless requests and demands (mostly, it seemed, not to teach the Wolf Pack), and having a most unpleasant spat with Mike Pitts, who hadn't taken kindly to criticism of his timetable.

'Then do it yourself.'

'No,' countered Janna bravely, 'it's your job to put it right.'

She had fared little better with Sam Spink, the union rep, who had very short hair shaved at the back, a large bottom and an even larger sense of her own importance. Her straining brown leggings stopped at mid-calf leaving a hairy gap above her Winnie-the-Pooh character socks, which seemed to give out signals that she was not all work and no play, and clearly regarded herself as a bit of a card. She proceeded to lecture Janna at great length about not prolonging the school day by a second. Remembering yet again Stew's instruction about not antagonizing colleagues unnecessarily, Janna just managed to keep her temper.

She then had to welcome two newly qualified teachers—NQTs or Not Quite Togethers, as they were known—pretty, plump, earnest Lydia who taught English, and pale Lance, teaching history. They were so full of hope and trepidation that Janna couldn't bear them to be bludgeoned by the weary cynicism of the other staff and spent longer than she should discussing Thomas Hardy country and the battlefields, where they had respectively spent their holidays in order to glean fascinating information to relay to their classes. Thus she was still talking and in jeans and a T-shirt when Rowan Merton put her sleek dark bob round the door:

'Two minutes to kick-off, headmistress.'

'Why didn't you warn me?' screamed Janna.

'You insisted on not being bothered.'

Janna only had time to sling on a denim jacket and slap on some blusher—God, she looked tired—before belting down the corridor. Across reception, at her instructions, Wally had strung a brightly coloured banner saying: 'Welcome back all Larks teachers and children'.

'So demeaning to refer to the students as children,' grumbled Sam Spink.

The meeting was held in the non-smoking staffroom. Outside, a muttering band of lefties, headed by the black-eyed, wild-haired Robbie Rushton, drew feverishly on last fags. Inside, Debbie the cleaner had pulled a blinder. The place was gleaming. Janna made a mental note to buy Debbie a box of chocolates. Gallant Wally had, in addition, attacked the immediate garden and a smell of mown grass and newly turned earth drifting in through the window gave an illusion of spring and fresh starts.

The Dinosaurs had clearly been emailed by a furious Mike Pitts. Having bagged most of the dingy chairs and chuntering disapprovingly about 'heads in jeans squandering the budget on drink', they were getting stuck into the red. Mike Pitts ostentatiously asked for a mineral water. Skunk Illingworth, who taught science, stank of BO and wore socks, sandals and shorts, had just cut himself a huge slice of quiche and filled up a pint mug with white.

'She's going to have the students out of uniform and calling us by our Christian names in a trice,' he grumbled.

Heart thumping, Janna glanced round at the sea of faces: appraising, hostile, suspicious, waiting for someone to make a move. Thank God, Phil Pierce, who'd befriended her at her interview, rushed straight over, kissing her on both cheeks and apologizing profusely for not being in touch.

Like most teachers, he looked fifteen years younger after the summer break. His kind eyes were clear, his hair bleached, his bony face dark tanned. He and his wife had just come back from Kenya, he said. He'd popped in earlier, but Rowan had stressed that Janna was tied up. He hoped she was OK. Then he introduced Miss Cambola of the large bosom, piled-up hair and stage make-up, and Janna scored immediate brownie points by remembering she taught music, was a fine mezzo

31

and sang with the Larkminster Operatic Society.

'You must join us,' said Miss Cambola. 'Wally tells me you have a beautiful voice. We're doing *Don Giovanni* in November and have yet to cast Zerlina.'

'I'm afraid I won't have time,' said Janna wistfully.

'Well anyway, come to supper. Have you met Mags Gablecross? She teaches French part-time.'

'And has a wedding in the offing,' said Janna, shaking hands with a sweet-faced woman in her fifties.

'You are well briefed.' Mags smiled. 'Your predecessor hardly recognized his staff.'

'Oh, thank you,' stammered Janna, 'and your husband's the great detective.'

'He'd like you to say so. He said to call him if you get any hassle.' Margaret popped the Chief Inspector's card into Janna's jacket pocket. 'You must come to supper and meet him.'

Vastly cheered, Janna worked the room, enquiring after new babies, congratulating on engagements and new houses, expressing sorrow over deaths and hearing endless complaints about the new Year Nine and the Wolf Pack.

She was aware of Mike Pitts skulking in a corner not meeting her eyes and Cara Sharpe also avoiding her. In a scarlet dress, which clung to her rapacious, elongated body and matched her drooping vermilion mouth, Cara looked far more attractive than she had at Janna's interview. Her ebony hair seemed softer and curlier, but her face was still as hard as the earth in those poor dead potted plants.

She was also busy upstaging other teachers over

their GCSE results. 'How did Mitzi do in geography?' she called across to Miss Basket: one of the Dinosaurs who had buck teeth, a pale, wispy fringe and a twitching face shiny enough to check one's make-up in, and who promptly stepped back into the Christmas decorations with a loud crunch, replying that Mitzi had only got a D.

'You amaze me, she's so easy to teach,' mocked Cara. 'She got A stars in drama, English and English lit. for me.'

Bitch, thought Janna and promptly told a crestfallen Miss Basket, 'You did brilliantly with those asylum-seekers, getting C grades in such a short time.'

Miss Basket blushed with passionate gratitude. Cara looked furious. Then Janna spoilt it by congratulating Basket on a new grandson.

'I never married,' squawked Basket.

Everyone suppressed smiles except Cara Sharpe, who laughed openly before turning glittering eyes on Lydia, the NQT who was the most junior member of her department:

'You've got Year Nine E tomorrow, Lydia, you'll find them a doddle.'

Janna swung round in horror. Year Nine E included the Wolf Pack, Monster and Satan, not to mention autistic, often violent Rocky. They'd eat poor Lydia for the breakfast their parents probably wouldn't provide.

'You must look out for Paris Alvaston,' Janna advised Lydia as Wally topped up their glasses. 'I hear he writes wonderful stories.'

'With respect,' sneered Cara, 'Paris is a no-hoper, like all the Wolf Pack. You have to tell them five times to do anything, they're always late or don't come in at all, and never do their homework. Paris, arrogant little beast, does what he pleases and the others follow suit.'

'Not a doddle then, as you promised Lydia,' flared up Janna, quite forgetting about keeping her trap shut. 'That's a very negative attitude.'

'I'm entirely on Cara's side. The Wolf Pack are beyond control.' A tall man with blond curls and smooth golden-brown skin had joined the group. 'Pearl's a hell-cat and Kylie Rose a nympho. If I'm going to teach them, I want a chastity belt and CCTV in the classroom.'

This must be Jason Fenton, alias Goldilocks. He was certainly pretty, his regular features marred only by rather bulging blue eyes, as though the transformation from frog into Prince Charming had not been absolute.

'We mustn't let past behaviour dictate the future,' Janna said firmly. 'The Wolf Pack are clearly forceful characters.'

'You can't make a difference with that lot,' drawled Jason, 'they're too damaged.'

The room had gone quiet, quivering collectively with expectation.

'If you feel like that,' said Janna furiously, 'you shouldn't be teaching here.'

'I couldn't agree more.' Jason smiled into her eyes. 'I've been trying to see you all day to hand in my notice.' Over the gasps of amazement he added: 'But Rowan Merton wouldn't let me cross your threshold,' and, shoving an envelope into Janna's hand, he turned towards the door.

A striking strawberry blonde in a non-existent skirt and a clinging pink vest glued to her worked-out body, whom Janna recognized as Gloria, the deputy head of PE, gave a wail: 'When are you going, Jase?'

'If one resigns on the first day of term, one can be over the hills and far away by half-term.'

'And *where* are you going?' hissed an incensed, wrong-footed Cara.

'To Bagley Hall as head of drama,' said Jason, filling up his glass on the way out.

'That's an independent,' thundered Sam Spink.

'I know,' murmured Jason. 'Adequate funding, nineteen weeks' holiday, a decent salary and no Wolf Pack: need I say more? Here's to me,' and, draining his glass, he was gone.

Over a thunderous murmur of chat, Janna had to pull herself and the meeting together. Clapping her hands for quiet, assuring everyone she wouldn't keep them long, she then had to express great regret that Larks had had to bid farewell to ten teachers she had never met. There were broad grins when she described a former ICT master as a 'tower of strength', when he'd evidently jumped half the female staff and impregnated two supply teachers, and laughter when she expressed deep regret at the death of some former head, who'd only emigrated with his wife to Tasmania.

'Mike Pitts wouldn't have slipped up like that,' muttered Skunk Illingworth, the science Dinosaur, refilling his pint mug.

'I will get to know you all soon,' apologized Janna. She took a deep breath and looked round. Somehow she must rally them. Then Jason returned. Seeing him grinning superciliously and lounging against the wall, Janna's resolve was stiffened and she kicked off by attacking her staff for their atrocious GCSE results.

35

'We must start from this moment to improve. If we can get our children to behave, then we can teach them, and they will behave if they're interested.' She smiled at Lydia in the front row.

'They will also behave if this is a happy school and they have fun here as well as learning. We must give them and the school back its pride so they'll stop trashing and graffitiing the place.

'Wally has worked so hard restoring the building over the holidays. Debbie has worked so hard cleaning up in here. Frankly, it was a tip.' Out of the corner of her eye, she saw Wally clutching his head. 'In turn,' she went on, 'I'd like you all to work hard transforming your classrooms. We want examples of good work on the walls and the corridors and colour and excitement everywhere.' Then, beaming at the furious faces: 'And will you all start smiling around the place, particularly at the children, making them feel valued and welcome.'

Only Phil Pierce, Lydia and Lance, Mags Gablecross and Miss Cambola, the busty music mistress, smiled back.

As Janna took a fortifying slug of white, she heard a loud cough to her left and, glancing round, saw Sam Spink tapping the glass of her watch.

'You were saying?' snapped Janna.

Marching over, Sam said in a stage whisper that could be heard in the gods at Covent Garden: 'People have been in school since eight-thirty, nearly nine hours, working flat out to get everything shipshape. Many colleagues need to collect kids from childminders, others have long journeys home and want to be alert for their students tomorrow. I'm sure you're aware that

36

anything over eight hours is unacceptable. Any minute they'll walk out of their own accord.'

'OK,' muttered Janna, turning to her now utterly captive audience, 'we'll call it a day. I'm afraid it's been a very long one. Thank you all for coming. I look forward to working with you,' then she hissed at Sam Spink, 'and I'll personally string you up by your Winnie-the-Pooh character socks if you ever cheek me in public like that again,' before stalking out.

'Remember always to smile around the school,' Cara Sharpe called after her.

'Never thanked me for taking Year Ten to Anglesey in July,' repeated Skunk as he petulantly emptied bottles, then glasses into his mug.

Phil and Wally were kind and complimentary, but Janna knew she'd blown it.

'This place needs shaking up,' said Phil. 'Would you like to come home for a bite of supper?'

'Oh, I'd love to,' said Janna longingly, 'but I've got so much to do.'

She still hadn't written her speech for assembly and her in-tray, to quote Larkminster Rovers's battle hymn, was 'rising, rising, rising'.

She was also jolted to realize that in the old days, before she'd become part of the high-flying team at Redfords, she'd have probably been out hassling senior management like Sam Spink: was poacher turning keeper?

The full moon, like a newly washed plate, followed her home—perhaps she *should* buy the staffroom a dishwasher. Jubilee Cottage was cold, smelt musty and didn't look welcoming because she still hadn't unpacked her stuff or put up any pictures. Most of them, admittedly, were adorning her office at Larks. Poor little cottage, she must give it some TLC along with five hundred disturbed children and at least twenty-eight bolshie staff.

A large vodka and tonic followed by Pot Noodles wasn't a good idea either. She'd promptly thrown up the lot. Then she washed her hair. Nagged to present a more respectable image by her fellow teachers at Redfords, she had had her red curls lopped to the shoulders, then defiantly invested in a pink suit decorated with darker pink roses which should jazz up tomorrow's proceedings.

As heads covered up to ten miles a day policing their schools, she had also bought a pair of dark pink shoes with tiny heels. She laid everything out on a chair. By the time she'd showered and put on a nightie, it was half past twelve.

She fell to her knees. 'Oh please, dear God, help me to save my school.'

If you banged your head on the pillow and recited something last thing, you were supposed to remember it in the morning.

'Feral Jackson, Paris Alvaston, Graffi Williams, Pearl Smith, Kylie Rose Peck . . .' The faces of the Wolf Pack swam before her eyes throughout the night.

Then she overslept and didn't get to school until eight-fifteen.

At the bottom of the drive, in anticipation of a new term, were already gathering lawyers' assistants waiting to hand out leaflets encouraging disgruntled parents to sue the school, pushers lurking with offers of drugs or steroids, and expelled pupils hanging around to duff up pupils they'd been chucked out for terrorizing.

On her desk, Janna found a pile of good-luck cards, but nothing from Stew, not even a phone message. She was also outraged to receive a card on which Tory blue flowers—bluebells, flax and forget-me-nots—were intertwined and exquisitely painted by someone called Hanna Belvedon. Inside was a handwritten note from Jupiter Belvedon, presumably the artist's husband and Larkminster's Conservative MP, welcoming Janna to Larkshire and hoping she'd ring him if she needed help. As if she'd accept help from a rotten Tory.

Out of the window she could see pupils straggling up the drive, smoking, arguing, fighting. Several posters and the welcome-back sign had already been ripped down. There was a crash as a brick flew through a window in reception.

Two minutes before assembly was due to start, Rowan Merton bustled in quivering with excitement:

'You might like to open this before kick-off.'

It was a beautifully wrapped and pink-ribboned bottle of champagne. Darling Stew had remembered. Turning towards the window, so Rowan couldn't look over her shoulder, Janna opened the little white envelope and was almost winded with disappointment as she read: 'Dear Miss Curtis, This is to wish you great luck, I hope you'll lunch with me one day soon. Yours ever, Hengist Brett-Taylor'.

'Who the hell's Hengist Brett-Taylor?'

Rowan was so impressed, she forgot for a moment to be hostile.

'Don't you know? He's head of Bagley Hall.' Then, when Janna looked blank: 'Our local independent school—frightfully posh. He was on *Question Time* last Thursday making mincemeat of poor Estelle Morris. Livens up any programme.'

'Not Ghengist Khan,' whispered Janna in horror, 'that fascist pig?'

'Well, I don't approve of Hengist's politics,' said Rowan shirtily, 'but he's drop-dead gorgeous.'

'He's an arrogant bastard,' who, now Janna remembered, had just poached Jason Fenton, another arrogant bastard. They'd suit each other. She was about to drop the bottle of champagne in the bin, when the bell went, so she put it in the fridge. She might well need it later.

Applying another layer of pale pink lipstick, she defiantly drenched herself in Diorissimo, buttoned up her suit to flaunt her small waist, and jumped at the sound of a wolf whistle.

'You look absolutely gorgeous,' sighed Phil Pierce, who'd come to collect her, 'roses, roses all the way. The kids are going to love you.'

Hearing the overwhelming din of children pouring down the corridor into the main hall, Janna started to shake. The task ahead seemed utterly awesome.

5

Dora, the eleven-year-old sister of Larkminster's Tory MP, Jupiter Belvedon, had heard that the young headmistress starting at Larks, the local sink school, was an absolute cracker. Dora thought this most unlikely. Schoolmistresses in her experience were such old boots that anything without two heads and a squint was described as 'attractive'.

Dora had therefore risen at seven to ride her skewbald pony Loofah along the River Fleet and into Larkminster to check Janna out. Dora also needed to think. She was very exercised because she was starting boarding at a new school, Bagley Hall, in a week's time. Dora's mother, Anthea, kept saying Bagley Hall was like Chewton Glen or the Ritz, but to Dora it was prison—particularly as she'd be separated from Loofah and Cadbury, her chocolate Labrador, who bounded ahead of them putting up duck. Dora was worried about both Loofah and Cadbury. Her sweet father, who'd been dotty about animals, would have looked after them, but alas, he'd died recently and her mother regarded both animals as a tie and a needless expense.

Dora sighed and helped herself to blackberries in the hedgerows. Loofah was much too small for her. He'd need lifts soon to stop her feet scraping the ground. He also bucked, sat down and bit people, but she loved him far too much to sell him. Life was very hard when you had so many animal dependants. Dora edged a KitKat out of her jodhpur pocket to share with the two of them. Her

41

mother, Anthea, was always warning Dora she'd get spots and never attract a boyfriend.

Who wanted soppy boyfriends? thought Dora scornfully.

Dora had thick, flaxen plaits and even thicker curly blonde eyelashes, which seemed designed to stop the peak of her hard hat falling over her turned-up nose. Her big eyes were the same drained turquoise as the sky on the horizon. Slender, small for her age, she was redeemed from over-prettiness by a determined chin and a mouth frequently pursed in disapproval.

And Dora had much to disapprove of. Her beautiful mother, Anthea, in appearance all dewy-eyed softness, was in reality catting around with loads of boyfriends, including an awful old judge and a rose-grower—both married—and playing the disconsolate, impoverished widow for all she was worth. Fed up with the school run and anxious to enjoy an unbridled sex life, Anthea clearly wanted Dora out of the way, locked up at Bagley Hall.

The sole plus for Dora was that for several years she had been augmenting her income by leaking stories to the press. Her mother's romantic attachments had provided excellent copy.

Bagley Hall should prove even more remunerative. Hengist Brett-Taylor, the head, whom her mother fancied almost as much as Rupert Campbell-Black, was never out of the news. Her twin brother Dicky, who'd been boarding since he was eight and was so pretty he was the toast of the rugby fifteen, had torrid tales of the antics of the pupils.

But alas, her chilly eldest brother, Jupiter, as well

as being MP for Larkshire, was chairman of the governors at Bagley Hall and, petrified of sleaze, had already given Dora a stern lecture about keeping her Max Clifford tendencies in check: 'If I hear you've been tipping off the press about anyone at Bagley or in the family, particularly me, there'll be big trouble.'

Jupiter was a beast, reflected Dora, appropriating the family home and all the money when her father died, so Dora, Dicky and their mother Anthea were now crammed into tiny Foxglove Cottage in Bagley village.

Ancient trees stroked the bleached fields with long shadows as Dora reached the outskirts of Larkminster. As she crossed the bridge, the cathedral clock struck eight. Ahead, she could see the beautiful golden houses of the Close, the market and the thriving bustling town. Trotting past St Jimmy's, the highly successful boys' school, entering the Shakespeare Estate, Dora was overtaken by an Interflora van heading nervously towards Larks Comp.

No one drove through the Shakespeare Estate by choice because of the glass and needles all over the roads. Screaming and shouting could be heard issuing from broken, boarded-up windows. Discarded fridges and burnt-out cars littered the gardens. An ashen druggie mumbled in the gutter. A gang of youths, hanging round a motorbike, hurled abuse at Dora as she passed.

Dora didn't care. She called off Cadbury who was taunting a snarling pit bull on a very short lead and looked up enviously at the satellite dishes clustered like black convolvulus on the houses. Her mother was too mean to install Sky in Foxglove Cottage.

Next door to the Shakespeare Estate, as a complete contrast, was a private estate called Cavendish Plaza, which was protected by huge electric gates, security guards and a great abstract in the forecourt, sculpted by Dora's gallery-owning father's most awful artist, Colin Casey Andrews, which was enough to frighten off any burglar, thought Dora sourly.

Cavendish Plaza was one of the brainchildren of developer Randal Stancombe, who was slapping houses, shops and supermarkets all over Larkshire and whom her mother also thought was frightfully attractive, but whose hot, devouring, knowing dark eyes made Dora's flesh crawl.

Cavendish Plaza had its own shops and access to the High Street on the other side. Dora, riding on, came to a chip shop with boarded-up windows and a pub called the Ghost and Castle, then stiffened with interest as she saw the notorious Wolf Pack slouching out of the newsagent's, loaded up with goodies. Feral Jackson was breaking the cellophane round a chicken tikka sandwich.

Everyone knew Feral. Although not yet fourteen, he was already five feet nine with snake hips, three-foot-wide shoulders and a middle finger permanently jabbing the air. He'd been up before Dora's mother at the Juvenile Court in the summer for mugging.

'And gave me such a disgustingly undressing look when we remanded him in custody,' her mother had complained.

In the end Feral had been sent for a month to a Young Offenders' Institute, and if he recognized her as her mother's daughter he'd probably knife her as well. Dora shot off down a side road.

Janna's arrival at Larks was, in fact, causing universal excitement.

Rod Hyde, head of St Jimmy's, picked up a magnifying glass to look at a photograph of Janna in the *Larkminster Gazette*. She had nice breasts and an air of confidence that would soon disappear. Pride comes before a fall. Rod Hyde was full of such little homilies. 'Good schools are like good parents,' he was always saying, 'caring and demanding.'

Rod Hyde was very bald but shaved his remaining hair. He had a firm muscular figure, a ginger beard, and believed in exercise and cold baths. St Jimmy's' results had been staggeringly good this year and they were edging nearer Bagley Hall in the league tables.

As a local super head, Rod Hyde was certain his friends, who ran S and C Services, would soon send him into Larks on a rescue mission. He would much enjoy giving Janna Curtis guidance.

*   *   *

Randal Stancombe, property developer, finished working out in his rooftop gymnasium. Before having a shower, he picked up his binoculars and looked down with pride on Cavendish Plaza, his beautiful private estate with its mature trees, still-emerald green lawns and swimming pools, where topless tenants were taking advantage of the Indian summer.

Randal's hands, however, clenched on his

binoculars as he turned them towards Larks Comp. He could see all those ruffians straggling in, scrapping, stopping to light fags or worse. Randal's tenants were constantly complaining about stolen cars and streets paved with chewing gum.

Janna Curtis looked pretty tasty in her photograph in the *Gazette*, decided Randal. She might make bold statements about turning the school round, but this Lark had two broken wings. S and C Services were bound to keep her so short of money, she'd soon be desperate for sponsorship. Interesting to see how long she'd take to approach him. Randal loved having power over women.

Randal's daughter Jade, a very attractive young lady, rising fourteen years of age, was starting her third year at Bagley Hall and dating a fellow pupil, Cosmo Rannaldini, the son of Dame Hermione Harefield, the globally famous diva. One forked out school fees mainly for the contacts. Randal would soon ask Dame Hermione to open his hypermall outside Birmingham.

*   *   *

Over at Bagley Hall, Hengist Brett-Taylor, who'd just spent five weeks in Umbria to avoid the middle classes and those with new money, was drafting a speech for the new pupils' parents.

'May I first issue a very warm welcome to all of you here tonight,' he wrote. 'But also point out what will rapidly become clear to you as the years roll by: that the headmaster of Bagley Hall is rather like the figurehead on an old wooden sailing ship. It is vaguely decorative and there is a clear understanding that one really ought to have one if

46

one is to be seen doing the proper thing, but it is of course of absolutely no practical use whatsoever and does nothing.'

Hengist's glow at nearing the top of the country's league tables in both A and GCSE levels was slightly dimmed by having to face several more massive hurdles at the start of term. In addition, he had to address the first staff meeting, the first assembly, the drinks party or 'shout-in' for new staff, not to mention keynote speeches to new pupils and sixth-formers and finally the first sermon in chapel on Sunday week.

The problem was to avoid repeating oneself or descending into platitudes, which was why Francis Bacon's essays, full of invigorating epigrams, was open on his desk. Hengist, who was terrified of boredom, was simultaneously drinking black coffee, listening to Brahms Symphony No. 2 on Radio 3, watching a video of Bagley's first fifteen's recent tour of South Africa and fondly admiring a white greyhound fast asleep on her back on the window seat.

Thank God all the holiday activities—sport and foreign trips—had passed without mishap. 'Toff school goes berserk in convent on rugger tour' could leave a huge clear-up job at the beginning of term.

Hengist gazed out at a sea of green playing fields broken only by the white rugger posts and a little wood, Badger's Retreat, in the distance, to which he kept adding young trees.

The Brahms had finished. Bagley's first fifteen had reached half-time. Picking up the *Larkminster Gazette*, Hengist looked at Janna's picture and shook his head:

47

'Poor, poor little lamb to the slaughter.'

*   *   *

The Bishop of Larkminster, on his knees in his bedroom in the Bishop's Palace overlooking the River Fleet, was praying without much hope that Janna Curtis, only a child herself, would be able to tame those dreadfully disturbed children who came from such appalling backgrounds. Next moment, he jumped out of skin still pink from his bath as a football parted the magnolia grandiflora and crashed against a pane of his Queen Anne window.

Creaking to his feet and bustling to the window, the Bishop caught a glimpse of white teeth like the crescent moon in a wicked laughing black face as, having retrieved his ball, the invader dropped back into the road. Here his companion, with a can of blue paint, was changing the 'u' in 'Please Shut the Gate' to an 'i'.

'Little buggers,' thundered the Bishop.

*   *   *

The Wolf Pack had no intention of going into school. The grass was too long to play football. So they played in the street. Fists were shaking and windows banged in fury as their ball shed the petals of a yellow rose, then snapped off the head of a tiger lily, before knocking down a row of milk bottles like ninepins.

Feral had finished his chicken sandwich but was still hungry, as he and Paris argued the merits of Arsenal and Liverpool. They once had a fight over

48

whether Thierry Henry was a better player than Michael Owen that had gone on for three days. Feral and Graffi were careful not to mention programmes they had watched last night in front of Paris. Viewing in Paris's children's home was strictly limited. The television was switched off at nine and monitored for sex and violence, which meant no *Big Brother*, *EastEnders*, or *The Bill*.

Pearl Smith, in a vile mood, was kicking a Coke tin. One of the few pupils at Larks who looked good in the hard crimson of the school uniform, she wore a skimpy crop top in that colour instead of the regulation sweatshirt. Her arm throbbed where she'd cut herself last night, after her mother's boyfriend had pushed her across the room for pinching her new baby sister.

Graffi, who'd appropriated another can of paint, was writing 'Stancombe is an asshole' on an outside wall of Cavendish Plaza.

'Very limited vocabulary,' mocked Paris, opening a stolen bar of Crunchie.

'Fuck off, professor,' replied Graffi. 'Teach me some new words then.'

Feral, meanwhile, had opened a nicked *Larkminster Gazette* and was studying Janna's picture.

'Don't look much,' snarled Pearl. 'Crap 'air, crap figure.'

'Oh, I don't know,' said Graffi, to wind her up.

Next moment, Kylie Rose, the fifth member of the Wolf Pack, carrying a pregnancy kit stolen from the High Street, joined them.

'I only got Mum to babysit Cameron by promising I'd go into school,' she told the others, then, peering at the *Gazette*, 'A-a-a-a-h. Janna says she's looking forward to meeting us. Isn't she pretty?'

'Let's go and take the piss,' said Feral, handing the paper to Paris. 'Wally might have mowed the grass.'

Feral could do anything with a football and now, seeing Dora Belvedon approaching, drove it between the conker-brown legs of her pony, Loofah, who reared up. Only Dora's excellent seat kept her in the saddle. Enraged, she rode straight at the Wolf Pack. As he leapt out of the way, Feral slashed at Loofah's reins with a knife, adding in a hoarse deep voice: 'Fuck off, you snotty little slag.'

Next moment Cadbury, the Labrador, came storming to the rescue, barking furiously. Feral, who was terrified of dogs, bolted, followed by the others. Only Paris, who protected and looked after Robin, the old fox terrier who lived at his children's home, stood his ground with hand outstretched, until Cadbury wagged his tail and licked the Crunchie crumbs off his fingers.

He had the palest face Dora had ever seen.

'Don't you dare suck up to my dog,' she yelled.

'Fuck off, you stuck-up bitch,' hissed Paris.

His face stayed with Dora. Apart from the curled lip and gelled, spiky hair, he looked like the ghost on the inn sign of the Ghost and Castle.

6

Assembly at Larks was held in the main hall. On the walls in between doorways leading to classrooms hung bad portraits of former heads: bearded gentlemen in wing collars or wearing cravats with their hair brushed forward. There were also boards listing head boys and more recent heads. How cross Mike Pitts, skulking at the back, must have felt not to have made it up there.

Moth-eaten bottle-green velvet curtains flanked the platform, whose only props included a lectern, a few chairs and, to the right, a grand piano. Behind, having remarkably escaped the school vandals, soared a stained-glass window depicting a languid Archangel Michael with his flaming sword raised to kebab an inoffensive little dragon.

The dragon et moi, thought Janna, unless I catch this mob by the throat. The butterflies in her tummy had grown into blindly crashing pterodactyls as she stood in the wings, trying to concentrate on Phil Pierce's flattering introduction. Although there were only three hundred children after the register had been taken, there seemed an awful lot of them. Above her, chewing gum and surreptitiously chatting into their mobiles, Years Ten and Eleven hung over the balcony rail. In the body of the hall stood Years Eight and Nine, who'd struggled to their feet when prodded by their various form tutors, who ringed them with arms folded like riot police anticipating trouble.

With a thud of relief, Janna thought how

attractive the children looked with their bright, curious faces: brown, black, yellow, pink, white, deathly pale, a few tanned, but now tinged with glowing ruby, emerald, violet, sapphire and amber by the light streaming through the stained glass. Both Wally and Phil crossed fingers behind their backs as she bounded up on to the platform, wearing an orange builder's hat.

'Good morning, everyone.' She beamed round at her astonished audience. 'I couldn't decide whether to wear this or a bullet-proof vest, but you all look so friendly, I needn't have worried, so let's kick off with one of your favourite songs.'

Crossing the platform she sat down at the piano and strummed out the introduction to the Larkminster Rovers battle hymn, then, with her sweet, pure voice ringing round the hall, launched into the first verse.

As she reached the second, Miss Cambola, head of music, ran up the platform steps and, in a rich mezzo, splendid bosom heaving, joined in: ' "Europe ain't seen nuffink yet." '

After a stunned silence, everyone else joined in, roaring out the chorus to loud whistling, cheering and stamping of feet.

How at ease she is with the kids, thought Wally as he uncrossed his fingers. And how bonny she looked in her rose suit, with her flaming red curls and her freckles breaking through her make-up.

After a second encore, Janna shut the piano, bowed, then whipped off her hat and held it out to a smiling Phil Pierce, who dropped in a pound coin to roars of laughter.

Janna turned to her audience. 'I'm so pleased to be here.'

'We're not,' shouted a voice from the gallery.

Janna laughed: 'Give me time.'

'She is very pretty,' whispered Kylie Rose, 'and nice.'

'She's ancient,' snarled Pearl.

'I was going through your personal files last night,' continued Janna, 'and discovered some truly excellent work.'

She then praised several children who'd done well in exams and in class.

'I particularly want to commend Aysha Khan's progress in science, and Paris Alvaston's essays, and Graffi Williams's artwork.'

'You can see it on walls all over the town,' shouted a wag.

'I want us to build on these wonderful successes, "rising, rising" like Larkminster Rovers till we get to the top. I'm determined to find what each one of you is good at. Everyone's a star at something. Never be afraid to ask for help or to pop into my office to tell me your problems. I and the other teachers are here to help.'

Seeing Cara Sharpe turn green like the witch in *Snow White* and raising her eyebrows to heaven, Janna took a deep breath:

'I'd like to tell you a story about some begonias, which are kinds of bulbs I planted in pots on the window ledge in my classroom at my last school. I planted seven. They were red, yellow, orange, pink, crimson, cream and white.'

'Oh, get on,' yelled a bruiser Janna recognized as Satan Simmons.

'These bulbs grew very fast on my window ledge,' she went on, 'except one little white one, which didn't put out a single shoot. I was sure it was

53

dead. Days passed and all the others bloomed in wonderful colours, red, yellow, orange, pink, crimson and cream.'

'Cream ain't a colour,' shouted Pearl.

'OK, OK,' went on Janna. 'But as Christmas approached, all the six had finished flowering. I was about to store them for next year and chuck the little white one in the bin, when suddenly it put out leaves and grew and grew until it flowered just at Christmas, when there were no flowers around. And it gave more pleasure than any of the other begonias. So if you're a late developer, don't worry, your time will come.'

Now she'd got their attention, she went on: 'You're all good at something—there are all sorts of exciting new GCSEs. Have you thought of taking one in child development? All you need do is study a little brother or sister.'

'Christ, no,' sneered Pearl, lighting a fag.

Janna's eyes flashed.

'And you're good at smoking, Pearl Smith,' she yelled in sudden outrage. 'You're only thirteen; how dare you ruin your lungs?'

Pearl dropped her cigarette, staggered that Janna knew her name and age.

'I want to see you in my office immediately after assembly,' said Janna ominously. 'You're Pearl's head of year, aren't you, Mrs Sharpe? Please see that she's there.'

*   *   *

Cara Sharpe was hopping. So was Pearl when she reached Janna's office. Her breath was coming in great gasps lifting her little crimson crop top even

54

higher above her groin-level mini.

She seemed to be deliberately breaking every school rule. Her hair drawn back into a cascade of ringlets was dyed more colours than the begonias. Studs gleamed from her belly button, nose and ears, from which, in addition, hung big gold loops. A silver cross nestled in her cleavage. A cat tattoo crawled under a gold ankle bracelet. More alarmingly, scars laddered her arms where she'd cut herself.

Yet with her wide-apart stick legs above killer heels, her sharp nose and chin, her shiny dark eyes, which kept glancing sideways at Janna, and her savage perkiness, she resembled nothing so much as a robin.

'How d'you know my name?'

'Because I care about you,' said Janna gently.

'Don't know me.'

'I want to very, very much.'

Pearl looked sullenly up at the photograph of smiling, waving Redfords pupils. 'Your last school?'

Janna nodded.

'Where is it?'

'Yorkshire.'

'Never been there. Miss Basket, our crap geography teacher, has never been to London.'

Janna suppressed a smile.

'We were the worst school in Yorkshire, right at the bottom,' she said.

'Like us.'

Janna went to the fridge. 'Would you like a Coke?'

'OK. Mrs Sharpe's a bitch.'

'In what way?'

55

'Blames it on us that she didn't get your job. If our SATs had been better, she would have. She never says anyfing nice when she marks our stuff.'

'How's your new baby sister?' asked Janna.

'Mum wanted to put her in my room—screams all night—and expects me to babysit so she can go out with her toyboy. I said no fucking way. I used to live with my boxer dad, but he's inside for burglary to feed his habit.'

A depressing smell of unflavoured mince was drifting up from the kitchens. I must do something about the food, thought Janna.

'I had a sister who trashed my room,' she said, 'but we get on now. I've heard you're very bright.'

'Paris is the clever one,' said Pearl. 'If he wasn't so cool, he'd get bullied for being a boffin.'

They were interrupted by screams and yells; next minute, Kylie rushed in in high excitement. 'Quickly, miss. Feral and Monster are killing each other in classroom G.'

Not yet wired up, with no thought of summoning back-up or enlisting help from other staff, Janna hurtled down the corridor.

'Christ, she's fast,' gasped Pearl as she and Kylie Rose panted after her.

Half Year Nine E was standing on desks, cheering on the protagonists; occasionally they got so heated, they started punching each other. Graffi was grinning broadly and offering two to one on Feral winning. Paris lounged against the wall pretending to be reading *David Copperfield*, but watching and waiting to jump to Feral's aid.

Young Lydia, suffering a baptism of fire in her first lesson, cringed in a corner, a book called *Dealing with Disruptive Students in the Classroom*

56

sticking out of her pocket.

Janna promptly pummelled and shoved the audience out of the classroom, but they rushed round outside and continued to peer in through the window, applauding and egging on their heroes.

'C'mon, Feral.'

'C'mon, Monster.'

Monster was as huge as a sea lion; Feral, lithe as a panther, prowled round, taunting him, hitting Monster in the eye, which started bleeding, then skipping out of the way as Monster tried to punch him in the stomach. Now they were locked, throwing blows, Feral wincing as he was crushed by Monster's brute strength. Noticing Feral's hand stealing down his jeans, followed by a flash of silver, Janna dived between them.

'Stop it,' she screamed over escalating shrieks and yells. Next moment Feral's knife was thrust in her face, halting within an inch of her nose.

'Pack it in, Feral,' repeated Janna, 'and you too, Monster.'

Chivalry was not in Feral's code, but he admired guts. The rest of the class crept back in through window or door.

'You have a very sexy mouth, Feral,' observed Janna. 'If occasionally you raised it at both corners, and showed your beautiful teeth in a smile rather than an animal snarl, you could look very attractive. And please give me that knife.'

Feral put down his knife and started to laugh, so everyone else did too.

'She's OK,' muttered Pearl.

'I said she was nice,' said Kylie.

'You're wasted on Larks, miss,' observed Graffi,

'you should be refereeing Man U or Arsenal.'

Janna turned to a quivering, ashen Lydia. 'All right, love?'

'F-f-fine.' Then, with hero-worship in her eyes: 'You're the bravest person I've ever met.'

Phil Pierce and Mike Pitts, who were waiting in the passage, were not of the same opinion.

'You stupid fool,' said Phil. 'You could have been killed. Why in hell didn't you call for back-up?'

'I forgot my radio mike,' said Janna, jolted by his rage.

'Well, for God's sake, don't forget it again. This school is not the place for suicide missions.'

Back in her office, Janna was greeted by a smug Rowan.

'I've been trying and trying to page you. Both the Bishop of Larkminster and Mrs Kamani from the corner shop have been on the phone complaining about the Wolf Pack playing football and shoplifting. Evidently Pearl raised her skirt and distracted Mrs Kamani's young son while the boys helped themselves. Next time she's going to press charges.'

*   *   *

It was after six-thirty. People had been banging on Janna's door all day, wanting a piece of her or to give her a piece of their minds. News of her breaking up a fight had whizzed round the building, opinion dividing sharply as to whether she had been incredibly brave or glory-mongering.

Crispin Thomas, ringing from S and C Services, no doubt tipped off by Mike Pitts or Cara, was in the latter camp.

'Feral could have been up on a murder charge and the school brought into disrepute because of your thoughtless irresponsibility,' he snuffled in his asthmatic, pig-like voice. 'And what's this about singing football songs in assembly?'

Janna decided to call it a day and go home.

'Thank you,' she said to Rowan as she took Hengist Brett-Taylor's bottle of champagne out of the fridge, 'you've been a great support.'

Rowan, who knew she hadn't, had the grace to blush.

In reception, Wally was mending windows.

'You did triffic,' he told her. 'Don't listen to the others. Mike Pitts downloaded all his assemblies off the internet. The kids loved you. Just promise to wear that radio mike.'

'It bulks out my skirt at the back,' grumbled Janna.

'Better be wired up than washed up, when you're doing so good,' said Wally.

Maybe, but every poster she'd put up in reception had been ripped down. As she went towards the car park, she discovered someone spraying a large penis in dark browns, purples and pinks on a newly painted wall.

The artist was poised to bolt when Janna called out:

'I don't know how many penises you've seen in your short life, Graffi Williams, but normally the glans is longer. Those testicles, in my experience, are too big, although the wrinkling of the scrotal sac is masterly.'

As Graffi's jaw and his spray can crashed to the ground, Janna went on:

'I've got a spare wall in my lounge at my new

59

cottage. I've been wondering how to decorate it. Would you have a moment to pop over at the weekend and give me some ideas for a mural? I'll pay you, but I'd rather you didn't do cocks. There are enough of them crowing in the farm across the fields. Bring Paris, if you like. I'll clear it with the children's home.'

7

After the dark, frenzied intensity of her day, Janna was astonished by the tranquil beauty of the evening. Beyond the hedgerows, slate-blue with sloes and festooned with scarlet skeins of bryony, newly harvested fields rose in platinum-blond sweeps to woods so lush and glossy from endless rain that they appeared to have spent the summer in some expensive greenhouse.

Janna was trying to decide if the orange-gold sheen on the trees was the first fires of autumn or gilding by the setting sun when she plunged like a train into one of Larkshire's dark tunnels: hawthorn, hazel, blackthorn and elder, rising thickly from high banks and impenetrably intertwined overhead by traveller's joy. Down and down she went, until she emerged blinking into the village of Wilmington, passing the duck pond and the village green bordered with pale gold cottages, swerving to avoid a mallard and his wife ambling down the High Street in the direction of the Dog and Duck.

Jubilee Cottage was the last house on the right. As she parked her new pea-green Polo in the street, because the garage was still filled with unpacked boxes, Janna thought she had never been so tired. She'd survived, but the prospect of tomorrow terrified her. Getting out, she caught sight of her neighbour deadheading roses in the mothy dusk, who called out:

'How did you get on? I've been reading about you in the *Gazette*. Come and have a drink, if you're not too tired. I'd have asked you earlier, but I've been away. My name's Lily Hamilton.'

Lily must be well into her seventies, thought Janna, but she was still very beautiful, with gentian-blue eyes, luxuriant grey hair drawn into a bun and a poker-straight back.

'What a lovely garden,' sighed Janna, admiring white geraniums, phlox and roses luminous in the dusk. 'Mine's a tip.'

'You've been far too busy. I always think one tackles gardens the second year. I'm afraid it's like the Harrods' depository,' she went on, leading Janna into a drawing room crammed with furniture, suggesting departure from a much larger house. Pictures covered every inch of wall. Over the fireplace hung a very explicit nude, with far more rings and studs piercing her voluptuous body than Pearl Smith. Dominating the room was a lovely pale pink and green silk striped sofa, whose arms had been ripped to shreds. The culprit, a vast fluffy black and white cat whom Lily introduced as the General, was stretched out unrepentantly in one corner. In the other lay an even larger stuffed badger. Seeing Janna's frown of disapproval, Lily explained the badger was already stuffed when she acquired him.

'He was in an auction, looking so sad and unloved, I got him for fifteen shillings.'

Wondering if Lily was a bit dotty, Janna waved Hengist's bottle of champagne. 'Why don't we drink this?'

'Tepid champagne is a crime against nature,' observed Lily. 'Let's cool it in the deep freeze and first drink this stuff, which is much less nice.' She filled Janna's glass with white.

Parked between cat and badger, Janna admitted the day had been rough.

'The older staff are so antagonistic, and they're not giving any lead to the younger teachers.'

Then she explained who'd sent her the champagne, which deteriorated into a rant against independent schools and 'fascist bastards' like Hengist Brett-Taylor in particular.

'All those facilities wasted on a few spoilt kids, whose rich parents are too selfish to look after them and just pack them off into the upper-class care of a boarding school.'

'I don't think children in care jet home to Moscow or New York at the weekend,' said Lily. 'Or race up to London. And I promise you, Hengist is a charmer. I'm sure you'd like him if you met him. He doesn't take himself at all seriously, he's awfully good-looking, and he's worked wonders with Bagley. They were a pack of tearaways five years ago. Now they're near the top of the league tables.'

'Perhaps he could give me a few tips,' said Janna sarcastically. 'Although it can't be difficult with all that money and tiny classes and vast playing fields for the kids to let off steam. How d'you know him?'

'My nephew Dicky's a pupil, Dora his twin sister starts this term and Rupert Campbell-Black's children go there as well.'

Which sent Janna into more shivering shock-horror:

'Rupert Campbell-Black's the most arrogant, spoilt, foxhunting, right-wing bastard.'

'But again, decidedly attractive,' laughed Lily, topping up Janna's glass. 'He does have—even more than Hengist—alarming charm.'

The General heaved himself on to Janna's knee, purring and kneading.

'I must get a cat,' sighed Janna, rubbing him behind his pink ears.

'Do,' said Lily, 'then we can catsit for each other. Why did you take on Larks?'

After a second glass on an empty stomach, Janna found herself telling Lily all about Stew.

'He swore he was going to leave Beth, his wife, and marry me. He just had to see his son graduate, then it was his daughter's wedding, then Beth's hysterectomy, then it was going to be the moment Redfords came out of special measures.

'But the afternoon we found out, he immediately rang up Beth: "Darling, we've done it, put a bottle of bubbly on ice," and booked a table at the Box Tree. They went out to celebrate with the deputy head and his wife. I realized then he'd never leave her.'

'You poor child.' Lily patted her hand. 'For many married people, particularly men, adultery is merely an amusing hobby.'

'He really was a bastard,' mused Janna.

'But a left-wing one this time,' observed Lily.

Janna burst out laughing:

'I was so desperate to get away from the situation, and so longing to be a head, it rather blinded me to Larks's imperfections. Shall we tackle that bottle of bubbly now? And you can tell me why Hengist Brett-Taylor is so attractive and also about Wilmington.'

'Very much "Miss Marple" territory,' said Lily.

'Who's the handsome old gentleman who lives five doors down?'

'That's the Brigadier, Brigadier Christian

Woodford. He always salutes my General'—Lily nodded at the cat on Janna's knee—'when they meet in the street. His wife died recently; nearly bankrupted himself paying her medical bills. She needed twenty-four-hour nursing at home. I don't know if he'll be able to afford to stay.

'He had a terrific war. He's very well read and knows a huge amount about natural history, particularly wild flowers.'

'Like you do,' said Janna, looking at the autumn squills and meadow cranesbill in a vase on top of the bookshelf and the wild-flower books in the shelves. Glancing up at a watercolour of meadowsweet and willowherb, she added, 'I recognize that artist.'

'Hanna Belvedon, married to my nephew Jupiter.' Then at Janna's raised eyebrows, 'Our local MP.'

'Your nephew? But he's another sneering—'

'Right-wing bastard. Here I entirely agree with you,' smiled Lily and then confided that it was Jupiter who had chucked her out of her lovely house in Limesbridge when Raymond, his father and Lily's brother, had died last year. 'He needed the rent money to boost his political campaign.'

'I told you he was a bastard,' said Janna indignantly.

'I shouldn't have sneaked,' sighed Lily, 'but I do think you should have lunch with Hengist. He's got an awfully nice wife and a daughter about your age. You must meet some young people. We're rather a geriatric bunch in Wilmington.'

'I love Wilmington,' protested Janna. 'It's the sweetest village in the world.'

'What fun you've come to live here. Are you

65

desperately tired or shall we have some scrambled eggs?'

*   *   *

Dew soaked Janna's legs. The planets Saturn and, appropriately, Jupiter were rising, glowing green and contained by mist like lights from the angels' electric toothbrushes, as she tottered home after midnight.

What a darling Lily was. After the death of her sweet mother, Janna had plunged into work, and never properly mourned her loss. How wonderful if Lily could become a friend.

Tripping over a boot rack, Janna fell on top of a large bunch of pink and orange lilies wilting in the porch.

'Good luck,' said the card, 'missing you terribly, all love, Stew'.

8

Janna was woken by a raging hangover and torrential rain and things went from bad to worse. She found Wally sweeping up more glass from two broken windows. Two door handles had been broken off in the lavatories. The walls in reception had been attacked with a hammer and rain poured in through the roof into the main hall and several classrooms.

Adele, who taught geography and had two children and no husband, rang in sick, so there was no one to take her classes. Another teacher, who hadn't turned up yesterday, wrote saying she'd taken a job in Canada. Ten of the children, believed to be truanting, had evidently gone elsewhere. This hardly put Janna in carnival mood to welcome the new intake of Year Seven: eleven-year-olds fresh from their primary schools.

Leaving Mags Gablecross, who had a free period, to show them round and explain their timetables, Janna took refuge in an empty classroom to fine-tune what she was going to say to their parents. The cleaners had piled the chairs on the tables to show they had swept the floor. Next moment, a tall, handsome hellraiser from Year Nine, known to be a staunch BNP supporter, staggered in with glazed eyes.

'Good morning, Johnnie Fowler,' called out Janna, proud she'd remembered his name.

Johnnie immediately grabbed a chair and hurled it at her. Just missing her head, it crashed into the whiteboard.

Radio mike forgotten, Janna fled into the corridor, slap into Phil Pierce. She collapsed against his dark blue shirt.

'Help,' she yelped.

For a moment his arms closed around her and she snuggled into him, heart hammering, breath coming in great gasps, then they both pulled away.

'Johnnie Fowler hurled a chair at me.'

Phil went straight into the classroom, slowly calming Johnnie and sending him back to his own classroom.

'He was coming down from crack.'

'He ought to be excluded or at least suspended,' raged Janna.

'If he goes home, it won't do any good. He'll be out on the street thieving. He mugged an old lady last term. Mother's on her own and can't control him, poor woman.'

Janna felt ashamed. Phil was such a good guy, who had a true empathy with the kids. She was horrified how much she'd enjoyed having his arms round her.

Janna then addressed the new Year Seven parents, who were touched, assuming her frightful shakes were due to nerves at meeting them rather than hangover or Johnnie Fowler.

'Your children will always have a special place in my heart,' she told them, 'because I'm starting at Larks at the same time as they are. We'll go up the school together, and I will learn as much from them as I hope they will from me. I will do everything to make them really enjoy learning. Any problems, please come to me and I hope to welcome you all at parents' meetings.'

She smiled round. The Year Seven parents

smiled back. Most of them had been disasters at school and had been phobic about crossing the threshold. Largely from the Shakespeare Estate, they looked like children themselves. If they'd had these kids in their early teens, they need only be in their mid twenties now, which made Janna feel dreadfully old.

As she finished speaking, Mags Gablecross brought in a little girl with huge slanting dark eyes and straight black hair. She was adorable, but sobbing. Mags explained that she came from Paris Alvaston's children's home and had just arrived from Kosovo. Her mother had died in a shootout. Her father was missing, believed killed, in the war. She didn't speak any English and was called Kata.

'Now, which of you is grown-up and kind enough to look after Kata?' Janna asked the children.

Every hand went up.

Afterwards, having just managed to keep down two Alka-Seltzer and feeling incapable of tackling not one, but now two buckling in-trays, Janna informed Rowan Merton she was going to sit in on some classes. Armed with her radio mike, Janna went on to the corridors, fantasizing she was June in *The Bill* or, more likely, a sapper moving from minefield to minefield. She was aware of children roaring past her, swearing, fighting, chatting on their mobiles, drifting in late.

Out of a window, she noticed rabble-rousing Robbie Rushton and Gloria the gymnast creeping in through a side door. They should have been taking geography and PE. No wonder the kids were running wild.

A nice change, however, was Miss Uglow's RE class. 'Ugly', who refused to teach anything but the

Bible, was held in equal proportions of terror, respect and love by her pupils.

'Jesus clothed the naked, fed the hungry, and educated the ignorant,' she was telling an enraptured Year Eight, 'which is what I'm doing now.'

Janna smiled and moved on. Rounding the corner, she went slap into Mike Pitts. Obviously tipped off by beady Rowan, he was spluttering to Miss Basket, the menopausal misfit who taught geography.

'As a dedicated professional for twenty-five years, I'm not having some chit of a young woman sitting in on my lessons.' Catching sight of Janna, he turned an even deeper shade of magenta.

Miss Basket melted into the Ladies. Janna followed Mike into his office.

'Could we have a word?'

Mike glanced at the clock. 'I'm teaching in five minutes.'

Clearly a bit of a handsome dandy, judging by past cartoons of him as a cricketer and footballer on the walls, Mike looked dreadful now: his puffy face as bloodshot as his eyes; snowfalls of scurf on the shoulders of his blazer. Joss sticks glowed on his desk. His hands shook as he fussily shoved papers into a blue folder.

Poor man, thought Janna, I usurped him.

'We ought to try and get to know each other,' she stammered. Then, on wild impulse: 'Would you like to come to supper on Sunday?'

'My wife and I prefer to forget school at the weekend.'

Janna flushed. 'Well, perhaps a drink during the week?'

70

'Quite frankly, I'm too drained. I find if one has fulfilled one's professional commitments, socializing at the end of a working day is not on the agenda. Now, if you'll excuse me.'

Bastard, thought Janna. Feeling the parched earth of a drooping jasmine on the window ledge, she instinctively picked up the green watering can beside it.

'Don't,' yelled Mike, adding hastily, 'I like to look after my own plants. Women overwater.'

That's gin in that watering can, thought Janna, catching a whiff.

Mike glared at her, daring her to confront him.

'We have to work together . . .' Her voice trailed off.

'I must go.'

'I'll come with you,' insisted Janna.

In his classroom, they found a sweet-faced Indian girl in a pale blue sari: a teaching assistant who helped the slower pupils, particularly the foreign ones with poor English, by explaining questions to them and showing them how to write the answers. She was now laying out worksheets and consulting an algebra textbook, and told Janna she had been at Larks for four terms. She loved the job because it was so rewarding seeing understanding dawning on the children's faces and how the slow ones blossomed if you took time to explain things.

'I'd like to start an after-school maths club.'

'Wonderful idea. Come and see me.'

'We must get on,' interrupted Mike, 'the students will be here in a minute.' Tetchily, he handed the Indian girl a page of squares and triangles. 'Can you get me some marker pens and photostat this?'

'She's great,' said Janna as the girl left the room.

'What's her name?'

'I've no idea.'

And Janna flipped. 'This is disgraceful. She's the only black teacher in the school, she's been here a year and you don't know her name.'

'She's only a teaching assistant.'

'Working her butt off for you and the kids. You ought to know everyone in your department and what they're up to, and in the school, you're deputy head, for God's sake.'

'I will not be spoken to like that.'

Both jumped at a knock on the door. It was Rowan Merton, dying to find out what was going on.

'Phone for you, Janna.'

'I'm busy.'

'It's Russell Lambert, our chair of governors. Says its urgent.'

Bitterly regretting her outburst of temper and aware she had made an even more implacable enemy, Janna ran back to her office.

Russell, whom Janna could still only think of as Babar, king of the elephants, head of the Tusk Force, was at his most portentous.

'Good morning, Janna, bad news I'm afraid. Harry Fitzgerald, head of a school in the north of the county, has had a coronary. Ashton Douglas, head of S and C, has just phoned. They want Phil Pierce to take over as head immediately.'

'Can't they take Mike Pitts and his joss sticks?' wailed Janna unguardedly.

'You'll need your deputy head,' reproved Russell. 'You'd be very weak on the maths front if Mike goes.'

*   *   *

'I'll never survive without you,' Janna moaned later to Phil, who had the grace to look sheepish.

'I'm sorry, Janna, I hate to let you down, but I can't resist the chance to be a head.'

He didn't add that Janna had been disturbing his sleep recently: she was so brave but so vulnerable. He loved his wife; safer if he took himself out of harm's way.

'Anyway, Harry Fitzgerald will probably pull through and I'll be back in a few weeks.'

'I'm only cross because Skunk Illingworth will have to be promoted to head of science. He'll be so up himself. When are you going?'

'Tomorrow.'

Crispin Thomas from S and C Services rang later.

'You're providing a bloody sight more challenge than support, swiping my best teacher,' stormed Janna.

Crispin laughed fatly. 'We know, we know. We're going to send Rod Hyde, the super head from St Jimmy's, round to give you a hand next week.'

Outside, rain was still tipping down; the awful playground was filling up with puddles.

'I don't need Rod Hyde. I was hired to run this joint. Our playground needs a makeover for a start,' and Janna hung up because of more screams and yells coming from the direction of the history block.

Running into the classroom, Nine E again, she found tin soldiers and a model battlefield scattered all over the floor. Next moment, a display of shrapnel and shell splinters, the collection of

Lance, the newly qualified teacher, went flying. Lance and his teaching assistant were cringing in a corner and the appalling Monster Norman, no doubt feeling he had lost face after his fight with Feral yesterday, had taken centre stage as he menaced a terrified sobbing Asian girl.

'Teacher's pet, teacher's pet,' he hissed. 'Paki swot, Paki swot.'

His victim was Aysha Khan, who'd made such progress after two terms that Janna had singled her out in assembly.

The children, diverted by fights—this was their theatre—had formed a four-deep circle round the participants.

'Black rubbish, black shit,' taunted Monster, then spat in Aysha's face.

'Stop that,' shouted Janna, pushing her way through the crowd, too enraged to be frightened.

Monster, who she noticed had a shadow of moustache on his sweating upper lip, had a lit cigarette in his hand.

'Go home, fucking Paki bitch,' he yelled and was about to burn her arm when Janna dragged his hand away, grabbing the cigarette, stamping on it and turning on him.

'How dare you!'

'Go on,' mocked Monster, 'touch me, hit me, you try it. I'll get you fired, you'll never work again, you sad bitch.'

'You loathsome thug.' Caution had deserted Janna once more. 'Get out of here, you revolting bully.'

'Go on, miss, 'it 'im,' yelled Pearl.

'My mum's a governor.' Monster's evil, sallow, pasty face was disintegrating like goat's cheese in

74

liquid as he gathered saliva in his mouth.

'I don't care. Out, out!'

'Well done, miss,' cheered the children as Monster, already on his mobile to his mother, pummelled his way out of the classroom.

'Are you all right, miss?' asked Kylie Rose. 'Shall I get you a cup of tea?'

In the doorway, Wally was shaking his head again. 'When will you learn, Janna?'

A hovering Jason 'Goldilocks' Fenton was also highly amused.

'Wherever you go, there's a rumpus. So exciting. I might not hand in my notice after all.'

Janna turned on him furiously too. 'Out,' she yelled.

*   *   *

She was picking up toy soldiers and sorting out a mortified Lance—'I wanted to defend you, but I couldn't somehow. Not sure I'm cut out to be a teacher'—when there was a further rumpus in the corridor.

'Where's Miss Fucking Curtis?' bellowed a voice and Monster Norman's mother, predictably nicknamed 'Stormin'', square, massive and enraged, with a whiskery jaw thrust out, came barging in.

'Why are you always picking on my Martin?'

She raised her fist. Janna got out her mobile.

'If we can't discuss this, Mrs Norman, I'm calling the police. Your Martin was sadistically bullying another pupil.'

Only Wally seizing Mrs Norman's arm stopped her punching Janna in the face.

To Janna's horror, the following day, two

75

governors (Russell Lambert and Cara Sharpe), Crispin Thomas from S and C and Mike Pitts (as deputy head), overturned Monster's exclusion, mostly on Cara's testimony.

'Martin's a sweet, caring boy,' she cooed, 'I've never had any trouble with him.'

'Nor have I,' agreed Mike, who was wearing a purple shirt to match his nose as he helped himself to another extra strong mint.

'He abused Aysha in the most revolting and racist way,' raged Janna. 'He terrorizes half his classmates. We'll never get a happy school with kids like him around.'

'Don't forget you incur a hefty five-thousand-pound fine every time you permanently exclude a pupil,' snuffled fat Crispin, accepting a mint. 'It's not as though you're oversubscribed or rolling in money. You really must be more restrained in your attitude. I'm getting complaints from all over and you've only been here three days. Calling Martin a "loathsome thug" is hardly the way to address challenging behaviour.'

Monster was suspended for three days.

*   *   *

The children were devastated when they heard of Phil Pierce's defection. Their favourite teacher had become just another rat leaving a sinking ship.

9

On Saturday morning, Janna sneaked into Larks to tackle her towering in-tray unobserved by Rowan Merton. Following Stew's maxim that if anything's important, people will write a second time, she chucked ninety-five per cent of her 'bin-tray' into six black dustbin bags. Perhaps Mike Pitts had a 'gin-tray'—he'd locked his office, so she couldn't check his watering can.

Yesterday afternoon, Miss Cambola had flung open the staffroom door and, rattling the teeth of the Dinosaurs and nearly bringing down the whole crumbling building, sang at the top of her voice: 'Thank God it's Friday.'

She had also written on the back of a postcard of Caruso: 'Congratulations! You have survived a whole week and done well, Regards, Maria Cambola', reducing Janna to tears of gratitude.

Having fired off thirty emails, mostly thanking people who'd sent her good-luck cards, Janna made the decision to hold a prospective-parents' evening at the end of the month. This would give her the clout and everyone the incentive to smarten up the school, painting as many classrooms as possible and papering walls and corridors with some decent kids' work, even if she had to write and draw it herself. Full of excitement, she first wrote copy for an ad in the *Larkminster Gazette*, inviting prospective parents to the event, then secondly, a glowing report of Larks's progress and plans for the future. These she delivered to the *Gazette* on the way home.

Earlier in the week, she had rung Mr Blenchley, the care manager of Oaktree Court, Paris's children's home, who sounded bullying and humourless and who had a thick clogged voice like leftover lumpy porridge not going down the plughole.

Little Kata from Kosovo was adjusting to the regime, he said, and it was all right for Paris to come to tea with Graffi:

'But as the lad pleases himself, I doubt he'll show up.'

*   *   *

It was one of those mellow, hazy afternoons only September can produce. Midges jived idly with thistledown. The field at the end of the village was being ploughed up, two men in yellow tractors sailing back and forth over the Venetian-red earth and waving at Janna as she sat in the garden worrying about her first governors' meeting on Monday. There was so much that needed tackling: permission to fire three-quarters of the staff for a start.

A flock of red admirals was guzzling sweetness from the long purple stems of a buddleia bush, but ignoring the honeysuckle next door—like pupils flocking to St Jimmy's and Searston Abbey rather than Larks, she thought sadly. She was just wondering how to galvanize the staff at Monday's morning briefing when the doorbell rang.

To her delight and amazement, it was Graffi, bringing both Paris and Feral. As they swarmed in, laughing and larky as the players in *Hamlet*, Janna suspected they had been enjoying a spliff or two on the way.

'How grand to see you. No Kylie and Pearl?'

'Kylie's minding baby Cameron,' said Graffi, 'giving her mum a day off. Pearl's got a hairdressing job. Don't think she'd have got here on those heels, anyway.'

'Did you walk all the way?' asked Janna, and then thought: How stupid, how else could they have afforded to come?

Taking Graffi by the arm, she led them down the hall into the kitchen, newly painted buttercup yellow and brightened by good-luck cards and framed children's drawings.

'Are you starving? I was planning to give you "high tea", as we call it in Yorkshire, a bit later,' she asked, getting out dark green mugs and a big bottle of Coke.

Opening a jumbo bag of crisps with her teeth, then bending down to pull out a blue bowl into which to decant them, she found all three boys staring at her. Barefoot, wearing tight jeans and a clinging blue-striped matelot jersey, with her wild russet curls escaping from a tartan toggle, she didn't look remotely like a headmistress.

'I don't bother to dress up much at weekends,' she stammered.

'Nice Aga.' Graffi patted its dark blue flanks. 'My mum's ambition's to have one.'

'It was already there when I moved in,' said Janna hastily.

She loved the Aga, but felt, like the burglar alarm, it was rather too middle-class.

'Why don't you explore?'

As she put knives, forks and willow-patterned plates on a tray, the boys careered round the

79

house, opening doors and cupboards, picking up and examining ornaments.

'It's fucking tiny,' said Paris, who was accustomed to Oaktree Court, a great house once belonging to the very rich, now ironically inhabited by children who had nothing.

'This bed's fucking large,' agreed Graffi and Feral, who were used to sharing with several brothers and sisters and sometimes a drunken father or fleeing mother, when they discovered Janna's attic bedroom.

Hung with blue gingham curtains, the four-poster only left room for triangular shelves slotted into one corner, a television, fitted cupboards and a dressing table which Janna had to perch on the bottom of the bed to use.

'Fink there's a bloke in her life?' asked Feral.

'Hope not,' said Graffi, breathing in scent bottles.

'Wouldn't mind giving her one,' said Feral.

'Oh, shut up, you're incorrigible,' snapped Paris, who was examining the books, mostly classics, on either side of the bed.

'Whatever that means. This bed's fucking comfortable,' said a bouncing Feral. Then, glancing sideways at Stew's photograph, which, after Monday's flowers, was on show again: 'That must be her father.'

Joyous as otters, they bounded downstairs (emptying the crisp bowl en route) out into the garden, fascinated by reddening apples, French beans hanging from wigwams, potatoes and carrots actually growing in the ground.

'What the hell's that?'

'It's a marrer,' said Graffi. 'My nan used to stuff

them.'

Holding it against his groin, Feral indulged in a few pelvic thrusts. 'Looks as though it orta do the stuffing.'

While Paris stopped to stroke Lily's cat the General, who was tightroping along the fence, Graffi and Feral began kicking a football round the lawn. Watching their antics from the kitchen, Janna thought how perfectly they complemented each other. Paris, ghostly pale, seemed lit by moonlight, Feral by the sun. Feral was so arrogant, like George Eliot's cock, who thought the sun had risen to hear him crow. It wasn't just the lift of his jaw, or the swing of his hips, or the lean elongated body that made a red T-shirt, cheap fake leather jacket and black jeans look a million dollars. He'd make a fortune as a model. The long brown eyes curling up at the corner, with thick lashes creating a natural eyeliner, were haughty too; even the huge white smile said, 'I'm superior.'

But, despite this hauteur, like a feral cat he constantly glanced round checking for danger. Made edgy by the alien territory of the countryside, he shot inside when a dozy brown and white cow put her nose over the fence, and ran upstairs to watch football.

Physically, Graffi was a mixture of the two and, with his stocky build, olive skin and wicked dark eyes, needed only a black beret on his unruly dark curls, a smock and an easel to be having *déjeuner sur l'herbe* with naked beauties.

Janna took him into the low-beamed living room, which was painted cream with a pale coral sofa and chairs. Set into one wall was a stone fireplace filled with apple logs. The second wall was mostly a

81

west-facing window overlooking fields and woods. Against the third was an upright piano and floor-to-ceiling shelves for Janna's books, music and CDs. The empty fourth awaited Graffi's genius.

Blown away that Janna trusted him, Graffi borrowed paper and pencil and started sketching. How would she like a view of the cathedral, houses in the Close, softened by lots of trees, a few cows paddling in the river to 'scare Feral away', people walking their dogs on the towpath?

'That sounds champion, as long as you don't graffiti the buildings.'

'Make it look more lived in. Nice place this. My da's a builder, does a lot of work for Randal Stancombe. If you want anything done, he could hide it.' Then, going back to the wall: 'It'll take a few Saturdays.'

'That's fine. You could come Sundays as well.'

'Nah, I'm busy Sundays. Going to look at them cows.' And he wandered off to kick a ball on the lawn with Feral.

Chests of books were lying round, so Paris took them out and put them on to the shelves, his face growing paler as he kept stopping to read. Janna helped him, pointing out favourites: *Rebecca*, *Middlemarch*, *Wuthering Heights*, giving him spare copies of Byron, *Le Grand Meaulnes* and *The Catcher in the Rye*.

Paris found the cottage blissfully quiet after Oaktree Court, where someone was always sobbing, screaming and fighting, and wardens or social workers were always asking questions or needling him: 'Get your long nose out of that book. Come on, open up, open up.'

'How long have you loved reading?' asked Janna.

'Since I was about nine. Head teacher of my school in Nottingham put me in charge of the library, so I could borrow all the books I wanted. I saved up to buy a torch and read under the bedclothes all night. That torch lit up my life.'

Children in care are usually attention-seekers, or, like Paris, internalize everything. Looking at the cool, deadpan face, its only colour the eyes bloodshot from reading, few people realized the raging emotional torrents beneath the layers of ice.

Paris had been two when his mother dumped him on the door of a children's home in Alvaston, outside Derby. He had been clinging on to a glass ball containing the Eiffel Tower in a snow storm— still his most treasured possession. On his royal-blue knitted jumper was pinned a note: 'Please look after my son. His name is Paris.'

No one had ever found his mother. Early adoption was delayed, hoping she'd come forward. Afterwards, there was no one to sign the papers.

Every so often, when the moon was full, longing for his mother overwhelmed him, and he went searching for her on trains round the country. When he was twelve, he had suffered the humiliation of putting his photograph in the local paper advertising for a family. The photograph, taken in the fluorescent light of the children's home, made him look like a death's head. Paris for once had dropped his guard and written the accompanying copy, which Nadine his social worker had rejigged: 'Paris is a healthy twelve-year-old, who has been in care for a number of years. He has a few behaviour problems and needs firm handling,' which, translated, meant trouble with a capital 'T'.

Paris, affecting a total lack of interest, had hung around waiting for the post, expecting Cameron Diaz or Posh and Becks to roll up in a big car and whisk him off to love and luxury. But there had been no takers.

Feral and Graffi had carried him during this humiliation. He, in turn, had carried Feral when his older brother Joey dissed the head of a rival gang, who took him outside and shot him dead. Feral's mother, Nancy, had emerged briefly from a drug-induced stupor to achieve fleeting fame bewailing the loss on television. But as it was only black killing black, the public and police soon forgot and moved on to another tragedy. Nancy turned back to her drugs.

Feral was dyslexic and, ashamed he wrote and read so poorly, truanted persistently. Paris, who was very clever, translated for him and explained questions.

'He's my one-to-one teaching assistant,' boasted Feral.

Out of eighteen homes and eleven schools, Paris's three years at Larks and Oaktree Court had been his longest placement. Terrified of being dragged away to a new care home in another part of the country, he tried not to complain or rock the boat.

'I've got two copies of *The Moonstone*, so here's one for you,' said Janna, 'and here's Lily coming up the path.'

Lily was in high fettle. She had just won a hundred pounds on the three o'clock and been making elderflower wine. Feral and Graffi came scuttling down the stairs for new diversion.

'Boys, this is my friend Lily Hamilton who lives

84

next door, and Lily, these are my friends, Graffi, who's painting me a mural, Paris, who's sorting out my bookshelves, and Feral, who's an ace footballer.'

'Really?' said Lily. 'My nephew Dicky is besotted with Man U; I confess a fondness for Arsenal.'

'That's cool, man,' said Feral approvingly.

'I'm about to watch them on Sky,' said Lily. 'Would you like to come and have a look and test this summer's elderflower wine?'

Needing no more encouragement, Feral and Graffi bounded after her.

10

Paris preferred to stay with the books and Janna. With her sweet face and rippling red hair, she was like those beautiful women in pre-Raphaelite paintings. He tried not to stare. As she handed her books and their hands touched occasionally, she told him about her parents' evening.

'I want the place to look so good, people will really want to send their children to Larks.'

Paris said nothing. Oh God, she thought, he has no parents, I'm a tactless cow. Changing the subject hurriedly, she said she was planning a project on the lark.

'In literature, art, music and real life. I don't know if larks are singing at the moment, but we could take a tape recorder into the fields. I'm going to call the project "Larks Ascending" to symbolize our climb out of special measures.'

' "To hear the lark begin his flight, And singing startle the dull night," ' murmured Paris, handing her a tattered copy of *Anna Karenina*.

' "From his watch-tower in the skies, Till the dappled dawn doth rise," ' carried on Janna, clapping her hands. 'Fantastic, exactly the kind of stuff we need. Will you copy it out for me and perhaps write a poem about a lark yourself?'

Larks were always having to move on because of tractors ploughing and harrowing, and people sowing seed and spraying pesticides and fertilizers, thought Paris bitterly, just like him moving from home to home.

Whoops and yells from next door indicated that

Arsenal must have scored.

'Tell me about Graffi,' said Janna as she slotted *Northanger Abbey* between *Emma* and *Persuasion*.

'His dad earns good when he's in work. Nice bloke but the money seems to evaporate in the betting shop or the pub. Graffi's got two elder brothers and a sister; then, after him, his mother had a Downs Syndrome baby, and all the attention goes on her. Graffi gets the shit kicked out of him by the elder kids, but his mother—when she works in the pub evenings and Sundays—expects Graffi, because he's easy-going, to look after his sister. Graffi loves her to bits but he gets jealous and worries she'll be bullied when she goes to primary school next year.'

'Where does he live—on the Shakespeare Estate?'

'Hamlet Street. Feral's Macbeth, Kylie's Dogberry, Pearl's Othello—which figures: she's dead jealous. Monster Norman's Iago, which figures too.'

'Is it really rough?'

'If you want respect, the only way is to act tough and deal drugs,' said Paris. 'Randal Stancombe's sniffing round the place, wants to offer it a leisure centre.'

'So young people have somewhere to go in the evening to keep them off the streets,' volunteered Graffi, returning at half-time.

'I like the streets,' grumbled Feral. 'I don't want no youth club woofter teaching me no ballroom dancing.'

'More walls to draw on,' said Graffi. 'I like that lady next door. She's got terrific pictures on her wall, that nude over the mantelpiece looks straight out of a porn mag. That elderflower wine's not bad neiver; she said it didn't matter as we wasn't driving.'

Out of the corner of her eye, Janna saw Feral pick up a very pretty pink and white paperweight, put it in his pocket, then put it back again.

'What d'you want to be in life, Feral?' she asked.

Feral gave her his huge, charming, dodgy smile.

'Twenty-one, man.'

'I beg your pardon?'

'If you live on the Shakespeare Estate, it's an achievement to stay alive to the weekend,' explained Graffi. 'I've done this drawing of Lily's cat.'

'That's so good.' Janna took it to the light. 'You must give it to Lily. When you get back from the second half, I'll have your tea ready.'

While Paris became immersed in *The Catcher in the Rye*, Janna produced a real Yorkshire tea, with lardy cake, dripping toast, jam roly poly, crumpets and very strong tea out of a big brown pot.

As a returning Feral and Graffi helped her carry it to the table outside, Feral looked up at the kitchen beam. 'What's that long thick black thing called?' he asked.

'Feral Jackson,' quipped Graffi.

'Fuck off, man,' said Feral, who was in a good mood. Arsenal had won resoundingly.

The sinking sun was turning the stubble a soft mushroom pink. Housemartins and swallows gathered on the telegraph wires; rooks were jangling in the beeches; a purple and silver air balloon drifted up the valley, like a bauble escaped from a Christmas tree. As the boys sat down on a rickety old garden bench and devoured everything, helicopters kept chugging overhead.

'Is there an air show on or something?'

'Naaah,' sneered Graffi, 'it's toff kids being taken back to Bagley Hall.'

With only a slight stab of guilt, Janna realized none of her emails had been to thank Hengist Brett-Taylor for his bottle of champagne.

'That dark blue one'—Graffi pointed towards the sky—'belongs to Rupert Campbell-Black, who my dad hero-worships because Rupert's given him so many winners. And that's Randy Scandal,' he added as Rupert's helicopter was followed five minutes later by one in dark crimson bearing Randal Stancombe's name in gold letters and his logo of a little gold house.

'Randal's got a hot daughter called Jade,' said Feral. 'I wouldn't mind giving her one, wiping the smug smile off her face.'

Paris shivered. Oaktree Court was a grand old building set back from the main road on the way to St Jimmy's and Searston Abbey. Randal Stancombe's henchmen had been spotted in the grounds. Converted, it would make splendid luxury flats in the catchment area of the two schools, and once again Paris's security would be blown.

Seeing the shiver, and how inadequately Paris was dressed in his thin nylon tracksuit and trainers with the soles coming off, Janna suggested they went inside.

'It's nice here,' said Graffi.

'Nadine, your social worker, rang me yesterday,' Janna told Paris.

'Nosy old bitch,' said Paris flatly.

'She spoke well of you,' laughed Janna. 'She said you told the other children fantastic stories at bedtime. Why don't you write them down?'

'Did once. Cara Sharpe said they were crap.'

'That's only her opinion,' said Graffi. 'She's head of drama as well as English but I don't fink she's read a play since she left uni.'

'I told her I wanted to be an actor and she pissed herself.' Paris gave a cackle. 'She said: "With an accent like yours, you've got to be joking." '

For a second, Janna gasped in terror.

'That was extraordinary. That was Cara's laugh and voice exactly.'

'Paris can do anyone,' said Feral.

'Do Mike Pitts,' said Graffi, wiping his hands on his jeans and picking up his pen to draw Janna.

Paris pursed his lips: ' "If it weren't for my professional commitment, I'd have left teaching yearsh ago and been earning a million a year running I-Shee-I." '

Janna gave a scream of laughter. Once again the imitation was perfect. Paris had even caught Mike's drunken slur.

Then he did Rowan: ' "Ay'm so busy juggling my job, my husband and my two little girls, I forget to have 'me' time." ' Paris looked up from under his lashes like Rowan did.

'You're brilliant,' cried Janna, 'you *must* become an actor.'

' "Moost I really? Thut's lovely, in fuct it's chumpion," ' said Paris.

'That's me,' giggled Janna. 'I thought I'd lost my accent a bit down here.'

Paris smiled—and Janna felt truly weak at the knees. He was like some Arctic Prince who'd strayed southwards and might melt any moment in the autumn sunset.

90

I will do anything to make his life better, she told herself.

They were reserved but not shy, these boys. Although only thirteen or fourteen, they were old before their time, hardened and aged by poverty, loss, lack of security and the contempt of others. But at the same time, they were all hunky: muscular from the fight to survive, and sure of their sexuality.

Overwhelmed with longing for both a lover and a child of her own, Janna was aware that Feral, Graffi and Paris fell halfway between the two. Suddenly she knew she had to send them home.

'We must decide a fee for the mural,' she told Graffi.

'Five grand a day,' Graffi grinned, looking round for the picture he had drawn of her, but Paris had already whipped it.

Janna gave Paris a carrier bag for his books and, for all of them, a big bag of Cox's apples from the tree at the bottom of the garden. But running upstairs for a cardigan, glancing out of her bedroom window, she saw them chucking the apples at each other. Paris, with his long nose still in *The Catcher in the Rye*, stretched out a hand to take a perfect catch as they sauntered up the lane.

Back in the kitchen, the laptop she'd been working on had been opened. Then she gave a gasp of horrified amusement.

To the words: 'Get rid of three-quarters of the teachers, I wish', someone had added, 'Why not start with Cara Sharpe, Mike Pitts, Skunk Illingworth, Chalford (you ain't met her yet), Sam Spink, Robbie Rushton and Hot Flush Basket for a start.' Janna's sentiments exactly.

She ought to work, but she was so pleased to be interrupted by a call from Lily saying she'd enjoyed the wine-tasting as much as Feral and Graffi: 'What delightful boys. Feral's going to help me make sloe gin and Graffi did an excellent drawing of General, caught the angle of his whiskers exactly. If I hadn't fallen out with him, I'd show it to my nephew Jupiter, who's a dealer when he's not being an MP. Feral gave me a spliff.'

'Lily,' said Janna shocked.

'I haven't had one since another nephew, Jonathan, got married. Come and have a drink.'

*　　　*　　　*

Janna slept fitfully. Outside her window, Mars blazed golden and angry, a ginger tom cat seeing off a fierce dog. I've got to fight and win, she thought.

11

With Mars in the ascendant, the battle raged on at Larks. On Monday, a physics supply teacher was so unnerved by her first encounter with Year Nine E that she fled down the drive with singed eyebrows and blackened fringe and was never seen again.

'Who was she covering for?' demanded Janna.

Rowan glanced up at the timetable: 'Sam Spink. She's gone to the TUC conference.'

'She never asked me.'

'She cleared it with Mike Pitts last term. There was a memo'—Rowan looked disapprovingly at Janna's dramatically diminished in-tray—'but it seems to have been chucked away.'

'How long's she gone for?'

'All week. Sam's awfully conscientious. She feels it's crucial to exchange views and keep up with modern legislation.'

'You bet she does, when it involves swilling brandy Alexanders all night in the Metropole.'

Returning from a shouting match in Mike's office, Janna caught Robbie Rushton and Gloria the gymnast sneaking in at midday, claiming that the boat on which they'd been sailing had run aground.

'So will you if you skive any more,' yelled Janna.

*   *   *

A day of hassle left her drained and defensive. Remembering the support the governors at Redfords had given Stew when the going got tough, she looked forward to pouring out her grievances to her own governors, who'd been so friendly at her interview and who were, after all, responsible for Larks's appalling state.

The meeting was held after school in A18, classroom of Robbie Rushton, who, for once in a hundred years, made a point of working late, so Debbie the cleaner had to sweep and arrange chairs and glasses of water around his martyred presence.

'Robbie's so conscientious,' cooed Cara to arriving governors, as he finally took himself and a huge pile of marking away.

Classroom A18 was one of the worst. Damp patches on the ceiling resembled the map of India and Bangladesh. A rattle of drips was filling up two buckets. Year Eleven, ironically, were studying the story of water: irrigation, the rain cycle, domestic canals and wells. Year Ten, on the other hand, were learning about earthquakes, photographs and diagrams of which also covered the peeling walls. It wasn't long before Janna wished the floorboards would split open and swallow her up.

Mike Pitts wasn't present, but his spies were. Rowan Merton, wafting Anaïs Anaïs, had changed into a clean white shirt and was taking the minutes. Cara, as a teacher governor, having saved Monster Norman from being expelled last week, was thick as thieves and parked next to his mother, Stormin' Norman, also a parent governor.

Bring me my bully-proof vest, muttered Janna.

Kylie Rose's mother, Chantal, another parent governor, held up the whole proceedings by saying: 'Can we discuss this?' at every new item and making eyes at snuffling Crispin Thomas, whom she didn't realize was gay and who looked fatter than ever.

Crispin was accompanied by his boss, Ashton Douglas, S and C Services' Director of Education, an infinitely more formidable adversary who utterly unnerved Janna. His handsome, regular features were somehow blurred like soap left too long in the bath. An air of vulnerability (created by a lisp and soft light brown curls flopping from a middle parting) was belied by the coldest green eyes she had ever seen. Languid as a Beardsley aesthete, Ashton wore a mauve silk shirt, a beautifully cut grey suit and reeked of sweet, cloying scent.

He was now murmuring to Sir Hugo Betts, the camel on Prozac. Sir Hugo was disappointed Janna didn't look nearly as bonny as at her interview, so there would be even less to keep him awake.

Russell Lambert as chairman droned on and on, loving the sound of his own voice and expressing sadness that Brett Scott, the jolly director of Larkminster Rovers, had resigned, not having appreciated the extent of a governor's workload. He had been replaced by a local undertaker, called Solly, who at least can bury us, thought Janna.

She longed to weigh in on the atrocious state of the school, but in a subtle shift of emphasis, she was now held responsible for all Larks's evils. Five other pupils had gone out of county to other schools. Attendance was down by sixty-seven.

'What plans do you have to impwove the situation?' asked Ashton Douglas silkily.

Janna told them about her prospective-parents' evening.

'Hope it's not an *EastEnders* night,' warned

Chantal Peck.

Russell then expressed the governors' horror at the disastrous league-table results, with commendable exceptions—they all nodded deferentially at Cara Sharpe. What was Janna intending to do about that?

'I need a massive increase in funding,' said Janna, 'and must smarten up the school. Take this classroom. If you're into virtual reality, we can re-create the monsoon season every time it rains. If we don't mend the roof, we'll need an ark. And moving to Australia'—she tore a peeling strip of paper off the walls—'we can re-create the eucalyptus.'

No one smiled.

'No, it isn't funny,' agreed Janna. 'We also need hundreds more textbooks; we need to replace four computers. We need an IT technician.

'On the non-teaching side, we need a part-time gardener to sweep up the leaves, which will soon be cascading down from the trees—the only proud thing in this place. Above all we need a decent cook'—both Cara and Rowan Merton were frantically making notes—'to give the children a really nourishing hot meal in the middle of the day. Dinners here are the only food many of them can rely on, but they're so disgusting, most of the kids won't eat them.'

'Mrs Molly does her best with limited resources,' protested Cara.

'There was a blood-stained plaster in the shepherd's pie on Friday.'

'The shepherd must have cut himself shearing,' murmured Solly the undertaker with a ghostly chuckle.

96

'And most of all'—Janna plunged in feet first—'we need some more teachers. Ten of them, including my head of history, Mrs Chalford, whom I've never even met, are off with stress. The only way to attract new talent is to pay them better.'

But no more money was forthcoming.

S and C Services, Ashton Douglas reminded her smoothly, had been brought in by the Government because the local education authority couldn't balance the books. Janna must learn, like everyone else, to economize.

'We must have more money.' Janna banged the table with her little fist. 'You're a private company. You're not in this for love but to make a fat profit, that's why you don't want to give any extra to me. But it's so defeatist to let us self-destruct.'

There was a horrified pause and a flicker of amused malice in Ashton Douglas's cold green eyes.

'Your job, my dear, is to sort out the mess.'

'I've been here a week. If I'm going to sort out this "mess" I need your support. I lost my best teacher last week.' She daren't in front of Cara and Rowan say that Mike Pitts was useless. 'The junior staff are utterly demoralized. The children—'

Clearing his throat, Ashton Douglas cut right across her.

'With wespect, we shouldn't be discussing teaching matters in fwont of Mrs Sharpe. If you need funding, I suggest you look for sponsors in the town: Wandal Stancombe, or Gwant Tyler, our local IT giant. Get the local community on side.'

'Why not mobilize your parents?' suggested Crispin Thomas, smiling at Stormin' Norman and Chantal. 'Last year Searston Abbey and St Jimmy's raised fifteen and twenty thousand pounds respectively.'

'They've got hundreds of middle-class parents who aren't struggling to pay any school fees,' raged Janna. 'Of course they chip in. We don't have middle-class parents at Larks.'

'Ay take exception to that,' bridled Chantal Peck.

'That uncalled-for wemark should be struck from the minutes,' said Ashton. 'If you attwacted more pupils, we could allow you more money. So concentrate on your prospective-parents' meeting. Wod Hyde will also be here to advise you next week.' Then, at Janna's look of outrage: 'You'll find him a bweath of fwesh air.'

'An image that conjures up icy winds blasting in from Siberia,' snapped Janna, 'blowing everything that matters out of the window. I don't want Rod Hyde telling me what to do. I just need more money.

'The children need some treats,' she pleaded. 'They have such bleak lives. We should offer them rewards: a fun day out to look forward to and in recognition of good behaviour.'

'What did you have in mind?' asked Crispin sarcastically.

'The London Eye perhaps, or Tate Modern. A lot of them have never been to the seaside or inside the cathedral or a museum.'

'You'd trust them in a museum?' said Cara incredulously.

'Once they realized we did, they'd start behaving better.'

'Which brings me to behaviour management,' said Russell Lambert. 'We notice you've introduced a new system of mentors.'

98

'It worked very well at Redfords,' said Janna defensively. 'Means any kid can go to a mentor if they're being bullied or have a problem. I had ten of the more responsible members of Year Eleven photographed last Thursday. Their pictures are now up in the corridors.'

'A needless expense.' Ashton smiled thinly. 'Surely they could have brought photogwaphs from home.'

'It made it more of an honour,' said Janna. 'They look really good.'

There was a knock on the door. It was Kylie Rose, come to collect her mother Chantal and bearing Cameron, a sweet jolly baby who'd inherited his mother's blond, blue-eyed beauty. His charm was lost on Crispin Thomas, however, when his besotted grandmother thrust him into the deputy educational director's arms, particularly when Cameron threw up on Crispin's cream suit.

'Come and see the mentors' photographs,' said Janna hastily, leading everyone off to admire the display, only to find the photographs had already been adorned with moustaches and squints, with the names crossed out and replaced by 'Wanker' and worse.

Janna promptly lost her rag again and shouted at anyone within range. She was just calming down when kind Kylie Rose tugged her sleeve.

'You're easily the best teacher in the school, miss.'

'Am I?' Janna was marginally mollified.

'Easily the best at shouting,' said Kylie Rose.

The governors smirked.

'Phone for you,' called Rowan from Janna's office.

'I'm busy.'

'Says he's an old friend from Redfords.'

Janna shot into the office.

'I tried the cottage,' announced Stew. 'Somehow I knew you'd be still working.'

'Oh Stew.' How lovely to hear the broad, warm, measured Yorkshire accent.

'How are you getting on, love?'

'Horribly. It's hell.' Janna kicked her door shut. 'I hate most of the staff. They gang up. There aren't enough of them. The only nice guy's been hijacked to head up another school. The deputy head's a total lush.'

'What about the kids?'

'Animals, most of them.'

'That's not like you, Janna. What about your PA? She sounded friendly enough on the phone.'

'Worst of the lot. She sneers, sneaks and pumps up my in-tray to demoralize me.' Swinging round, Janna went scarlet; Rowan who must have quietly opened the door was standing outraged in the doorway. 'I've got to go, Stew, ring me later at home.'

But Stew didn't ring back. Why had she moaned so much?

Laugh and the world laughs with you, weep and you weep alone, her mother had always told her. If only she were still alive.

*   *   *

The fall-out was awful. Cara, backed up by Rowan, was straight on to Mike Pitts and the rest of the staff, reporting everything that had been said.

No one would meet Janna's eye the next day.

Molly the cook walked out. Even Wally, her dear friend, looked at her reproachfully, until she explained that she wanted to get in some gardening help, to free him for more important tasks.

That same morning, however, Debbie the cleaner, who'd been blown away by the big box of chocolates Janna had given her for blitzing the staffroom, came blushing into the head's office. As she got on so well with Molly's other assistants, how would Janna feel if they took over school dinners on a month's trial?

'Profoundly relieved,' replied Janna. 'Oh, Debbie, thank you, that's the best bit of news I've had for ages. Start today.'

'You deserve some luck,' said Debbie. 'Lots of us think you're 'uman.'

Ironically, Janna was saved by the greatest tragedy. Towards the end of the day, which was 11 September, she was trying to explain Arthur Miller to a sullen group of fifteen-year-olds, who seemed only interested that he'd been married to Marilyn Monroe, when Rowan rushed in to say the World Trade Center had been hit.

Mike Pitts and Cara thought the school should carry on as normal. Janna insisted that this was history and the children must see it.

In no time, Wally had rigged up the big screen attached to a television in the main hall. The excited pupils lugged chairs in from the dining room to watch the terrible events unfold. At first, these were like so many Hollywood films, it was hard for them to understand it was the real thing. But they were soon screaming, sobbing and sometimes cheering. Janna stood to the side of the screen, explaining what was happening.

The Wolf Pack, when they first saw people leaping out of the flaming tower windows, exchanged glances, because they were always escaping that way, but here there was no wisteria to aid their descent, and horror gripped them too.

When it was time to go home, she called for a minute's silence to pray for America and the suffering of its people, thanking God for the courage of the emergency services and hoping as many people as possible had escaped to safety.

Next day at assembly she gave everyone an update on the tragedy and who was responsible, and when fights broke out between the Muslim children and the Hindus and the Christians, she tried to impress on them that ordinary people weren't to blame. She asked the senior classes to write poems about the tragedy. Paris's was marvellous.

As the days passed, a huge mutual interest developed as the children learnt about the courage of the firemen and the brave search-and-rescue dogs. Some of the children said their parents thought Bin Laden was a hero, and more frightful fights ensued.

Cara and Mike Pitts, however, were constantly on the telephone, stirring up trouble. When it was crucial to raise Larks's position in the league tables, why was Janna wasting the entire school's afternoon watching television?

'It's called global citizenship,' protested Janna when Ashton Douglas carpeted her.

'Wod Hyde will be with you tomorrow,' said Ashton nastily. 'He'll sort you out.'

12

Janna had always felt that one of the cruellest humiliations was when heads of very successful establishments known as 'beacon schools' were posted in to sort out failing schools, 'yanking them up by the hair' as the Education Secretary so charmingly put it.

Janna's russet curls were well and truly yanked by the smug and self-regarding Rod Hyde who, as head of St Jimmy's, had been forced to redesign his writing paper to accommodate all the awards and accolades his school had received.

Arriving at Larks, Rod immediately showed how well he got on with Janna's staff, joshing Mike Pitts, Skunk Illingworth and Robbie Rushton, kissing Cara on both hollowed cheeks and warmly quizzing Sam Spink about her week at the TUC conference.

'I'm sure you found it very empowering. You must debrief me over a few jars.'

Janna ground her teeth.

Known as Jesus Christ Superhead, Rod showed off his spare figure and muscular freckled arms by wearing short-sleeved shirts tucked into belted trousers. On colder days, he wore a rust-coloured cardigan to match his ginger beard.

A control freak, Rod received an emotional charge from acting as a 'critical friend', rolling up at Larks, telling Janna what was wrong with her and her school, attacking both her management skills and her teaching.

Janna, on the rare occasions she had time to

teach, delivered the national curriculum as if it had been freed from its chains. When, on Rod's first day, Lydia rang in sick at the prospect of teaching *Macbeth* to Year Nine E, Janna took over, refusing to be fazed when Rod parked himself at the back, busily making notes on his clipboard.

It happened to be the day when Rocky, the huge curly-haired autistic boy kept comparatively calm by Ritalin, was in one of his more eccentric moods. Wandering in, he took one look at Rod and shut himself in the store cupboard at the back of the classroom.

'The Macbeths were a glamorous career couple,' Janna was saying, 'like Tony and Cherie Blair or Bill and Hillary Clinton. We tend to think of them as middle-aged and childless, but probably they were young, young enough to have kids who might inherit the throne, which may have been why Macbeth told Lady Macbeth to "bring forth men children only".'

The class then had a spirited discussion on the right age to have children. Kylie Rose said 'twelve'. They then moved on to Macduff being ripped untimely from his mother's womb.

'That's a cop-out, miss,' volunteered Paris.

'I think Shakespeare meant that Macduff's mum had a Caesarean,' explained Janna, 'but you're right, Paris, it is a cop-out.'

How difficult not to be touched when she saw his pale face flood with colour.

'You must also remember Macbeth was a mighty warrior, a fantastic killing machine.'

'Like Russell Crowe in *Gladiator*,' said Pearl.

'Or Arnie in *Terminator*,' said a sepulchral voice from the cupboard.

The class giggled.

'Exactly, Rocky,' called out Janna. 'Macbeth was on a fantastic high having routed the terrorists who were trying to overthrow Duncan, the King of Scotland, who was also his wife's cousin. Mighty Macbeth had been on a killing spree that was hugely applauded. Like scoring a hat trick for Arsenal or Liverpool. The world was at his feet.

'Now tell me, what did Macbeth have in common with Stalin, Hitler and Saddam Hussein?'

'They all had moustaches,' shouted Pearl.

'Like Baldie Hyde,' called out the sepulchral voice from the cupboard.

More giggling as the class stared round at Rod.

'They all deteriorated into tyrants and mass murderers,' said Janna quickly. 'Now, for homework, you've got two choices, one of which may appeal more to the girls, particularly you, Pearl. If you were a costume designer and in charge of make-up, how would you kit out the Weird Sisters?'

'I'd put them in baggy, raggy, gypsy-style costumes,' said Pearl, 'wiv red and purple hair, blackened-out teeth and cruel scarlet mouths.'

'Like Cara Sharpe,' intoned Rocky from his hideout.

'That's enough,' said Janna firmly. 'The other choice is to imagine you're a war correspondent like John Simpson or Kate Adie, and write a script telling the viewers at home about Macbeth's first victory, bringing in the routing of the rebels, the Norwegian support and the butchering of the treacherous Thane of Cawdor, ripping him open or unseaming him "from the navel to the chaps". If you've got time, you could list questions for an interview with Macbeth or Banquo and add Macbeth's possible answers.'

Year Nine E were gratifyingly enraptured and groaned when the bell went. Throughout the lesson, however, Janna had kept seeing Rod Hyde's tongue, green as a wild garlic leaf, as he pointedly yawned. Afterwards he couldn't wait to tick her off.

'You're far too familiar, and if you digress all the time, you'll never get them through their exams.'

'They're not taking GCSEs for nearly three years. I want them to enjoy Shakespeare.'

'And you talk too much,' Rod consulted his clipboard, as they walked back to her office. 'Try to be a listening head rather than a talking one. Don't take this personally,' he added when Janna looked mutinous, 'it's for your own good.

'And you must stop blowing your top. I know we redheads are volatile'—he crinkled his small eyes—'but you lose dignity every time you raise your voice to students and colleagues. Ashton tells me you displayed unedifying aggression at the governors' meeting. Has it occurred to you that you're the reason so many of your staff are off with stress?'

Janna dug her nails into her palms and counted to ten. Next moment, she and Rod were sent flying by a yelling gang from Year Ten, stampeding like buffaloes towards the playground.

'Don't run,' howled Janna.

'Don't run,' said Rod quietly.

Infuriatingly the gang mumbled, 'Sorry, sir,' and shambled off.

'You must instil discipline here.' Rod shut her office door behind them. 'Coloured hair, beaded

106

necklaces, particularly for boys, rings in the navel or the tongue, and shaved heads must all go.'

Ten days ago, Janna would have agreed with him, but he was irritating her so much, she said she liked children expressing themselves.

'And you should cut down that wisteria, which seems the accepted escape route for most of your hooligans.'

'That wisteria's older than me or even you, and much more beautiful.'

'Dear Janna'—Rod pursed his red lips—'you're not helping yourself. Caring Cara Sharpe also tells me'—he turned back to his clipboard—'you've been working here until eleven at night. Terribly unfair to Wally, who has to lock up after you. He does have a life.'

'Wally's never complained,' stammered Janna.

'He's too nice,' said Rod pompously. 'Start thinking of other people. You wouldn't have to work so late if you organized your day better. Now stop sulking and turn on that coffee machine.'

Somehow, Janna managed not to rip him from navel to chaps with her paper knife, but she cried herself to sleep that night. Were the children and staff really acting up and demoralized because she was such a bitch?

*   *   *

For his next visit, Rod called a breakfast meeting at 8.00 a.m.

'You provide the croissants. I'll provide the pearls of wisdom.'

He'd been jogging and dripped with sweat when he arrived. Janna had to watch him getting butter,

107

marmalade and crumbs all over his red beard as he poured scorn on Larks's place in the league tables.

'It'd help if you and Searston Abbey didn't cream off all the best pupils,' snarled Janna. 'Think how disadvantaged our kids are. Most of them have no quiet room at home to do their homework and no one able to help them. Unemployment's at an all-time high on the Shakespeare Estate, so the kids, as well as helping out with the shopping, have to take evening and weekend jobs to make ends meet. Poor little Graffi fell asleep at his desk this morning.'

'Probably been doing drugs all night,' said Rod dismissively. 'You must get your parents on side. Ours were in school all weekend, installing benches in the playground—that's one reason our results are spectacular. We'll be catching up with Bagley Hall in a year or two and then Hengist B-T will have to look to his laurels. No parent will want to fork out twenty-odd thousand a year only to get thrashed by a maintained school.'

'What's Hengist like?' Janna was annoyed to find herself asking.

'Terminally frivolous and arrogant,' snapped Rod. 'Typical public-school Hooray Henry, far too big for his green wellies.'

As Janna bent down to retrieve a pen, Rod suppressed an urge to pull down her panties and smack her freckled bottom. Sheila, his 'superb wife' of twenty-seven years, an ex-nurse, who called him 'head teacher' in bed, didn't excite him quite enough. One day Janna Curtis would express gratitude for the way he'd imposed discipline on her and her school.

'I shall be spending one to one and a half days a

week with you from now on,' he announced.

'How d'you find the time?' asked Janna sulkily.

'I delegate. Ask a busy person.'

On the following day, Rod rolled up in a big black hat, which he left in Janna's office. Later in the morning, passing Year Nine E's history lesson, he found Paris wearing it and doing a dazzling imitation of Rod addressing the troops:

' "As part of our caring and supportive ethos . . ." '

Rod was outraged and snatched back his hat.

'Others make allowances for you, Paris Alvaston, because of your unfortunate circumstances, and you abuse it,' he shouted. 'I shall speak with Mr Blenchley.'

'Mr Blenchley'll make Paris's life hell,' protested Janna.

The Wolf Pack, who also thought Rod's remarks were below the belt, started pelting him with textbooks and pencil boxes and banging their desk lids when he tried to shut them up.

Nor was Rod's impression of Larks improved later in the day, when Graffi caught him whispering to Cara Sharpe just inside the huge stationery cupboard and locked them both in.

Only after an hour did Rowan hear banging and let them out.

Rod had gone maroon with fury. 'How dare you?' he bellowed at Graffi, who was now wearing the hat.

'You and Mrs Sharpe was saying horrible things about Miss,' said Graffi and, jumping out of the window, slithered down the wisteria and ran laughing down the drive.

'This school deserves to be closed down,'

exploded Rod.

*   *   *

Janna, meanwhile, was working on her Larks Ascending project for her prospective-parents' evening.

'We need to put everything about larks, how high up they sing, how they nest on the ground, how because of modern farming, they're getting fewer and fewer.'

'Like Larks's pupils,' said Feral.

Janna and Paris raided the dictionary of quotations for poems about larks. Cambola searched for music. Graffi did a wonderful drawing of Rod Hyde as Edward Lear's Old Man with bird droppings on his head and with owls, larks, hens and wrens nesting in his beard. Graffi also helped Janna cover the corridor walls with pictures by the children and torn-out paintings by Old Masters. They tried not to laugh when Mike Pitts wandered in after a lunchtime session at the Ghost and Castle and remarked:

'That Modigliani's not a bad painter. What class is he in?'

Janna knew she ought to sack Mike for drinking, but who would back her up? She ought to sack him for perfidy too. When she came back unexpectedly from a meeting, she found him whispering into her telephone. Seeing her, he flushed even redder and hung up.

Janna had immediately pressed redial, and an answering voice had said, 'Ashton Douglas.'

Janna was so thrown, she revealed who she was and instantly received a bollocking for her

110

treatment of Rod Hyde.

'As part of his caring, supportive ethos, Wod gives of his valuable time and you put up disgusting paintings of him on the wall and treat him with twuculence and disrespect.'

'He's a bloody clipboard junkie who upsets the kids.'

'Your school is spiralling out of control,' said Ashton coldly.

'Ashton to Ashton, dust to dust,' screamed Janna, slamming down the telephone. When it rang again, she was, for once, able to snatch it up before a suspicious Rowan.

'Janna Curtis,' she snapped.

'This is Hengist Brett-Taylor.' The deep lazy voice was laced with laughter. 'I wonder if you'd like to have lunch this week.'

Janna was about to refuse when she saw Monster Norman's mother charging up the corridor, and abandoning her open-door policy, kicked it shut and leant against it.

'Yes, please.'

'How about Wednesday?'

She had a finance meeting at four-thirty, so she could escape early.

'That's OK.'

'I thought we'd go to La Perdrix d'Or in Cathedral Street. Shall I pick you up?'

'No, I'll meet you there.'

'At one o'clock, then. I really look forward to it.'

13

Janna looked forward to lunch with Hengist less and less. She had her prospective-parents' evening the following day and shouldn't be skiving. Nor should she be fraternizing with the enemy with Rowan clocking her every move, particularly when Janna came in in her rose-festooned pink suit, with her newly washed russet curls bouncing around her shoulders.

But, by the time a German teacher and a lab assistant had given in their notice, the boys' lavatories had blocked yet again and Satan Simmons had been carted off to hospital after an encounter with a broken bottle, Janna was ready for a large drink.

Only when she had driven past the Ghost and Castle did she pull in to tart up, not helped by her trembling hands zigzagging her eyeliner, spilling base on her pink satin camisole top and drenching her in so much of Stew's Chanel No 5, big-headed bloody Brett-Taylor would be bound to construe it as a come-on. In an attempt to look school-marmish, she groped furiously for a hairband in the glove compartment, and scraped back as many of her curls as possible. Then she jumped as, in the driving mirror, she caught sight of Rowan, Gloria the gymnast and perfidious Jason Fenton sloping off for an early lunch, no doubt to bitch about her. It was debatable who blushed most when they recognized her car storming off.

Janna grew increasingly flustered because she was late and Cathedral Street long, punctuated with cherry trees and composed of seemingly identical eighteenth-century shopfronts and she'd forgotten the French name of the restaurant—something like Pederast's Door. She was scuttling up and down, when Hengist, who'd been looking out, pulled her in from the street.

'You are absolutely sweet to make it.'

And Janna gasped because he was a good foot taller than she was and undeniably gorgeous-looking, with thick springy dark hair, unflecked by grey, brushed back and curling over the collar. In addition, he had heavy-lidded, amused eyes, the very dark green of rain-soaked cedars, an unlined face still brown from the summer, a nose with several dents in it, a square jaw with a cleft chin and a wonderfully smooth smiling mouth, framing even white teeth, most of them capped after the bashing they had received on the rugger field.

He was conventionally dressed in a longish tweed jacket, dark-yellow cords, an olive-green shirt and an MCC tie, but as his lemon aftershave mingled amorously with Chanel No 5 on the warm windless autumn air, he seemed utterly in the heroic mould. Casting Hector or Horatius who kept the bridge for a Hollywood epic, you would look no further. Beneath the languid amiability, he exuded huge energy, and after the Hydes and Skunks, who'd been her fare for the last month, he seemed like a god.

Janna bristled instinctively:

'I've got a finance meeting; I haven't got long.'

'Then the sooner you have a large drink the better.'

Hengist ordered her (without asking) a glass of champagne and, picking up his glass of red and the

113

biography of Cardinal Mazarin that he'd left on the bar, he led her through a packed restaurant to what was clearly the best table, overlooking the water meadows and the river.

'The view's breathtaking, but you must sit with your back to it, because it's so good for my street cred to be seen with you and it means that all the fat cats lunching here will think: how pretty she is, and pour money into your school.'

'I wish,' sighed Janna.

'I've brought you a present,' said Hengist.

In a blue box tied with crimson ribbon was a long silver spoon.

'I know you feel you're supping or lunching with the devil,' he said, laughing at her. 'I've read all about your views in the *TES* and the *Guardian*— "upper-class care" indeed—but I promise I won't bite except my food, which is excellent here. Thank you, Freddie.' He smiled at the spiky-haired young waiter who'd brought over Janna's champagne and the menu.

'Now get that inside you,' he went on. 'You'll need it to endure the appalling Russell Lambert and the even more appalling Crispin and Ashton. What a coven of fairies you've surrounded yourself with.'

'I don't want to discuss my governors,' said Janna primly and untruthfully.

'I've cracked the governor problem,' confided Hengist. 'We have two meetings a year. One over dinner at Boodle's, my club in London, which they all adore. Then, in early November, they all come down to Bagley for dinner and the night. Sally, my wife, is a fantastic cook. Wonderful smells drift into the boardroom throughout the meeting, so

114

they're desperate to get through it and on to pre-dinner drinks. Then they push off first thing in the morning.

'But my pièce de résistance has been to get the most ravishing mother on to the board, a divorcee called Mrs Walton, so we always get full attendance and all the governors are so busy looking at her boobs, they OK everything.'

Janna tried and failed to look disapproving.

'Sally and I call her the governing body, but she'd be wasted on Ashton or Crispin,' said Hengist idly. 'You'd do better with Brad Pitt.'

'Or Jason Fenton,' snapped Janna.

'Oh dear, I'd forgotten him.'

'Self-satisfied little narcissist. I passed him bunking off with two other teachers today when they thought I'd left for lunch. He'd have been admiring himself in the shop windows if they weren't all boarded up round Larks. I'm over the moon you've taken him off my hands.'

'At least I've done something right.'

Hengist looked so delighted, Janna burst out laughing.

La Perdrix d'Or itself seemed to be celebrating both golden partridge and the guns who killed them. Paintings of partridge or sporting prints of shooting parties in autumn, with birds and yellow leaves cascading out of the sky, adorned the dark-red walls. There were silver partridges and vases of red Michaelmas daisies on the white tablecloths and, like Sally B-T's governors' dinners, the most delicious smells of wine, herbs and garlic were drifting up from the kitchen.

The menu was in French, always Janna's Achilles heel, but Freddie the waiter charmingly translated

115

for her.

'The goat's cheese fritters are out of this world,' said Hengist, 'although they might give you even worse nightmares if you fall asleep during your finance meeting.'

'And the Dover sole's fresh in today,' said Freddie.

'I'll have that,' said Janna with a sigh of relief.

Janna always liked people who looked straight at you, but Hengist unnerved her; those amused appraising eyes never left her face. He was just *so* attractive. Determined not to be a partridge to his twelve bore, she went on the offensive.

'You can't order venison. Poor deer.'

'A poor deer got into the garden last night and demolished the remainder of Sally's roses. He'd have gobbled up your lovely suit in seconds.'

Getting hotter by the minute, Janna was too embarrassed about the make-up on her camisole top to undo her jacket.

'How did you turn Bagley round?'

'Fired a lot of masters. Found several old codgers already dead in the staffroom, which saved me the trouble. We were horribly under-subscribed. Every time the telephone rang, it was someone resigning or removing a pupil. The children were running wild.'

'Sounds familiar.'

'They're still pretty wild,' admitted Hengist. 'You think you've got delinquents at Larks. I've got the offspring of celebrities and high achievers, who are often just as neglected and screwed up. The divorce rate among the parents is frighteningly high.

'My first move was to set off the fire alarm at

116

midnight on my first Saturday of term,' he went on. 'Ten Upper Sixth boys were so drunk, they couldn't get out of bed. In chapel on Monday, I named them all, then fired the lot. The parents, whom I'd alerted, were waiting outside. Then I told the rest of the school, "Your last five days of bad behaviour are up." I think it shocked them. None of the boys kicked out were very bright,' he added. 'One should never fire clever pupils.'

Janna didn't know how to take this patter. Hengist, like jesting Pilate, flitted from subject to subject, never waiting for an answer.

Then he switched tack, unnerving her further by asking her all about herself, her cottage and about Larks. She was too proud to tell him about the antagonism of the staff, but he was so sympathetic, interested and constructively helpful and the cheese fritters were so delicious, particularly washed down by more champagne, Janna was having such a nice time she was ashamed.

'How d'you cope with the workload?' she asked.

'I have a brilliant PA, Miss Painswick, who's a dragon to everyone but me and drives my wife Sally crackers. I appointed a deputy head, Alex Bruce, from the maintained system, who understands red tape and I've no doubt one day will strangle me with it like Laocoön. He *likes* filling in forms. He's a friend of your nemesis, Rod Hyde, same awful class. And I've got a brilliant bursar, Ian Cartwright; he's just back from Africa having extracted two years' unpaid school fees from a Nigerian prince.'

'With so many people looking after you,' asked Janna waspishly, 'what on earth do you find to do?'

'Given the quality of my staff,' murmured

Hengist, 'my job consists largely of keeping out of the way,' and again smiled so sweetly and unrepentantly Janna melted.

'Do you have many women teachers?' she asked as she attacked her sole.

'Alex Bruce's wife, an Olympic-level pest, teaches religious studies, which includes everything except the Bible. Miss Wormly teaches English and we've got a head of science with absolutely no sense of humour, known as "No-Joke Joan". She also runs our only girls' house: Boudicca, a "thankless task". Miss Sweet, the undermatron of Boudicca, takes sex education, poor thing. The girls, who are sexually light years ahead, help her along.'

He's got a divinely deep husky voice, even if I do disapprove of everything he says, thought Janna, unbuttoning her jacket.

'You ought to employ more women,' she said fretfully.

'I'm sure. You don't want a job, do you?'

'I'd rather die than work for an independent school.' Then, feeling she'd been rude: 'This sole is wonderful. How can I stop truancy? It's shocking among the boys.'

'What do they like best?'

'After Hallé Berry, probably football.'

'Start a football club.'

'We haven't got any pitches. Lots of land, nearly ten acres, but we can't afford to have it levelled.'

'I'll introduce you to Randal Stancombe. You're so pretty and he's so rich, he'll give you some money.'

'Do you have a football club at Bagley?'

'No, we're a rugger school.'

'Of course,' said Janna sarcastically. 'I suppose

118

you played rugby for *your* school.'

'Mr Brett-Taylor played rugby for England,' said Freddie. 'Everything all right, sir?'

When he'd gone, Janna asked if there were lots of drugs at Bagley.

'Probably. We only expel on a third offence. Why squander twenty thousand a year? A boy was sacked from Fleetley last week because they found cannabis in his study. He's expected to get straight As and is an Oxbridge cert, so we took him straightaway. His parents are so grateful, they'll probably pay for a new sports pavilion.'

'I can't afford to exclude,' said Janna crossly. 'I get fined five grand every time.'

'Whatever happened to the word "expel"?' sighed Hengist. He quoted softly:

> 'Shall I come, sweet Love, to thee,
> When the evening beams are set?
> Shall I not excluded be?'

Stretching out a big suntanned hand, on the little finger of which glinted a big gold signet ring, he gently stroked Janna's cheek.

'Pretty, you are. Don't work yourself into a frazzle over Larks.'

'Don't patronize me.' Blushing furiously, Janna jerked her head away. 'We're just hopelessly underfunded. Bloody rural Larkshire. Can you really introduce me to Randal Stancombe?'

'Of course. Randal wants to build us a vocational wing. When I was young, vocation meant pretty girls becoming nuns and plain ones going off to be missionaries in Africa. Now it means thick boys training to be plumbers and thick girls learning to run travel agencies.'

'I know what "vocation" means,' spat Janna. 'I didn't know you took any thick children.'

'Rupert Campbell-Black's son Xav is destined to get straight Us,' confessed Hengist. 'In compensation, it wildly impresses parents to catch a glimpse of Rupert on Speech Day.'

Janna was getting so flushed with drink, she took off her jacket—sod the spilt make-up. People kept stopping at their table to say hello to Hengist, and praise something he'd written in the *Telegraph* or said on television.

Each time, he introduced Janna, then gave the other person twenty dazzling seconds of charm, before saying they must forgive him, but he and Janna had things to discuss.

'My children aren't thick,' protested Janna when they were alone again. 'They know the players and fixtures of Larkminster Rovers inside out. All I want to do is make a difference to children in a community who don't have the advantages I had. Education is about empowering children to access parts of themselves they haven't accessed,' she concluded sententiously.

Hengist raised an eyebrow. 'Can it really be English language you teach?'

'Oh, shut up,' said Janna so loudly lunchers looked round. 'No, I don't want any dessert. My teachers stop talking when I come into the room: would I had the same effect on the children. Show them any kindness and they spit and swear at you. But now, the wildest of them all, Feral Jackson, comes to tea with me on Saturdays,' she added proudly, 'with Graffi and Paris. Paris is a looked-after kid, I must show you some of his poems, they're brilliant.'

Poor little duck, she's adorable when she gets passionate, thought Hengist, only half listening, examining Janna's glowing freckles, the fox-brown eyes, the full trembling mouth, the piled-up Titian hair, which seemed to want to escape as much as she did. Lovely boobs too, quivering in that pink satin thing.

'My children have such terrible lives,' she was saying. 'My old school, Redfords in the West Riding, was an oasis of warmth and friendliness. I want that at Larks.' Tears were now pouring down her cheeks. 'I'm so sorry.' She blew her nose on her napkin.

'I know your old head, Stew Wilby,' said Hengist. 'Met him at conferences. Brilliant man, a visionary but a pragmatist like me.'

He took Janna's hands, stroking, comforting, as if she were a spaniel frightened by gunfire in one of the sporting prints.

'I'll help all I can. S and C Services worry me. I'm not sure they're kosher.'

'Ashton Douglas's vile, and Rod Hyde's a bully,' sniffed Janna.

'Sally likes most people, but she can't bear him,' agreed Hengist. 'Says he's so pompous and stands too close, with terrible coffee breath.'

'How did you find someone as lovely as Sally?' asked Janna wistfully.

'Have you time for another drink?' Hengist waved to Freddie.

'Oh, please. Could I have a gin and orange instead, please?'

Anything, she was appalled to find herself thinking, to extend lunch. Hengist was like the

121

kingfisher or the rainbow, you longed for him to stay longer. Without realizing, she pulled the toggle off her hair.

'Sally, at twenty-one,' began Hengist, bringing her back to earth, 'had so many admirers. She was so pretty—still is—but her father, another head, didn't approve of me. Thought I was a bit of a rugger-bugger and hellraiser, appalled when I didn't get a first. Anyway, Sally turned me down. I was devastated. My own father, however, told me not to be a drip. Said Sally was the best girl I was likely to meet, I must try again.

'So I invited her to the dogs the following night. She wore a pale blue flowing hippy dress. We backed a brindle greyhound called Cheerful Reply. After a drink or two in the bar, we joked that if Cheerful Reply won, Sally would marry me.

'Darling, it was a photo finish between Cheerful Reply and a dog called Bombay Biscuit. So we had several more drinks and a nail-biting quarter of an hour waiting for the result, which was Cheerful Reply ahead by a shiny black nose.

'Euphoric, probably at winning all that money, Sally agreed to marry me. I've never known such happiness: even better than being selected for England.'

'Lucky Sally,' sighed Janna.

'Lucky me. My parents were living in Cambridge at the time,' went on Hengist. 'I took the Green Line bus home, sitting up with the driver, so excited and tanked up, I told him everything and he said:

' "Isn't it amazing how racing dogs influence events?" Wasn't that perfect?' Hengist burst out laughing. 'Sally and I have had greyhounds ever since.'

'What a wonderful story.' Janna shook her head. 'I'd love a dog, but I'm out all day.'

'Take it into school, you're the head, the children would love it. Homesick children at Bagley are always asking if they can take Elaine, our greyhound, for a walk.'

He waved for the bill. As Janna gulped her gin and orange, he paid with American Express, then got a tenner out of his notecase for Freddie.

'Thank you so much,' Janna told the boy. 'Is this a full-time job?'

'No, I'm starting at New College next week.'

'Well done. Where did you go to school?'

'Bagley Hall,' said Freddie.

'One of our nicest boys,' murmured Hengist as he and Janna went out into the sunshine. 'His father walked out, so his mother worked all hours to pay the fees.'

'Why the hell didn't she send him to a comprehensive?'

'Because Freddie was happy with us. A lot of our parents are poor,' said Hengist sharply. 'They just believe in spending money on their children's education rather than cars, holidays and second houses.'

Wow, he can bite, thought Janna.

'Don't forget your spoon.' Handing her the box, Hengist smiled down at her. It was as though the sun had shot out from the blackest cloud. 'Come and see my school,' he said. 'Please.'

'Well, very quickly,' said Janna ungraciously. 'I'll follow you in my car.'

14

I am way over the limit both physically and mentally, thought Janna as, determined to keep up with Hengist, she careered down twisting, narrow, high-walled and high-hedged lanes made slippery by a recent shower of rain.

Bagley Hall, surrounded by exuberant wooded hills, sprawled over a green plain like one of those villages glimpsed from a train where you imagine you might start a thrilling new life.

The school itself was dominated by a big, golden Georgian house, known as the Mansion, which formed one side of a quadrangle. Behind were scattered numerous old and carefully matched modern Cotswold stone buildings, to accommodate 800 pupils and at least 150 staff.

Girls and particularly boys craned to look as Hengist whisked Janna round endless, many of them surprisingly pokey, classrooms. These were compensated for by a library to rival the Bodleian, entire buildings devoted to music or art, a magnificent theatre and a soaring chapel with Burne-Jones windows glowing like captured rainbows.

'Science etc. is over there.' Hengist waved dismissively at an ugly pile through the trees. 'A subject about which I can never get excited; besides, it's the domain of my deputy head, Alex Bruce.'

Outside, he showed her a swimming pool nearly as big as Windermere, running tracks and a golf course. Smooth green pitches stretched eastwards to infinity. To the north, a large bronze of a fierce-looking general on a splendid charger looked out on to an avenue of limes.

'That's General Bagley, our founder, famous for putting down troublemakers after the Black Hole of Calcutta and being effective at the Battle of Plassey.

'Our house is two hundred yards to the west, hidden by the trees,' he added, 'and very pretty. We're very lucky. You'll see it when you come to dinner.' Then, when she raised an eyebrow at his presumption: 'To meet Randal Stancombe. That's Rupert Campbell-Black's adopted son, Xavier, originally from Bogotá.' Hengist lowered his voice as a sullen, overweight black boy surrounded by a lot of chattering white thirteen-year-olds splashed past through the puddles on a cross-country run.

'Xavier's acting up at the moment,' explained Hengist. 'Hard to fade into the background if you belong to such a high-profile white family. Adolescents so detest being conspicuous and Xav's not helped by having a ravishing younger sister, Bianca, of a much lighter colour.'

'Poor lad being saddled with such an uncaring father.' Janna was getting crosser by the minute. 'Having plucked him out of Bogotá, how could Rupert have shunted him off to the vile prison of a boarding school?'

'He wanted to come here,' said Hengist mildly. 'People do, you know, and his stepbrother and -sister both did time.'

When he showed Janna the new sports hall, she really flipped.

'It's a disgrace, kids getting such privileges because they've got wealthy parents. No wonder society's divided. Think how Graffi would thrive in the art department and Paris in the library. Think how Feral would scorch round those running tracks.'

'There's no reason why they shouldn't.'

But Janna was in full flood: 'Why should rich kids have such an easy route in life?' Furious, she snarled up at him, an incensed Jack Russell taking on a lofty Great Dane.

'Janna, Jann-ah,' drawled Hengist, 'by "easy route", I presume you mean being put into "upper-class care". Surely you don't want your precious Larks children subjected to such a "vile prison"? That ain't logic.'

'Stop taking the piss. You know exactly what I mean. I want kids of all classes to go to day schools together, have access to these kinds of facilities and fulfil their potential. All this system does is make your odious stuck-up little toffs despise my kids and make them feel inferior.'

'Dear, dear,' sighed Hengist, stopping to pick up a Mars bar wrapper. 'So it's wicked of me to improve my school because it demoralizes children who don't come here.'

Then he noticed the tears of rage in her eyes and the violet circles beneath them. They had reached a lake fringed with brown-tipped reeds. Falling leaves were joining golden carp in the water. Next moment, a chocolate Labrador surfaced, shaking himself all over Hengist's yellow cords.

On the opposite bank, a blonde head appeared between the fringed branches of a weeping willow and shot back again.

'Dora,' shouted Hengist.

Very reluctantly, a pretty little girl with blonde

plaits and binoculars round her neck emerged, followed by an even prettier one, with dark gold skin, laughing brown eyes and glossy black curls.

They were poised to bolt back to school, but Hengist beckoned them over:

'Meet two of my odious stuck-up little toffs, Dora Belvedon and Bianca Campbell-Black, two new girls this term. How are you both getting on?'

'Really well,' said Dora, eyes swivelling towards the chocolate Labrador, who was now chasing a mallard.

Both girls were wearing sea-blue jerseys, white shirts, blue and beige striped ties and beige pleated skirts, which Bianca had hitched to succulent mid-thigh.

'This is Miss Curtis, the new head of Larks,' Hengist introduced Janna. 'Shouldn't you be playing some sort of game?'

'PE, but we both had headaches and needed fresh air.' Frantic to change the subject, Dora turned to Janna, 'How are you getting on at Larks?' she asked politely.

'Very well,' lied Janna. 'Are you Sophy Belvedon's sister-in-law?'

Dora brightened. 'I am.'

'Sophy and I taught at a school in Yorkshire,' explained Janna.

'She and my brother Alizarin have got a sweet little baby called Dulcie. All my brothers are breeding,' sighed Dora. 'I'm an aunt four times over; such an expense at Christmas!'

'How's Feral Jackson?' asked Bianca. 'I think he's cool.'

'So does Feral,' said Janna.

'That was an excellent essay you wrote on Prince

Rupert, Dora, you obviously liked his dog,' said Hengist. 'And I've been hearing about your dancing, Bianca, I hope you're going to teach me the Argentine tango.'

'It's dead sexy. Women dance really close and rub their legs against men's. Daddy wants to learn it.'

'Is he going to win the St Leger?'

'I hope so.'

'I don't recognize this dog,' Hengist patted Cadbury, who'd bounced up again. 'Whose is it?'

'One of the masters, we don't know all their names yet,' said Dora quickly. 'But we offered to walk him. We'd better get back, he might be worried. Bye, sir. Bye, Miss Curtis. Best of luck at Larks.'

Dog and children scampered off.

'That was a near one,' muttered Bianca. 'We'd better dye Cadbury black. Do you think Mr B-T and Miss Curtis fancy each other? She's very pretty, and he's not bad for a wrinkly.'

Janna, however, was off again. 'How can Rupert Campbell-Black send that adorable scrap to a boarding school?'

'Bianca's a day girl,' said Hengist.

'I thought they all boarded.'

'Not at all. We've got several day pupils, and lots of them go home at weekends, so they can drink and smoke unobserved.' Then he added: 'Come and see my pride and joy.'

The gold hands of the chapel clock already pointed to twenty to four.

I ought to go back. Why am I allowing myself to be swept away by this man? thought Janna as she ran to keep up with his long, effortless stride.

Hengist, who loved trees passionately and was

always sloping off in the spring and autumn to rejoice in the changing colours, led her down the pitches to a little wood called Badger's Retreat, which was filled with both newly planted saplings and venerable trees. On the far side, as a complete surprise, the ground dropped sharply down into a broad green ride with beech woods towering on either side and a glorious view of villages, fields and soft blue woods on the horizon.

Janna gasped.

'Lovely, isn't it? Some criminal idiot back in the fifties gave planning permission to build here.' Hengist's voice shook with anger. 'Desirable residences with a view. Every time Bagley runs into trouble, there's talk of selling it off. The moment I got here, I planted more trees to discourage this. Those enormous holes are badger sets. If anyone built houses, the badgers would burrow up through the floors.

'This is what we call the Family Tree,' he added, pointing to a huge sycamore with a single base, out of which three separate trees hoisted a great umbrella of yellowing leaves into the sky. Like three bodies locked in muscular embrace, their trunks gleamed from the recent rain.

'This is the father.' Hengist tapped the biggest trunk, which, from behind, was pressing its chest and pelvis against the mother trunk, with its branches around her and around the child trunk, which was leaning back against its mother. The branches of all three were stretching southwards towards the sun, many of them resting on the ground, as though they were teaching each other to play the piano. The bark, acid green with lichen, was cracked in many places to reveal a

129

rhubarb-pink trunk.

'How beautiful,' breathed Janna, 'like a marvellous sculpture.'

'Like a family, struggling for freedom,' said Hengist, 'yet inextricably entwined and protecting each other. When we first came here, we noticed it, the way families cling together and hide their problems. It was May, and the new leaves were thick and overlapping, like parrots' plumage, concealing trunks and branches.

'We have a daughter, Oriana, who works for the BBC as a foreign correspondent. We did have a son, Mungo, but he died of meningitis.'

Betraying his desolation for only a second, Hengist pulled off a sepia sycamore key.

'I used to tell Oriana she could open any door with one of these and you can too, my darling.' He put the key in Janna's hand, closing her fingers over it.

I must not fancy this man, she told herself.

'Oh look,' said Hengist, 'the Lower Sixth has been here.'

In the long pale grass lay an empty vodka bottle and several fag ends. 'The retakes must have been harder than expected,' he added, picking up a couple of red cartridge cases.

As Janna glanced at her watch and said, 'Help, it's nearly a quarter past four,' Hengist could feel a black cloud of depression engulfing her.

'Thank you for lunch and the spoon,' she stammered as he opened her car door.

'I'd like to help, and I hope it's not just facilities you and I are going to share,' said Hengist, kissing her on the cheek.

'Hum,' said Dora Belvedon, nearly falling out of

the biology lab window, 'Mr B-T definitely fancies her.'

15

Hengist Brett-Taylor had been born fifty-one years ago in Herefordshire. His parents were upper-middle-class Liberals and academics: his mother specializing in plants, his father a revered early English history don at Cambridge, hence the choice of Hengist's Christian name. Hengist had been educated at Fleetley and, between 1969 and 1972, read history at Cambridge. Here he got a double Blue for cricket and rugger and later played rugger for England, clinching the Five Nations Cup with a legendary drop goal from just inside his own half. As a result of too much sport and an overactive social life, Hengist, to his parents' horror, only scraped a 2.1.

At a May Ball at Cambridge, Hengist met Sally, a headmaster's daughter, as beautiful as she was straight. Their wedding took place in the chapel at Radley, where Hengist had started teaching history in autumn 1972. A daughter, Oriana, was born in 1973. Hengist had hoped for a son who would play rugger for England and whom he intended to call Orion.

Hengist prospered at Radley and was overjoyed in 1976 when Sally produced a son, Mungo. The birth was so difficult that Sally and Hengist decided two children were enough.

In 1979, Hengist returned to teach history and rugger at his old school, Fleetley, which now rivalled Winchester and Westminster in academic achievement. Fleetley's head, David 'Hatchet' Hawkley, was determined to keep the school single sex, believing that girls distract boys from work.

In 1984, tragedy struck when little Mungo died of meningitis. This nearly derailed Sally and Hengist's marriage, particularly as Sally had just discovered that her husband had been dallying with David Hawkley's ravishing and promiscuous wife, Pippa.

Although Fleetley took only boys, as a huge concession, because Hengist and Sally couldn't bear to be separated from their now only child, David Hawkley had allowed the eleven-year-old Oriana into the Junior School. A contributory factor was that Oriana was far brighter than any of the boys in her class.

Gradually, Sally unfroze and she and Hengist mended their marriage. In 1989, however, Pippa Hawkley had been killed in a riding accident and, going through her desk, a hitherto unsuspecting David Hawkley discovered passionate letters from Hengist, which also contained the odd dismissive crack about David himself. Hengist, therefore, departed from Fleetley under an unpublicized cloud, which not even Oriana gaining straight As in twelve GCSEs could lift.

In 1995, later than if he hadn't screwed up at Fleetley, Hengist had been appointed headmaster of the notorious and wildly out-of-control Bagley Hall. Applying the same foxiness and energy that he displayed on the rugby field, Hengist miraculously turned Bagley round in six years.

Bagley was now snapping at Fleetley and Westminster's heels in the league tables, and lynching every other school at rugger and cricket. Hengist had signed on for another five years until summer 2005 but, easily bored, was looking for new challenges. His ambition was to thrash David Hawkley in the league tables and take over Fleetley when David retired. But he was also toying with the idea of politics. His chairman of governors, steely Jupiter Belvedon, the great white Tory hope, was only too aware that Hengist, as a media star, would add a desperately needed dollop of charisma to the party.

Oriana, meanwhile, had got a first at Oxford and joined the BBC. Although attached to her parents, she couldn't handle the claustrophobia of their love and expectation, and had pushed off abroad as a foreign correspondent. Despite a somewhat contentious relationship, Hengist missed Oriana dreadfully.

One of the reasons Hengist had turned Bagley round was because he was a genius at recruitment. He had so many celebrities among his parents that, in summer, the school helicopter pad wore out more quickly than the wickets.

Interviews with prospective parents took place in Hengist's study, usually in front of a big fire with papers spread all over his desk and everyone relaxing on squashy sofas. Hengist also insisted on the prospective pupil being present and addressing him or her as much as the parents.

To the fathers, who remembered catches flying into his big hands like robins and his dark mane streaming out as he thundered like the Lloyd's Bank horse down the pitch at Twickenham, Hengist was an icon. The mothers just fantasized about sleeping with him. The children said, 'I like that man, I'd like to go to that school.'

As a result Bagley was overbooked until 2010.

Hengist was a great teacher because he was a

great communicator. But, because it involved too much hard work, he preferred to leave the GCSE and A level pupils to his heads of department and teach the new boys and girls so he could get to know them. Hengist believed in praising, and always fired off half a dozen postcards a day telling staff or pupils they had done well.

He was a genius at inspiring staff and delegating, but hopelessly bored by admin and red tape, which was why, to relieve himself of this burden, he had appointed Alex Bruce from the maintained sector as his deputy head.

*   *   *

Hengist was aware that the charitable status awarded to the independent schools, which saved them millions of pounds a year, was under threat from the Government unless they could prove they were sharing their facilities with the community and in particular with the local state schools.

Bagley already had a distinguished history of pupils helping in neighbouring hospitals. From the Lower Fifth onwards, each child was allotted a couple of OAPs whose gardens they weeded and errands they ran. But this wasn't quite enough.

What more charming and advantageous diversion, reflected Hengist, to mix philanthropy with pleasure and help out Larks and that adorable crosspatch. And it would so irritate the heads of the other local schools.

16

Larks was revving up for its prospective-parents' evening. All the displays were in place. There was terrific work on the walls, including Pearl's A star essay on dressing the three witches in Macbeth. Year Ten had turned a room into a spaceship. Year Eight were doing agriculture in geography, and although Robbie Rushton had been far too lazy and bolshie to provide any input, his deputy Adele, whom he'd employed to disguise his imperfections, had weighed in and, with the help of the children, created a farm with coloured cut-outs of animals, machinery and a farmhouse kitchen with bread, milk, butter, cheese and a ham on the table.

Graffi, who fancied Adele and had drawn most of the animals and a farmer and his wife, had also created a glorious country scene in reception. This included wild flowers and trees, and larks in their nest, in the young emerald-green wheat or soaring into a red-streaked sky. In the east, he had painted a yawning sun crawling out of bed, and in the west, weary stars wriggling thankfully under the duvet.

Janna had craftily made it seem a great privilege for forty of the better-behaved children to be allowed back into school to welcome and provide tours for visiting parents. Those who'd helped put up displays had been rewarded with Mars bars and letters home requesting their presence.

This had caused sneering from the troublemakers, who'd not been chosen, but who, when a smell of roasting chicken crept out of Debbie's kitchen and Bob Marley began booming over the tannoy at going-home time, felt that they might be missing something—if only the chance to trash.

Feral had been truanting again, but Graffi, Pearl and Kylie had been among the chosen. Alas, Mr Blenchley, angry with Paris for cheeking Rod Hyde, had refused to let him out. Without Paris and Feral, Graffi needed to defend his work more fiercely than ever and, like a little tiger, prowled up and down reception.

The staff had divided into helpers and hinderers. Among the former were Miss Cambola and Mags Gablecross, who had taken children into the fields to try and record trilling larks.

'He's too high, miss,' was the considered opinion, but everyone got muddy and had a laugh.

Wally had painted till he dropped. Countries of the World in lime green now decorated the turquoise corridor walls. Even languid Jason had come to Janna's aid.

'I gather you had lunch with Hengist. How did you find him?'

'With difficulty. I got terribly lost.'

'Charming bloke.'

'If you like arrogant Adonises.'

'Did he mention me?'

'He feels you'll fit in very well.'

Missing the sarcasm, Jason looked delighted.

'Any help needed this evening, I'll be around.'

'If you could provide some evidence of work in progress in the drama department?'

Once Jason decided to lend a hand, Gloria and all the other pretty women on the staff did too.

Lance, although unable to galvanize his class, had himself created a project of life in Tudor

England and spent days blackening beams and colouring in doublet and hose.

The hinderers were in a state of mutiny because Janna had ordered them to be on parade. Mike Pitts had left everything to Jessamy, his little Asian teaching assistant. Robbie was sulking because Adele had done so well. Skunk Illingworth carried on reading the *New Scientist*.

Around teatime, Janna caught Cara bitching into her mobile. 'Nobody'll turn up. I'll be away by eight.'

'That is such a defeatist attitude. You've made no effort,' Janna had told her furiously. Shaking with rage, she returned to her office. 'I'm going to kill Cara Sharpe.'

'Kill her tomorrow,' said Debbie, putting a plate of chicken sandwiches, a blackberry yoghurt and a cup of tea on Janna's desk. 'You must keep up your strength.'

'You are champion, the most champion thing that's happened to Larks, your food's utterly transformed the place, and you've added tarragon.' Janna bit gratefully into a sandwich. Then, picking up the *Gazette*: 'Let's look at our ad.'

But, to her horror, there was nothing there: no advertisement nor any part of her glowing report on Larks's future plans.

'I cannot believe it!' The *Gazette* flapped like a captured seagull as she flipped through it a second and third time—nothing. Even more galling, there were big ads and reports on the splendour and overflowing rolls at Searston Abbey, St Jimmy's and the choir school, who were all having parents' evenings this same night.

Colin 'Col' Peters, the *Gazette* editor, was all

injured innocence when Janna called him.

'We never received any copy, Miss Curtis.'

'I put it through the letterbox.'

'I'm sorry. We have no record. If we had, we'd have billed you. We're not in the habit of turning away business.'

'I don't believe you. At least send a reporter down here this evening.'

'I'm afraid they're all on other jobs. *Such* a busy night.'

Janna smashed the telephone back on its cradle. What was going on in this town? Keep calm, count to ten, she told herself as she changed into a new dress, the blue of grape hyacinths, which had long, tight sleeves and clung to the bust and waist before flowing into a full skirt. It was demure, but very sexy. Sadly, she felt as sexy as a corpse. Her face, in the mirror, was drained of all colour and confidence.

Smile, Janna, even when you're playing to empty houses.

She hadn't even the heart to chide Gloria who, to wow any fathers, had rolled up in a pink vest and a white groin-length skirt showing off a shocking pink thong.

'Gloria certainly believes in transparency,' observed Mags Gablecross.

As she waited in reception, Janna's mood was not improved by the arrival of Monster Norman and Satan Simmons.

'Who told you to come along?'

'Mrs Sharpe,' sneered Satan.

'I've come to meet my mother,' said Monster.

'If you put a foot out of line . . .' hissed Janna.

'Everything looks splendid,' boomed Miss Uglow,

139

taking up residence in her RE classroom with the latest P. D. James and a bag of bulls' eyes.

'Just remember to be polite to the new parents,' Janna urged the children. 'Show them you're proud of your school, so they'll want to send their kids here.'

The coffee was brewing. Debbie's chicken sandwiches and homemade shortbread were laid out on plates. Fresh rolls awaited the sausages warming in the oven for people who'd come straight from work. The church clock struck seven-thirty.

'Shall we dance?' asked Jason Fenton to Gloria the gymnast, as over the tannoy Bob Marley reassured them that every little thing was going to be all right.

But it wasn't, because no one came. You couldn't even blame the weather. It was a lovely evening, dove grey in the east, rose doré in the west and the first stars competing with Wally's lights up the drive.

'People'll turn up soon. They'll have seen our "Welcome to Larks" sign outside,' Janna reassured the children.

After ten minutes, Graffi abandoned his display in reception and ran down the drive to check. Immediately, Satan and Monster moved in.

' "Due to pesticide and fertilizer, there are few larks about these days," ' read Satan in a silly voice.

'And even fewer prospective parents,' wrote Monster underneath with a marker pen, just as Graffi returned, gloomily shaking his shaggy head.

'No one's coming, miss. Street's empty.'

'They'll probably come on to us from other

schools.'

'Here's someone,' cried Kylie Rose in excitement.

But it was only Cara, Mike, Robbie, Sam and Skunk, trooping in from the Ghost and Castle.

'I hope you're not going to insist we hang around if no one turns up,' said Mike.

'Those are for the parents,' protested Pearl as Robbie and Skunk started wolfing chicken sandwiches. 'Tell them off, miss.'

Janna couldn't bear seeing the excitement draining out of the children's faces. Even worse, Rod Hyde kept ringing up.

'We've had two hundred already and they're still flowing in. How are you doing?'

'Oh, go away,' said Janna, fighting back the tears.

'What a waste of money heating the school on such a warm night,' chided Cara.

The boys, also believing in transparency, had started flicking water at the white shirts of the girls, revealing their bras underneath. There was a crash as a window was smashed. Any moment there would be a mass exodus down the wisteria.

Unwilling to take on Graffi, Monster led Satan off to trash Year Eight's farm and, spitting at a cringing Adele, ignoring the screams of the girls, they swept everything off the farmhouse table and hurled a bread board and a papier mâché loaf out of the window. Chucking the farmer and his wife on the floor, they stamped on pigs, sheep and hens, kicked over milk pails and ripped the beautifully constructed tractor to pieces.

'Don't,' yelled Janna, racing up and seizing Monster's arm. Next moment, Graffi erupted into the room, hurling Satan to the ground.

141

'Fight, fight, fight,' yelled Year Eight, tears drying on their faces as they gathered round.

'Someone's coming,' squealed Kylie Rose.

'It's your mother, Monster,' yelled Graffi, catching him off guard and smashing a fist into Monster's round, pasty face.

Not wanting to have his ears boxed (Stormin' Norman could be as tough on her son as on other people's children), Monster scrambled to his feet, wiping his bloody nose.

Downstairs, Russell Lambert, Ashton Douglas and Crispin Thomas walked into comparative calm. Ashton had gone casual, wearing a beige cashmere V-necked jersey next to his pink-and-white skin, which made his features more formless than ever. Crispin ducked as a cardboard pig flew over the stairwell.

'This is very disappointing,' said Russell as Janna ran downstairs to meet them. 'Sam Spink tells me you've had no one in.'

Crash went another window.

'Turn up the volume,' hissed Janna to Mags Gablecross.

' "Hark, Hark! the Lark",' sang Bryn Terfel, fortissimo, making everyone jump out of their skins.

'Is it a good idea'—Ashton looked disapprovingly at Paris's copied-out poems and Graffi's countryside mural—'to gwaffiti newly painted walls?'

Explosions from the science lab indicated Year Ten were having fun. As Debbie and her helpers put plates of hot dogs and more chicken sandwiches on the table, Skunk, Robbie and Sam fell on them.

'How caring of Debbie to realize we'd missed supper.'

'Those are for the parents,' repeated Pearl indignantly.

'What happened to the advertisement in the *Gazette*?' asked Ashton.

'They didn't print it, claimed they never got it.'

'It's always wise to check these things,' said Russell heavily, 'shame to squander so much money and time on displays which no one sees.'

I must not cry, Janna told herself.

Five minutes crawled past. Mike Pitts was nose to nose with Ashton Douglas.

'Shall we call it a night?' he was saying. 'Frankly, I've got better things to do.'

'So glad I didn't waste time glamming up my department,' sneered Cara; then, shooting a venomous glance at Janna: 'Some people accused me of letting Larks down.'

'Ay had to pay someone to mind Cameron,' grumbled Chantal Peck. 'Ay'm going to put in expenses. Told you it would flop on an *EastEnders* night.'

'Please give it another five minutes,' begged Janna.

Noticing the ill-suppressed satisfaction on the faces of Ashton, Crispin and Russell, she told herself numbly: I don't understand why, but they are willing me to fail.

17

Then, suddenly, like the Angel Gabriel emerging from a day in the City, resplendent in a pinstriped suit, dark blue shirt and pretty pink and yellow checked tie, eyes sparking with malice, in sauntered Hengist Brett-Taylor.

'Janna, darling, how are you?'

Striding down reception, he took her hands and, bending down, kissed her on both cheeks.

'It all looks fantastic. My God, you've cheered this place up, and this mural is simply breathtaking. Of course, it's "Larks Ascending"— and the music too,' as, on cue, the tape launched into Vaughan Williams. 'Who's responsible?'

'Well, everyone, but the mastermind's been Graffi Williams here.'

'Brilliant, brilliant.' Hengist grasped Graffi's hands. 'I love the sun and the stars and that beautiful Shelley quote: "The world should listen then, as I am listening now", the prayer of all writers, me included. This is inspiring stuff.' Then he gave a shout of laughter. 'I love the old man with the beard, got that pompous ass Rod Hyde to a T.'

Hengist had been buoyed up by a very successful meeting with two of his high Tory conspirators, who were standing in the doorway and whom he now beckoned over.

'First, this is Jupiter Belvedon, your MP and chairman of my governors at Bagley.'

'Oh, goodness.' Janna found herself shaking hands with a dark, thin-faced, haughty-looking man in his early forties, familiar from posters all round the town, and forgot to bristle because she was so grateful to see anyone. 'Hi,' she gasped, 'welcome to Larks.'

'And Rupert Campbell-Black,' added Hengist.

'Blimey,' whispered Pearl.

'Wicked,' sighed Kylie. 'Oh, wicked!'

'Wicked indeed,' breathed Janna, because Rupert was so beautiful: like moonlight on the Taj Mahal or Monet's *Irises*, or a beech wood in autumn sunshine, which you'd dismissed as clichés because you'd seen them so often in photographs, in the flesh, they—and he—took your breath away.

The antithesis of Ashton Douglas, there was nothing soft in Rupert's face, from the smooth, wide forehead, the long watchful Oxford blue eyes, the hard, high cheekbones, Greek nose, short upper lip and curling but determined mouth. Around Hengist's height, somewhere up in the clouds to Janna, he was broad-shouldered, lean and long-legged.

Only his voice was soft, light and very clipped as he said:

'You don't look like a headmistress. I wouldn't have run away from school at fourteen if they'd looked like you.' Then, glancing down at the battered cardboard collie under his arm: 'Have you lost a dog? This one just flew out of the window.'

Prejudice evaporating, Janna burst out laughing.

'Would you like some shortbread?' asked Gloria.

'Or a chicken sandwich?' said Debbie the cook.

'Or a coffee?' said Rowan.

'Or an 'ot dog?' Chantal Peck rushed forward with a plate.

'I've got one already.' Rupert patted the collie's

145

head.

'I'd adore one, I'm starving,' said Hengist.

'So am I,' said Jupiter.

Rupert shook his sleek blond head. 'I'm OK.'

'You bet you are,' murmured Gloria.

Even Cara Sharpe was looking quite moony.

Jason was feeling very upstaged, particularly as Hengist hadn't recognized him.

'Rupert, as you know, is one of my parents, and a director of Venturer Television,' Hengist told a stunned Janna.

'Has Venturer been in yet?' asked Rupert, who'd noticed Janna was trembling. 'No? I'll give them a ring.'

'Nor have any prospective parents,' said Monster Norman smugly. 'You're the only people who've shown up.'

'D'you have any kiddies, your honourable?' Chantal asked Jupiter.

'One boy.'

'Thinking of sending him to Larks?'

'He doesn't really talk yet.'

'We've got an excellent special-needs department.'

'Even so, he might have difficulty keeping up,' said Jupiter gravely, 'he's only fourteen months.'

'Same as my grandson, Cameron. Frankly, Jupiter, I wouldn't send Cameron anywhere else than Larks.'

Crash went another window. Overhead, it sounded like elephants playing rugby.

'How are you, little one?' Hengist murmured to Janna.

'Hellish. They've trashed the farm we built upstairs; no one's come. I've let the kids down.'

146

'Leave it to me. You're right about Paris Alvaston. I've just read his poem about a lark; it's miraculous.'

'Hi,' murmured Rupert into his mobile, 'I'm at Larks, get your asses down here.' Then, after a pause: 'Can you rally some parents?' Switching off, he turned to Janna. 'They were on their way to St Jimmy's; they won't be long.'

'I want to see round the school,' said Hengist, who was now talking to the children, praising and discovering who'd done what. 'Are you all going to take me? What's that, England?' He pointed to one of Wally's newly painted acid-green countries.

'No, Africa, dumb-dumb,' giggled Pearl.

'God, these are good.' Grabbing another hot dog, Hengist set off like the Pied Piper, trailing children, all wanting to hold his hand. Reluctantly, Ashton, Russell and Crispin followed him.

Going into classroom B20, he found a scene of total devastation, and Adele trying to comfort the sobbing twelve-year-olds.

There was a pause, then Hengist said, 'This is absolutely brilliant. Look, Ashton, look, Russell, they've re-created a farm in the Balkans.' Putting huge arms round the sobbing little girls, he went on, 'Of course you're sad your farm's been bombed, but you've really captured the pathos of war.

'Look at the poor farm animals and birds.' Hengist pointed with half a hot dog. 'Animals are always the first casualties of war. Look at that poor lamb with its legs blown off and the cow who's been disembowelled, and everything's been swept off the table.'

Hengist righted the farmer and his wife who'd

147

lost an arm. 'They were just enjoying their tea, poor darlings, when the bomb fell. So sad.'

'Are you responsible?' He turned to a shell-shocked Adele. 'I can only congratulate you; such vision and courage, to destroy something so precious. That tractor's wonderful too. What's your name? Miss Stevens, just the kind of primitive machinery they'd have in Bosnia.'

'Graffi made that,' piped up Janna proudly.

'We did it too.' Monster and Satan edged forward. 'We trashed it.'

Janna was poised to annihilate them, but wily old Hengist pumped their hands. 'Well done, a real team effort.'

Robbie was simply furious, longing to push forward to take credit, but Hengist had moved on to Life in Tudor England and, as a fellow historian, was praising a blushing Lance:

'Just the right scarlet for that doublet, a very Elizabethan scarlet.'

Jupiter, meanwhile, was hell-bent on discomfiting Russell, Ashton and Crispin, who were all allied to the hung Labour/Lib Dem county council, who so frustrated his Tory ambition.

'And we'll hang them out to dry at the next election,' he murmured to Rupert as they paused to admire Mrs Gablecross's French café and enquire after her husband, the Chief Inspector, an old friend of them both.

Word had, by this time, got around that Rupert was at Larks and there was a further chance to get on telly, so there was a mass exodus from the other schools with parents and children storming up the drive. A reporter who'd only been at the *Gazette* for a week, tipped off by a Venturer cameraman, also belted over to Larks with his photographer. Hengist immediately introduced them to Janna, then took them by the arm, showing them the Larks Ascending display and the bombed farm.

Satan Simmons and Monster Norman were soon being interviewed.

'We built it up, then trashed it to create a wartime situation,' Monster was saying.

'Like the Chapman brothers or Rachel Whiteread,' said the reporter.

'Yeah, yeah, whatever.'

Photographs were also taken of Rupert, Jupiter and Hengist with Janna. Parents were everywhere, demanding autographs: 'You sending your kids here, Rupert? How's Taggie? Any tips for Cheltenham?'

'We didn't get food at St Jimmy's or Searston Abbey,' said the other parents as they fell on Debbie's hot dogs. 'Lovely atmosphere here. I like these old buildings. More ambience. Hello, Jupiter. He's our MP.'

Jupiter, who reminded Janna of the lean and hungry Cassius, told the *Gazette* that as Shadow Education Minister and Larkminster's MP, he took a great interest in local schools.

'I am delighted Janna Curtis appears to be turning round this one, after only a few weeks. Good to have a young, energetic and charismatic head. You're to be congratulated, Ashton.' He smiled coolly at a seething Ashton Douglas. 'I hope you're providing adequate financial support. Janna tells me she needs textbooks, computers, playing fields and a new roof.'

'We can't have raindrops falling on our head or anyone else's,' said Rupert, looking up from the

Evening Standard.

Janna got the giggles.

'Ashton, well done,' said Hengist, coming out of a side door, trailing children. 'You must be delighted you chose Janna. I've never seen such a change.'

Ashton looked as though he'd swallowed a wasp.

Venturer Television arrived, filmed the sea of parents and then interviewed Hengist about his interest in Larks.

'Janna and I have been discussing plans to share our facilities,' Hengist told them. 'The council sold off Larks's playing fields, so we'd like to offer them access to ours, and to our libraries, art departments, science labs and running tracks. We're very early in discussions, but it's an exciting project. We'll both learn from each other.'

'We'll teach them fist-foiting, shooting and Formula One driving,' yelled Graffi and was shushed.

'When will this happen?' asked the Venturer presenter.

'I'm off to America and we've got half-term, but very soon after that, I hope. To merit our charitable status, we independent schools must increasingly demonstrate we're of benefit to the community,' Hengist concluded smoothly. 'We've always offered bursaries to bright children; we're merely carrying on a tradition.'

'First I've heard of it.' Russell Lambert was puffing out his cheeks.

'Janna and I'—Hengist smiled in her direction— 'had a working lunch yesterday. She's made a great start, but as one who had problems at the beginning with Bagley, I'd like to offer my support.'

150

'Rod Hyde's already doing a grand job,' snapped Ashton, 'and I'm not sure how Larks staff will feel about bonding with an independent.'

'We'll have to find out,' said Hengist coolly, 'but three heads are always better than one.'

'Come on, I need a drink.' Rupert was getting bored. 'Can I keep this dog?'

Briefly, Hengist drew Janna aside: 'Pretty dress. "At last she rose, and twitched her mantle blue: tomorrow to fresh woods, and pastures new."'

'I don't know what you're playing at,' muttered an utterly confused Janna, 'but thank you for rescuing us.'

'I'll ring you tomorrow.'

'Goodbye, goodbye.' Reluctantly, the children waved Hengist off.

'I'll be in touch,' Jupiter told Janna, then, handing his card to Graffi: 'I'd like to see more of your stuff.

'That was rather injudicious,' he added a minute later as the black polished shoes of the three men rustled through red and gold leaves towards the car park. 'Do you honestly want Bagley overrun by a lot of yobbos?'

'I want the world to know how good and philanthropic my school is. Caring conservatism must show it has balls,' said Hengist mockingly.

'Are you sure Bagley won't corrupt those innocent Larks hooligans?' asked Rupert. 'Do you really want bricks heaved through your Burne-Jones windows?'

' "We must love one another or die",' replied Hengist sanctimoniously.

'I hope you don't want to get into Janna Curtis's knickers,' warned Jupiter, pressing the remote

151

control to open the doors of his Bentley. 'The Tory party can't afford any more sleaze.'

'I like this dog.' Rupert patted his cardboard collie. 'It can round up the Tory unfaithful.'

* * *

Paris lay on top of his bed at Oaktree Court. A girl in the room opposite had been screaming for nearly an hour. Fucking Blenchley, not to let him out, when Janna had been kind enough to pin up his poem beside those of Shakespeare, Milton and Shelley. He murmured longingly:

> 'Teach me half the gladness
> That thy brain must know;
> Such harmonious madness
> From my lips would flow,
> The world should listen then, as I am
>   listening now.'

He would have liked to shag Benita who slept next door, but if ever he left his room, a red light went on in the warden's office.

Shutting his eyes, he dreamt of making love to Janna: 'such harmonious madness'. He must get out of this place.

* * *

Waving the *Gazette* next morning, Gillian Grimston, head of Searston Abbey, telephoned Rod Hyde. 'That swine Hengist Brett-Taylor's never offered us a blade of grass. It's just because Janna Curtis wears tight jumpers and bats her

152

eyelashes.'

'Hengist has always been a ladies' man.'

'I'd hardly call Janna Curtis a lady.'

'It'll all end in tears,' said Rod Hyde grimly, thinking of his stolen hat.

Nor was Randal Stancombe pleased. He didn't fork out £20,000 a year for Jade's school fees only for her to mix with riff-raff.

18

The following evening, Janna recounted the latest events to her new friend Lily Hamilton as they sat at Lily's kitchen table making sloe gin, selecting blue sloes from a pile Lily had picked earlier in the day, pricking each one with a needle before dropping it into a waiting bottle. Lily was progressing much faster because Janna kept pricking her fingers or missing the bottle whenever she got on to the subject of Ashton or Cara or Russell.

'They were foul. If Hengist and his friends hadn't rolled up . . .'

Lily smiled. 'I told you Hengist was nice.'

'I reckon he was more interested in bugging Ashton,' said Janna firmly, but the glow of gratitude still warmed her.

'You're returning your sloes to the pile,' chided Lily.

'Oh help, sorry.'

Just as she was topping up their glasses, Janna's mobile rang.

'Is that Janna?' asked an incredibly plummy voice. 'It's Sally Brett-Taylor. We were wondering if you'd come and dine on October the twenty-sixth. Hengist so enjoyed his lunch with you, and we'll try and rustle up some fun locals for you to meet. As it's a Friday, we won't bother to dress.'

And be running around nude, reflected Janna, then said she'd love to.

'Lovely, eight for eight-thirty, bye-ee.'

'Bye-ee, bye-ee,' muttered Janna as she hung up.

'That was Mrs Brett-Taylor,' she told Lily. 'She sounds very jolly hockey sticks.'

'She's a sweet thing,' said Lily. 'Terribly kind, keeps Hengist on the rails, remembering names, edging him out of parties if he's getting drunk or indiscreet.'

*   *   *

Janna was further touched on Monday to receive a cheque for three thousand pounds from Venturer Television.

'Hope this might buy a few textbooks,' Rupert had written, 'and your children might enjoy this film.'

It was *Gladiator*, which Janna allowed all the excited children to watch that afternoon as a reward for their good behaviour.

As a result of the prospective-parents' evening, thirty parents put their names down for Larks in autumn 2002 and the editor of the *Gazette* nearly sacked his news editor when a most flattering piece about Larks Comp appeared on the front page. This was accompanied by a smiling picture of Rupert, Hengist, Jupiter and Janna.

Inside were pictures of Graffi, Pearl, Monster and Satan surveying the trashed farm and a large headline: 'Larks Ascending'.

An overjoyed Janna bought twelve copies of the paper and sent photocopies to all the parents. Even more excitingly, the *Gazette* published Paris's poem 'To a Skylark', no longer a blithe spirit, whose trill was a burglar alarm, warning of the pillaging of the countryside.

'Paris Alvaston', wrote Hengist in his diary.

Poor Paris was unmercifully ragged at the children's home.

Sam Spink, meanwhile, called a union meeting to protest against Larks accepting any favours from the private sector. Alex Bruce, deputy head of Bagley, who'd come from the maintained sector, was equally unamused. His friend Rod Hyde had briefed him on the 'challenging behaviour' of Larks's pupils.

'Do we really want these hooligans to invade Bagley? You're always complaining of overwork, Senior Team Leader,' he reproved Hengist. 'Why not let me mentor Janna Curtis? I could slot in a visit to Larks on Fridays.'

'I'm only overworked by things I don't enjoy and Janna Curtis is very pretty,' said Hengist and laughed in Alex's shocked face.

After the parents' evening, Hengist had telephoned Janna as promised.

'I'm deadly serious about Larks and Bagley getting together. But I've got a hellish October. Lectures in Sydney and Rome, a headmasters' conference in Boston, not to mention half-term, so let's aim at early November.'

With that, he had drifted off and, like everyone else, been distracted by the American bombing of Al-Qaeda in Afghanistan, particularly as his daughter Oriana was reporting for the BBC from there.

Larks's pupils, whose spirits had been lifted by Hengist's visit and watching *Gladiator*, fell back into their old ways. Janna seemed to spend her time wrestling with red tape, refereeing fights, putting buckets under leaks and sparring with Rod Hyde, who said:

156

'Typical Hengist B-T behaviour, swanning in to cash in on the publicity. That's the last you'll see of him.'

It was so humiliating to have nothing to report when the *Gazette* and other papers rang for news of the bonding, and heartrending when the children kept asking when they'd get a chance to play football on a decent pitch. Janna was too proud to call Hengist, but as the leaves changed colour and tumbled from the trees, she felt enraged he hadn't rung and was determined to look as glamorous as possible at his wife's dinner party.

This was preceded by a day from hell.

In the morning, guilty that she hadn't tapped any local fat cats for sponsorship, Janna had visited Grant Tyler, a Larkminster electronics giant who, with his long, yellow face ending in a pointed chin, looked just like a parsnip.

'And what do I get out of sponsoring Larks?' he had demanded rudely.

'Some of our clever children could do work experience here,' said Janna brightly, 'and might want to work for you as a career.'

Mr Tyler's face had turned from parsnip yellow to the purple of aubergine. 'If you think I'd let your ragamuffins over my threshold—' he had roared, and Janna had walked out leaving him in mid-sentence.

Later in the day she gave Cara Sharpe a final warning for bullying a little Bangladeshi pupil who'd been unable to produce a note explaining her absence because her mother didn't speak or write English.

Janna was also worried about Feral, who'd been

157

truanting persistently. She'd sort him out next week. But tonight she was leaving on time to shower and wash her hair at home and remove the red veins in her eyes with an iced eye pad, before putting on a lovely new off-the-shoulder black dress: all the things she had had time to do before a date with Stew in the old days.

As she came out of Larks, fireworks, anticipating a forthcoming Bonfire Night tomorrow week, were popping all over town. Walking towards the car park, she heard a terrified whine, followed by shouts of laughter. Tiptoeing further into the garden, stumbling down Smokers' Bank, she froze in horror to discover Monster Norman and Satan Simmons in the long, pale grasses above the pond. No doubt carried away by their success in trashing the cardboard animals, they were now trying the real thing and torturing a little dog. They had tied its front legs together; Monster was winding a rope round its muzzle. Satan was swearing as he tied a large rocket to its tail. Monster was also smoking. Having stubbed his cigarette out on the shoulder of the desperately writhing animal, he groped for a lighter and set fire to the rocket's blue paper.

'Stop that,' screamed Janna as both boys leapt out of the flight path.

Seeing her storming down the bank, they bolted, howling with laughter, down the hill over the wall. Next moment, the rocket exploded. Unable to soar into the air, it thrashed around on the ground, shooting out green and bright pink stars, dragging the dog with it.

Whipping off her coat, Janna flung it over the wretched animal, gathering it up, dunking it in the pond. As the sparks finally fizzled out, the dog wriggled. At least it was alive. In the gloom she could see its red and white fur singed on its face, sides and paws. It was a small mongrel with brown ears and a brown patch over one eye. Freeing its muzzle, untying the rocket with frantically trembling hands, Janna carried it up the bank to her car. It was hardly breathing now. Finding Wally and help would waste time. Laying the dog on the back seat, trying not to upset the poor little thing by sobbing, soothing it with: 'Good boy, brave boy, hang on a bit longer, darling,' she hurtled round to the Animal Hospital, off the High Street.

Here a sympathetic vet said it was their first Guy Fawkes casualty, but they were expecting a lot more; that the dog had been very badly burned and would probably lose his tail and an eye.

'It's only just breathing, hasn't got a collar, probably a stray, terribly thin, kinder to put it down.'

The dog, who suddenly seemed to symbolize Larks, gave a whimper.

'Try and save him,' pleaded Janna.

'I'll see what I can do.' The vet looked regretfully at her watch. 'I'm supposed to be at a dinner party.'

'Oh Christ, so am I,' said Janna. 'Can I drop by later?'

'Ring if you'd prefer. You'd better get something on those burns.'

Weeping with rage and horror, Janna plunged into the night. At least she had a proper reason to exclude Monster and Satan, except they'd both deny it. There was plenty of the dog's blood on her, but probably not on them.

Heavens, it was a quarter past eight. She had no

time to change or wash her hair. In a lay-by, she ripped off her bloodstained T-shirt, leaving on her old olive-green cardigan and black skirt. Her stockings were laddered to bits. She'd look as poor and scruffy as the toffs would expect a state-school teacher to be, she thought savagely.

She was so distraught, she didn't reach Bagley until nine, where her animosity escalated as various incredibly polite children gave her directions.

'If you like, I'll hop in and guide you,' a little Hooray Henry said finally. 'Should get a good dinner. Mrs B-T's a terrific cook.' Then, noticing the bloodstained T-shirt in the back, he reached nervously for the door handle, until Janna told him about the dog.

'They ought to be shot, or rockets tied to their dicks. That's diabolical. We always give our greyhounds tranquillizers at home when there are fireworks around—at least we did,' he said sadly.

'Here we are,' he announced as the headlamps lit up brilliant red and crimson dogwood and maple and drifts of white cyclamen on either side of the drive.

As they passed arches trailing last year's roses and yew hedges cut into fantastic shapes, including a greyhound, Janna knew she'd come to the right house, which reared up, greyish yellow, shrouded in creeper, with some sash and some narrow casement windows, topped by roofs and turrets on different levels.

'It's a bit of a mishmash,' said her companion. 'Part Elizabethan, part Queen Anne, but very nice.'

A mongrel of a house, thought Janna, but

160

strangely appealing, like the little dog fighting for his life.

'I hope your dog recovers,' said the boy, running round and opening the door for her, 'and you have a good evening.'

'Thank you so much. What's your name?'

'Dicky Belvedon.' As he rang the bell for her, she realized he was Dora's twin.

'How are you getting back?'

'I'll walk. It's not far, and I can have a smoke in peace.'

A plump, middle-aged woman answered the door. Relieved that Hengist's wife wasn't glamorous, Janna was about to apologize for being late, when a truly pretty blonde ran out.

'Hello, Janna, I recognize you from your picture, I'm Sally B-T.'

After her, slipping all over the floorboards, wagging her tail, dark eyes shining, long nose snaking into Janna's hand, came Elaine, the white greyhound. Seeing such a happy, healthy dog, Janna burst into tears.

'You poor darling.' Sally turned, waved to the crowd in the room behind her to have another drink and whisked Janna upstairs. 'What's happened?'

Collapsing on the four-poster in the prettiest blue, lilac and pink bedroom, Janna explained about the dog.

'They're operating now. He was so defenceless and it was Larks children that did it. What can have happened to kids to turn them into such brutes?'

'They don't know any better. But poor little dog, and you've burnt your poor hands. They must be

161

agony. We'll ring the sick bay and get something for them.'

'I'm fine, honestly. I'm so sorry I didn't have time to change.'

There was a knock on the door, and a large glass of gin and orange, followed by Hengist, came round the door.

'Everything OK?'

'No! Poor Janna's had the most awful time.'

Sally, decided Janna—all her antagonism evaporating—was simply sweet. She was terribly Sloaney in her pie-frill collar and tartan blanket skirt, with wonderful rings on her rather wrinkled hands. But she was so friendly and kind.

'Now, please, borrow anything,' she told Janna. 'I'm afraid my make-up's not very exciting. A dash of lipstick and mascara is about my limit, but help yourself. And here's a nice cream shirt, if you're too hot in that cardigan. The bathroom's next door. Don't hurry.'

Having downed half the gin and orange, Janna felt perkier and the urge to spy. The curtains of the huge four-poster were patterned with sky-blue and pink delphiniums. On Sally's bedside table were Joanna Trollope and Penny Vincenzi, on Hengist's, French poetry and a biography of Louis XIV. A big dressing gown in forest-green towelling (to match his eyes) hung on the bathroom door. Janna imagined it wrapped round his hot, wet body. *The Joy of Sex* and *Fanny Hill* were well-thumbed in the shelves. Old maps of Greece and Italy covered the bathroom walls. Water gushed out of a lion's mouth into a big marble basin.

Janna took her hair down, but it looked so lank and straggly she put it up again. Sally's base was too pink, so she merely applied a little cherry-red lipstick to her mouth and blanched cheeks, and took off the shine with a pale blue swansdown powder puff dipped in a cut-glass bowl.

She now needed some perfume. Beautiful was pushing it. She'd smelt it on Sally. Instead, she slapped on a cologne called English Fern and was immediately transported back to La Perdrix d'Or and the wonder of her lunch with Hengist.

Comus, with damp, crinkled pages, was open beside a glass vase of yellow roses. 'What hath night to do with sleep,' read Janna.

You could say that again. She glared at her hollow cheeks and even hollower eyes. Sally's cream shirt falling to her knees like a nightdress made her look even more drained, but anything was better than the dreary cardigan.

Pale but interesting, Janna, she told herself. If that dog pulls through, I'm going to keep him.

19

Hearing the neighing and yelping of the upper middle classes three drinks up, Janna nearly turned and ran. Entering the double doors she found everyone up the other end examining some picture and paused in reluctant admiration because the huge lounge was so warm and welcoming.

Flames leapt merrily in the big stone fireplace. A crimson Persian carpet covered most of the polished floorboards. Battered sofas, armchairs and window seats in fading vermilion, old rose and magenta begged her to curl up on them. Poppies, vines and pomegranates rioting over the scarlet wallpaper battled for space with marvellous pictures. Was that really a Samuel Palmer of moonlit apple blossom? In bookshelves up to the ceiling fat biographies, history, classics, lots of poetry, gardening and art books, all higgledy piggledy and falling out, pleaded to be read. More books jostled with photographs of former pupils on every table, music scores rose from the floor in piles around the grand piano.

Any space left was crammed with family memorabilia: an old-fashioned gramophone with a convolvulus shaped speaking trumpet, a papier mâché HMV dog, busts of Wagner and Louis XIV, a staring female figurehead taken from a nineteenth-century fishing ship, a ravishing marble of Demeter with a sweat band restraining her curls—every object with a story.

This blaze of colour was reflected in a wooden mirror over the fireplace and softened by lamplight falling on great bunches of cream roses.

Never if I pored over *House & Garden* for a million years could I produce a room as beautiful, thought Janna wistfully, then angrily that independent heads must be grossly overpaid to afford places like this.

Hengist seemed to have read her mind, because he swung round and bore down on her with another vat of gin and orange.

'You poor darling, poor little dog, bloody bastards, I'd like to ram great lighted rockets up their arses.'

He was wearing a shirt in ultramarine denim, which turned his dark-green eyes a deep Prussian blue. From the breast pocket he produced a tube and a silver sheet of pills.

'The sick bay sent this over for your poor hands. Let me put some on at once.'

'It's only one hand, and it's fine.' Janna snatched the tube, knowing she'd tremble far more if he touched her.

Hengist's suntan had faded; his face was sallow and rumpled rather than golden and godlike. The trips to the States and Sydney must have been punishing, but his spirits were high and his eyes filled with amusement and expectation.

'It's so nice to see you again. I can't wait to open my facilities—such a dreadful word—to your children and particularly you.'

Bloody patronizing Little Lord Bountiful, thought Janna, wincing as she applied the gel, then wiped her hands on her skirt.

'Now swallow these,' ordered Hengist, pushing out two Anadin Ultra. When Janna looked mutinous he added, 'Or I'll hold your nose and stroke your throat.'

Feeding the pills into her mouth, letting his fingers rest on her lips a second too long, he held out the gin and orange for her to wash them down.

'Good girl. Now what are we going to argue about this evening: dyspraxia, ethnic diversity, gifted children?'

'Are my kids ever going to be allowed to play on your pitches?' asked Janna furiously.

'Oh, sweetheart, of course they are.'

'No one believes you.' The hurt and humiliation poured out of her. 'Ashton Douglas, Rod Hyde, Mike Pitts, Crispin Thomas are all sneering at me.'

'Bugger Ashton,' said Hengist, 'although he'd rather enjoy it. I swear the first—no, second week in November. The red carpet awaits. Feral, Graffi, Paris, whoever you like.'

Janna, who'd been staring fixedly at his strong, smooth neck and emerging six o'clock shadow, raised her eyes and found such affection and tenderness on his face, she was quite unable to speak. Thank God, Sally rescued her.

'Janna, come and meet everybody. Be careful, this carpet is a high-heel hazard. You've met Elaine?'

'I have.' Janna ran her hand over the pink silken belly; Elaine, showing herself off to advantage on a russet chaise longue, opened a liquid dark eye and waved a tail in greeting.

The buckets of gin and orange were kicking in and Janna was cheering up, there was so much to look at. The watchful, saturnine Jupiter Belvedon actually pressed both planed cheeks against hers before telling her how much he'd enjoyed visiting her school. He then introduced Hanna, his lovely blonde Norwegian wife, who was as warm and curvy as he was cold and thin, and who must be a colossal asset to him in his constituency.

'Hanna's responsible for those exquisite flower paintings in our bedroom,' explained a hovering Sally.

'They're beautiful,' said Janna. 'My next-door neighbour, Lily Hamilton, has lots of them too.' Then she blushed as she remembered how cruelly Jupiter had turfed Lily out of a lovely house. Fortunately Jupiter, having parked her, had moved off so Janna was able to reassure Hanna that Lily was fine and a wonderful neighbour.

'What's she up to?' asked Hanna.

'Making sloe gin. Keeping us all entertained.'

'I miss her so much,' sighed Hanna.

I am behaving really well at a smart Tory dinner, Janna told herself in amazement. Then, goodness, jungle drums! Sally was introducing her to Randal Stancombe.

Just as black panthers and leopards, sighted in woods and along river banks and terrorizing whole communities, often turn out to be domestic cats with fluffed-out winter fur, Stancombe, despite his fearsome reputation, was in the flesh much less alarming than she'd imagined. He was certainly sexy, with a handsome predator's face, scorching dark eyes that seemed to burn off Janna's clothes, blow-dried glossy black curls and a mahogany suntan, set off to advantage by a linen shirt even whiter than Elaine. Asphyxiated by his musky aftershave and blinded by his jewels, Janna snatched away her burnt hand before it was crushed by his rings.

'Delighted to meet you, Jan, Henge says you're

doing a great job at Larks, catch up with you later,' and he turned back to his companion, quite understandably, because she was the most glorious, pampered, expensive-looking beauty with shining chestnut hair, creamy skin, wide hazel eyes and luscious smooth coral lips.

This ravishing adventuress, Hengist whispered in Janna's ear, was *the* Mrs Walton he'd enticed on to the Bagley board as a parent governor, to ensure not only full houses at governors' meetings, but also that the other governors were so distracted by lust that they OKed all the decisions already made by Hengist and Jupiter.

'Very different from *my* parent governors,' giggled Janna, thinking of Chantal Peck and Stormin' Norman. 'When did they meet?'

'About ten minutes ago.'

Feeling his laughing lips against her ear, Janna experienced a surge of happiness. Sally then whisked her off to meet Gillian Grimston, head of Searston Abbey, who had a lot of teeth like a crocodile whose mother had failed to make it wear a brace, and who was asked out a lot because of her ability to offer the Larkshire middle classes an excellent free education, rather than for her charm or good looks. She was patronizing but amiable, and commiserated with Janna on having Rod Hyde on her back.

'He's so conceited and bossy.'

She then banged on about her workload, which had cost her her marriage, and Searston Abbey, which had already raised thousands for Afghanistan war victims, thus giving Janna plenty of opportunity to watch Stancombe freefalling down Mrs Walton's cleavage and only just disguising his irritation when Jupiter joined them.

Determined to crack every aspect of society, Stancombe was not only pressing Hengist to make him a Bagley governor, but having watched Jupiter's rocket-like ascent was anxious to buy into that camp and be a formative influence in Jupiter's breakaway Tory party. Jupiter, who liked Stancombe's money better than Stancombe, was playing hard to get.

'The Afghan Fund is part of our caring ethos,' droned on Gillian Grimston, wishing Mrs Walton were one of her mothers.

'I'd rather have an Afghan hound,' giggled Janna. Oh dear, she was getting drunk again.

'Dinner,' announced Sally.

The dining room was equally seductive, with bottle-green jungle-patterned wallpaper, and chairs upholstered in ivy-green velvet round an oak table as dark and polished as treacle toffee.

Light came from red candles flickering amid more white roses and a chandelier overhead like a forest of icicles, which set the regiments of silver and glass glittering.

Ancestors under picture lights looked down from the walls, except for a portrait by Emma Sergeant over the wooden fireplace, which showed the young Hengist, solemn-faced, dark eyes raised to heaven, poised to kick his legendary drop goal at Twickenham. Pausing to admire it, Janna felt Sally's arm through hers.

'I insisted on hanging it there. It was painted some time after the event. Hengist thinks it's awfully showing off, but I so love it. Hope you didn't get too stuck with Gillian. She's a good old thing and probably a useful ally. Are you OK?

169

Hands not too sore?'

'You are kind,' sighed Janna.

Even kinder, Sally had invited two single men to sit either side of Janna. One was Emlyn Davies, a blond giant with a battered face who taught history and rugger. The other, Piers Fleming, was head of English. Dark and romantic-looking, like Shelley's younger brother, wearing a steel-blue smoking jacket, he confessed he had great difficulty keeping the Bagley girls at bay.

'I'd screw the lot, if I weren't going to be banged up for under-age sex. Some of them are so gorgeous and so precocious, and worst of all'—he nodded across at Stancombe, who was being reluctantly prised away from Mrs Walton—'is Randal's daughter Jade, and no one can expel her because Daddy's poised to give the school a multi-million pound science block—bloody waste of money.'

They then got on to the more edifying subject of English literature.

Noticing Hengist at the head of the table flanked by lovely Hanna Belvedon and even lovelier Mrs Walton, whose taffeta dress, the stinging emerald of a mallard's head, seemed to caress her body with such love, Janna's spirits drooped. Then Hengist smiled at her and mouthed, 'Everything OK?' And suddenly it was.

Two big glass bowls of glistening black beluga caviar resting on crushed ice were placed on the table, eliciting moans of greed all round. Accompanying them were little brown pancakes, bowls of sour cream, chopped shallot, hard-boiled egg and wedges of lemon.

'Oh, thank you,' said Mrs Walton, as her glass

steamed up with the addition of iced vodka. 'Thank goodness I'm staying here and can get legless.'

'Shame with such lovely legs,' Stancombe leered across the table.

How the hell do I eat this lot? wondered Janna.

As if reading her panic, Sally called down the table, 'Do make up Janna's blinis for her, Piers, her hands must be so sore.'

'My favourite food,' confessed Jupiter.

'Where did it come from?' asked Gillian Grimston.

'Moscow,' said Hengist. 'Anatole, one of our pupils and the son of the Russian Minister of Affaires, chucked an empty vodka bottle out of an attic window and nearly concussed the chaplain—'

'And was, I presume, excluded?' Gillian looked shocked.

'Good God, no,' said Hengist, 'Anatole's a lovely boy. Always pays his own school fees in cash— probably laundered—out of a money belt. If only other parents were as prompt.'

'My cheque's in the post,' murmured Mrs Walton.

'Anyway, Anatole's mother was so grateful, she immediately sent us a ton of caviar.'

'Jupiter would kill for caviar,' said Hanna as her husband put two huge spoonfuls on his plate.

And much else, thought Janna. Not Cassius, she decided, he's more Octavius Caesar to Hengist's Mark Antony.

Janna wasn't sure about the caviar. She drowned it in lemon juice and took huge slugs of vodka. Perhaps she should give hers to the emaciated man across the table, who had a tired, bony face and flopping very light red hair, and was already piling a second helping on to his blue glass plate.

'Rufus Anderson, head of geography.' Piers lowered his voice. 'Head in the clouds, more likely, always leaving coursework on trains. Eats hugely at dinner parties because his wife, Sheena, doesn't cook and whizzes up to London to a high-powered Fleet Street job, leaving Rufus to look after the kids. Note his sloping shoulders weighed down by baby slings.'

'Then they should get an au pair,' said Janna sharply. 'Her career is just as important as his.'

'Not at Bagley, it isn't. Wives are expected to be helpmates. Sheena's hopping that Emlyn on your left was offered a job as a housemaster last year and Rufus wasn't. Rufus is miles cleverer than Emlyn or me. Sheena doesn't appreciate she's the only thing in the way of her husband's advancement. That's her down the table hanging like a vampire on Stancombe's every word.'

As Mrs Walton was soft, passive and voluptuous, Sheena Anderson was rapacious and hard. She had sleek black jaw-length hair, a hawklike face only adorned by eyeliner and a lean, restless body. No jewellery softened her short sleeveless black dress.

'I'd love to interview you for the *Guardian*,' she was telling Randal Stancombe.

'They always give me a rough time.'

'Not if I wrote the piece. You could approve copy.'

Like Jack-the-lad-in-a-box, Stancombe kept texting, emailing, doing sums on his palm top, leaping out of his seat to telephone or receive calls, leaving his mountain of caviar untouched.

'We could do it one evening over dinner,' urged

172

Sheena.

But Stancombe was checking his messages. 'Bear with me a minute, Sheen,' and he shot into the hall again. Through the doorway, he could be heard saying, 'Sure, sure, great, great, call you later.' Switching off his mobile, he punched the air. 'Yeah!'

'Good news?' enquired Sally as he slid back into his seat.

'Just secured a plot of land in Colorado, Sal, a ski resort to be exact.'

Janna caught Jupiter's eye and just managed not to laugh.

Gillian Grimston, who'd been subjected to Stancombe's back, was not used to being ignored. 'Where is this resort?' she asked.

'I'm not at liberty to reveal as yet, Gilly.' Stancombe flashed his teeth. 'In fact, bear with me again, Sal and Henge, if I make another call,' and he retreated again.

'That's how he keeps his figure,' said Piers.

Sheena, much to Sally's disapproval, had whipped out and was muttering into a tape recorder.

'How did you get started?' she asked when Stancombe returned.

'As a barrow boy. One of my customer's husbands gave me a job as an office boy in a property company. Kept my ear to the ground. Gave the CEO hot tips until he promoted me to head of the agency division. Two years later I took away all my contacts and started Randal Stancombe Properties. Rest is history. According to the Rich List, in Central London alone we own eight hundred buildings let to blue-chip companies.'

Everyone was listening.

'Despite heavy borrowings at the last count the portfolio must be worth more than two billion.'

Mrs Walton was gazing across the table in wonder. That would sort out the school fees.

'How many million times a million is that?' hissed Janna. 'He should be on the stage.'

'Better on television,' hissed back Piers. 'You could turn him off.'

'To what do you attribute your success?' asked Sheena, who'd left the tape recorder running.

'Hard work, seven days and seven nights a week.'

Stancombe checked his messages again. It was his thin line of moustache, Janna decided, like an upside-down child's drawing of a bird in flight, which gave him a gigolo look.

'Don't you ever play?' purred Mrs Walton.

'According to Freud,' said Janna idly, 'work and love are the only things that matter.'

'And children.' Hanna smiled at Jupiter, thinking how she'd like to paint those white roses.

Stancombe glanced down at his abandoned coal heap of caviar, realizing everyone had finished.

'I've had sufficient. I OD'd on beluga in St Petersburg last week.'

'Christ, what a waste,' exploded Jupiter.

'Did you buy a resortski?' enquired Janna.

Sheena was well named, she decided; she had a sheen of desirability about her but was very opinionated. As conversation became general and moved on to the war, she kept regurgitating whole paragraphs from a piece she had written on American imperialism earlier in the week.

'Hell, isn't she?' muttered Piers.

As he moved on to William Morris on October:

174

'How can I ever have enough of life and love?' Janna had noticed a sweet little girl gathering up the blue glass plates. Then she realized it was Dora Belvedon, Jupiter's stepsister, who'd emerged from the weeping willow by the lake with Bianca Campbell-Black, the day Hengist had shown her over Bagley.

Now she was bringing sliced roast beef in a rich red wine sauce round on a silver salver.

'Hello, Dora, you'd better tell me what fork to use.'

Dora's mouth lifted at the corner.

'It's very good, I tried some in the kitchen. I hear you met my brother Dicky earlier. I do hope that poor dog recovers.'

Dora loved waiting for Hengist and Sally. If she lurked and kept quiet, guests often forgot she was there, and revealed lots of saleable gossip.

Stancombe for a start was utterly gross, but good copy, and there'd been a lot about Janna Curtis in the press recently. She didn't look pretty tonight with that schoolmarmish hair and shapeless white smock. Mrs Walton, on the other hand, was gorgeous. Stancombe clearly thought so, which might make a story: Dora bustled back to the kitchen, and taking a pad out of her coat pocket wrote 'Randy Randal' and vowed to ring the papers tomorrow.

20

The beef and the creamy swede purée were so utterly delicious, Janna, Sheena and Mrs Walton all simultaneously vowed to take more trouble.

'Thomas Hood's also brilliant on autumn,' Piers was saying.

'You mustn't monopolize Janna,' Sally called down the table.

'He wasn't, we've had a smashing time comparing notes,' protested Janna, who had deliberately concentrated on Piers because the man on her other side was shy-makingly attractive. Outwardly unruffled as a great lion dozing in the afternoon sun, he had a spellbinding voice: deep, lilting and very Welsh, a square, ruddy face, thick blond curly hair, and lazy navy-blue eyes which turned down at the corners.

'Welcome to Larkshire,' said Emlyn Davies as she turned towards him. 'How are you enjoying being a head?'

'Not as much as I'd hoped,' confessed Janna. 'I keep looking back wistfully to the times when my biggest worry was getting a class through GCSE.'

Encouraged by his genuine interest, she was soon telling him all about Larks.

'I made Paris and Feral mentors,' she said finally. 'I thought giving them some responsibility might make them more responsible. You know Feral?'

'Everyone knows Feral.'

'He and Paris are so gorgeous. All the girls are dying to be mentored by them, but Feral's never in school and Paris has his nose in a book and tells them to eff off.'

'Can you buttle, Emlyn?' asked Sally a shade imperiously, 'No one's got a drink at your end.'

'Feral's a dazzling footballer,' continued Janna when Emlyn returned. 'If this bonding between us and Bagley takes off, would you keep an eye on him?'

'I teach rugby.'

'Feral could adjust, he's so fast and can do anything with a ball. If he felt he was achieving, he might come in more often. If Feral stays away, half the school does too and we'll never rise in the league tables.'

Emlyn put a huge hand over hers. 'League tables are shit, so many heads fiddle them. Schools like St Jimmy's and Searston Abbey don't improve: they just reject low achievers. Why should anyone want difficult children if they push you to the bottom?

'When you think of the disadvantages with which your kids from the Shakespeare Estate start, it's as much a miracle to get five per cent of them through as it is for us and St Jimmy's and Gillian to clock up ninety per cent. League tables are about humiliation, delving into laundry baskets and washing dirty linen in public.'

Janna was delighted by the rage in his voice.

'How does an independent teacher understand these things?'

'I taught in comprehensives for nearly nine years.'

'How could you have switched over?' cried Janna in outrage.

'A number of reasons. I like teaching history and the national curriculum's so prohibitive. Nor do I like being bossed around by the Council of Europe. I also like teaching rugby. Bagley was unbeaten last season. Gives you a buzz. I like the salary I get. I adore Hengist and I'm very idle. Here, I get plenty of time to play golf and fool around—"displacement activity" our deputy head Alex Bruce calls it.' He smiled lazily down at her.

'Most Welshmen are small, dark and handsome,' he added, patting his beer gut. 'I'm fair, fat and funny.'

Not handsome, decided Janna, but decidedly attractive.

She hoped he'd ask her out. As if reading her thoughts, he said, 'You must come out with us one evening. We drink at the Rat and Groom. If you're going to be coming to Bagley a lot, someone ought to give you a minibus.'

'I'm not very good at getting sponsorship,' sighed Janna, remembering Mr Tyler who'd looked like a parsnip. 'I get bogged down by administration.' She took a slug of red. 'I'm even wearing my admini skirt.'

Then she noticed the red and white hairs on the black wool, gave a sob, and told Emlyn all about the poor little dog.

'I'm going to call in on the way home. Oh dear.' As she wiped her eyes, smudging Sally's mascara, her elbow slid off the table.

'I'll drive you, I haven't drunk much,' said Emlyn, adding, with a slight edge to his voice, 'Don't want to screw up in front of the boss and his wife.'

'How *kind* of you,' cried Janna, hoping Emlyn might stop her thinking so much of Hengist.

'Can I come too and see this dog?' asked Dora, who was hovering with second helpings. 'Have

178

some more potatoes, Mr Davies, keep up your strength. We had a Labrador called Visitor,' she told Janna, 'who adored fireworks, saw them as coloured shooting. He used to sit barking at them, encouraging them on.'

'Get on, Dora,' ordered Hengist, 'and you move on too, Emlyn, I want to sit next to Janna.'

All the men moved on two places, which meant Randal ended up on Janna's right and, to his delight, on Mrs Walton's left.

Hengist was shocked how wan Janna looked. He didn't tell her about the uproar there had been from Bagley parents reluctant to have Larks tearaways let loose among their darlings.

'How are your hands?'

'Numbed by booze and painkillers. I'm having a lovely time tonight, sorry I snapped at you earlier.'

'It was fear biting.'

'Everything's been getting on top of me.'

Except a good man, thought Hengist. Then he said, 'There's a dinner at the Winter Gardens—tomorrow week—to plan Larkminster's Jubilee celebrations. All the local bigwigs'll be there. Sally can't make it. Come with me; I've got to speak so I can officially announce the twinning of Larks and Bagley.'

'How lovely. Sure I won't lower the tone?'

'Don't be silly. That's a date then. How did you like Emlyn?'

'Wonderful.'

'He is. We didn't lose a match on the South African tour; the boys had a ball but never overstepped the mark. They call him Attila the Hunk. A lot of people raised eyebrows when I tried to make him a housemaster, but the boys adore

179

him and so do the parents. Sadly he refused—said the rugger teams give him enough hassle. You know he played rugger for Wales?'

'Goodness,' said Janna.

'He used to be very chippy, but with success the chips go.'

'Am I chippy?'

'Very, that's why I want to ensure you're wildly successful.' And he smiled with such affection, Janna had to smile back.

'Oh dear, dear,' Piers muttered to Sheena. 'Little Miss Curtis is going to get hurt.'

'What d'you think of Stancombe?' Hengist had lowered his voice.

'Challenging,' said Janna.

'And deeply silly. Parents have to kill to get into one's school; once in, men like Stancombe compete to build science blocks, sports pavilions.'

'And an indoor riding school,' said Dora, putting out pudding plates.

Hengist laughed and patted her arm. 'Dora keeps me young.'

Stancombe had moved on to art. 'I'm a big art person, Ruth. I frequently make large donations to the Tate; they're talking of naming a staircase after me.'

'I'll slide down your banister any time,' murmured Mrs Walton.

'How about making a generous donation to Larkminster Comp?' asked Emlyn idly. 'And give them a minibus.'

'Oh, hush,' said Janna, blushes surging up her freckles.

'What a good idea.' Mrs Walton smiled. 'Then they could name the bus after you.'

'Even a second-hand one,' suggested Hengist. 'If Larks is bonding with Bagley, they'll need transport.'

'I'll think about it.'

'Oh, go on, Randal,' cooed Mrs Walton.

Stancombe was trapped. A muscle was rippling his bronzed cheek, but he was so anxious to impress her.

'Right, you're on, Jan.'

'Oh, thank you,' gasped Janna. 'Thank you so much.'

'Make a note of it, so you don't forget,' insisted Mrs Walton.

'Larks minibus,' wrote Stancombe on his palmtop, then looked across at Mrs Walton, the hunter setting the deer in his sights. 'You owe me,' he mouthed.

'I hope he won't pull out of this science block,' whispered Hengist. 'Alex Bruce insists it'll look good on the prospectus, but oh dear me, builders in hard hats here for over a year and a sea of mud. I'll probably have to take Stancombe's dunderhead son as a quid pro quo, but I'm not having him on my board. And if he wants to get into Boodle's, he'll have to buy the building.'

'Why are you so ungrateful?' asked a shocked Janna.

'At heart, I don't trust him.'

A vibration in Stancombe's trouser pocket signalled an incoming call. Fascinated by Stancombe's mobile, the very latest model, which could actually take pictures and even flashed up on the screen a little photograph of who was calling, Dora shimmied forward to offer Stancombe more wine. Then she nearly dropped the bottle as a

181

disgusting photo of a naked blonde with her legs apart indicated one of Stancombe's girlfriends was on the line. Stancombe hastily killed the call, and started taking photographs of everyone at the table, which gave him the excuse to immortalize Mrs Walton.

All the same, thought Dora, it was a wonderful invention and would hugely help her journalistic investigations to have a little camera inside her mobile. What a good thing too that revolting Stancombe was off his grub. His untouched beef would make a terrific doggie bag for Cadbury, who didn't like caviar.

'My daughter Jade is in a relationship with Cosmo Rannaldini, Dame Hermione Harefield's son,' Stancombe was proudly telling Mrs Walton. 'Dame Hermione was very gracious when Jade went to visit. As Milly and Jade are good friends,' he continued, 'I hope you'll be able to make a long weekend skiing before Christmas.'

'I'm sure we could fit it in.' Mrs Walton's exquisite complexion flushed up so gently, Stancombe could just imagine her generous, sensual mouth round his cock.

'Come home with me tonight,' he whispered.

'I can't really, Sally's offered me a bed.'

*   *   *

'It's awfully kind of you to offer us a minibus,' Janna told him when he finally tore himself away to talk to her. 'I hope you haven't been compromised.'

'No way, I come from a poor family myself, Jan, seven of us in a tiny flat. Your kids deserve a leg-up.'

'I'm particularly grateful for Feral Jackson's sake . . .' began Janna.

Stancombe choked on his drink. He'd been so knocked sideways by Mrs Walton, he'd been manoeuvred, without realizing it, into benefiting his bête noire Feral Jackson, who rampaged through the Shakespeare Estate and nearby Cavendish Plaza terrifying tenants and, only this evening, chucking around lighted fireworks.

Twigging he wasn't exactly flavour of the month, Janna suggested Feral would behave much better if he had a focus in his life.

'It'd better not be my Jade,' snarled Stancombe.

'Rugger channels boys' aggression in an awfully positive way,' said Sally, scenting trouble.

Fortunately Stancombe was distracted by Dora. He liked her shrill little voice, her gaucheness, untouched by masculine hand, her antagonism, her tiny breasts pushing through her blue dress, her figure which hadn't yet decided what it was going to do with itself. He wondered if she had any pubic hairs yet. He'd met Anthea, her mother, at Speech Day, a tiny, very pretty lady. Dora was larger than her mother already. That sort of thing made a young girl feel lumpy and elephantine. Dora would benefit from a little attention.

Dora was serving white chocolate mousse with raspberry sauce when she noticed Stancombe's hand burrowing under Mrs Walton's green silk skirt and was so shocked she piled an Everest of mousse on to Mrs Walton's plate.

'Heavens, Dora,' cried Mrs Walton, tipping half of it on to Stancombe's plate, 'are you trying to fatten me up?'

Dora watched appalled as Stancombe removed his hand to spoon up his mousse, then shoved it back up Mrs Walton's skirt.

Marching furiously back to the kitchen, Dora made another note on the pad in her coat pocket, before returning with a brimming finger bowl, which she plonked in front of Stancombe. 'Like one of these?' she hissed.

Emlyn glanced over and roared with laughter. Everyone else was distracted by a querulous knock on the door.

One of Hengist's tricks for keeping people on the jump was to exclude from dinner parties those who felt they should have been invited. A case in point was his deputy head: Alex Bruce, a fussy-looking man with spectacles and a thin, dark beard which ran round his chin into his brushed back hair, edging his peevish face like an oval picture frame. He now came bustling in:

'A word please, Senior Team Leader.'

'It can't be that important.' Hengist patted a chair. 'Have a drink and sit down. You know everyone except Janna Curtis, the marvellous new head at Larks. Janna, this is Alex Bruce, the superpower behind the throne.'

Alex nodded coldly at her, and even more coldly at Mrs Walton, whose presence on the board, making things easy for Hengist and Jupiter, he bitterly resented.

This must be Hengist's cross, thought Janna, the man he feared was going to strangle him in red tape. He certainly looked cross now.

'Joan Johnson's just been on the phone,' Alex told Hengist. 'She caught Amber Lloyd-Foxe and Cosmo Rannaldini snorting cocaine. Dame

184

Hermione was incommunicado when I tried to call, but I took the liberty of suspending Amber Lloyd-Foxe. When I phoned her mother, Jane, she complained it was the middle of the night—it's actually only eleven-thirty—and when I appraised her of the situation, she said: "How lovely, Amber can come to the Seychelles with us." I don't believe Jane Lloyd-Foxe was entirely sober; anyway she refused to drive over and collect Amber.'

Typical, uncaring, public-school parent, thought Janna disapprovingly.

'I'm afraid I hit the roof, Senior Team Leader,' went on Alex.

Cosmo Rannaldini up to no good with Amber Lloyd-Foxe? Randal was also looking furious: was his precious Jade being cheated on?

'Shall we go upstairs?' said Sally, glancing round at the women.

Do they still keep up that ritual? thought Janna, outraged to be dragged away, particularly when she heard Alex recommending exclusion, and Hengist replying in horror that Cosmo was an Oxbridge cert.

21

Upstairs, Sally drew Janna aside on to the blue rose-patterned window seat. 'My dear, it's so nice you're here. Jolly tough assignment, Larks, but I'm sure you'll crack it. You will come to me if I can be of any help?'

Advise me how not to fancy your husband, thought Janna.

'I'm so glad you got on with Emlyn,' went on Sally. 'You must go to the cinema with him and some of the other young masters. I'm awfully fond of naughty little Piers. And you must meet our daughter.' Sally pointed to a photograph in a silver frame on the dressing table.

'Oriana Taylor,' gasped Janna. 'My God! But she's an icon. So brave and so brilliant during September the eleventh and the war in Afghanistan. Hengist never said she was her. I didn't realize. I'd die to meet her, and so would our kids.'

'We must arrange something next time she's home. Oriana is rather left-wing,' confessed Sally. 'Bit of a trial for her father. Having profited from a first-rate education, she now thinks we're horribly elitist.' Sally smiled. 'I expect you do too. She gets into dreadful arguments with Hengist.'

'Does she live in New York full time?' asked Janna.

Sally nodded: 'We had a son; he died.' Oh, the sadness of those flat monosyllables. Sally pointed to a photograph of a beautiful blond boy with Hengist's dark eyes. 'So Hengist misses her

186

dreadfully.'

'I'm so terribly sorry,' mumbled Janna.

'I know you are,' said Sally. 'I'm just nipping downstairs to organize drinks and coffee and pay Dora.'

After that, Janna sat on Sally's four-poster and talked to Mrs Walton, who was really a joy to look at and to smell—great wafts of scent rising like incense from her body.

'Emlyn's very attractive, isn't he?'

'Extremely, but sadly spoken for.'

'He is?' asked Janna in disappointment.

'He's going to marry Hengist's daughter Oriana.'

'A shrewd career move—lucky Oriana.'

'Lucky indeed. Emlyn's so bats about her he agreed to wait until she'd tried being a foreign correspondent. Alas, she's been so good at it, she seems to have lost any desire to settle down.'

'Oh, poor Emlyn.'

'Sally isn't that displeased by the turn of events; she doesn't think Emlyn's quite good enough,' confided Mrs Walton as she repainted her lips a luscious coral. 'Despite his amiability, he's very left-wing. Hates the Tories, hates the royal family, and hates rich spoilt children. He didn't get a first either, although he's a wonderful teacher. Hengist dotes on him. They have rugger in common, but Sally feels that macho Welsh rugger bugger tradition isn't for Oriana—she needs someone more subtle and better bred. Sally tries not to show it because she's such a gent,' went on Mrs Walton, 'but she also feels Oriana isn't bats enough about Emlyn. I mean, if you had a hunk like that, would you base yourself in New York pursuing all those terrifying assignments?'

187

Sally wants me to go to the cinema with Emlyn because she knows I fancy Hengist rotten, decided Janna, and if I get off with Emlyn it will free Oriana and get me out of Hengist's hair.

Suddenly, she felt very tired. 'I must go.'

'Let's have lunch,' said Mrs Walton.

'I can't really get away.'

'Well, come to supper then.'

'I'd like that.'

'I'll ring you at Larks.'

At that moment Mrs Walton's mobile rang. It was Stancombe from downstairs.

'I'll call you,' she mouthed at Janna.

How can I ever have enough of love and life, thought Janna as she put on her dreary green cardigan.

Downstairs, she found Jupiter talking to Hengist, who had lucky Elaine stretched out on the sofa beside him with her head in his lap.

Sheena, having dispatched Rufus home to relieve the babysitter, was arguing with Piers and waiting to get a lift from Stancombe who was still on his mobile.

Then Janna started to laugh.

'All part of our caring ethos,' Gillian Grimston was droning on to Emlyn, who had fallen asleep in an armchair.

'Caring Ethos,' mused Hengist. 'Sounds like a fifth Musketeer, the priggish older brother of Athos or Porthos. Caring Ethos.' He smiled at Janna, gently setting aside Elaine's head so he could get up. 'Have a drink.'

'I'm off,' she said, 'I'll drive very slowly.'

'You will not, you've had a horrid shock. Emlyn is going to take you,' said Sally firmly.

As they left, Hengist imitated the Family Tree, standing big, strong and dark behind Sally's fairness, his arms wrapped around her: we are an item.

'Will you be home tomorrow afternoon?' he asked Janna. 'I'll drive your car back, and we can discuss where we go from here—put Saturday night in your diary.'

Everything out in the open, so unlike Stew, thought an utterly confused Janna.

'I'd like a word, Sheena,' said Sally as she closed the front door.

*   *   *

Trees brandished their remaining leaves in the wind like tattered orange and yellow banners. Janna tried to quiz Emlyn about Hengist and Sally but, guilty he'd spent half-term and so much money in New York with Oriana rather than with his mother and sick father in Wales, he was uncommunicative.

He didn't say much but he was sweet to make a long detour into Larkminster via the Animal Hospital. The little dog hadn't come round from the anaesthetic, said the nurse, but should pull through. They had saved the eye but probably not the tail. He'd need to spend a few days in hospital.

'And then I'll come and collect him,' said Janna.

I'm going to call him Partner, she decided, then if anyone asks me if I've got a partner, I can say yes.

Most of the Sundays carried lurid accounts of Amber Lloyd-Foxe and Cosmo Rannaldini being suspended for drugs, and everyone blamed the leak on Sheena Anderson.

22

Janna knew that if confronted Monster and Satan would deny torturing Partner. Instead she decided to unnerve them by relating the incident in detail at assembly the following Monday.

'Animals feel pain just as we do. They're more frightened because they have no idea why such evil things are happening.' Her voice broke: 'Partner was such a trusting little dog.'

'Bastards,' spat Pearl.

'Murderers,' sobbed Kylie Rose.

'The bad news is that it was so dark I'm not sure which Larks pupils were involved but the good news is I rang the hospital this morning and despite his horrific burns Partner's getting better all the time. He may still lose his tail but when he comes out of hospital he's moving in with me.'

Cheers from the children.

'I'm going to bring him into school because I know you'll love him and I'm sure he'll recognize the evil bullies who tortured him and we can report them to the police and RSPCA.'

Five minutes after assembly, Rowan gleefully reported that Satan and Monster had been seen belting down Smokers' and over the wall.

'One pair I don't mind truanting,' said Janna.

Feral, on the other hand, was another matter. Each day he missed he slipped further behind. There was no point setting up minibuses, pitches and running tracks if he wasn't there to profit from them.

Paris and Graffi went vague when questioned so

Janna dropped a line to Feral's mother asking if she might pop in to discuss her son on the way to Hengist's civic dinner. At least it would give her a chance to check out the dreaded Shakespeare Estate.

Outside she could see shrivelled pale brown leaves tumbling out of the playground sycamores and imagined them falling from Hengist's Family Tree revealing the interlocked incestuous grapplings to the white sky.

She tried not to get excited about Saturday's dinner, for hope would be hope of the wrong thing. At least it would be a change from paperwork and she could finally give her slinky new off-the-shoulder dress an airing. The night before she rubbed lots of scented body lotion into the shoulder that was going to be exposed before falling into a rare and blissful eight-hour sleep.

Waking with optimism, she popped into the hospital to take Partner a bowl of chopped chicken. Still heavily sedated, he greeted her with barks of joy and shrieks of pain as he wagged his poor burnt tail. He really was a sweet little dog, with one ear pointing skywards, a freckled fox's face, a pink nose, sad chestnut-brown eyes, short legs and a rough red and white coat.

'We'll be two short-arsed, mouthy redheads living together,' she told him, 'and exploring the country instead of working all weekend.'

Having measured his neck size and promised she'd fetch him home tomorrow, she spent a fortune in Larkminster's pet shop on a sky-blue collar and lead, a name disk, dog food, pig's ears, a blue ball and a blue quilted basket decorated with moons and suns.

191

Out in the street, rustling through shoals of red and gold cherry leaves, her happiness evaporated as she caught sight of a *Gazette* poster: 'Is Janna Curtis turning her back on failing Larks?'

Buying a paper, she found a smiling photograph of herself, Hengist and Jupiter at the prospective-parents' day on page three. Accompanying it was a snide story saying she was being wooed by the independent sector and had recently dined with the Brett-Taylors, Jupiter Belvedon, his wife and property tycoon Randal Stancombe. How much longer would she bother with a bog-standard school she had failed to improve?

With a scream of rage, Janna scrunched up the paper, sending three pigeons fluttering up into the rooftops. Why in hell hadn't the piece mentioned Gillian Grimston had been at dinner too?

*   *   *

Larks was always left open on Saturdays for the rare members of staff who might want to catch up or prepare lessons. Fortunately no one seemed to be around when Janna arrived so she would have time to prepare a denial. But as she walked down the corridors, rejoicing in the colour and vitality of the children's work on the walls—Larks was *not* failing—she heard crashes and screams coming from her office and broke into a run.

She was greeted by devastation as a hysterical Pearl, who'd already pulled the books out of the shelves and thrown every file on the carpet with Janna's in-tray scattered on top, was now upending desk drawers.

Her spiky rhubarb-red hair was coaxed upwards

192

like an angry rooster, her coloured make-up was streaked by tears and studs quivered like the Pleiades on her frantically working face.

'Bitch, cunt, slag!' she howled, catching sight of Janna. 'I know you've got the 'ots for Feral, you 'orrible slag, wiv your cosy little tea parties.'

She ripped Janna's date calendar off the wall: pointing a frantically trembling finger at 3 November: ' "Feral's mother seven p.m." You never bothered visiting my mum.' She started tearing the calendar to pieces.

'Stop it.' Janna tried to stay calm. 'Steady down. Whatever's brought this on?'

But a screaming Pearl had started on the pictures. Crash went *Hold the Dream* and *Desiderata* over the back of a chair, followed by the big photographs of Fountains Abbey and the Brontës' house at Haworth.

'For God's sake, you'll get glass in your eyes,' pleaded Janna, wondering the best way to grab her.

Crash, sending out another fountain of splintered glass, went Stew's photograph of all the children at Redfords.

Pearl then hurled Janna's Diorissimo against the window smashing both with a sickening crunch, followed by a bottle of ink against the white wall which spilt down over the flower-patterned sofa. Then she picked up Stew's little Staffordshire cow.

'Oh please, no,' gasped Janna.

'You sad bitch!'

Crash went the cow, hitting the fridge and fragmenting into a hundred pieces. Pearl, like a cornered cat now, rather than a furious rooster, was clawing, screaming, spitting. Slowly, slowly

Janna talked her down.

'Please tell me what's the matter. I'm not cross, I'm here for you,' until Pearl collapsed sobbing on the ink-stained sofa.

'Thought you liked us, miss, but the paper says you're leaving us for those stuck-up snobs.'

A tidal wave of relief swept over Janna.

'Then they'll have to carry me out in a coffin. I love you at Larks. You're my children and I'm going to take a big photograph of you all and put that on the wall.'

Sally and Hengist, she explained, had kindly invited her to dinner to meet other teachers and people who might help Larks.

'So we can buy more textbooks and go on more jaunts and invest in some fun, young, new teachers. I'd rather live in a cage full of cobras than teach in an independent school.'

'What about the cow?' sniffed Pearl, picking up a fragment of horn from the carpet. 'Was that precious?'

'Not any more,' said Janna, realizing it was part of a past that had gone away. 'And the only reason I haven't asked you over to the cottage is because of your Saturday job, and I'm not sure how you'd cope with the walk in those heels. The boys are coming tomorrow afternoon instead to meet my new dog. Please come too, and be very gentle with him, boys can be a bit rough. Look at what I bought him at the pet shop.' She opened the carrier bags she'd left in the corridor. 'And let's have a coffee and a chocolate biscuit.'

Later, as, chattering, they made an effort to straighten the room, Pearl noticed the invitation to the civic dinner which Hengist had posted to

Janna.

'That's tonight. "Jubilee Dinner". Looks a posh do. I hope we can have a street party. My mum's always going on about how great they was in seventy-seven. Look, to make up for this'—Pearl waved a blue-nailed hand round the devastation— 'I'll make you up for tonight, do your hair, give you a make-over, like. It'd be really cool. Then I could photograph you, put it on the wall like Graffi's pictures and Paris's stories and fucking goody-two-shoes Aysha's chemistry project.' Pearl was suddenly wildly excited. 'I'll find you a dress too.'

'That would be champion,' said Janna. Anything not to shatter this rapprochement. 'Let's meet at five-thirty.'

'Make it earlier,' said Pearl, suddenly authoritive. 'I did the morning stint at the salon. That's where I read the *Gazette*. I need time to do it proper. You go home and have a nice bath. I'll meet you back here at four.'

When Janna dutifully returned, Pearl refused to work her magic in front of a mirror.

'It stresses me to be watched.'

So Janna tugged her desk chair into the middle of the office and got stuck into planning the next human resources meeting, which would cover staffing.

She was sure Ashton Douglas and Crispin would demand redundancies or her budget would never balance. But with any luck the dinosaurs like Mike Pitts, Basket, Skunk, even Cara Sharpe might consider early retirement.

'She's an evil bitch, that Cara.' Pearl peered over Janna's shoulder as she cut her hair.

'If I'm not allowed to look, neither are you,'

195

reproved Janna, 'and not too much off.'

'My mum always says that. I'm going to lift the colour with a few highlights.'

'Not too tarty,' pleaded Janna, 'I'm trying to be an authority figure,' then cautiously enquired about the Shakespeare Estate.

Pearl shrugged. 'Council uses the place as a bin bag to dump all the bad families. Most of the dads are in the nick like mine or on nights and never see their kids.'

Finally, having washed Janna's hair in the Ladies, blow-dried it and made her up from a range of colour that would have been the envy of Titian, Pearl sprayed gold dust on her shoulders. Then, dismissing the black off-the-shoulder number Janna had brought in as too mumsy, she helped Janna into an incredibly short fern-green handkerchief dress which gave her a cleavage worthy of Mrs Walton.

'You look wicked, miss.' Pearl held up Janna's hand mirror, about the only thing unsmashed. 'Now you can look.'

Janna didn't recognize herself. Even under the office strip lighting she looked absolutely gorgeous.

'That can't be me. I look like a film star.'

'Good material to work on,' conceded Pearl.

She had covered Janna's face in light-reflecting moisturizer, then put shimmering highlights on her cheekbones, and narrowed and rounded Janna's squarish chin with blusher, before blending in sparkling powder.

To make the eyes huge and vulnerable she had drawn black along the upper lash line, mingled all the golds, oranges and russets on the lids, then

196

thickened the lashes with three layers of brown mascara.

Most seductive of all, on Janna's big mouth, instead of pale pinky coral, she had used a deep plum red gloss.

'Weee-ee.' Janna shook her head, swinging rippling cascades of rose red, emerald green and chestnut hair. 'Which flag of the world am I? You're a genius.'

'You look amazing, miss,' said Pearl happily. 'Go out and pull.'

'Where did you find all this incredible make-up?' asked Janna, suspecting it had been knocked off.

'They often pay me in make-up at the salon,' said Pearl airily.

Janna was far too kind to put Pearl down by saying the whole thing was completely OTT and was vastly relieved when Pearl wrapped a long, tasselled flamingo-pink shawl round her shoulders.

'This is lovely and the dress too.'

'My mum's,' said Pearl hastily.

'Won't she mind?'

'Doesn't know—it's my babysitting fee.'

*   *   *

It was only when she was driving to the Winter Gardens, praying none of the big shop owners would recognize their stolen wares on her that Janna remembered she'd promised to pop in on Feral's mother at 12 Macbeth Street. She'd been crazy to pick this weekend. It was like entering a war zone, as coloured stars exploded in dandelion clocks and rockets hissed into the russet Larkminster sky, crashing and banging to a counterpoint of jangling fire engines and screaming police sirens.

How could the people of Afghanistan cope with incessant American bombing—or was she twice as scared because she'd had a baptism of fireworks with Partner a week ago?

The Shakespeare Estate was a concrete hell, hemmed in by a high circular wall, which separated it from the beautiful, prosperous golden town, the serenely winding river and the lush countryside beyond. Cul-de-sacs named after Shakespearean characters ran like spokes in a wheel from this circular wall into a bald piece of land, known as the Romeo Triangle, which had a much graffitied pub, broken seats and a boarded-up newsagent's. Gangs of youths in hoods with sliding walks prowled the streets chucking stones or bangers at Janna's green Polo as she drove past. Rasta and R and B music fortissimo, blaring televisions, couples having violent domestics were interrupted by the screams of prostitutes. Fireworks lit up the crazed emaciated faces of Ixions chained to the wheels of their addictions.

'Never get out of your car and walk,' Pearl had warned.

But there was no space outside number 12, so Janna was forced to park fifty yards away and totter up Macbeth Street on her high heels. All the windows of number 12 were broken or boarded-up. The front garden contained stinking, unemptied dustbins, an old fridge and a burnt-out BMW. No one answered the door, the paint of which was blistered and dented with kicks. Youths, gathering on the pavement, were hurling fireworks into next door's garden. A curtain flickered and Janna

198

caught a glimpse of a terrified old man.

Although number 12 was in darkness, she could hear a ghetto blaster. Perhaps Feral was hiding upstairs. Ducking in terror as a rocket hissed past her head, she ran back down the garden path slap into a very large black man. He had a shaved head and was wearing black leather, a large diamond necklace, ear studs and lots of aftershave, which mercifully blotted out the stench of dustbins.

'What yer doing?' a bass voice with a soft Jamaican accent rumbled menacingly up from his chest.

'Looking for Feral Jackson.'

The big guy gave Janna, as made over by Pearl, the once-over and made an understandable mistake. 'Bit long in the tooth for him.'

'I actually have an appointment with his mother.'

'Pull the other leg—and get off my territory if you don't want your pretty face rearranged.'

Janna winced as he yanked her head upwards and flicked on his lighter. 'On second thoughts I'll forget it if you show me a good time.'

'I beg your pardon?'

'I won't cut you up'—he threatened her eyelashes with his lighter—'if you give me a fuck.'

Whereupon Janna rose in outrage to her five feet one inch plus four-inch heels. 'How *dare* you. I am Feral's head teacher.'

The big guy looked initially flabbergasted then became very, very cosy and introduced himself as Feral's Uncle Harley.

'And you don't look like an 'ead teacher, little darling.'

'Feral hasn't been in school for three weeks.' Janna tried to steady her trembling legs. 'I'd like to see Mrs Jackson.'

'She's not in; family's gone to the pitchers to see *Shrek*.'

'I just want someone to get him up in the morning and see he does his homework.'

'Look no further,' murmured Uncle Harley.

As he walked her back to her car, approaching gangs of youths retreated like smoke. A prostitute stopped screaming at Janna and slid away like a snake.

'Feral's such a wonderful athlete,' urged Janna. 'A group of Larks children have been invited over to Bagley Hall so he'll get an opportunity to play football on decent pitches and try out their running tracks.'

'He's a lucky young man.' Uncle Harley grew even cosier. 'You got time for a drink?'

'I should be at the Winter Gardens already.'

'Sorry I mistook you.' Uncle Harley took her keys to open the car door, then, adding with massive irony, 'Not safe round here for a nice young lady,' he kissed her hand.

'I hope to see you at one of our parents' evenings.'

'Try and keep me away.'

23

Still shaking with hysterical laughter, Janna reached the Winter Gardens. The dinner was held in a side hall, whose high ceiling was covered with nudging, pinching cherubs reminiscent of the playground at Larks. In one half of the room, tables were laid for dinner and speeches. In the other, because a Lib Dem/Lab hung council had no intention of squandering ratepayers' money, indifferent red or white was being offered to a crowd of bigwigs.

Hengist had not yet arrived, but Pearl's make-over was soon having a dramatic effect. The Mayor, wearing a chain Uncle Harley would have killed for, blamed the Winter Gardens' poor acoustics for the fact he had to bend right over Janna's boobs to hear what she said.

Next minute, parsnip-faced Mr Tyler rushed up with two friends and was just apologizing for his rudeness the week before last when Stancombe appeared by her side, looking sleek and glamorous in a dinner jacket and far more relaxed than he'd been at Sally and Hengist's. 'I can't handle teachers, Jan; so patronizing, do my head in. Don't count you as one; not tonight, particularly. You look very tasty.'

He got out his mobile, took a picture of her and texted it to one of his friends, showing her the message: 'How lucky am I to be invited to functions with ladies like this?' Then, to show off further to Tyler and the Mayor: 'The minibus will be with you by a.m. Wednesday, what colour d'you fancy?'

'The coolest colour, please.' Janna accepted a top-up of white. 'You are kind, it will give our children such street cred.'

'I'm donating a minibus to Larks,' boasted Stancombe to the others, 'so Jan can transport her kids to matches and things.'

'I'll send in the boys to sort out your computers,' countered Tyler.

'I'll pick up the bill for any sports kit,' said one of his friends.

'That would be fantastic,' beamed Janna.

Thank you, Pearl, she thought, sidling away as the Mayor pinched her bottom. She'd never had such an effect on men. Tyler and his mates were clearly irked by the way Stancombe muscled in, but they all deferred to him.

Then Hengist swanned in, instantly stealing Stancombe's thunder: 'Darling, sorry I'm late. Christ, you look amazing.' He kissed her on both shimmering cheeks. 'What have you done?'

'Pearl gave me a make-over.'

'We'll make her head of make-up when we do our joint Larks–Bagley play.' He took a gulp of red and nearly spat it out.

'Christ, that's disgusting.' He waved to a waiter who scuttled over. 'Can you get me a bottle of Sancerre and a large whisky and soda, no ice, and take this arsenic away.' He handed the boy his and Janna's glasses.

'It can't be that bad, Hengist,' grumbled the Mayor.

'It's much worse,' said Hengist, putting an arm round Janna's shoulders. 'Jesus,' he added as the flamingo-pink shawl fell away.

'I'm having a Mrs Walton moment,' giggled Janna.

Hengist couldn't stop laughing.

'I can't work out if you look ten years older or younger than the little teenager you normally resemble. Come and meet everyone important. Oh dear, here come Super Bugger and Sancho Pansy from S and C,' as Ashton and Crispin paused to have their picture taken by the *Gazette*.

Crispin had put on more weight and with his petulant baby face he looked like the bullying older brother of the cherubs rampaging over the ceiling. Ashton's bland pink and white face had been given more definition by a dinner jacket and a black tie but his thinly lashed eyes were as cold green as a frozen fjord. Waiting until Hengist had been distracted by some Tory councillor, he and Crispin cornered Janna.

'You look very Chwistmassy.' Ashton examined her hair. 'Does it wash out?'

'Yes, but I don't.'

'The *Gazette* says you're joining Bagley,' snuffled Crispin.

'When did that rag ever tell the truth? Gillian Grimston was at the same dinner party. Sally invited me to meet some locals, which is more than Mike Pitts, Rod or either of you have ever done.'

'And how's the Bagley bonding going?' asked Ashton.

'Starts next week.'

'Doesn't it threaten your left-wing pwinciples to accept largesse from an independent?'

'Beggars can't be choosers. My children have been let down too often.' Janna's voice rose: 'And it's not as if you're giving us any money.'

203

Ashton put his head on one side. 'You should weally take a course in anger management.'

'Doesn't she look gorgeous?' It was Hengist back, waving a bottle of Sancerre, topping up Janna's glass. 'Pearl Smith did her hair and make-up. I think we've got another Barbara Daly on our hands. You should let her have a go at you, Ashton, next time you've got an important date,' he added insolently.

'I'm from the *Western Daily Press*, Miss Curtis,' announced a hovering photographer. 'Can I get a picture of your new look? I'll take care of your shawl,' he added whisking it away and arranging her next to a marble vestal virgin with downcast eyes.

'Sacred and profane love,' murmured Hengist. 'I know which I prefer.'

'Can we have you in the photograph too, Mr B-T?' said a second photographer. 'I'm from *Cotswold Life*.'

Ashton and Crispin were hopping. So was Rod Hyde. How dare Janna look so desirable! She deserved a good spanking. Rod had rolled up with Alex Bruce and, like Alex, had rejected the right-wing regalia of a dinner jacket. Gillian Grimston immediately sat down beside them.

'As the leading professional at the Brett-Taylors' dinner party,' she said indignantly, 'why didn't the *Gazette* mention I was there?'

Why wasn't I asked in the first place? thought Alex and Rod darkly and simultaneously.

'Who's that toad-like man with bulging eyes who's just waddled in?' Janna whispered to Hengist.

'Colin "Col" Peters. Editor of the *Gazette*, failed

Fleet Street, now enjoying being a big toad in a small pool.'

Janna downed her third glass of wine. 'I'm going to kill him.'

'Not tonight you're not,' said Hengist firmly.

'And the smiley-faced woman in the red trouser suit talking to him looks familiar.'

'That's Cindy Payne, the Labour county councillor in charge of education, hand in glove with Ashton Douglas. Looks like a cosy agony aunt, but she's a snake in sheep's clothing.'

'Snakes eat toads. Col Peters better watch out.'

*   *   *

At dinner Janna found herself sitting next to a CID Chief Inspector with a square, reddish face softened by beautiful long-lashed green eyes, and was enchanted when he turned out to be the husband of her languages teacher, Mags Gablecross.

'Such a lovely woman. If only she worked full time.'

'She says you're working wonders and the kids adore you.'

'I wish the teachers felt the same. They're so terrified of Cara Sharpe.'

'Get her out,' advised Chief Inspector Gablecross. 'She's bad news.'

After a good bitch about Cara, Janna told the Chief Inspector about her encounter with Uncle Harley, which really shocked him.

'Don't ever go near the Shakespeare Estate alone again. Harley's really dangerous and hell-bent on taking the drug trade to new markets all over the

West Country.'

Janna drew in her breath. 'Oh dear.'

Across the room she saw Stancombe getting up, making apologies to his table and waving to Janna on the way out.

'See you Wednesday morning, Jan. Give the garage a spring clean.'

'Stancombe's got his eyes on the Shakespeare Estate,' observed the Chief Inspector. 'Always the same procedure. He vows he's going to build cheap houses for first-time buyers—teachers and nurses—then he razes the place to the ground and, like mushrooms, desirable residences spring up.'

He looked down in disgust at his first course of roast vegetables. 'You used to be able to turn down these things with your main course. Now they're everywhere.' He patted his gut.

Janna, who hadn't eaten all day, was tucking in.

'I was worried Stancombe might be after Larks—all those acres of lovely land,' she admitted, 'but I misjudged him, he's just given us a minibus.'

'*Timeo Danaos*,' warned the Chief Inspector.

'Will you come and talk to my kids?' asked Janna.

On Janna's left was a trendy estate agent called Desmond Reynolds, nicknamed 'Des Res', because he found so many middle-class parents desirable residences in the catchment areas of St Jimmy's and Searston Abbey.

He had little chin, talked through clenched teeth and, having discovered she came from West Yorkshire and didn't know the Lane-Foxes or the Horton-Fawkeses, lost interest.

'Five per cent of the properties I sell each year are driven by parents' desire for a better school. Stands to reason,' he went on languidly. 'Pay three hundred thousand for a house in the catchment area of St Jimmy's. In seven years you've not only saved at least a hundred and forty K per child you would have spent on Bagley school fees, but also your house will have trebled in value because you're in the catchment area of such a cracking good school.'

'Why's St Jimmy's so good?' Sulkily, Janna speared a roast potato.

'Because Rod Hyde's a cracking good head.'

'Do your children go there?'

'No, Eton.'

'I suppose people never want to buy houses in the catchment area of Larks?' asked Janna wistfully.

'Never,' said Des Res with a shudder. 'Beats me why Hengist's pairing up with them.'

Glancing round, Hengist caught the desolation on Janna's face and immediately swapped places with Des Res.

Janna took a huge gulp of wine and then a deep breath.

'Stancombe's promised the minibus for Wednesday morning.'

'Come over on Wednesday afternoon then.'

'How do I know your little toffs won't take the piss out of my kids?'

'Send the best-looking. The Wolf Pack are such celebs they'll get badgered for autographs.'

Hengist's flippancy enraged Janna but when she told him about her visit to the Shakespeare Estate he went white.

'Promise, promise never to go there again. Planes may not disappear from the Romeo Triangle but people do.'

'Uncle Harley promised to get Feral back into school.'

'Probably wants him to flog drugs to our "little toffs" when he visits Bagley.'

'Oh God, I hope not.' Then, stammering and angry: 'Desmond Reynolds said he couldn't think why you were wasting your time on Larks.'

'Ah.' Hengist forked up one of her potatoes, 'Because I believe in improving the state system. When I'm old, I want well-educated, positive, happy young adults running this country.' He smiled. 'Or it could be that I fancy you rotten.'

Janna's blush came through Pearl's war paint.

'Stop taking the piss.'

'And because you remind me of Oriana.'

'She's wonderful.'

'And terribly tricky. If only she'd take a nice job with the BBC in Bristol instead of being addicted to trouble spots.'

'I'm amazed she can tear herself away from the Shakespeare Estate.'

Hengist laughed. Then, as waitresses stormed on with strawberry pavlova: 'I'd better get back to my seat.'

*   *   *

Against the colourful banners of the Boys' Brigade, the Rotary Club, the Parish Council and the Honorary Corps of Elephants and Buffaloes, the chairman of the county council made a colourless speech laboriously outlining Larkminster's plans for the Jubilee.

He wasn't anticipating a visit from Her Majesty but there were plans for a Jubilee mug and the

208

shops would be decorating their windows. No street parties were planned.

'My children would love a street party,' shouted a now drunk Janna and was shushed.

Noticing Ashton shaking his head and exchanging a pained, what-did-you-expect glance with Crispin and Rod, Hengist thought angrily: They're willing the poor child to screw up. More resolute than ever he rose to his feet.

Miss Painswick had typed out his speech in big print, so he didn't have to wear spectacles; a lock of black hair had fallen over his forehead. As he thanked the waitresses and waiters for all their hard work, they crept back into the dining room to hear him.

'The Queen has been on the throne for nigh on fifty years,' he said warmly, 'never put a foot wrong, and deserves to be celebrated. And, like myself,' he went on slightly mockingly, 'she believes there is no privilege without responsibility.

'We in the independent sector have always recognized there is no justification for our work if pupils grow up to use the benefits of their education only for their own advancement and profit. We at Bagley Hall have a tradition for community work: we go into hospitals, we give concerts in the cathedral, members of the public and other schools use our golf course and our park for cross-country running. We are also clearing ponds around Larkminster and carrying out conservation in the Malvern Hills.'

Then he launched into an attack.

'I appreciate many county councils and education authorities are actively opposed to private education. Larkshire's LEA, in the past, was too busy to answer our letters and ignored our offers of help. S and C Services have shown themselves equally pigheaded. So we approached Janna Curtis direct and to our relief found she puts her children at Larks before her prejudice.

'Larks has been described as a "head's graveyard",' went on Hengist idly. 'One might almost believe S and C and Councillor Cindy Payne are frightened of Janna breaking the mould.'

'Prepostewous. Nothing could be further from the truth,' spluttered Ashton.

'Good,' said Hengist smoothly. 'Just to let you know that Larks will be paying their first visit to Bagley on Wednesday.'

'Oh, goodness.' Janna clapped her hands in delight.

Col Peters was writing furiously.

'This has nothing to do with Janna Curtis or helping her students,' hissed Councillor Cindy Payne to Ashton, 'it's Hengist establishing himself as a dove. If Jupiter takes over the Tories, he'll find Hengist a quick seat and give him Education and God help us all.'

Glancing over to the enemy table, Janna noticed Alex Bruce quite unable to hide his jealousy. Hunched like an old monkey throughout Hengist's speech, he had mindlessly wolfed his way through an entire plateful of petits fours. A denied Crispin was almost in tears.

No sooner had Hengist finished, to mixed applause, than the press gathered round him, except for Col Peters, editor of the *Gazette*, who pulled up a chair beside Janna, plonking a bottle of red on the table. Close up he really did look like a toad, his eyes glaucous, fixed and bulging.

'What did you think of that, Miss Curtis?'

'Fantastic.' Janna raised her glass. 'Hengist has been marvellous to us, which is more than you have. Why are you always slagging off Larks? Don't you realize my kids read your rotten paper and are utterly demoralized by your lies?'

A good row was boiling up when Janna was distracted by the peroxide-blonde wife of the chairman of the Rotary Club, who'd drunk even more than she had, and who, passing Councillor Cindy Payne in the gap between the tables, called out: 'Thank God we got Lottie, our grandchild, into Searston Abbey, Cindy, or we'd have had to go private or out of county rather than end up at that dreadful Larks.'

'They'll probably bid for specialist status now they've got Hengist B-T on board,' joked Cindy, who must have been aware of Janna's proximity.

'Crime's Larks's only speciality,' sneered the Rotary chairman's wife. 'They hold their old school reunions in the nick.'

'How dare you slag off my school!' Janna jumped to her feet. 'And you, Councillor Payne, haven't even had the courtesy to visit Larks.'

Seizing Col Peters's bottle, she was tempted to give Councillor Payne's mousy hair a red rinse, when Hengist grabbed her wrist, increasing pressure so violently she gasped and dropped the bottle, spilling red wine all over Pearl's mother's lovely dress.

'Now look what you've made me do.' She turned, spitting, on him. 'Get off me, you great brute.'

Loosening his grip only a fraction, Hengist dragged her out into the corridor and let her have

211

it:

'When are you going to learn to behave?' he yelled. 'Have you got some sort of death wish? Do you want to wreck everything we're doing to save your school?'

Bursting into tears, Janna fled into the night.

24

Janna woke to find herself on the settee, her breath rising whitely as a reproving sun peered in through the window to dissect her hangover without the aid of anaesthetic. Pearl's mother's green handkerchief dress was her only protection against the bitter cold.

Whimpering and wailing, she pieced together last night's broken dreams. How could she have nearly tipped wine over Cindy Payne, sworn at Col Peters and Hengist, who'd made such a lovely speech about her, then driven home plastered?

As a contrast to such anarchic behaviour, she caught sight of the green and gold serenity of Graffi's mural of Larkshire. He had worked so hard. But now she had stormed out on Hengist, Graffi and his pals would no longer get the chance to run joyously on Bagley's green and pleasant pitches or blossom in art studio, library or concert hall. She had blown it for them and she'd never see Hengist again.

Staggering to her feet, she noticed Pearl's make-up all over the recently upholstered coral settee. Why did she ruin everything? Tottering into the kitchen, wondering if she could keep down a cup of tea, she fell over a padded blue basket and gave a moan of horror as she took in the tins of Pedigree Chum on the window ledge and the blue collar and lead with the newly engraved disk: 'Partner Curtis'. In the fridge was a Tesco's cooked chicken to tempt his appetite.

Glancing at the clock she realized she was due to collect him in three-quarters of an hour. Rescued dogs, particularly ones as traumatized as Partner, needed calm, relaxed owners and she hadn't had the decency to stay sober the night before his arrival. Bloody Larkshire Ladette. And what the hell had she done with Pearl's mother's shawl?

*   *   *

Partner's delighted wagging when he saw Janna was still punctuated by whimpers. His tail, which they'd managed to save and had wrapped in a net gauze dressing, was still very raw and sore.

'Bathe it constantly with cold water,' said the nurse, 'and he'll need antibiotics and painkillers for another fortnight. We ought to keep him in longer, but he's pining in here. He'll do better in a home environment.'

As Janna sank to the floor holding out her arms, Partner crept into them, licking away her tears as they poured from her reddened eyes. 'He needs me as much as I need him,' she whispered.

'Be happy for him,' said the nurse, handing her a box of medicine. 'He's such a brave little dog; we'll all miss him.'

Reluctant to leave at first, Partner perked up in the car, resting his roan nose on Janna's shoulder all the way home. He peed in excitement over the stone kitchen floor before wolfing a huge chicken lunch.

Janna's hangover was hovering like an albatross. She must plan tomorrow's staff meeting. Still cold, she lit a fire. Determined to start as she meant to go on with Partner, she brought his basket into the lounge. Ignoring it, he jumped on to the sofa beside her.

214

'Not on my new settee,' she said firmly, then caught sight of the streaked make-up and relented.

'Agenda for staff meeting', she read. On top was a note that Mrs Chalford, head of history, who'd been off all term with stress, would be back in school on Monday. Evidently she was a dragon and a bossy boots. The file dropped from Janna's hand.

* * *

She was woken by furious barking. Partner, although he was taking refuge under the sofa, was defending his new home against an enchanted Lily.

'What a charming dog. Part corgi, part Norwich terrier, I would say.' Then as Partner, cheered to be attributed with such smart origins, crawled out to lick her hand: 'Oh, your poor little tail. How are you feeling?' she asked Janna.

'Terrible.'

'I've brought you a hair of the dog.' Lily brandished a bottle of last year's sloe gin.

Janna shuddered. 'I'd never keep it down.'

'It's to celebrate Partner's arrival. What are you going to do with him during the day?'

'Take him and his basket to Larks.'

'It's too soon. I'll look after him here until his tail mends.'

'Oh Lily, you're an angel. Are you sure?'

'I expect he'll tree the General to start with, but the old boy needs a bit of exercise.'

'OK, I will have a glass,' said Janna.

As they toasted Partner, Lily said, 'You look terribly tired. What happened last night?'

Janna was about to tell all, when to her horror Partner went into another frenzy of barking and up

215

rolled Graffi, Feral, Paris and this time Pearl. Janna had completely forgotten they were coming.

*   *   *

From Paris's point of view, the afternoons spent at Jubilee Cottage had been the happiest of his life. Afterwards, the memories of gentle football, picking apples and sweeping leaves and twigs for bonfires would be suffused by a golden glow. Best of all had been his hours by the fire with Janna toasting marshmallows and crumpets, the long, leisurely conversations about books, the quiet after the needy, anguished clamour of the children's home. Often, when younger, he had pretended to be his mother and read out loud to himself. Sitting on the floor, not quite letting his head fall on to Janna's little jeaned knees, he had listened to her reading from the *Aeneid*, Aesop's *Fables*, *Paradise Lost*—'With thee conversing I forget all time'— with no other sound except the swish of Graffi's brushes and the crackle of Lily's apple logs.

Paris had never loved anyone as he loved Janna, but never by the flicker of a pale eyelash would he betray his feelings or embarrass her. He never had any difficulty attracting girls—they lit up like road signs in his headlights as he approached—but it was only an illusion that faded once he'd passed. For, however much they ran after him, inside him was desolation. He must be worthless and unlovable if his mother hadn't wanted to keep him.

Paris didn't have to be back at Oaktree Court until eight o'clock—nine, when he reached fourteen in January—so as the evenings closed in, he would wander the streets of Larkminster:

wistful, lonely, pale as the moon, gazing into rooms lit up orange like Halloween pumpkins, bright with books, pictures, leaping fires and mothers, arms round their children's shoulders, as they helped them with their homework.

Bleakly aware that he was incapable of expressing the love that would make him lovable, that he had nothing to offer emotionally, longing for a family would overwhelm him and he would howl at the night sky, reaching for the stars beyond the branches.

What terrified Paris was once Graffi's mural was finished, there would be no excuse for them to roll up at Janna's every weekend, so he kept dreaming up extras for Graffi to include: 'Put Rod Hyde in the stocks.'

As the Wolf Pack rolled up that Sunday, blown in like dry, curling leaves, Paris tried not to feel resentful at having to share Janna with Graffi, Feral and a chattering, first-among-equals Pearl as well as Lily, who was puffing away on the sofa, already stuck into the booze with a fox on her knee, who promptly shot terrified under the sofa.

'Meet Janna's new dog,' said Lily.

'Is it all right if we come today?' asked Graffi.

'Sure,' said Janna weakly.

In agony, Paris noticed her swollen, reddened eyes, ringed by vestiges of Pearl's eyeliner, and loved her more than ever. Had she had bad news? He'd kill anyone who hurt her. Instead he knelt down by the sofa and began to coax out the little dog.

'Come on, good boy.' At least Graffi could string out a few more afternoons adding Partner to the mural.

Janna took a reviving slug of sloe gin. 'You must all speak very quietly,' she begged, 'and avoid any sudden movements. Partner's scared of humans.'

'And I'm scared of dogs,' said Feral, keeping his distance and defiantly bouncing his football.

'It's lovely to see you again,' Janna told him, but noticed in dismay a purple bruise on his cheekbone and that one of his eyes had closed up. She prayed that Uncle Harley hadn't done him over. He was wary of her today, with no sign of that wide, charming, dodgy, insouciant smile.

Later, when conversation moved on to the subject of films, Janna asked if anyone had seen *Shrek*. They all shook their heads, which meant Uncle Harley had lied about Feral's mother taking Feral and the other children to the cinema last night.

While Graffi got down to work, Pearl, her shiny black eyes darting, wanted to hear all about last night. Janna told her, omitting the indecent proposal from Uncle Harley, the row with Col Peters, the attempted wine-drenching of Cindy Payne and the screaming match with Hengist.

'Everyone thought I looked fantastic. Lots of people didn't recognize me. Others who'd previously ignored me were all over me. I felt like a princess.'

'Meet any nice guys?' said Pearl.

Shut up, Paris wanted to scream.

'Think there'll be anything in the paper?'

'Well, they took my picture with Hengist B-T and he told a reporter about your brilliant make-up.'

'Nice guy, Hengist,' observed Graffi, mixing rose madder with burnt sienna to paint in a copper beech. 'Like to see him again.'

218

'Knowing the *Gazette*,' said Janna quickly, 'they're bound to print the most hideous pictures, but I'll try and get some prints. I'm afraid I spilt wine over your mother's lovely dress and left the shawl behind. I'll get it dry-cleaned.'

'Don't matter,' said Pearl.

'Probably nicked,' murmured a grinning Graffi.

'Shurrup,' snarled Pearl.

Feral was examining the mural. It had come on since his last visit, with a wedding spilling out of the cathedral, dog walkers in the water meadows and otters and fish in the turquoise river.

'It's cool,' he said, then, aggressively bouncing his football, sent Partner under the sofa again.

'Stop it, you're scaring the dog.' There was such ice in Paris's voice and eyes that Feral stopped.

'Why don't you play in the garden?' suggested Janna.

Lily struggled to her feet. 'I'm off to watch Arsenal. You coming, Feral?'

Janna was feeling really ill—perhaps Ashton had spiked her drink. She wasn't up to cooking for this lot and there was nothing in the fridge except Partner's cold chicken.

'How'd you like a Chinese?'

'Wicked,' said Pearl. 'I'll come and help you.'

Paris could have knifed her.

Looking at Pearl's heels, Janna decided to drive.

'Why don't you come with us?' Pearl asked Paris.

'I'll stay with the dog,' said Paris sulkily.

'Oh, would you?' Janna's face lit up. 'He's really taken to you. You're an angel.'

Paris thought he would live after all.

*   *   *

The increasingly bare woods seemed to have been invaded by swarms of yellow and orange butterflies as leaves drifted down. The sun was already sinking.

'Everywhere you look, the colours make you want to be a fashion designer,' observed Pearl as they drove towards Larkminster.

'I met Feral's Uncle Harley last night,' said Janna.

There was a long pause, then Pearl said, 'He's not a real uncle. He's kind of scary, laughing one moment, crazy wiv rage the next. People say he's got Feral's mother hooked on crack'—her voice faltered—'so he can do what he likes wiv her.'

Listen, listen, listen, Janna urged herself, let Pearl stumble into more indiscretion.

'Don't tell anyone I told you, miss, but Harley's the Shakespeare Estate supplier. Also collects rents for Randal Stancombe. You don't want to be late paying or Uncle Harley cuts you up.' White-knuckled, Pearl's little hands were clenched on her thin thighs.

'He seemed keen for Feral to stop truanting.'

'Only so Feral can push drugs. 'Spect he heard about us bonding wiv Bagley. Means Feral'll have access to rich kids.'

Oh dear. Hengist had said the same thing.

'Uncle Harley gave Feral's brother Joey a gun for his sixteenth birfday, same as a deaf warrant. You didn't hear this from me, miss.'

As they waited outside the Chinese takeaway for their order, which included a double portion of sweet and sour prawns for Feral, Pearl grew more expansive.

'My boxer dad got a prison sentence for burglary, feeding a drug habit. He's convinced Harley shopped him. Last year'—Pearl lowered her voice, shiny robin's eyes darting round for eavesdroppers—'Feral ran away because Uncle Harley beat him to a pulp. No one went looking for him. Frozen, bleeding to death and half starving, he was forced to crawl home. He's so proud, Feral. Never asks for help, feels he's got nuffink to offer in return. Don't say anyfing, miss. I'm not supposed to know these fings, picked them up, listening.'

'You've been so helpful, Pearl, this'll be our secret.'

'Did they really like my make-up?' asked Pearl.

When they got back to the cottage, Partner only barked once, wagging his tail as Janna went into the sitting room but staying put on the sofa beside Paris.

'Oh look,' shrieked Pearl. 'Sorry, sorry, Partner,' she whispered. 'Graffi's drawn him into the fields wiv you, miss. You've both got the same colour hair.' Then she started to giggle because Graffi had painted in Mike Pitts, Cara, Skunk and Robbie: instantly recognizable as gargoyles.

Janna tried to look reproving. 'I'll never be able to ask any of them for a drink now. Did anyone ring?'

Paris shook his head, noticing how she kept checking her mobile for messages and how she now pounced on the telephone when it rang.

Janna felt herself winded by disappointment when, instead of Hengist, it was the shrill voice of Dora Belvedon.

'You probably don't remember me, Miss Curtis. I

221

was waiting at table when you came to dinner with Mr and Mrs Brett-Taylor and we met by the lake. I'm having tea with my Aunt Lily, she says your new dog has arrived. Could I come and see him and bring your shawl back? And I've got a letter for you from Mr Brett-Taylor . . . Miss Curtis?'

But Janna was out of the house in a flash.

Dora had been dying to steam the letter open but wily old Hengist had sealed the blue envelope with green wax, imprinted with his crest of a griffin and a lion.

Dora felt only mildly guilty she had sold the story about 'Bagley beckoning Janna Curtis' to the *Gazette*. Janna would be far happier teaching at Bagley than that horrible Larks.

'I've heard of a new CD that stops dogs being frightened of fireworks, Miss Curtis. You play it every day when they're having their dinner and they get used to the bangs.'

But Janna wasn't listening, she had torn open the envelope and it wasn't just the setting sun reddening her face.

'Darling Janna,' Hengist had written. 'Sorry I bawled you out. I just want to open every door of your advent calendar for you. Very much looking forward to seeing you on Wednesday afternoon. Bring about sixteen to twenty children; they can play football and case the joint and have tea together. I'll ring you this evening. Love, Hengist.'

She was brought back to earth by Dora's gasp of delight. 'Oh, what a sweet dog, he looks like Basil Brush.'

Suddenly Janna's hangover had vanished.

'We're coming over to Bagley next week,' she told Dora. 'Paris and Feral are indoors, and Pearl and Graffi. Do come and meet them.'

Dora sidled away. 'I've come to see Aunt Lily. She misses the family since my horrible brother Jupiter chucked her out of her house. Another time. That is a very cool dog.'

Dora had not forgiven Paris for telling her to fuck off or Feral for kicking his football between her pony Loofah's legs.

*   *   *

Birds were singing agitatedly as the day faded. It was getting cold, so they had tea in the kitchen. It amazed Janna that so much food should vanish so quickly. Feral had cheered up; he'd been at Lily's sloe gin, Arsenal had won convincingly and he was delighted to have an extra helping of prawns. Partner, exhausted by his social afternoon, snored in his blue basket among the moon and stars.

Radiant, able to eat and even keep down a glass of wine, Janna broke the news of the trip on Wednesday.

'Randal Stancombe's been really kind and given us our own minibus to enable us to go to plays and rugby and football matches against other schools, so please stop writing rude things on the walls of Cavendish Plaza.

'And on Wednesday,' she went on, 'a bus load of Larks pupils has been invited over to Bagley on a recce.'

'Wreck will be the operative word,' snapped Paris.

'Send Johnnie Fowler,' taunted Pearl. 'He'll break the place up. I wouldn't want to meet those stuck-up snobs,' she added sulkily.

'How would you all like to go?' said Janna.

'You'd send us?' asked Graffi slowly.

'Yep.' Janna smiled round at their incredulous faces. 'And some pupils from Year Ten, just to look round and have some tea and see what we'd like to do in the future: playing golf, using the running track. The art and the music rooms are to die for; they've even got a rock band.'

'I don't want to go,' said Paris flatly.

'You wait until you see the theatre and the library.'

'Can Kylie come?' asked Pearl.

'I don't see why not.'

'Why us?' muttered Feral. 'We're the school dregs.'

'No you're not,' said Janna crossly. 'I want to show Bagley what attractive, talented pupils Larks has and that, once and for all, our manners are just as good as theirs.'

'Yeah, right,' said Feral, licking sweet and sour sauce off his knife and rolling his huge eyes at Janna, so everyone burst out laughing. From his basket, Partner wagged his gauze-wrapped tail.

'I'd like to go,' said Graffi. 'I'd like to see Hengist again.'

'He really liked your work, Graffi, and your poems,' she added to Paris. 'Please come.'

'OK,' said Paris, 'but what's in it for them?'

'They want to break down conventional social barriers,' said Janna hopefully.

*   *   *

After they'd gone, Lily popped in with some lavender oil. 'Put a few drops on your pillow and

224

you'll fall into a deep sleep. You look much better already.'

Janna was floating on air. She had a bath and sprinkled lavender oil all round her room and on her pillow, then she took Partner out for a last pee and put him in his basket in the kitchen. 'Stay there, love,' she said firmly, then forgot everything because Hengist rang.

'I'm so sorry,' she babbled, 'I just lose it when people attack Larks. I should never have said those awful things to Col Peters.'

'You were suffering from toad rage,' said Hengist.

When she floated upstairs five minutes later, she found Partner out like a light, his ginger head on her lavender-scented pillow. Even his snores didn't keep her awake.

25

Forgetting her own violent antipathy towards private education, Janna was taken aback by the fury produced by the proposed visit to Bagley. The matter was thrashed out at Monday's after-school staff meeting by which time most of the participants had digested as deadly poison the *Gazette* piece with a headline: 'Brett-Taylor confirms Bagley–Larks bonding'.

The copy, which included flip remarks from Hengist about the need to get chewing gum and hooligans off the streets, was accompanied by a glamorous photograph of himself and Janna in front of a vestal virgin. Janna was smiling coyly. Hengist's lazy look of lust was so angled as to be aimed straight down her cleavage.

'Just as though they were playing Valmont and Madame de Merteuil in some amateur dramatics,' spat Cara.

The piece ended with a paragraph about Janna's make-up being created by a Year Nine student, fourteen-year-old Pearl Smith.

' "We like to encourage enterprise in Larks's pupils," joked Miss Curtis.'

Pearl had borrowed a fiver off Wally and rushed out and bought ten copies and a cuttings book.

As staff gathered in explosive mood, down below they could see Janna drifting round the playground chatting, laughing, bidding farewell to the children, adding a last handful of crumbs to the bird table, and praising the new litter prefects who were shoving junk into bin bags.

As she came in Wally, who'd been making garage space for the new minibus, warned her the mood was ugly:

'Don't take any nonsense.'

Already two minutes late, Janna was further delayed by a telephone call.

'It's Harriet from Harriet's Boutique. We were so delighted to see you in today's *Gazette* in one of our gowns.'

'It was a present,' stammered Janna, convinced now that Pearl had nicked the dress. Harriet's was very pricey.

'You looked so lovely,' went on Harriet, 'we wondered if as a great favour, we could blow up the photograph and put it in our window—it would be such a boost to our Christmas display.'

Janna was still laughing as she went into the staffroom. The wind had whipped up her colour and ruffled her hair. She looked absurdly young.

The subject for discussion had been going to be the creation of a Senior Management Team (SMT), or lack of it, because Janna was dragging her heels about appointing a second deputy head to succeed Phil Pierce. If she'd had a flicker of support from any of the heads of department besides Mags Gablecross and Maria Cambola, she might have made more effort.

Now the staff had additional cause for outrage. Rain lashed the windows and relentlessly dripped into three buckets. The only cheery note was a blue vase of scarlet anemones which a grateful parent had given Janna, and which she had plonked in the middle of the staffroom table.

On Janna's right, Skunk Illingworth nearly gassed her with his goaty armpits. On her left,

Mike Pitts crunched Polos to hide any drink fumes. Why in hell didn't he kill two birds and drink crème de menthe?

Beyond Mike was Cara Sharpe, who had ripped up the *Gazette* piece. Now, shivering with fury, she was marking essays on the sources of comedy in *A Midsummer Night's Dream* with a red Pentel. Beyond her, Robbie Rushton was spitting blood and applying for a new driving licence. Opposite him presided a returning Mrs Chalford, whom Janna already disliked intensely.

A self-important know-all, she had a smug oblong face and wore a brown trouser suit with a red Paisley scarf coiled round her neck like a python. Insisting on being called 'Chally', she looked as likely to have been suffering from stress as a Sherman tank.

Next to her sat Miss Basket, the menopausal misfit, who had not forgiven Janna for refusing two invitations to supper. She was so red in the face Janna wanted to shove her outside to provide autumn colour.

'Restore work/life balance', 'No one forgets a good teacher', shouted posters on the wall. The younger staff were waiting expectantly for fireworks. Mags Gablecross looked up from the blue and purple striped scarf she was knitting for her future son-in-law and winked at Janna; Jason was reading *The Stage*, Gloria *Hello!*, Cambola the score of *Beatrice and Benedict*. Trevor Harry, head of PE, shook with righteous rage. How dare that shit Brett-Taylor suggest the only exercise Larks pupils got was running away from the police? Old Mr Mates, who taught science, was asleep.

As a heavyweight and official spokesman, Mrs

Chalford kicked off. 'I wish to object in the strongest possible terms to learning future plans for our school from the pages of the local rag: future plans which are anathema to the majority of my colleagues who are opposed to any partnership with the private sector. To take only sixteen students is also totally against our caring ethos of equal opportunity for all.'

'The idea has been around since the prospective-parents' meeting,' said Janna reasonably, 'when Mr Brett-Taylor visited Larks.'

'Such bonding is a flagrantly right-wing initiative,' accused Mrs Chalford.

'Not at all, it's a New Labour initiative.'

'I agree with Chally,' butted in Robbie Rushton, who used every steering group or meeting to puncture the atmosphere. 'It is a disgrace that schools charging parents twenty thousand pounds a year should be subsidized for bonding with their impoverished state-school neighbours. Any Labour Government worth its name should be working night and day to abolish the educational apartheid of the independents.'

'Sin-dependents,' murmured Janna.

'As a socialist, I am amazed you're committed to the project,' added Sam Spink.

'Think of the children,' said Janna. 'There is no playing field here where they can let off steam and build up team spirit. Every suggestion box is filled with pleas for more football, more games with other schools. Nor do I want our children to turn into grossly overweight couch potatoes.'

'I object,' said Trevor Harris.

'Later, Trev.' Janna raised her hand. 'As S and C won't help, we have to go elsewhere. If Bagley are prepared to share their facilities with us, we should be gracious enough to accept them for the sake of the children.'

'How are we going to get there?' snapped Mike Pitts.

'Randal Stancombe has given us a minibus,' said Janna. 'It's arriving on Wednesday.'

'That capitalist snake,' hissed Robbie.

'As someone from a desperately deprived background who has clambered out of the poverty trap, I think Randal should be applauded for giving others a chance in life,' snapped Janna.

'Why doesn't he set a good example by sending his children to maintained schools?' said Chally.

'You'll get a chance to ask him on Wednesday; we're having a photo call at Bagley.' Janna took a gulp of water. 'The minibus arrives at midday. We're going over to Bagley in the afternoon. I'd like volunteers to pioneer this first trip.'

The dead silence that followed was only broken by the furious scratch of Cara's pen.

'Hopeless. 1/10', she scrawled across an essay that looked suspiciously like Paris's.

'You amaze me,' she said shrilly. 'After the way you've constantly complained about the cost of supply staff, you're now prepared to impose a further drain on the budget?'

'It'll only be Wednesday afternoons to begin with,' said Janna. 'Later we're going to aim for Saturdays.'

'You cannot expect dedicated, overworked professionals to squander valuable time on something of which they utterly disapprove,' intoned Chally.

'Hear, hear,' agreed most of the room.

230

'Quite frankly, if I left my post for half a day to commit to this project, which I don't believe in anyway,' said Mike Pitts, 'I'd return to worse problems.'

'I'm sure we'd all like an afternoon off and a chance to see the Burne-Jones windows, but I, for one, thought we were trying to restore work-life balance, not jeopardize it,' pronounced Chally.

'What's in it for Lord Bountiful?' sneered Robbie.

'If you mean Mr Brett-Taylor,' said Janna icily, 'he genuinely wants to help.'

'Rubbish,' hissed Cara. 'He's only interested in his charitable status. Caring conservatism is a classic oxymoron.'

Janna's fingers drummed in counterpoint to the rain dripping into the buckets.

'She's about to lose it,' murmured Jason to Gloria.

'You cannot expect instant decisions without adequate consultation,' reproved Chally.

Mags Gablecross got another ball of mauve wool out of her bag:

'I'd like to go,' she said. 'I'm off on Wednesdays so it won't disrupt the timetable.'

'I'd like to go too,' said Miss Cambola, who was now orchestrating 'Ding, Dong, Merrily' for the Christmas concert. 'I gather the acoustics for the new music hall are stupendous. I'd like some of our young musicians to join the Bagley orchestra. Cosmo, son of my late countryman, Roberto Rannaldini, is their conductor. His mother, Dame Hermione Harefield, has the most beautiful voice of her generation.'

'Oh, thank you both.' Janna tried to control her

shaking. 'We need one more.'

'I'd like to go too,' drawled Jason. He'd score brownie points if he were seen to be giving support to Hengist's pet scheme.

'You've already gone over to Rome,' hissed Cara.

'Thank you, Master Fenton,' sighed Janna.

'I'd like to go as well,' piped up Gloria to Robbie's rage. 'Chance of a lifetime to see their facilities, pick up good practice, must be open-minded, I had an aunt who went to public school.' She smiled adoringly at Jason. 'I'd like to see Bagley.'

'So would I,' sighed Lydia, and was bleached pale by a laser beam of venom from Cara, who then turned on Jason, hissing, 'Who's going to cover for you, Jason?'

'I will,' said Lydia.

She turned even paler when Cara added viciously, 'You know it's Year Nine E.'

'Not quite as challenging as it sounds.' Janna smiled at Lydia. 'The Wolf Pack are coming to Bagley.'

'The Wolf Pack?' Cara's mad escalating laugh made everyone jump. The grey-green roots of her lank black hair gave an impression of poison welling out of her skull. Her red mouth was slack and twitching; her mad malevolent eyes rolled in every direction. Selecting an anemone from the blue vase and ripping off its petals with scarlet talons, she hissed, 'The Wolf Pack? D'you want Larks to be even more of a joke?'

'I've chosen kids who don't normally get recognition and whom I trust,' said Janna simply.

'Just because they've been enjoying cosy weekend tea parties at your cottage. They'll trash the place.'

232

'Other kids are going: several from Year Ten, plus Aysha, Rocky and Johnnie Fowler.'

'Johnnie Fowler!' said Skunk incredulously.

'Johnnie hasn't been in trouble since he chucked a chair at me on my second day. He's a marvellous cricketer.'

'Who's going to control them?' mocked Cara, selecting another anemone.

'They're very fond of Hengist and have huge respect for Wally who's going to drive the bus.'

'Wally as well?' snapped Mike. 'Without a by-your-leave you hijack our site manager. What happens if there's a fire or a fight?'

'Fend for yourself for a change,' snapped back Janna. 'Use the fire extinguisher on both.'

'I wish to register a protest against our students being exposed to snobbish and reactionary peer pressure,' said Robbie pompously.

'Have you got parental permission?' accused Chally.

'I was on the phone first thing this morning,' said Janna triumphantly, 'and didn't get a single refusal. Even Aysha's mother agreed. Parental consent forms have gone home with the kids this evening.'

'How long will you be at Bagley?' demanded Sam Spink, who'd been making copious notes.

'We'll arrive after lunch, at about one-fifteen, and be home about half-five.'

'That could be two and a half extra hours. I'll have to consult the branch secretary. Unfortunately I'm away on Wednesday.'

'What takes you away this time?' said Janna irritably.

'A course on self-assertiveness.'

'Whatever for?' Jason grinned. 'You're far too bossy as it is.'

'How dare you?' spluttered Sam.

Janna decided she was rather going to miss Jason when he moved to Bagley.

Chally looked at her watch. 'It's nearly five o'clock, which leaves no time to discuss the lack of a Senior Management Team. We must have more democratic rule and the opportunity to make informed decisions.'

Her scarf looks set as fast as Hengist's sealing wax, thought Janna. I'm going to see him the day after tomorrow. She fell into a daydream.

'Sorry to railroad you,' she piped up two minutes later as Chally paused for breath, 'but I'm convinced it will boost the children's morale. We're planning a joint play next term.'

Cara gave such a howl of rage, teachers on either side shrank away. 'As head of drama and English I should be consulted on every development.'

'Loosen up, Cara,' drawled Jason, 'it's a great idea.' Then, smiling round the room: 'Means I won't lose touch with you when I move to Bagley.'

'Shall we call it a day?' asked Mike Pitts, who needed a drink.

'Have the rest of Nine E been given the option of going or just your Hell's Angels?' asked Robbie.

Janna gathered up her files. 'That's uncalled for.'

'I'm sure Simon Simmons and Martin Norman would love to go,' said Cara ominously.

'They wouldn't,' replied Janna sweetly. 'Both Mrs Norman and Mrs Simmons told me categorically Monster and Satan don't do detentions on Wednesdays, so I hardly think they'd be available to go to Bagley.'

Then she regretted it, instinctively crossing herself as Cara shot her a look of pure loathing. Ripped anemone petals lay like drops of blood on the table. She wants to kill me, thought Janna.

26

Hengist, who, unlike Chally, regarded debate as the enemy of progress and had no desire to discuss anything with his (dreadful word) colleagues, often used chapel to issue orders to subordinates who couldn't answer back.

It was thus on Tuesday morning that he broke the news of the Larks invasion. He softened the blow by asking Primrose Duddon, form prefect of the Lower Fifth, to read a specially selected lesson from St Luke's Gospel.

Primrose Duddon was clever, earnest, noble-browed and already ample-breasted, which ensured normally inattentive schoolboys listened as she read about the Lord throwing a party and, when all his smart friends refused, dispatching his servants into the lanes to invite 'hither the poor, and the maimed, and the halt and the blind'.

'Like some ghastly soup kitchen,' observed Dora Belvedon.

Primrose, reflected Dora, who was sitting in the choir stalls, didn't need the exquisite silver lectern decorated with oak leaves framing the Bagley emblem of a lion sheltering a fawn; she could have rested the Bible on her boobs.

Dora loved chapel. She loved the carved angels in the niches, the flickering lights attached to the dark polished choir stalls, the soaring voices echoing off the wooden vaulted ceiling and the luminous glowing windows, particularly the one opposite, full of birds and animals inhabiting the Tree of Life.

' "For all the saints who from their labours rest," ' sang Dora.

Because she could sight-read and sing in tune, she had been picked for the choir and could thus observe the feuds and blossoming romances of both staff and pupils. Opposite sat her favourite master, Emlyn Davies, far too big and broad-shouldered for his choir stall. Black under the eyes from worry about his darling Oriana who was reporting from Afghanistan, he was surreptitiously selecting the rugby teams for a needle match against Fleetley on Saturday.

Next door were his friends, the elegant, charming head of modern languages, Artie Deverell, who was reading the *Spectator*, and Theo Graham, head of classics, who was bald, wrinkled and sarcastic but revered by his pupils because his lessons were so entertaining.

Next to Theo, looking pained, sat deputy head Alex Bruce, known as Mr Fussy because he was always whingeing about something and who was now pinching the bridge of his nose between finger and thumb. Next to Alex was *his* friend, Biffo Rudge, head of maths, who got so carried away coaching the school eight, he was always riding his bike into the River Fleet. Biffo, a cherry-red-faced bully, with bristling hair like an upside-down nail brush, had a crush on Dora's poor twin brother, Dicky, and (if Dicky were to be believed) dressed up in a black leather dress very late in the evening. Next to Mr Fussy and Biffo was their ally, Joan Johnson, No-Joke Joan, Dora's housemistress, who was hell-bent on making Boudicca, the only girls' house, outstrip the boys' houses academically.

There was no way Joan was going to let Dora rest from her labours like the saints.

In the row in front, romantic-looking Piers Fleming, head of English, was asleep. Not surprising. When Dora had crept out at six o'clock to walk her chocolate Labrador, Cadbury (who was currently living a clandestine existence with the school beagles), she had seen Piers scuttling in, probably from shagging Sheena Anderson in London. Sheena's husband Rufus, head of geography, having dressed and fed himself and his children, and got them to school, was now frantically preparing his first lesson. Piers smelt of Paco Rabanne, reflected Dora, Rufus of baby sick. One could see why Sheena preferred the former.

If she leant back, Dora had an excellent view round the silver lectern of the Lower Fifth—Bagley's equivalent of Year Nine—and the naughtiest form in the school.

Although it contained boffins like Primrose Duddon, and 'Boffin' Brooks, who was both geek and boffin, the Lower Fifth boasted the luscious, long-limbed Bagley Babes. Otherwise known as the Three Disgraces, they included Dora's heroine, Amber Lloyd-Foxe, who had a mane of flaxen hair, exeats on Saturday morning to hunt with the Beaufort and who was now reading love letters from boys at Eton, Harrow and Radley. The second Bagley Babe was Milly Walton: emollient, charming and auburn-haired but overshadowed by her ravishing mother Ruth.

Making up the trio was Jade Stancombe, Randal's 'little princess', who had long, shiny dark hair and was as bitchy as she was beautiful. Jade's street cred had rocketed because of her on-off relationship with Cosmo Rannaldini and because she'd been recently rushed from a party to hospital with alcoholic poisoning to blot out the 'pain of my parents' separation'. Jade had in fact been spoilt rotten all her life, and was miffed because her parents were, for a second, thinking of their impending divorce rather than her.

Everyone was scared of Jade. Milly and Amber loved her for her cast-offs—she seldom wore even cashmere twice—and for trips in the Stancombe jet, though you had to be prepared to endure Randal's groping.

The Bagley Babes indulged in lots of hugging and kissing and, from the humming of vibrators after dark, you'd think bees were swarming. As a new girl, Dora got fed up with making toast and running errands for Jade, and applying fake tan to the small of her very sleek back. She drew the line at shaving Jade's Brazilian.

As well as the Bagley Babes, the Lower Fifths were enlivened by Lando France-Lynch, the Hon. Jack Waterlane and Amber's twin brother, Junior Lloyd-Foxe, who all had Coutts cheque cards and accounts at Ladbrokes and whose sparse intellect was compensated for by their dazzling athletic ability, which had led them to forming their own cricket team: the Chinless Wanderers. With life also revolving round the school stables where they kept their horses and the beagle pack, little time was left for academic pursuit.

And if Babes and Wanderers weren't enough in one form, there was Cosmo Rannaldini, machiavellian master of the universe, and his pop group the Cosmonaughties. Jade Stancombe thought Cosmo was 'sex on cloven hoofs'. Dora thought he was the most horrible boy in the school.

Known as the Bagley Byron, Cosmo had the same lustrous black curls as the poet, but his pale, cruel face was leaner and his dark, soulful eyes less protruding.

'Oh God, our help in ages pissed,' sang Cosmo. Only five foot seven, our little Prince of Darkness had two bodyguards. The first was Anatole, son of the Russian Minister of Affaires, whose vodka bottle chucked out of an attic window was responsible for the glazed expression on the chaplain's face. The second was Lubemir, from Albania, who claimed his family were asylum-seekers, but whose safe-breaking skills and habit of paying school fees with rare works of art suggested rather an affiliation with the Mafia. Pupils tended to seek asylum as Lubemir approached. No one was going to beat up Cosmo with those two around.

Next to the Cosmonaughties sat Xavier Campbell-Black, hunched and miserable. Dora tried to like him because he was the brother of her best friend Bianca, but she'd been horrified recently to see him beating up his horse. Although if you were fat and ugly, and had a heart-rendingly pretty sister after whom every boy in the school lusted, you probably had to take it out on something.

Last hymn over, Dora fell to her knees and really prayed for the safety of Cadbury and Loofah and her dear Bianca, who kept waving and giggling at her from the body of the chapel, and for her brother Dicky, who was always being bullied or jumped on because he was so small and pretty.

Dicky had a much better voice than Dora, but

had deliberately sung flat at the compulsory audition, because he'd get even more jumped on if he had to wear chorister's robes.

'Grant me lots of good stories to sell,' prayed Dora.

The twenty pounds from the *Gazette* for the story of Janna dining with the Brett-Taylors wouldn't keep Cadbury in Butcher's Tripe or pay the massive mobile bill from chattering to Bianca. How could she talk to her press contacts without a phone? Life was very hard.

The glazed chaplain was just blessing everyone, when a hitherto absent Hengist swept in, bounding up the steps of the pulpit, as always raising blood pressures and fluttering pulses as he smiled round.

'If I may keep you a moment,' he began in his deep, infinitely thrilling voice. 'You all heard the lesson: "Go out quickly into the streets and lanes of the city, and bring in hither the poor, and the maimed, and the halt, the blind."

'Well, just as the Lord invited the poor to his party, we will be inviting those less fortunate than you to our school tomorrow, when sixteen pupils from Larkminster Comprehensive will spend the afternoon with us.'

A rumble of mirth, interest, disapproval and incredulity swept round the chapel.

'These are children often from tragically impoverished backgrounds, who have only played football on concrete between tower blocks, who often care for handicapped, senile, abusing or drug-addictive parents, who after long days at school have to clean the family home, look after brothers and sisters, iron, cook, shop and hold down evening or weekend jobs to make ends meet.'

Glancing round, moved by his own eloquence, Hengist noticed Cosmo Rannaldini, long lashes sweeping his high cheekbones, playing an imaginary violin, and snapped:

'Save that for the orchestra, Cosmo. Sixteen children from Years Ten and Nine will visit us,' he went on. 'You will recognize them from their crimson sweatshirts and black tracksuits.'

'And yobbo accents,' said Jade Stancombe.

'Takes one to know one,' murmured Amber Lloyd-Foxe.

'A list of both staff and pupils selected to look after our visitors will be found on the noticeboard,' added Hengist. 'I know you and Larks have been sneering at each other for generations, but tomorrow you will have a chance to break down traditional class barriers, and to treat your visitors with the kindness and consideration of which I know you are capable.

'As those selected are too old to kick off with Pass the Parcel, and too young—officially that is'— Hengist raised a thick black eyebrow—'to break the ice with a large vodka and tonic, we will begin with a team-building exercise in Middle Field, supervised by Mr Anderson and Mr Fleming, which I think you'll enjoy, followed by a tour of the school in general and early supper in the General Bagley Room.

'Tomorrow is only a recce. In future Larks will be spending more time with us and sharing our magnificent facilities. So please look out for anyone looking lost in a crimson sweatshirt and remember our Bagley emblem of the lion protecting the fawn and our motto: "May the strong defend the weak".'

242

Dora was absolutely livid when she consulted the noticeboard and discovered the Bagley Babes, the Cosmonaughties and the Chinless Wanderers had been chosen to entertain Larks rather than her form. Think of the stories she'd miss.

She was not, however, as furious as Alex Bruce when he saw the list of staff and pupils and realized Hengist had ridden roughshod across his timetable.

Fortunately Miss Painswick, the dragon who guarded Hengist, was off with flu, and Alex was able to storm into Hengist's darkly panelled book-lined office, which was on the first floor of the Mansion and, like the bridge of a ship, enabled Hengist to overlook the playing fields and escape if he saw anyone he didn't like coming up the drive.

Alex's mood was not improved to find Hengist reading *The Times* and listening to some noisy symphony on Radio 3.

'I must protest, S.T.L., on the peremptory way you have imposed your will, hijacking members of staff without any consultation. Who is going to take Piers and Rufus's classes now?'

'Oh, go away, Alex,' said Hengist irritably. 'We must try and learn how the other ninety-five per cent live in this country.'

Alex cracked his knuckles. 'Before you rush into this scheme, S.T.L., we should apply to join the Government Building Bridges programme which for a start would entitle us to some funding.'

'Any initiative from this Government involves far too much red tape.'

'Our parents will be understandably displeased,' continued Alex. 'How can we justify putting up our fees—I got a most offensive letter from Rupert Campbell-Black this very morning—if we reject potential funding?'

Then, as Hengist turned to the crossword:

'I don't expect you realize, grant money could be particularly advantageous to the maintained school involved, funding transport costs and cover for teachers. If you're anticipating any expensive joint productions, you could be depriving your' – Alex was about to say 'precious' but changed it to—' "friend" Janna Curtis of fifty thousand pounds.'

'Good God.' Hengist put down his pen. 'That's not bad.'

'And there's no reason we ourselves shouldn't apply for a grant retrospectively.'

'Then look into it, you're so good at that sort of thing. Now, if you please.'

But Biffo Rudge, also unchecked by Miss Painswick, had barged in, redder in the face than ever, bellowing, 'Our parents will be up in arms that fees they're struggling to raise are being squandered on the very students from whom they wish their children to be distanced.'

Bringing up the rear, like Boudicca leading her troops into battle, came No-Joke Joan, who had just learnt from the noticeboard that the Bagley Babes, none of whom were working hard enough, had been enlisted. Nor did she trust them with Feral Jackson or Paris Alvaston. Couldn't Hengist select three other young women?

'My decision is final,' said Hengist, turning up Brahms's First.

'But S.T.L. . . .' Joan longed to defy Hengist, but

244

her ally Alex Bruce, who'd got her in post at Bagley, was shaking his head.

'Make a note of it—our time will come,' he murmured as a delighted Hengist swooped on an incoming call, then to his horror realized it was Dora's mother, the awful Lady Belvedon whom Painswick would never have let through.

'Quite frankly, Hengist,' she was squawking, 'I don't bankrupt myself as a poor widow in order that Dicky and Dora pick up common accents. The late Sir Raymond would turn in his grave. I also insist the party doesn't include Feral Jackson, who's been up before me and spent several weeks of the summer holidays in a Young Offenders' Institute; a most vindictive fellow.'

Hengist filled in five across and let her run. If he kept saying, 'Yes, yes, yes,' a glowering Biffo, Alex and Joan might go away.

*　　　*　　　*

Having ascertained from the noticeboard that the Cosmonaughties, the Chinless Wanderers and the Bagley Babes were all rather surprisingly included in the party to entertain Larks, Cosmo Rannaldini decided to give physics a miss.

Humming Prokofiev's Piano Concerto No. 1, which he was playing and conducting in a concert at the weekend, he sauntered across the quad to the school office to discover Painswick, Hengist's secretary, was off sick. She must be ill to desert Hengist. Instead, Painswick's junior, the ravishing but daffy Jessica, whom Hengist only employed to keep visiting fathers sweet and because her typos made him laugh, was in charge. Jessica was an old friend of Cosmo, having worked as a production secretary on his late father's last film. Jessica wanted to pop down to Bagley village to buy a birthday card for her nan. So Cosmo offered to man the office.

Having checked the weekly bulletins and Hengist's diary, he tapped into Painswick's computer to find out who was coming from Larks, and whistled. Talk about the dregs: not just Johnnie Fowler and his hell-cat girlfriend Kitten Meadows, and Rocky who went berserk if he didn't take his Ritalin—that had possibilities—but all the Wolf Pack.

Feral was four inches taller than Cosmo and had once hit him across Waitrose's drink department. Cosmo did not want his crown as the Byron of Bagley taken away.

He therefore proceeded to email the entire school and most of the parents in histrionic terms, listing the dramatis personae, warning that barbarians were at the gate and that Bagley could anticipate the worst mass rape since the Sabine Women.

'A marauding army of Sharons and Kevs will plunder your cattle and your mobiles. Lock up your Rolexes, iPods and your credit cards; pull up the drawbridge; get the oil boiling on the Aga: we will fight to the death.'

He was just enlarging Janna and Hengist's photo in the *Gazette* to stick on the noticeboard when Dora Belvedon sidled in.

'What do *you* want?'

'To be part of the welcome party when Larks comes over,' said Dora piously. 'It's so important to break down social barriers.'

'Bollocks,' said Cosmo, 'you want to flog the story to the press.'

Unlike his current squeeze Jade Stancombe who considered Dora to be 'a mouthy disrespectful brat', Cosmo rather liked little Miss Belvedon. Her blond plaits were coming untied, her blue-green eyes were suspicious and disapproving and her little nose stuck in the air, but her pursed mouth was sweet. He liked her fearlessness, resourcefulness and jaundiced view of life. She could be trained up as a useful accomplice. And if he won over Dora he could gain outwardly unthreatening access to the desirable Bianca.

'You were waiting at dinner when Janna dined with the B-Ts,' said Cosmo, offering Dora one of Painswick's humbugs.

'So?'

'Must be something going on between Hengist and Janna for him to allow scum like this in here.'

'If you'll stop bullying my brother Dicky . . .'

'Yeah, yeah, whatever. So what gives with Janna and Hengist?'

'She's got a ginormous crush on him. I delivered a sealed love note to her house on Sunday; it was like chucking petrol on a bonfire: whoosh!'

'Is Randal Stancombe after her too?' Cosmo got a fiver out of the inside pocket of his tweed jacket. 'Giving her that minibus?'

'No.' Dora accepted the fiver. 'He was showing off to Mrs Walton. He had his hand up her skirt all dinner—disgusting letch.'

'Lucky Stancombe.'

Dora accepted another fiver, and another after the revelation that Piers Fleming had come in at six that morning.

247

'Piers likes Sheena Anderson. He put his hands between her bosoms when no one was looking. Thank you.' She shoved yet another fiver into her bra.

'What a decadent world we live in,' sighed Cosmo. 'If we can instigate a punch-up or, better still, a broken jaw tomorrow, it'll make every national. You pick up what you can behind the scenes. Here's my mobile number. I'd better have yours. If you're good, I'll buy you a mobile that takes photographs, then you can photograph the Duddon valley in the shower.'

Sally Brett-Taylor picked up a telephone and rang Larks.

'Janna, my dear, we're so looking forward to seeing you tomorrow. Tell me, what do your chaps really like best to eat?'

Sally was such a brick, reflected Janna, you could chuck her through a window.

27

The morning of Larks's visit began for Hengist with a glorious fuck. His favourite breakfast aperitif was going down on his beautiful wife, licking her clitoris, seeing it and the surrounding labia swelling pink, hearing her squeaks and gasps of pleasure, then her breath coming faster until she flooded into his mouth, so slippery with excitement that he could instantly slide his cock inside her.

Sally was like a clearing in the jungle no one but he had ever discovered. No one else knew the joy of making love to her. No one had warmer, softer, sweeter-smelling flesh, or higher, more rounded breasts and bottom, or prettier legs.

Sally's clothes were so straight. No one seeing the silk shirts tucked into the wool skirts which fell just below her knees suspected the luscious underwear: the suspender belts, French knickers and pretty bras in pastel satins; the Reger beneath the Jaeger. Strait is the gate; once through it was all pleasure, which left Hengist purring and utterly relaxed.

Downstairs he switched on the percolator, threw a croissant into the Aga, later smothering it with Oxford marmalade, chatted to Elaine the greyhound and turned on BBC 1 to hear Oriana's latest brief bulletin from Kabul, protesting on the plight of Afghan women. Thank God, she was alive.

Sally knew her husband was excited about Larks's visit. In turn, recognizing the slight widening and worry in Sally's eyes, Hengist murmured that Janna was only an Oriana substitute. 'I like someone to spar with—chippy, chippy, bang, bang—and she's so desperate to make Larks succeed.'

Sally understood Hengist's craving for novelty. She watched his confident lope, head thrown back, wind lifting his dark hair, shoulders squared. Last leaves were tumbling out of the trees, tossed in every direction, gathering round the bole of a big chestnut, whirling like the tigers circling until they turned into melted butter in *Little Black Sambo*. Sally's heart swelled as she saw Hengist suddenly dance and skip as he rustled through the dry leaves.

She must get on. There was lots to do: organizing smoked salmon and scrambled egg and puds for the Larks pupils; arranging a wrapped bottle of champagne and a light lunch for Randal Stancombe; and masterminding an Old Bagleian reunion dinner this evening.

*   *   *

Swinging out of sight, Hengist ruffled the hair and asked after the parents of two Upper Fourth boys, before grappling briefly with the second fifteen's scrum half and then discussing with him Bagley's chances against Fleetley on Saturday.

'We'll bury them, sir.'

Mist was curling ghostly round the last fires of the beeches as he stopped to joke with gardeners, busy putting the flower beds to rest; ferns hanging limp and dark and a few pinched 'Iceberg' roses being the last inhabitants.

Robins and blackbirds stood round indignantly glaring at a squirrel who, having taken over their bird table, was wolfing all their food. Hengist shooed it off. It was after all the duty of the strong to protect the weak.

It was going to be a beautiful day. The sun was breaking through as he settled into his big office chair, upholstered in burgundy leather, which had once belonged to the Archbishop of Singapore. Radio 3 was playing Brahms's Third Symphony, written when the composer was hopelessly in love, as Hengist leafed through his post. He so adored not being pestered to do things by Miss Painswick.

Then his telephone rang. Jessica wasn't good at fielding calls. This one was from a father, furious that his tone-deaf daughter hadn't been awarded a music scholarship.

No sooner had Hengist put down the telephone than Jessica rushed in to say the *Daily Telegraph* was on the line.

'We wondered what had happened to your copy,' asked John Clare, the hugely respected and influential education editor.

'What copy?'

'On the contribution of competitive sport to the public-school ethos.'

'Christ, when was it due?'

'Yesterday.'

'Jesus, I'm sorry.'

'I can give you till four o'clock.'

'Fuck, fuck, fuck,' yelled Hengist. Painswick would have reminded him. He dialled Emlyn Davies. 'You'll have to kick-start this Larks operation.'

'I've got rugby all afternoon.'

'Not any more you haven't. I'll get shot of this piece as fast as I can.'

251

'Absolutely fucking typical,' roared Emlyn as he slammed down the telephone.

Next Hengist dialled Alex Bruce.

'I've got to borrow Radcliffe. Someone's got to type this piece.'

'Why can't Jessica?'

'Jessica's not safe. Remember "There's no such word as cunt"?'

Alex Bruce winced. 'High time you learnt to use a computer.'

'You know technology makes me cry.'

'Absolutely typical,' screamed Alex slamming down the telephone and, turning to Mrs Radcliffe, his PA: 'Hengist wants you to type out his article.'

Mrs Radcliffe tried not to look pleased. Hengist was so attractive and so appreciative.

Rufus then rang in and said he wouldn't be able to organize the team-building exercise as one of his children had chicken pox and needed looking after.

'Why can't your wife do it?' snapped Hengist.

'She's in London.'

28

'What is the dress code?' Gloria had asked for the hundredth time.

'Trousers, jumper, warm jacket and flat shoes to run around in,' Janna had replied firmly.

Then, early on Wednesday morning, watched by a bleary-eyed Partner, she had proceeded to wash her hair and scatter rejected clothes all over the bedroom before settling for shiny brown cowboy boots, cowgirl dress in woven pink and blue wool and a dark red jacket with a rich red, fake-fur collar. It looked wacky but sexy and elicited wolf whistles from all the children when she arrived at Larks.

'You said we had to wear trousers,' reproached Gloria, who'd shoehorned herself into her tightest jeans, but added a Sloaney twinset, Alice band and Puffa.

Jason, rolling up in a tweed jacket, grey flannels, a striped shirt and round-necked dark blue jersey, looked as though he'd already crossed over. Mags Gablecross, in a lilac coat and skirt that reminded everyone what a pretty woman she was, was having great difficulty not laughing at Cambola, who looked equipped for a Ruritanian shooting party in a moss-green belted jacket, plus fours and a Tyrolean trilby trimmed with a bright blue jay's feather.

Knowing the other staff were waiting for things to go wrong, Janna had organized everything to the nth degree. Then Chally came bustling smugly into the office. 'Cara's just rung.'

253

'Yes?' said Janna through gritted teeth.

'The poor dear's sick.'

'Is she ever anything else,' said Janna, instantly regretting it as Chally bridled.

'Let's pretend you never said that. Cara's been signed off with stress for at least a week.'

'She could have rung in earlier,' snapped Janna, thinking of a hundred children with their minds and mouths open and only young Lydia and martyred Basket to cope.

'It was perhaps a mistake for both you and Jason to desert the English department.'

'Cara was perfectly OK last night.'

'Outwardly, perhaps,' reproved Chally. 'Inwardly she was humiliated by your announcing a joint play with Bagley. She feels her authority slipping away—we all do.'

Janna was tempted to throttle Chally with today's bright orange scarf. It was too late to get in a supply teacher.

Instead Wally rigged up a new film of *A Midsummer Night's Dream* in the main hall for the children to watch and then write an essay about.

Janna hugged him. 'Thank God for you.'

*   *   *

Stancombe's minibus was already twenty minutes late. The selected children were getting edgy. No matter that they'd knocked off Bagley's caps for generations. That had been on the streets of Larkminster. Now they faced an away fixture in toff country. Those not chosen to go were jealous and taunting. Fights were breaking out all over the playground.

Matters weren't helped by Kylie Rose turning up in a pretty mauve pansy-patterned wool dress and a little blue velvet jacket, saying she hadn't realized they had to wear uniform.

'And you look wicked, miss,' she added to get the attention off herself.

'She just wants to hook a toff boyfriend,' said Pearl furiously, 'and we're stuck in bloody uniform.'

'That's enough, Pearl,' said Janna. 'And take off those hoop earrings. A dog could jump through them. All right, Aysha?'

Aysha, the cleverest girl in the school, nodded. Despite dark hair hidden by a headscarf, her features were serene and lovely. Inside she fought panic. Her father, in Pakistan on business, was due back any day. Her much more liberal mother had bravely signed today's consent form. If her father found out he would beat both of them.

The boys, wearing massive trainers and tracksuits with the hoods up, were swigging tap water from Evian bottles, unwilling to reveal they couldn't afford spring water.

'Have you taken your Ritalin, Rocky?' asked Janna.

Other boys had discovered that crushed Ritalin snorted gave you a high as good as cocaine and had been offering Rocky ten quid for his daily intake. Rocky liked money to buy chocolate and fizzy drinks, which made him even crazier.

Rocky also had a huge crush on Kylie who led him round like a great curly-polled red bull.

'I want to go on the bus,' he was now grumbling.

'We all do.' Trying to keep her temper, Janna got out her mobile to learn that Stancombe had an important lunch in London, but would arrive at Bagley around three-thirty, officially to hand over the bus, which would be arriving any second.

'It's not coming, it's all a hype,' taunted Monster Norman.

Graffi, Feral and Paris retreated behind a holly bush for a cigarette, which became a second and a third as they all waited.

Then, just when they'd given up, Kylie shouted:

'Here it comes, here it comes, and it's ginormous!'

The bus, the same crimson as Larks's sweatshirts, had black leather upholstery, an upright lavatory like an upended coffin, a television and seated at least twenty-four. On the sides, so no one could mistake its benefactor, was printed in gold letters: 'Larkminster Comprehensive School Bus donated by Randal Stancombe Properties'. On the front the destination said: 'Bagley Hall'.

'Wicked!' yelled the children.

But as they surged forward, struggling to be first up the steps, Satan shouted: 'Yer mother,' to Feral. Next moment Feral had jumped on Satan and Monster on Johnnie Fowler, at the same time aiming a kick at Paris. Graffi leapt to Paris's defence. Everyone was yelling and pitching in, when suddenly the driver climbed down out of the bus. Instantly every child retreated in terror. Then, as he swept off his baseball cap, revealing a dark, shaven head and lighting up the grey day with his diamonds and his white teeth, Janna recognized Feral's Uncle Harley.

'Miss Curtis.' He took her hand. 'As beautiful as ever.'

'What are you doing here?'

'I do a bit of work for Mr Stancombe. Sorry I'm late, the garage was changing the number plates.'

'It's wonderful, thank you so much,' cried Janna as the selected children climbed on in a most orderly fashion.

Janna was about to leap on too, when Rowan came running across the playground: 'Toilets are blocked again, and Mrs Norman's on the warpath.'

A second later, Stormin' Norman came charging across the playground.

'Why isn't my Martin on that bus? Why's he bein' discriminated against, you cheeky cow?' The fist poised to smash into Janna's face stopped in mid-air. 'Mornin', Harley, just discussin' logistics wiv Janna.'

'Fuck off,' ordered Harley, who'd been showing Wally how the bus worked.

Amazingly, Stormin' Norman did.

'You wouldn't like a job here?' asked Janna.

Harley flashed his teeth and advised her to get going. He'd sort everything this end.

'He's dead sexy, your uncle,' said Gloria as Feral tried to get lost against the black leather.

'Quick, miss. Baldie Hyde's just driven up,' shouted Graffi.

Janna needed no further encouragement. Cheered off by other pupils who ran down the drive, banging its sides, the bus pulled away, quite jerkily at first, as Wally became accustomed to the gears.

'I'm going to be sick,' announced Kylie. 'Can we open a window?'

'Nah,' said Pearl. 'It'd fuck my hair.'

As the bus crossed over the River Fleet into the country, pupils charged up and down, trying out the coffin lavatory, fiddling with the windows, standing on the seats to test the luggage rack.

Mags Gablecross, knitting a shawl for a prospective grandchild, handed round a tub of Heroes. Miss Cambola got everyone singing: first 'Swing Low Sweet Chariot', then 'It really ain't surprising That we're rising, rising, rising.'

'Up the fucking social scale,' sang Graffi to howls of laughter.

Outside, the red ploughed fields were covered in flocks of birds having staff meetings.

'Miss, miss, Johnnie Fowler and Kitten Meadows have been in the toilet for five minutes,' cried Kylie.

Janna smiled and walked up and down encouraging everyone.

Paris, ecstatic to be in her company for a whole day, thought she'd never looked more beautiful. The red fur softened her little freckled face. Her perfume made him sneeze and his senses reel, particularly when she sat down and took his hand.

'You'll flip when you see the library. Have you written any more poems?'

'Not a lot.' Actually he was wrestling with one about Janna herself called 'Perihelion'. Such a beautiful word, it meant the point in its orbit when a planet was nearest the sun. He was the planet that craved its moment of perihelion close to his sun: Janna, her flaming hair spread out like the sun's rays.

Love had sabotaged his cool, but he tried to be more inscrutable than ever, gazing out at old man's beard glittering like cast-aside angels' wings in the hedgerows.

'Here's Bagley, playground of the rich,' said

Graffi, catching sight of the big gold house through the thinning trees.

Getting out her powder compact Janna took the shine off her freckled nose and, in the driving mirror, met Wally's wise, kindly eyes, which missed nothing. 'Be careful,' they said.

The bus swung left, through pillars topped with stone lions, up a drive past red and white cows, muddy horses, black-faced sheep, ancient trees in khaki fields; past heroic sculptures; past a signpost pointing the way to the bursar's office, the science laboratory, the music hall, the sick bay, the headmaster's rooms—Janna gave a shiver. Would there be room for her?

All around, Bagley pupils were walking to classes, girls in sea-blue jerseys, soft beige pleated skirts and slip-on shoes, the boys in tweed jackets and grey flannels. Passing eternal playing fields on the right and the big square Mansion on the left, Wally turned left, then left again up a little drive through a big oak front door into a quadrangle in the centre of which a bronze lion tenderly sheltered a fawn between its paws.

'Bleedin' 'ell,' said Feral, 'it's a fuckin' castle.'

'Bigger than Mr Darcy's house,' conceded Pearl.

'It's Goffic,' breathed Johnnie Fowler, gazing up at the pointed turrets and narrow windows.

'Ah, isn't that lion sweet,' cried Kylie.

As the bus doors buckled, aware of hundreds of eyes looking down at them from offices and classrooms, the Larks children swarmed out into the sunshine, steeling themselves for mockery.

Then, as though one of the heroic sculptures, perhaps Thor, God of Thunder, had come to life, curly-haired, square-jawed, massive-shouldered and battling to curb his fury, Emlyn Davies strode out to meet them.

On Saturday, the five Bagley rugby teams had away matches against Fleetley, the school from which Hengist had departed under a cloud and the one he most wanted to bury.

Emlyn had intended spending the afternoon fine-tuning each team, trying out different moves and combinations of players, before making a final selection. Hengist would be the first to raise hell if Bagley didn't wipe the floor with Fleetley, but had now dragged Emlyn away to oversee his latest self-indulgent distribution of largesse, leaving that pompous woofter Denzil Harper, head of PE, in charge. Sometimes Emlyn loathed Hengist. Everyone had to pick up the fucking pieces.

He had just broken the news that Hengist was irrevocably tied up all afternoon to a stricken Janna and her bitterly disappointed children, when Hengist made him look a complete prat by erupting into the quad, dark hair on end, ink all over his hands.

'*Mea culpa, mea culpa*. I'm so sorry, children. I failed to hand in an essay yesterday and have to stay in all afternoon to write it.' Then, seizing Janna's quivering hands, he kissed her on both flaming cheeks. 'Darling, I'm mortified, how delicious you look. Diorissimo, isn't it?'

Then he turned his spotlight charm on the other teachers—kissing Mags and telling her on what good form her husband Tim had been the other night; praising a piece on Boccherini Miss Cambola had written for last week's *Classical Music*: 'I'd no idea he was such a fascinating character!'; urging Gloria to try out the newest equipment in the gym: 'I'd so value your opinion. What pretty women teach at Larks! And young Jason, hello. I can't remember whether you're in Year Nine or Year Ten,' followed by a shout of laughter, which cracked up the children.

Jason, who'd quickly put his striped shirt collar inside the crew neck of his dark blue jersey because Hengist had, tried to be a good sport.

Then, turning to the children, Hengist explained that with Miss Painswick away and his excitement about their visit, he'd completely forgotten to write his piece for the *Telegraph* about 'the importance of competitive games'. 'You lot, being obsessed with football, know all about that,' he went on, shaking hands with each of them.

'I know Miss Curtis has only chosen special people: Johnnie Fowler, the great cricketer, you must try out the indoor school later. And Aysha, the budding Stephen Hawking, what part of Pakistan d'you come from? I know it well,' followed by a couple of sentences in Urdu.

'And Feral, the ace footballer, whom I am determined to convert to rugger, you're the right build. Lily Hamilton, an old friend, and a fan of yours, Feral, tells me you support Arsenal. And here's Graffi, another old friend, how's the mural of Larkminster going? Janna says it's fantastic. I've just bought a Keith Vaughan for the common room. I'll show it to you later.

'And here's Pearl, who transformed Janna last Saturday, an amazing effort, although you had a lovely subject'—quick smile at Janna—'will you help us with make-up for our play next term? We're planning to join forces. You must look at our theatre.'

'Yes, please, sir.' Pearl, the cross robin, had suddenly turned into a lovebird.

Yesterday Janna had emailed Hengist photographs of every child with little biogs, but never expected him to memorize them. She felt overwhelmed with gratitude.

Noting how she was blushing, Paris thought: the smarmy bastard, he's miles too old for her. Then Hengist swung round, his smile so warm and sympathetic.

'And you must be Paris. I love your poems. Janna showed me "The Spire and the Lime Tree". I gather you can also mimic anyone, so you must have a big part in our joint play. You'll find a terrific drama section in the library. Have a look at Wilde, Coward and Tennessee Williams, great writers, great dialogue, great parts for you.'

The boy's looks set him apart, thought Hengist. He has the same sad eyes, pallor, long nose and greyhound grace of Elaine, and I bet he can run away from life just as fast.

And Paris was bowled over like the rest.

Hengist was so good at putting people at their ease: he fired questions and used names to punctuate a sentence, to illustrate how clever he was to remember you out of the thousands of people he met. He had reached Kylie and rocked everyone by asking after little Cameron.

Kylie blossomed like the mauve pansies on her pretty dress. 'He's very well, fank you, sir.'

'Must be hard looking after him and getting your homework done, Kylie, but I gather you're coping brilliantly.'

Janna couldn't fault him. He had screwed up, but as she watched the antagonism and fear melt out

262

of her children, she could only forgive him.

'I'm going to leave you in the large, capable hands of Mr Davies who, until he wrecked his knee, used to play rugger for Wales, which won't impress you, Feral, but will our Welsh Graffi, look you. Everyone wants to be taught history by Mr Davies. His classes are hopelessly over-subscribed. He's easily our most popular master, and has taken the afternoon off to organize your fun and games.'

Emlyn, who'd just been told that Rufus, who'd set up the entire team-building activity, had ratted, refused to be mollified. He was also brick red with hangover and not nearly as attractive in daylight, thought Janna.

Emlyn, in fact, had got wasted last night because he was worried sick about Oriana. God knows what the Taliban might do to one so fearless and beautiful. Then Sally had had the gall to email him first thing. Oriana was safe and sent love. Why the fuck couldn't Oriana call him herself instead of ducking out, like her father, leaving someone else to break the news to the kids.

'Mr Davies will take you over to Middle Field to meet our Bagley lot,' Hengist was now saying. 'He's got some rather vigorous game to help you get acquainted. Randal Stancombe is jetting in during the afternoon, so you'll get a chance to thank him for that splendid bus. Then you're free to explore the school; someone will show you round. Don't forget the library, Paris. I'll see you all later. I better get back to my prep.'

'Isn't he awesome?' sighed Kylie Rose.

263

29

'I'm afraid I won't remember any of your names,' said Emlyn sarcastically as he led them out of the quad, past the lake and the River Fleet in the distance, down to a little white cricket pavilion. Behind this lay Middle Field, which divided Pitch One from the first holes of the golf course and consisted of four acres of rough grass dotted with little copses. Middle Field was also used by the CCF for training exercises. Bagley pupils enjoying peaceful smokes or snoggings were often disturbed by flying balls or invading armies.

On Pitch One, the armies of Larks and Bagley now lined up glaring at one another.

Feral, to appear more menacing, had, like Paris and Graffi, left up the hood of his black tracksuit. Then he clocked the three Bagley Babes, who looked as though they'd been fed on peaches and fillet steak all their lives, who had glossy hair cascading from side partings to below their boobs and gym-honed bodies in cobalt-blue tracksuits and pale ochre T-shirts, which evoked the sea and sand of endless holidays.

Nodding haughtily at Amber, then Milly, then Jade, Feral murmured, 'I am going to have that one, that one and that one.'

'No doubt yelling Sharpeville at the moment of orgasm,' murmured back Paris.

Then Feral reached for the knife in his tracksuit trousers as he recognized sneering, supercilious Cosmo Rannaldini flanked by his two heavies.

'I am Anatole from Russia,' announced the first

heavy in a voice as deep as the Caspian Sea, as his narrowed, dark eyes slid over Kylie, Kitten and Pearl.

'And I am Lubemir from Albania,' said the second, whose black hairline rested on his thick eyebrows like a front on the horizon and whose Slav face was rendered more sinister by dark glasses and even darker stubble.

'And we're Lando France-Lynch, Jack Waterlane and Junior Lloyd-Foxe, from the broom cupboard,' quipped Amber's mousy-haired, merry-faced twin brother.

'Those three are nice,' whispered Kylie, who was also vastly relieved that some of the Bagley contingent were quite plain. There was a boy called Spotty Wilkins who had more spots than face and a geek in granny specs with buck teeth and a huge air of self-importance, who, humming and swaying back and forth, introduced himself as: 'Bernard Brooks from East Horsley, but most people call me "Boffin".'

'Boffin from leafy East Horsley,' murmured Paris, catching Boffin's singsong curate's voice so perfectly, the Bagley Babes started giggling.

'Look at the knockers on that one.' Graffi gazed at Primrose Duddon in wonder. 'Stick out more 'n Boffin's teef.'

'And this is Xavier Campbell-Black,' announced Emlyn because Xav was too shy to introduce himself.

Remembering Rupert from the prospective-parents' evening, all the Larks girls swung round in excitement, which faded as they realized the heavy, hunched, sullen Xavier bore no resemblance to his gilded father.

Next moment the mighty unbeaten first and second fifteens pounded past.

'Sir, Sir,' they shouted to Emlyn, 'we've been dragged out on a fucking cross-country run. We're supposed to be practising ball skills.'

'Buck up, keep moving,' shouted Denzil Harper, head of PE, running effortlessly beside them. A recent Alex Bruce appointment, sporting a snow-white T-shirt and earrings, Denzil had a shaved head and a chunky, muscular body.

I'll kill Hengist and Rufus, vowed Emlyn, if that woofter Denzil injures any of them.

'I want you to split into groups of six,' he told the waiting children, 'mixing both schools as much as possible.'

This meant everyone chose their best friends. Instantly the Wolf Pack drew together, determined to show those fucking Hoorays (Lando France-Lynch indeed) how thick they were.

'Come on, Rocky.' Kind Kylie pulled him into their group.

'We don't want him,' hissed Pearl, 'Rocky couldn't build a team if it sat on his face. Grab Aysha.'

As Jade was Cosmo's girlfriend, the Bagley Babes automatically teamed up with the Cosmonaughties. Johnnie Fowler, who wouldn't let sexy Kitten Meadows out of his sight, formed up with four members of Larks Year Ten; the Chinless Wanderers—Lando, Junior and the Hon. Jack—with Bagley mates from the form above. Rejects like Spotty Wilkins and Xavier edged miserably together for comfort.

'A fat lot of mingling that is,' roared Emlyn and proceeded to number members in each group from

266

one to six, and to their outrage ordered the 'ones' to form one group, the 'twos' another, and so on until crimson sweatshirts and sea-blue tracksuits were totally mingled.

Outside the cricket pavilion on a trestle table lay a building pack for each group.

'These packs contain simple—depending on your intelligence—instructions on how to build your own hot air balloon,' shouted Emlyn, 'and as you can't fly a balloon without a control tower, here are newspapers for you to create one.'

'This is going to be fun.' Janna smiled anxiously at the mutinous, contemptuous, incredulous faces as Mags Gablecross and Jason rushed round handing out copies of the broadsheets.

'I can't understand papers like this,' grumbled Kitten, unenthusiastically opening the *Observer*, 'too many long words.'

'To build your balloon,' continued Emlyn, 'you'll also need coloured sheets of tissue paper, cardboard and scissors, which are assembled here on the table. But you win these by passing a number of tests.'

Then, as Janna and Gloria handed out pads of crosswords, puzzles and teasers, Emlyn explained: 'Every time you solve a page of these, you race up to us in the cricket pavilion and if it's correct you'll win yourself either cardboard, scissors or glue, or a sheet of coloured tissue paper. You'll need at least six of those to build your balloon.'

Like the labours of Hercules, thought Paris.

'The other way you can win the stuff you need,' called out Mags, who'd been reading the instructions, 'is by taking part in an orienteering treasure hunt.'

'We're not in the bloody Lower Fourth,' grumbled Cosmo.

'One would not know from your behaviour,' snapped Emlyn. 'You may not have noticed, but amid the autumn colour of Middle Field are hung fifteen orange flags with staplers and directions to the next map reference attached. Here are the maps.' He lobbed them at each team. 'In the frames round them you will find fifteen boxes which each need to be punched with the appropriate map reference. These will entitle you to more tissue paper, glue, etc.'

'Are we going to find treasure?' Amber eyed up Feral.

'Once you've built your balloons,' added Emlyn, 'and you've got an hour and a half, members of the staff will provide hot air.'

'Again,' shouted Junior Lloyd-Foxe to shouts of laughter.

'OK, joke over. Provide hot air to enable them to fly. And there'll be a competition to see whose balloon flies farthest, and for the prettiest and the first finished.'

'And to think I could be curled up in a nice warm classroom learning calculus and being molested by Biffo Rudge.'

'Shut up, Cosmo. Anyone undertaking the treasure hunt must go round in twos in case you get lost.'

'Sounds fun,' Amber smouldered at Feral. 'Shit, I forgot to ring Peregrine.' She groped for her mobile.

'Put that away,' roared Emlyn, 'we're about to start.'

'What is the matter with Attila?' sighed Amber.

Graffi, meanwhile, was immersed in the *Telegraph* racing pages.

Peering over his shoulder, Junior said, 'Singer Songwriter's a good horse.'

'Shining Sixpence's a better one,' said Graffi. 'My dad does work for his trainer. We orta have a bet.'

'I'll ring Ladbrokes,' murmured Junior. 'Hear that, Lando and Jack?' he called out. 'Shining Sixpence in the three o'clock.'

Next moment Lubemir and Anatole were also on their mobiles.

'Shall I put a tenner on each way for you?' Junior asked Graffi.

Aware it would feed the family for a week, Graffi said yes. He'd have to become a rent boy. That Milly Walton was hot.

'Blimey. "He left pubic hair on my mouse",' read Kitten, now engrossed in the *Observer*. 'I didn't know posh papers wrote about this sort of fing. What's "coprophilia"?'

'A kind of cheese, I fink,' said Kylie.

Janna turned on her angrily. 'Concentrate.' Emlyn's increasingly short fuse was getting to her. How on earth had she found him so attractive? With his gut spilling over too-tight chinos, blond hair like an electrocuted haystack, heavy stubbly jaw and angry bloodshot eyes, he looked more like Desperate Dan.

Seeing his beloved Kitten in the same group as evil Cosmo, Johnnie Fowler grabbed Cosmo's collar.

'Don't you lay a finger on my woman.'

'Don't insult my libido,' said Cosmo icily.

'Yer wot?' Johnnie clenched tattooed, ringed fingers.

Nonchalantly, Cosmo sidled off whistling Prokofiev One. Separated from Anatole and Lubemir, however, he felt vulnerable. He was, in addition, outraged to be teamed with not just Kitten but also Amber, who was making eyes at his arch enemy, Feral, and Lando, who was so thick he made pig shit look like consommé.

Deeply competitive, accustomed to automatic victory, Boffin Brooks was even more outraged to be lumbered with Lubemir, the Hon. Jack, Kylie and the unspeakable neanderthal Rocky, who refused to leave Kylie's side.

'For Christ's sake keep Rocky away from any glue or he'll sniff it,' warned Kylie. 'And the scissors too. If his Ritalin wears off, he'll cut your head off.'

Like a vicar doorstepped by the *News of the World*, Boffin shuddered.

Paris, icier and more remote by the minute to hide his shyness, was in a group which included the even more shy Aysha, monosyllabic Xavier Campbell-Black, Anatole who was reading Pushkin and swigging vodka out of an Evian bottle, and Jade Stancombe.

As Cosmo's friend and his girlfriend respectively, there was no love lost between Anatole and Jade, who made no secret of the fact she had joined the worst group.

' "Woman! when I behold thee flippant, vain, Inconstant, childish, proud, and full of fancies ..." ' murmured Paris, who'd been reading Keats. Jade was beautiful, but what a bitch.

270

How he envied Graffi who, oblivious of class difference, was creating his usual party atmosphere, laughing with the ravishing Milly Walton and Junior Lloyd-Foxe, whose father Billy worked for the BBC and brought home riveting gossip about celebs ('Richard and Judy are *so* nice').

Also in their group were Pearl and Spotty Wilkins.

'You could use a concealer on those spots,' Pearl was telling him kindly as they waited for the off.

'You start on those puzzles, Junior,' suggested Graffi, 'and win us some sheets of paper. Pearl's clever, she'll help you.'

'Five, four, three, two, one,' yelled Emlyn, brandishing the starting pistol, then as the chapel clock struck two he pulled the trigger, making members of both schools leap out of their skins, thinking the other had opened fire.

'You have a go at these brainteasers, Feral,' suggested Lando France-Lynch.

'Ain't got a brain to tease, man,' said Feral.

'Nor have I,' agreed Lando.

Amber smiled at Feral. 'Why don't you and I do some orienteering? Hand over the map,' she added to a furious Cosmo, 'you and Lando can work out the puzzles with Kitten and wind up her jealous boyfriend.'

*   *   *

'Ven two people stand on the same piece of paper in the same house and can't see each other, vere vould they stand?' A perplexed Anatole looked up from another page of puzzles.

271

'Haven't a clue,' said Jade in a bored voice.

'If they put the sheet of paper under a door, shut it and stood on the paper on either side, they couldn't see each other,' suggested Aysha timidly.

'Brilliant,' chorused Paris, Xav and Anatole.

Admiring her sweet blushing face framed by its black headscarf, Xav wondered what Aysha would look like with her hair unleashed. Not liking attention off her for a second, Jade announced she was going to build the control tower.

'Daddy's got several around the world,' she boasted, picking up the *Sunday Telegraph* business section. 'Oh look, there's a picture of Daddy.'

Ignoring her, Paris was whipping through the crossword even faster than Boffin Brooks.

'Despicable person, five letters beginning with "C"?'

' "Cosmo",' volunteered Lando.

Paris smiled faintly. 'Nice one, but I guess it's "creep". Pleasant facility, seven letters beginning with "A".'

' "Asshole",' drawled Lando.

Aysha blushed. 'Could it be "amenity"?'

'Could indeed, well done, Aysha.' Paris tore off the page, sending her and Xav scurrying off to claim more tissue paper.

*   *   *

The Threes were being held up by Graffi's desire to build a round balloon, rather than one in the recommended cylinder shape.

'It's the wrong way,' protested Junior.

'No it ain't.'

'Bloody is,' said Pearl. 'Graffi's so wilful.'

272

'Trust me, give me the fucking scissors, and go off and win some more tissue paper in case I screw up,' ordered Graffi.

* * *

Tempers and papers were beginning to fray. Under Boffin Brooks's fussy guidance, his team had concocted a scarlet and black cylinder from five sheets of paper, and were now trying to attach round ends to top and bottom.

'You stupid idiot,' screamed Boffin as Rocky's big fist went straight through the tissue paper.

'Don't pick on him, you great bully,' screamed Kylie.

* * *

Jade, bored of building her control tower, was putting the boot in.

'You stupid cow,' she cried as Aysha, trying to join their balloon's two emerald and royal blue sides together with trembling hands, also tore the paper.

'Don't talk to her like that,' yelled Xav.

Jade turned on him. 'I can talk to anyone however I like. You know who my boyfriend is.'

'I don't care,' lied Xav defiantly.

'You'll regret this,' hissed Jade.

'Kill each other later,' said Anatole, who was now immersed in the *Sunday Times* business section. 'Ve have balloon to build.'

'You're not being much help.'

A full dress row was quelled by the descent of Mags Gablecross, who chided them for wasting

273

their human resources.

'You've completed the puzzles. Anatole and Jade, go off orienteering; Paris, get on with the balloon and Xav and Aysha, help him after you've finished the control tower.'

*   *   *

Janna and Jason stood at the trestle table handing out tissue paper and cardboard, checking maps to see if each box had been punched correctly.

'You're cheating again, Lubemir, go back and get two to eight punched properly and you too, Rocky, these have all been punched with the same staple. You need fifteen different ones.'

*   *   *

Feral and Amber raced hand in hand through Middle Field, their footsteps muffled by the thick yellow and orange leaf patchwork. They had punched nearly all their map references and collapsed on the roots of a big sycamore to catch their breath.

Amber's tousled mane was falling over eyes, the rich ochre of winter willows. Her breasts heaved beneath her sand-coloured T-shirt.

'Lovely tan,' said Feral.

Amber stroked his cheek. 'Not as lovely as yours.'

Feral laughed, clapping her hand to his face.

'You been away,' teased Amber.

'Inside,' said Feral.

'Poor you, was it hell?'

'Hell, being banged up.'

'What did you do?'

274

'Mugged a stuck-up bitch; only took her bag and her mobile.'

'My father was always in gaol for hellraising on the showjumping circuit in the old days. You should compare notes. You're so sexy, Master Feral.'

Feral stretched out a hand and touched a nipple sticking through her bra and T-shirt and very gently ran his finger round and round it, until Amber was trembling with longing to be kissed. He had such white even teeth, such a wonderful smile, such curly black eyelashes.

'It's so important to overcome traditional barriers,' murmured Amber.

Feral found her colouring so exquisite against the yellow hazel, and faded tawny oak, he said, 'You suit autumn.' Putting a hand on her tracksuit trousers, he repeatedly tapped a finger against her clitoris. 'Like that?'

'Amazing.'

Unable to bear the tension, Amber leapt to her feet and stumbled deliberately in a rabbit hole, allowing Feral to catch her. For a second they gazed at each other, burst out laughing, then he kissed her. He smelled so lovely and tasted faintly of peppermint, his tongue flickering as delicately as his fingers had, then growing more and more insistent until her legs would have given way if his arms hadn't held her like steel bands.

'Oh Feral,' gasped Amber, 'talk about lift-off,' then, as his snake hips writhed against hers and his cock seemed about to burst through his trousers: 'I don't think you're entirely in control of your tower.'

'Stop taking the piss, man.'

'Oh, wow,' moaned Amber. As Feral's hand crept inside her T-shirt, her hand in turn slid down his flat belly and thighs and encountered hard steel.

'Ah,' she whispered. 'I see you also dress on the left.'

'I don't take chances.'

Letting her go, Feral whipped out his knife, running his finger down the blade, smiling at her. Amber stood her ground, determined to show no fear. Neither jumped much as they heard Boffin Brooks's strangulated whine.

'Number eight ought to be around here somewhere.'

Reaching up Feral cut through the string which tied stapler and flag to an overhead branch and chucked them into a wild rose bush. Then, putting away his knife, he pulled Amber behind a big oak tree, hand over her mouth to stop her laughing.

'We don't want Boffin catching up wiv us.'

'I've never snogged anyone black before,' murmured Amber, prising off his hand and pulling his head down. 'What have I been missing?'

30

Earlier, in London, Randal Stancombe and Rufus Anderson's wayward wife Sheena lunched on smoked salmon and champagne in one of his many apartments.

'It'll be an excellent photo opportunity,' Sheena reassured him, 'and brilliant for your profile both locally and nationally to help a school that serves an estate with such a high level of deprivation. People will recognize your sincerity about cleaning up the area. If the rest of the press are expected at Bagley at three-thirty I suppose we ought to go,' she added regretfully.

'We could have another drink,' said Stancombe, unbuttoning her dress. Sheena was very tasty and it was one way of finding out if she'd hidden a tape recorder anywhere.

*   *   *

Back at Bagley, the Lower Fourth were studying Tennyson. Poor Miss Wormley, whom the class referred to as Worm Woman, had made the mistake of asking Dora Belvedon for her views on the Lady of Shalott.

'Well, Sir Lancelot with his flowing black curls and his broad brow was pretty cool,' began Dora, 'like a young Mr Brett-Taylor. But next minute he's described as flashing into the crystal mirror. We had a flasher in Limesbridge when we lived there. Our gardener, actually. He was always waving his willy at people, so it must have been a shock for the Lady of Shalott, she'd led such a sheltered life. No wonder she suddenly got her period.'

'Don't be silly, Dora.' Miss Wormley had gone very pink.

'She did too. "The mirror cracked from side to side; 'The curse has come upon me,' cried The Lady of Shalott." They called a period "the curse" in medieval times when my mother was young, so she wasn't going to be much good to Sir Lancelot that day. No wonder he kicked on.'

Apart from Dora's brother Dicky, who had his burning face in his hands, the rest of the Lower Fourth were in ecstasy. They loved it when Dora got into her stride. Dora, however, was frantic to escape.

'I simply must go to the loo, Miss Wormley, I've got a frightful tummy upset. I'll burst all over the floor if I don't.'

And Wormley let her go. Anything to be spared more literary interpretation.

By the time the Lower Fourths had moved on to the next poem, about a snob called Lady Clara Vere de Vere, Dora was falling out of the lavatory window, binoculars trained on Middle Field as the teams shrieked, yelled and raced about.

There was Xavier Campbell-Black actually laughing—that must be a first—with a girl in Eastern clothes. Kylie Rose and the Hon. Jack were having a very heavy snog behind a holly bush. Jack was so dopey, Dora hoped he'd remember to use a condom. Lord Waterlane would go ballistic if he got Kylie pregnant. If only she had a camera, the *Mail* would love that story—talk about Posh and Complications. That dickhead Boffin was grumbling to Mr Davies about something. Dora could just make out Graffi and Milly Walton building a tower together. Janna was looking bleak, probably missing Hengist. And Amber, Dora's heroine, was sauntering out of Middle Field, doing up her bra, straightening her clothes, followed by—yuk!—Feral Jackson. How could Amber fancy him? She wouldn't if she knew he'd kicked a football through Loofah's legs. Dora got out her mobile to ring the press.

Great cheers rent the air as Junior Lloyd-Foxe got a text to say Shining Sixpence had won by five lengths.

'I'm terribly sorry I only got him at ten to one. That's a hundred and thirty quid I owe you,' he told Graffi. 'Thanks for the tip. Bloody good.'

Graffi's balloon would clearly be the most beautiful but not the first completed.

'Come on, Graffi, we must beat that twat Boffin,' pleaded Pearl.

'Rocky and Kylie'll hold him back,' muttered Graffi, gluing on extra strips of violet.

'We must beat that horrible Cosmo.'

'Feral and Lando will hold him back even more.'

'Feral makes up for it by running quick.'

*   *   *

Cosmo, in fact, was white with rage. He'd always fancied Amber, and she'd pushed off with that snake Feral, leaving him with Lando (who was immersed in week-old racing pages) and only Kitten Meadows to bully, who kept rolling her eyes, clapping her hands over her mouth and giggling.

'Why do you laugh when it's not funny?' he asked

evilly.

'Dunno.'

'That's not an answer.'

Kitten flushed, looking round for Johnnie to protect her, but Johnnie, part of Primrose Duddon's team, was gazing longingly at Pitch One. To hit a six on it would be really something.

*　　*　　*

Having cut out a doughnut-shaped piece of cardboard to reinforce the bottom disk of violet tissue paper, Graffi shoved his fist through the paper.

'This is where the hot air goes in, Milly.' He lowered his voice. 'You ever come into town?'

'It could be arranged. Here's my mobile number.' Milly wrote it on a fragment of daffodil-yellow tissue paper, shoving it into Graffi's jeans pocket, fingers splaying over his thigh.

'Stop wasting time,' said an envious Spotty Wilkins.

'Your balloon's the prettiest,' said Milly.

Graffi's smile was unwavering. 'No, you're the prettiest.'

*　　*　　*

To reinforce his team's balloon, Rocky had also been instructed to cut a piece of cardboard shaped like a doughnut and now pretended to eat it. Everyone laughed so Rocky started really to eat it.

'Stop that, you stupid idiot,' screamed Boffin.

'Leave Rocky alone, you great bully,' shouted Kylie. Then, as Rocky went on chewing the cardboard: 'Stop that, you stupid asshole.'

'Now who's being both bullying and offensive,' said a shocked Boffin.

'Rocky's my friend, I'm allowed,' snapped Kylie, adding as an afterthought: 'You're the asshole.'

'Very well said, Kylie,' brayed the Hon. Jack.

*　　　*　　　*

Jade Stancombe wasn't happy. Cosmo had ignored her all afternoon. Amber had pulled the divinely wayward Feral. Graffi was so busy gazing at Milly he'd put a fist through his balloon and was frantically patching. The enigmatic Paris, whose beauty was undeniable, was ignoring her. Paris was in fact watching Janna and Emlyn, wondering how that great ape could train his binoculars on a distant rugby game when the loveliest woman in the world stood beside him.

My poor father has spent a fortune on a bus to enable Larks and Bagley to indulge in an orgy, thought Jade furiously, and no one's asked me to join in.

'Why are you staring at me?' she rudely asked Paris, who shrugged and turned back to the balloon to which Lando and Anatole, delighted at their winnings, were proving surprisingly good at adding finishing touches.

Aysha and Xavier were also working well, Aysha deftly gluing the paper Xavier had cut out as they built a beautiful control tower, nearly three feet high with crenellated turrets.

*　　　*　　　*

281

The hour and a half was nearly up. Shrieks of rage, frustration and triumph rent the air.

'I feel like the end of a jumble sale,' said Mags, looking at the empty trestle table from which every scrap of tissue paper had been whipped.

'Finished,' yelled Primrose Duddon, whose team, even with Johnnie on board, had indulged in no dalliance or illicit boozing and had completed their orange and Prussian-blue balloon to loud cheers. As there was no sign of Stancombe, Emlyn presented Primrose with a red rosette.

'Well done,' he told her, then, turning to Janna: 'Should we release the balloons as they come in?'

'More impact if they all go off together,' said Janna, and was nearly sent flying by a furious Boffin.

'Sir, sir, someone's been cheating, cutting free the staplers in the wood so I've been unable to complete our map. Objection! Objection!'

'It's only a game,' said Emlyn, mindful of the gathering press. 'No one's getting any prizes.'

Graffi's round balloon, in diamonds of primrose yellow, shocking pink and violet, was judged to be the most beautiful; Xav and Aysha's control tower the finest; Cosmo's tower the biggest and tallest, which, everyone agreed, figured. Nearly all the participants were chatting and laughing now.

As the balloons were lined up on the edge of the cricket pitch, the chapel weathercock, which had been watching proceedings, swung away as the warm south wind, which would have swept the balloons over the golf course, changed to north-east. Now, with luck, it would carry them over the Mansion.

'Stick 'em up.'

Feral reached instinctively for his knife as Gloria ran out brandishing two hot-air paint-strippers, followed by Cambola, Jason and Janna bearing hairdriers. Emlyn then handed out cardboard tubes to plug into the cardboard hole in the bottom of each balloon.

'Too phallic for words,' muttered Cosmo as the nozzles of hairdrier and paint-strippers were applied to the lower end of the cardboard tubes.

Emlyn was studying the building pack.

'Are all staff wearing protective gloves and all balloons held firmly by a team member?' he shouted.

'Yes,' went up the cry.

'Well, turn on the heat.'

Scarlet and black, navy and emerald, Prussian blue and orange, shocking pink, violet and yellow, mauve and dark green: the balloons bobbed like tropical fish.

Mauve and dark green, held by Paris as Janna's hairdrier poured hot air inside it, quivered most. Jade put her hand round the cardboard tube, pretending to toss it off, then, encountering an icy look from Paris, blushed and let go.

'Do you like the bus my father gave you?' she demanded.

'It's absolutely wonderful,' cried Janna, 'it'll change our lives. We can't thank him enough.'

'The balloons should take four minutes to fill up,' advised Emlyn.

Kitten stood well back. 'I'm sure the glue's going to catch fire.'

'Out of nuffink, just bits of paper and glue, we've made somefing beautiful,' said Kylie in a choked voice. Like we could be, she thought.

The press had now arrived in force and, with no sign of Stancombe, photographed balloons and happy, excited children.

'Everyone ready?' yelled Emlyn.

'No,' protested Lando France-Lynch.

'He's never been able to get it up,' shouted Junior.

'They'll never fly either,' mocked Cosmo and, as everyone was concentrating on the balloons, whipped Amber's mobile from her pocket.

'Ten, nine, eight, seven, six,' shouted Emlyn. 'Five, four, three, two, one, lift-off.'

Away went the balloons, the tropical fish metamorphosing into a swarm of coloured butterflies, flying over the gold trees into the bright blue autumn sky.

Lubemir and Boffin's black and red balloon caught on the spikes of a sycamore, triggering off a stream of Albanian expletives until a gust of wind freed it to bob after the others. Sailing south-west over the Mansion, Primrose's orange and Prussian-blue prizewinner stalled on the gold weathercock.

'First time she's bounced on top of a cock,' giggled Amber.

'Let's see how far they go,' said Feral, taking her hand and together they raced through trees and school buildings, followed by a whooping Milly and Graffi, Lubemir and Pearl and, after exchanging shy smiles, by Aysha and Xavier.

'Black shit sticks together,' observed Cosmo. Jade laughed and slid her hand into his.

'Xav has just been very rude to me, I think he needs taking down a peg or two.'

'Or three, or four, or five,' agreed Cosmo. 'It will be arranged.'

284

'The Montgolfiers always maintained—' began Boffin.

'Oh, shut up, Boffin,' said Primrose.

Janna and Paris stood side by side watching until the last balloon floated out of sight.

'They're a symbol of Larks,' whispered Janna. 'We're going to take off and really fly and so will the partnership with us and Bagley—' Her voice broke.

Turning, Paris saw tears spilling over her lower lashes. Taking the hairdrier from her, he put it on a trestle table, then somehow his hand slid into hers and they smiled at each other.

'God speed,' cried out Janna, as the last emerald and navy balloon bobbed briefly between the tall chimneys, 'such a wonderful omen.'

Paris didn't know when to let go of her hand, so he left it to her.

Interesting, reflected Cosmo, who was standing behind them. Miss Curtis clearly likes toyboys as well as wrinklies.

The rugby fifteens, probably wrecked from all that pounding on hard ground, had gone in, so Emlyn also observed Janna and Paris. She's very near the edge, he decided, and so besotted with Hengist, she's unaware of the havoc she's wreaking on that poor boy.

'That was a great success,' he said loudly.

Janna let go of Paris's hand, and was soon telling the hovering press that 'Larks and Bagley's partnership couldn't have been illustrated taking off in a more romantic and beautiful way.'

31

Stancombe still hadn't turned up, but the Larks and Bagley balloonists, over orange juice and slices of Mrs Axford's cherry cake in the pavilion, were getting on much too well to care. Nor did they notice Cosmo slipping Amber's mobile into the pocket of Feral's tracksuit top, which he'd left hanging on the back of his chair.

Amber and Milly were wildly impressed when they discovered Pearl had done Janna's Winter Garden make-up.

'I mean she's pretty for a wrinkly today, but in that picture with Hengist, she looks like Meg Ryan, and you can see Hengist really, really fancies her,' said Amber.

'Will you make me up one day?' begged Milly.

'Pearl's going to do the make-up for a joint production,' said Amber.

'Then I can quite confidently play Helen of Troy,' giggled Milly.

Pearl was in heaven.

'What d'you want to see this afternoon?' asked Amber.

'The theatre, and Graffi's desperate to see the art department. He's dead talented.'

'Dead lush as well,' sighed Milly.

'Not as lush as Feral,' said Amber.

'Feral's my boyfriend,' said Pearl sharply.

'Ah,' said Amber.

If Feral were taken, which was indeed a body blow, she'd better call Peregrine. She patted her pockets. Where the hell was her mobile?

Johnnie Fowler, who'd been too uptight to have any lunch, had a fourth piece of cherry cake as he discussed safe-breaking and drugs with Lubemir.

'I tried to kill Miss when I were high on crack, so I went cold turkey.'

'Ve vould have allowed you to kill Alex Bruce,' said Lubemir. He turned to Feral: 'Vat vould you like to do this afternoon?'

'Amber Lloyd-Foxe.' Feral shook his head in wonder. 'She's the hottest girl I've seen in years.'

Amber, however, had slid out of the dining room, raided the art department and was racing towards the car park.

*   *   *

Dora, spitting with rage, was leaning out of the science lab window as Stancombe's crimson and gold helicopter finally landed on the grass, to be greeted by a diminished press corps fed up with waiting. As Larks's splendid minibus glided on to the field for the official presentation, no one realized that Amber Lloyd-Foxe had graffitied the back with silver spray paint.

Larks pupils lined up in two rows like ball boys at Wimbledon as Stancombe leapt lithely down on to the grass. Even today, when he'd cultivated an au naturel Richard Branson look—carefully ruffled hair, open-necked check shirt, designer jeans and a shadow of stubble, he didn't get it quite right. The tan was too mahogany and the Dolce & Gabbana label deliberately worn outside his belt.

Striding out to meet him, Alex Bruce explained why Hengist was tied up. Stancombe was incensed.

'You'd have thought . . .'

287

'I know, I know, I'm afraid our Senior Team Leader is a lawlessness unto himself.'

Next moment, Sheena Anderson had jumped down, and a gust from the helicopter took her black dress over her head to reveal black hold-ups, a neat Brazilian and a wodge of white loo paper shoved between her legs. This was greeted by whoops and wolf whistles. Cosmo whipped out his camera. Dora nearly fell out of the window as a furious Sheena tugged down her skirt.

'Funny place to keep your hanky,' observed Pearl.

'Stan came,' murmured Paris.

Feral laughed. 'You OK, mate?'

'We had a load of press here at three-thirty. They've rather drifted away,' Alex told Stancombe. 'Let's get on with the presentation.'

Rocky, who'd already torn the gold paper off the magnum of champagne, very reluctantly relinquished it so Kylie could present it to Stancombe who, accustomed to the tropical heat of his apartments, was now shivering uncontrollably in the north-east wind.

Janna then came forward to shake his hand.

'It's the most beautiful bus in the world, it's wonderful of you. We are all so grateful.'

A second later Jade, putting on a little girl's voice and crying, 'Daddy, Daddy,' ran across the grass to get in on the act.

'Hi Jadey, how's my little princess?' Stancombe kissed her lingeringly on the mouth.

'Gross,' muttered Milly.

'Can we have a photograph of you and Jade?' asked the *Gazette*.

Meanwhile the helicopter pilot, who'd been kept

waiting hours the other end, had charged off to the Gents, whereupon Larks and Bagley pupils swarmed on to the helicopter, examining, pressing buttons, bouncing on the pale beige upholstery, helping themselves to coloured cigarettes.

'Put it back,' said Paris furiously as Feral pocketed a gold ashtray. Sulkily Feral did. A second later, the same ashtray slid into Lubemir's pocket alongside a silver cigarette case. Everyone would blame the yobbos from Larks.

Outside Jade said, 'You know Amber and Milly, don't you, Daddy?'

'Of course.' Stancombe shook their hands. 'And I'd like you to meet Sheena Anderson.' Then, anxious to explain Sheena's presence to Milly: 'Sheen's doing an in-depth profile on me for the *Guardian*.'

'We know Mrs Anderson,' said Milly pointedly.

'How's Flavia?' asked Amber even more pointedly.

'Fine,' snapped Sheena.

'We heard she's got chicken pox even worse than Rebecca. She's got a temperature of a hundred and four,' Milly renewed the attack. 'Mr Anderson was so worried he had to duck out of supervising our balloon-building today.'

'Rufus is such a caring father,' said Jade, who always gave her father's girlfriends a hard time.

Sheena was simply livid.

'How's your mother, Milly?' Stancombe's voice thickened.

'She's really well.'

'Give her my best.'

Why the hell didn't the bitch answer his phone calls?

Bagley and Larks were getting bored. The press were getting restless.

'Why have you given Larkminster Comprehensive such a magnificent bus when you haven't been a huge supporter of the school in the past?' asked the Venturer presenter.

Stancombe, ruffling his hair for the camera, said: 'I feel it's important for disadvantaged youngsters to escape from the poverty trap and, as a consequence, a life of crime.'

As Larks faces fell or set into sullen lines, Janna's eyes met Emlyn's and was comforted to see rage. Stancombe then put an arm round Jade.

'My daughter is a very privileged young lady to be at a school like Bagley. But I've always taught her to treat those less fortunate with kindness.'

'You have, Daddy,' agreed Jade fondly.

'Jade sounds much posher than her dad,' Graffi whispered to Milly. 'Can you learn Posh as well as Spanish, French and German at Bagley?'

'That's what lots of the parents pay for,' said Milly.

Stancombe was kicking himself. By arriving late he had lost crucial coverage. He never should have shagged Sheena—and Larks kids had invaded his chopper. Feral Jackson had just leapt out, pulling at the elastic of a pair of black and red panties as though shooting a catapult at Paris, who was laughing his head off.

Then Stancombe gave a bellow. On the back of the minibus someone had sprayed the words 'Rough Trade Counter' in huge silver letters. The press was going mad photographing it. Alex Bruce was having a coronary.

Lurking in the bushes Amber chucked the can of

silver spray paint into the nettles. That would teach young Feral to make a play when he was already in a relationship—and yet, and yet, those kisses had been so magical ... And what the hell had she done with her mobile?

*   *   *

Fed up with Sheena sticking her tape recorder in everywhere, the press were packing up.

'We'd like the two heads with the pupils,' said a *Daily Telegraph* photographer. 'Any chance we can drag Hengist out?'

'He insisted on not being interrupted.'

'Then we'd better have you in the picture, Mr Bruce.'

Alex was just combing his beard in the minibus wing mirror when Hengist rolled up.

'Randal, you're a brick coming all this way.'

'Randal, you're a brick,' murmured Paris, cracking up Bagley as well as Larks pupils.

As Hengist, Janna, Stancombe and the Larks children, still humiliated and angered by his comments, posed together, a peal of bells floated across the soft autumnal air.

'How lovely,' sighed Janna. 'It must be Wally in the chapel.'

'Thought you only rang bells like that to warn people war had broken out,' quipped Stancombe.

'It already has,' said Paris bleakly.

'OK, chaps.' Hengist waved at the press. 'Got to get back to work. Help yourselves to a cup of tea and a piece of cake inside. Alex'll look after you. Randal, thanks for coming, and I'd like a word with you, Sheena.'

291

All amiability was wiped off Hengist's face as he drew her aside.

'Glad you're back. Rufus, as you're no doubt aware, is looking after your children, probably contracting chicken pox—or more likely shingles, after the pressure to which you subject him—which means he'll be off for more weeks. Now you're back, you can bloody well take over.'

Sheena flared up immediately. 'The *Guardian* have commissioned this piece. I'm flying straight back to London with Randal to file copy.'

'You can write it from home. Rufus was supposed to supervise operations today. He's paid to look after Bagley's children, not his own.'

Sheena glanced up at Hengist, so handsome, so hard, so contemptuous, and ached with reluctant longing.

'I earn four times as much as my husband,' she said furiously. 'Only way we can make ends meet on his piddling salary since you passed him over as housemaster.'

'Since we passed *you* over as a housemaster's wife. There's nothing wrong with Rufus. If you're capable of earning that kind of money, why the hell don't you get a nanny?'

Quivering with rage, Sheena caught up with Stancombe.

'That bastard B-T's ordered me home to look after the kids.'

'Got a point. Mother's place is with her kids when they're sick.'

'I can't write against that din.'

'You promised I could see copy.'

'I will if there's time; they want it this evening. I'm going to bury the Brett-Taylors if it kills me.'

32

Pearl and Graffi were in ecstasy. The drama department were doing *Bugsy Malone* and researching all that thirties kit and make-up. Graffi, having discovered the art department, was going berserk with a spray gun. Miss Cambola had already had a lovely time exploring the music library. Now, wandering round with Kylie, she suddenly heard a pianist pouring forth his soul in a ravishing fountain of sound. Miss Cambola stiffened like a pointer.

'This I must see.' Pushing her way into the music hall, followed by an enraptured Kylie, she found Cosmo at the piano, black curls flying, pale face maniacal as he thundered up and down the keys, producing notes of such crystal beauty, yet somehow managing with his head and occasional free hand to conduct the orchestra as well.

'Stop, stop.' The orchestra slithered to a nervous halt. Cosmo was hurling abuse at them when he heard a footstep and swung round. 'Get out,' he screamed. 'Get fucking out, out, out.'

But Miss Cambola strode on undeterred.

'Maestro,' she cried, sweeping off her Tyrolean hat like a principal boy and seizing Cosmo's pale hand. She kissed it lovingly. 'You can only be the son of Roberto Rannaldini, the greatest conductor of the twentieth century, if not all time.'

Cosmo was mollified. Whatever his contempt for humans, he loved music and was soon gabbling away in Italian. Miss Cambola then introduced Kylie Rose.

'She has an extraordinarily beautiful voice.'

'I must hear it. What instrument do you play, signora?'

'The trumpet,' replied Cambola.

'There's a spare here.'

*   *   *

'The Battle of Waterloo was won on the playing fields of Eton and various other good public schools,' wrote Hengist.

Normally he rattled off journalism. Today he was struggling, especially as Painswick wasn't here to do his research and find out how many acres of playing fields had been sold off in the last twenty years—or hectares. Stupid word. 'Hectors' ought to be sorting out Greeks on the ringing plains of windy Troy.

'Crash, bang, wallop, de dum, de, dah—de, dum, de dah,' anyone would think the Rolling Stones were warming up in the corridor. Hengist glanced irritably up at the timetable. 'Orchestra rehearsal: Cosmo Rannaldini.'

Sixty seconds later, Hengist roared into the music hall—

'For Christ's sake, Cosmo, take that bloody din down.'

Only to find Cambola, Tyrolean hat on the back of her head, jamming away on a trumpet.

*   *   *

Feral, who had a great capacity for kissing the joy as it flies, had just jolted Ex-Regimental Sergeant Major Bilson, who ran the small arms range, by

294

hitting everything in sight. Feral in turn had been fascinated to learn that the sixth-form pupils listed on the walls had sharpened up their shooting here before immediately setting off for two world wars to kill real people and be killed themselves.

Now he was playing golf in the fading light with his new friends Anatole, Lubemir and the Hon. Jack, who seemed a good bloke for a toff and who also supported Arsenal.

'You played before?' Jack asked Feral after a few holes.

'No, man.'

'Christ, well, keep practising, Tiger.'

'My father will sponsor you,' said Anatole. 'We will bury Americans.'

'Golf is excellent game,' said Lubemir. 'You can combine other pleasures, enjoy country air...' and, reaching into the bole of an oak tree, he produced what looked like a large stock cube wrapped in cellophane.

'Don't do drugs, man,' said Feral.

'Have a slug of this, then.'

'Nice guy, Emlyn,' observed Feral as neat vodka bit into his throat.

'Tough as sheet,' grumbled Lubemir. 'As punishment he make you run round the pitch in the middle of the night. But you can have a laugh with him. And he takes the teams to the pub when they win matches.'

'Good teacher,' Jack said, who was looking for his ball in the long pale grass. 'Annoying sometimes; always got a reason why the English didn't really win a battle.'

They were passing Badger's Retreat and the Family Tree, its three bodies writhing together in love and resentment. Down below in the valley, lights of farms and cottages were twinkling.

'Very left wing, Emlyn,' Jack went on disapprovingly.

'What's his woman like?' asked Feral.

'Good-looking but even more of a leftie than Emlyn. Wants to abolish public schools, hunting and the House of Lords—what the fuck would my father do all day?'

Feral was teeing up a ball, white as his eyeballs, squinting towards the distant green as he'd watched Tiger do so often on television.

'This is a five,' said Lubemir, passing the spliff to Anatole.

'Oriana is in Afghanistan,' said Anatole approvingly. 'Talking about war, always attacking American imperialism, very good girl.'

'Emlyn must be worried,' said Feral.

'That's why he's so bad-tempered.'

*   *   *

Johnnie Fowler, Kitten and Gloria were having a lovely time working out in the gym with Denzil. Alex Bruce, by contrast, was having a dreadful day. He'd failed to get on television. Hengist had stolen Mrs Radcliffe for another draft. He was furious with Emlyn for sloping off to fine tune the rugby team, leaving that coven of thieves playing golf with Feral Jackson. God knows what they were plotting. Alex had ordered Boffin Brooks, the one dependable boy in the school, not to let Paris Alvaston out of his sight.

Paris was now in the library. He had never seen such rows of temptation, magic carpets waiting to

296

fly him to distant worlds. He had found the plays of Noël Coward and Oscar Wilde. How could anyone be so funny? But Paris couldn't really concentrate; he wanted to write sonnets to Janna. She had held his hand and let him see her cry. If only Boffin would fuck off and stop rabbiting on about IT.

Paris took down a copy of Donne's poems.

> I am two fools, I know,
> For loving, and for saying so
> In whining poetry.

Summed it up really.

Boffin, bored with books, insisted on showing Paris the science lab. Here Dora, forcibly removed from the window by No-Joke Joan, was furiously writing an essay on 'The Journey of the Sperm'.

'The sperms venture inside the womb'—her Biro was nearly ripping the paper—'trying to swim towards the eggs—yuk—eventually they find them and fertilize them.'

'Do they do the breast stroke or do they crawl?' asked Bianca.

'Dog paddle, I would think. Just imagine all those tiny tadpoles swimming around to produce one. Yuk. Imagine our parents doing that.'

'Being adopted, I don't know who my parents were,' sighed Bianca.

'Must have been beautiful to produce you. My brother Dicky says you're the prettiest girl in the school. Oh, look, here comes that tosser Boffin and Paris Alvaston.'

Dora and Bianca watched Boffin sidle off to chat up No-Joke Joan.

'The old buzzard's looking quite starry-eyed.

297

Boffin's her favourite pupil.'

'He's gorgeous-looking, Paris,' observed Bianca.

Paris's face was as still as a statue, the white streak down the side of his tracksuit trousers emphasizing the lean length of his leg.

'Hengist said we've got to be nice to them,' said Dora, then, edging up to Paris: 'Would you like to take part in an experiment?'

'Depends.'

Dora handed him a piece of stiff white paper and a bottle of blue-black ink. 'Now, drop some ink on the paper.'

So Paris shook out a dark-blue blob, which trembled, then settled.

'Now dip the bit of paper in this flask of water.'

'What for?'

'Trust me. Good. Now watch.'

When the paper was removed from the water the dark blob had metamorphosed into a royal-blue, turquoise and olive-green oval.

'Look,' cried Dora in excitement, 'it's a peacock feather.'

'That's cool,' said Paris, examining it.

'You can all turn from blobs into peacock feathers if you work hard enough,' said a marching-up Joan. 'Now get on with your work, Dora. What are you writing?'

'The Journey of the Sperm.'

'Finding the eggs,' piped up Bianca. 'Dora wanted to know if the eggs were free range.'

'No, the sperm is,' said Paris.

Dora and Bianca got the giggles.

'Don't be sillier than you need be,' snapped Joan.

'I'm going to blow her up soon,' muttered Dora as she handed the peacock feather to Paris.

Paris put it in his pocket, thinking how nice it would be to have a little sister like Dora.

*   *   *

High tea was held in the General Bagley Room, which was used by the debating and literary societies, and for visiting non-crowd-pulling speakers. It was a charming room with flame-red walls, grey silk curtains, framed prize-winning pictures from the art department and a lovely view from the window of the General astride his charger gazing down the Long Walk.

As Hengist still hadn't finished his piece, Sally stood in for him and made the Larks children feel even more special by offering them a great mountain of delectable scrambled egg, dripping with butter and cream and served with smoked salmon and wholemeal toast. Larks, who had never tasted anything so delicious, went back for second and third helpings. A big cheese and onion pie had been set aside for the vegetarians, but everyone tucked into that too and into salads, slices of melon with glacé cherries, fruit salad and chocolate brownies.

'Yum, yum, yum,' said Milly. 'You must come over more often. We don't usually get food like this.'

'Such a happy day,' Mags Gablecross was telling Sally. 'I feel as though I've had a week's holiday. The kids are overwhelmed by such kindness.'

Mags was like a hot-water bottle on a cold night, thought Janna, who was ashamed of feeling so depressed when they were all enjoying themselves. Even Emlyn had shrugged off his ill humour. The teams looked sharper than he'd expected and he was electrified by Feral. If ever there was a natural talent ... That golf swing was utterly instinctive; he couldn't wait to get him on to the rugby field. Where was he? he wondered.

All around, the children were chattering nineteen to the dozen, arguing about GCSE subjects, football and clothes.

Boffin Brooks, who strongly disapproved of smoked salmon being wasted on such ruffians, noting Aysha and Xav sitting together, contented but not speaking, decided to join them. He was so caring about ethnic minorities.

'Mustn't neglect you two,' he said loudly.

Patronizing bastard, thought Xav, who'd never met anyone as adorable as Aysha. She had the same timidity and sweetness as his mother and he was sure she had the same rippling dark hair beneath her headscarf. He longed to tell her what he couldn't tell his parents: how lonely it was being black in a white family, particularly when, unlike Rupert, he wasn't good at anything.

'There is a myth that independent students don't work hard,' Boffin was saying sententiously. 'In fact I rise at six-thirty and am often still at my computer at eleven at night.'

And I clean the house, cook, wash, iron, shop, go to the mosque, learn from the Koran and do my homework, thought Aysha, and my father still beats me. But Xavier had protected her from Jade. She didn't know how to thank him. He had such a nice face when he wasn't scowling.

'Qualifications are indeed the only things that matter,' went on Boffin.

'No they ain't.' Graffi squeezed Milly's hand.

300

'Straight As don't teach you how to hang doors or unblock a bog.'

'I agree,' said the Hon. Jack. 'We're learning about agriculture in geography. Bloody waste of time. My father's got a farm. Rufus can't teach me anything new.'

Kylie felt Jack's big hand edging up her thigh. The hand of a lord's son. Her mother would be in raptures.

'I don't like maffs because I don't like our maffs teacher,' said Rocky in his hoarse voice.

'You wouldn't like ours any better,' said Amber. 'He shifts his cock from one leg of his trousers to another, and buries great silent sulphuric farts in his thick tweed trousers. He's called Biffo; ought to be "Whiffo".'

Rocky broke into his hoarse laugh and, unable to stop, lumbered to his feet.

'I'd like to fank everyone at Bagley for having us. Free cheers to Bagley. Hip, hip, hooray; hip, hip, hooray; hip, hip, hooray.'

'You *must* play Bottom next time we do a production of *A Midsummer Night's Dream*,' suggested Cosmo.

'Where's Feral?' said Pearl fretfully.

'You will come out wiv me, won't you?' Graffi murmured to Milly. After his winnings today he could take her to La Perdrix d'Or.

'Course I will. You've got the same lovely accent as Mr Davies. Everyone's got crushes on him, but you've got me over mine.'

33

Hengist felt drained but Christ-like. He had faxed his piece and the *Telegraph* loved it. One shouldn't be so dependent on approval. In the drinks cupboard he found a box of Maltesers given him by some pupil and, realizing he hadn't had any lunch, broke the cellophane and started eating them. His thoughts turned to Janna arriving with her children.

'Round about her "there is a rabble Of the filthy, sturdy, unkillable infants of the very poor",' he quoted idly. ' "They shall inherit the earth." '

Poor child, he'd neglected her shamelessly. He decided to text her: 'Settle your children, then escape and have a drink.'

*   *   *

Shiny-faced, shadowed beneath the eyes, lipstick bitten off, Janna longed to repair her face, but, scared Hengist would have pushed off somewhere else, loathing herself for such abject acquiescence, she was knocking on his big oak door five minutes later.

'How's it gone? I'm so sorry, darling.' Hengist thrust a large glass of gin and orange into her hand.

He'd remembered, but then he'd remembered Kylie had a baby called Cameron. It was so unprofessional to sulk, she must just be cool.

'Your kids have been so nice,' she began. 'The balloons were brilliant, and they've had a really

302

good time since then trying things out. I'm so proud of them,' she added defiantly.

'So you should be.'

His was such a beautiful room: rich dark panelling soaring into the ornate ceiling, William Morris animal tiles round the leaping log fire, red lamps casting a warm glow, lovely photographs on the desk of Sally, Oriana and Elaine, a stuffed bear in a mortar board, overcrowded bookshelves. Noting dilapidated, leather-bound copies of Horace, Aristotle, Saint-Simon and Gibbon, all containing bookmarks, Janna wondered if he'd really read and referred to them all.

Apart from the Keith Vaughan of a thundery twilight, yet to be dispatched to the Common Room, all other available wall space was covered by sepia photographs of past teams, past scholars, past heads, past glories. Such a stultifying emphasis on tradition.

'We've got an old boys' reunion tonight,' said Hengist. 'It's to encourage them to send their sons and daughters here.'

' "This is the Chapel: here, my son, Your father thought the thoughts of youth," ' quoted Janna scornfully.

She ran her hands over a bronze replica of the lion in the quad, dropping his head to lick the little fawn:

'More likely to gobble it up.'

'Debatable,' agreed Hengist.

He looked tired, with great bags under his eyes, but he seemed very happy as he abstractedly went on eating Maltesers.

On a side table Janna suddenly caught sight of a perfectly dreadful figurine of a headless naked

303

woman, with a noose around her long neck and forests of armpit and pubic hair.

'Goodness.'

'Goodness, as Mae West said, has nothing to do with it. Alex Bruce's wife made it for my birthday to remind me not to oppress women.'

'What's she like?'

'Gha-a-a-astly.' Hengist shuddered. 'She carries political correctness ad absurdum and has the relentless cheeriness and verbal diarrhoea of a weather girl. One longs to throw a green baize cloth over her.'

There was a pause. The room was so cosy after the chill winter evening, the flames dancing merrily.

'Dreadful forgetting the *Telegraph* piece, I'm so sorry.' Hengist upended the box of Maltesers.

'Did they like it?'

'John Clare said he did. It probably thumped the right tubs. I ought to write more.'

'I ought to read more,' Janna said fretfully. 'I haven't read a single novel since I came to Larks. I truly hate being a head.'

The guilt she felt about being away from school all afternoon was kicking in. She could no longer bury it beneath her longing to see Hengist again. He's not remotely interested in me, she thought bleakly.

'I don't deserve to be one,' she went on. 'I can't make peace with my staff. They'll never forgive me for having a lovely time today.'

'Don't be silly,' said Hengist gently. 'I like your children very much and I look forward to knowing them and their headmistress a great deal better.'

'You do?' Janna glanced up, and Hengist was

mortified to see her trembling bottom lip and the despair in her big brown eyes.

They were interrupted by an almighty crash, scattering glass everywhere, followed by a second and a further shower of fragments.

Janna screamed; Hengist leapt forward, pulling her against him and out of the way. For a few blissful seconds, his arms closed around her and she felt the softness of dark green cashmere and his heart pounding, and breathed in a faint smell of lemon aftershave and Maltesers.

Then he looked down and she looked up. Both for a second were distracted from the disaster as his beautiful mouth hovered above hers, then reality kicked in.

'Was that some kind of terrorist attack?' she gasped.

Something had smashed the vast bay window overlooking the pitches and to the splintered glass all over the floor were added the shattered remnants of Poppet Bruce's figurine.

'I've found a bit of bush.' Hengist brandished a fragment. 'At least Mrs Bruce's masterpiece is no more. It's an ill window, I suppose.' He grinned in such delight, Janna burst out laughing.

'This is the culprit,' Hengist fished a golf ball out of the fireplace. Striding to the now gaping window, he peered into the dusk, roaring: 'What the hell are you playing at? Christ!' he added as he slowly took in how far the ball must have travelled. Picking up his binoculars, usually used for birdwatching, he caught sight of a distant crimson sweatshirt and a huge, wide grin.

'Your Feral Jackson is the culprit behind the culprit.'

'Oh God.' Janna was appalled. 'We'll pay for it.'

'Feral can pay for it himself when he wins the Masters, if we haven't converted him to rugger by then. God, that was a long way.'

'I'm so sorry, I must take my children home.'

'Feral won't have had supper yet.'

'You've got your old boys' reunion.'

Hengist shrugged. 'We've always got something. Have another drink, it's only five o'clock.' He ran a hand over her hair. 'Sorry you were frightened, but it was a lovely hug.'

34

Over in the General Bagley Room, Graffi and Feral were chatting so much they hadn't noticed Paris's self-absorption.

Feral had come to Bagley determined to trash everything in sight, but he'd had fun; he'd outshot and outdriven everyone else; and he had a new friend called Amber who'd given him her mobile number. Would he have the guts to ring her?

Suddenly the jangling jolly theme tune of showjumping on the BBC rang out.

'That's my mobile,' cried Amber in delight. 'Where is it?'

'Here,' said Cosmo, picking up Feral's black tracksuit top and, before Feral could stop him, whipping a mobile out of the inside pocket. The room went quiet. Cosmo switched it on.

'Hi, is that Peregrine? Hang on a minute. What's your mobile doing in Feral's fleece?' he asked Amber.

'I never touched it.' Feral jumped to his feet, amiability turning to menace, fists clenched, Graffi and Paris beside him.

'I gave it to Feral to look after when we were racing round the wood,' said Amber quickly. 'It was safer with him.'

For a second she and Cosmo glared at each other.

'You said you'd lost it.'

'And now I've found it. Hi, Perry, how are you?'

Graffi pulled a protesting Feral back into his chair.

'I didn't take no mobile.'

'Cool it, man, she gave it to you to look after, she said so.'

'She didn't,' said Feral stonily. 'That was a plant to frame me.'

'What did you go inside for last summer, Feral?' asked Cosmo chattily. 'For nicking a mobile wasn't it?'

Paris stood up and, strolling down the row, pulled Cosmo to his feet. 'Don't even go down that road, you sick bastard,' he said softly. In a trice, Emlyn was beside him.

'It's Janna's day. Don't spoil it for her.'

Paris glowered round, slowly his fist uncurled and dropped to his side. 'You sick bastard,' he repeated.

Boffin, who'd missed this scrap, was still pontificating. 'We do a lot for charity,' he was telling Aysha in his nasal whine. 'We raised twenty thousand pounds for netball courts in Soweto with sponsored runs and cycle rides. Senior students act as mentors to the local primary school. Primrose is very active in this field. We run errands for senior citizens and tend their gardens. We raise a lot for the NSPCC, for cancer patients and other disadvantaged groups.'

Pausing for breath, he smiled smugly round at the Larks contingent. 'And of course today, we've set aside an entire afternoon to entertain you folks.'

'An entire afternoon to entertain you folks,' whined Paris in perfect imitation.

Milly's giggle immediately died. There was a terrible silence.

'Boffin,' said a horrified Amber.

308

Pearl rose to her feet, hoop earrings flying.

'You lot 'ad us over today,' she yelled. 'If you just did it for bleedin' charity, you can stick it up your ass'ole. In fact you're just a lot of fuckin' ass'oles. Upper class'oles in fact.'

'Upper class-holes,' sighed Cosmo in ecstasy. 'Isn't that perfect. Oh, Pearl of great price.'

Paris, however, had jumped on to the table, padded his way catlike through the debris of supper and leapt off at Boffin's side, lifting him up by his lapels.

'Take that back,' he hissed.

'Paris,' thundered Emlyn.

'How dare you patronize us.'

Next moment there was a crunch as Paris's knuckles connected with Boffin's buck teeth and hoisted him across the room.

'Stop it.' Emlyn grabbed Paris, clamping his arms behind his back; then, turning on Boffin, who was moaning on the floor, mouth filling up with blood: 'Get up, you deserve everything you got.'

Emlyn proceeded to whistle up Lando and Jack. 'Get him out of here quickly, take him to the sick bay.'

'Wait 'til my father hears about this,' mumbled Boffin, spitting out teeth.

'Save him the cash for a brace,' shouted Lando. 'You should send him a bill, Paris.'

Boffin's remarks had been so cringe-making that everyone cheered as Lando, aided by Jack, Mags and Jason, smuggled him out of a side door.

'Be quiet, everyone,' rapped out Emlyn as Hengist walked in with Janna, who looked as though a smoothing iron had been run over her glowing face.

'I just love being a head,' she was saying. 'It's like being a gardener with slightly too many plants to look after.'

Paris had felt no pain from Boffin's teeth, but he'd rather have roasted in hell than witness the adoring way Janna was smiling up at Hengist.

*   *   *

Out they swarmed into the twilight, rain like the spray from some giant waterfall cooling their hot faces.

Wally, who'd had a wonderful time trying out the bells, hobnobbing with Mrs Axford and talking to RSM Bilson about his son in Iraq, was revving up the bus.

The two schools were bidding each other fond farewells and the Larks pupils were surging on to the minibus when a BMW came hurtling up the drive, screamed to a halt and one of the prettiest women Paris had ever seen leapt out. She was very tall and slim with big anxious eyes and a mass of dark wavy hair. Jeans might have been invented for her.

' "Her eyes as stars of twilight fair; Like twilight's, too, her dusky hair",' he muttered in wonder.

'Christ, look at her,' gasped Feral.

'It's Rupert Campbell-Black's wife, Taggie,' cried an excited Kylie, a great reader of *Hello!*

For a moment, Taggie looked around in anguish, then Bianca came dancing down the steps into her mother's arms.

'I'm sorry, darling,' gasped Taggie. 'The traffic was terrible and I forgot my mobile. I'm so sorry,

310

how are you, how did the dance class go?'

Chucking her stuff in the back, running round to the other side, Bianca waved goodbye to Dora. 'See you tomorrow, I'll text you the moment I get home.'

For a second a shadow flitted across Taggie's face. 'Is Xav around?'

'No,' said Bianca, then irritably: 'He'll be doing prep or watching television. Come on.'

'OK,' sighed Taggie, slotting a seatbelt over the most delectable bosom.

'Oh, that I vas that seatbelt,' sighed Anatole.

'You did give Xav Daddy's and my love?'

'Yes, yes.' For a second, Bianca's sweet face hardened. 'Let's go, we're holding up the bus.'

Neither she nor Taggie saw Xavier lurking under a nearby oriental plant, desperate to catch a glimpse of his mother. He mustn't be a wimp and run to her. Cosmo, alas, had seen him.

'I hear you insulted Jade,' he said softly. 'Getting a bit above yourself, aren't you, black shit? You'll pay for it later.'

*   *   *

A furious Alex caught up with Hengist just as he was leaving his office. 'That window will cost a fortune to replace.'

'I know, but did you see how far the ball travelled? Boy's a natural, and surely we're insured.'

'Not for my wife's gift,' spluttered Alex. 'It's irreplaceable. I know how much care she put into it.' Then an almost coy expression flickered across his face. 'Although if you asked her *very* nicely, she might model you another one.'

'Sweet of her but I'm sure there are worthier recipients than I.'

You bastard, thought Alex.

'A very successful visit, I feel,' said Hengist, whisking off down the stairs.

* * *

On the journey back Wally stopped to pick up Graffi's balloon, which was roosting in a hedge like a bird of paradise. The children sang the whole time except when Janna went up to the front and clapped her hands.

'Thank you for behaving so beautifully. I'm right proud of all of you. The Bagley teachers were really complimentary, and thank you for mixing so well with the Bagley kids. Would you like to go back again soon?'

'Yes please,' rose the cry.

Paris didn't sing. He gazed out of the window at the skeletal trees against the russet glow of Larkminster and the cathedral spire, so like one of Rowan Merton's sharpened pencils that he wanted to pick it up and write volumes about his despair.

Imagine running out of school into the arms and soft bosom of a mother as loving as Taggie, who would ask him about his day and sweep him home to tea. Or think of turning right to Wilmington, feeding Partner, cooking supper with Janna and falling asleep in her arms: 'Pillowed upon my fair love's ripening breast'.

Oh God, he wanted a family and a home.

* * *

Rocky, after his exertions, had fallen asleep on Kylie's shoulder.

'I really like Jack Waterlane,' she was telling Pearl. 'He was so sweet to Rocky.'

'Same intellectual level,' muttered Graffi.

'Never seen such lovely men as that Emlyn, so macho,' gushed Gloria, 'and that Hengist and that Denzil, who I can assure you is not G.A.Y.'

Feeling there was safety in numbers Wally dropped the children off on the edge of the Shakespeare Estate. Janna shivered at the sight of Oaktree Court, a great Victorian pile with fluorescent lighting and bars on the windows. Paris jumped out, shuffling towards the front door without looking behind or uttering a word of thanks. He couldn't trust himself not to cry.

Humming Prokofiev One, Miss Cambola was joyfully ringing possible dates for a joint concert with Bagley.

'Time for a drink?' Mags asked Janna as they reached Larks.

'Just let me check my messages.'

'Mess' was the operative word. All the displays in reception had been trashed. Rowan had left a note on her desk:

'Did you mean to switch off your mobile? Ring Ashton the moment you get in. Ditto Russell. Ditto Crispin. Ditto Rod Hyde; he left at 6.30. Girl's toilets blocked as well now. Martin Norman rushed to hospital after fight in playground. Three windows broken. Satan on roof chucking down tiles.'

'I'll come and have that drink,' said Janna, just finding time to open a note from Lydia: 'Lovely

313

day; kids very good. We all missed you but heaven without Cara, please burn this.'

Mercifully the Ghost and Castle was empty, except for the skeleton propping up the bar. No disaffected Larks staff in sight. Funny how I lived in the pub when I was at Redfords, thought Janna. Her hair still felt on fire where Hengist had stroked it. Mags insisted on buying the drinks and, between gulps, carrying on knitting the scarf for her future son-in-law.

Mags had the beautiful complexion and sweet unruffled serenity, thought Janna, that a Raphael Madonna might have achieved in middle age if her life had not been torn apart by the tragedy of a son's death.

'Thank you ever so much for coming.'

Mags smiled. 'It was a huge success. You're right to be proud of your children. You've given them so much confidence. Both sides were amazed how much they liked each other.'

Mags prayed the saga of Boffin's teeth wouldn't reach the press. She wondered if she should tell Janna about it, then Janna put everything out of her mind by asking her if she'd like to be deputy head.

'You'd be so good, Mags. The kids love and trust you, and so do the staff. Your lessons are so popular and you don't grind axes all day.'

Looking at Janna's little face, at the pallor beneath the dark freckles and the eyes that never seemed far from tears these days, Mags was deeply touched.

'That's the sweetest compliment I've ever been paid. If you're part-time, people regard you as a dilettante. But truly two and a half days a week are

314

enough for me, so I can be there for Tim when he's on a big case and comes home wiped out, and for the children and soon, fingers crossed, the grandchildren who will all want a part of me and expect me to drop everything. And we've got Diane's wedding coming up. I'm better all round if I don't spread myself too thin.

'I'll support you all the way,' she went on, 'and the others aren't that antagonistic. Sam Spink is a troublemaking cow, but you get that in any school. Forget the Dinosaurs. The rest of the staff like you very much, they're just terrified and poisoned by Cara. You must get rid of her.'

'Hengist and your nice husband said the same thing.'

'Cara made a play for Hengist once, asked him to dance. He rejected her with a finesse only he's capable of.'

'Really?' Janna longed to know more, but didn't want to appear too keen. 'I think Cara's mad. Did you see her ripping apart those anemones? Do you think there's a conspiracy against me?'

Mags looked up, startled.

'The *Gazette* won't leave me alone. There was a piece yesterday about the staff leaving in droves. Russell and S and C deliberately thwart my every move. They seem to be willing me to fail.'

'I'll have a word with Tim,' said Mags thoughtfully. 'You know I disagree passionately with private education, but I have to say both teachers and pupils were terrific today.'

*   *   *

Over at Bagley, Cosmo, Lubemir and Anatole

were enjoying their game: shoving Xavier's dark head down the lavatory, holding him under as they pulled the chain.

'Might wash you white, black shit. Black shit should go down the bog,' taunted Cosmo, giving Xav a vicious kick in the ribs.

'Don't bruise him,' reproved Anatole.

'Bruises don't show up on black shit.'

'He is not getting whiter.' Lubemir yanked Xav out by the hair to examine his face. 'Try some bleach.' He emptied half a bottle of Domestos into the water before ramming Xav's head back again.

Xav squeezed shut his eyes so the bleach couldn't burn them but, forced to open his mouth to breathe, gulped and choked as bleach went down his throat.

Cosmo meanwhile, having wolfed down some muesli and a crushed bloc of lavatory freshener, retched and, yanking aside Xav's head, threw up into the lavatory bowl before shoving Xav back again.

'In you go, black bastard.'

Xav thought he'd choke with revulsion and his lungs would explode with pain. Death would be better than this.

Please God, let me die.

*   *   *

Mags had left her Renault outside the Ghost and Castle. As Janna wandered back to Larks's car park, she found the words: 'Go back to Yorkshire you dirty bitch', scrawled in scarlet lipstick across her windscreen.

I mustn't panic, she told herself. It couldn't be

316

Cara, she was off sick. Heart thumping, terrified her brakes had been tampered with, or a mad murderer might rise up in the back to strangle her, she drove very slowly back to Wilmington.

As she leapt out of her car, Partner hurtled out of Lily's house, then stopped at her feet, whimpering and crying.

'I'm so sorry to leave you so long, love,' she said, gathering him up, bitterly ashamed that he was trembling as violently as she was.

Lily admitted that the little dog had missed her dreadfully.

'He's fine with me for a bit, then he seems to panic you're not coming back.'

'I'll take him into Larks tomorrow,' said Janna. 'I guess I need a guard dog.'

35

Janna was so tired, neither terror of Cara nor dreams of Hengist kept her awake. It seemed only a second later that her alarm clock was battering her brain. Six o'clock already. Tugging a pillow over her head for five more minutes, she was roused at a quarter to seven by Partner tugging off her duvet with his teeth.

Thanking him profusely, showering, dressing, wolfing a piece of toast and marmalade, she took her cup of coffee, torch and dog out for a quick run across the fields, soaking her trousers with dew, tripping over molehills, splashing through streams.

'In winter I get up at night And dress by yellow candle-light.'

Partner charged ahead, barking joyfully, chasing rabbits, but as they returned to the cottage, his tummy dragged along the ground, his pointed ear and the remaining plumes on his tail drooped lower and lower at the prospect of Janna abandoning him.

'It's all right, darling, you're coming too.'

Hope springing eternal, Partner gazed up, ginger head on one side, onyx eyes shining, then went berserk, squeaking and jumping four feet off the ground. As she put his basket and a bag of biscuits in the car, he rushed off to collect his lead, then leapt into his basket in the back.

There was an apricot glow in the east. As they passed the signpost for Bagley, she wondered if Hengist ever thought of her. She kept remembering his powerful body thrust against

318

hers. She must find herself a boyfriend.

'I've got you,' she called back to Partner, who swished his tail, then as she crossed the bridge into Larkminster, her mobile beeped. Glancing at the screen, she read: 'Yr toff Bagley friends won't save you, you rancid old tart' and nearly ran into one of the Victorian lamp-posts. She must go to the police.

Shaking uncontrollably, moaning with terror, she sought refuge in the boarded-up newsagent's next to the Ghost and Castle. As she picked up the papers, she was fractionally cheered when the owner, Mrs Kamani, who was always grumbling about the children shoplifting, suddenly announced how delightful they'd been on television last night.

Having installed Partner with a Bonio in his basket under her desk, Janna distracted herself from the foul text message by checking on yesterday's press coverage. It was pretty good except for the *Gazette*, which angled its report on caring Stancombe giving Larks a £25,000 minibus and taking time out from his impossibly busy schedule to fly down to Bagley.

As the purpose of his generosity had been to rescue Larks pupils from the poverty of their ambitions and a life of crime, Stancombe had felt it sadly ironic that after these same pupils had stormed the helicopter during the opening ceremony, several gold ashtrays, a silver cigarette case and a bottle of champagne had gone missing.

'Rubbish,' howled Janna. 'The helicopter was also swarming with Bagley pupils.'

The piece was illustrated by a glamorous picture of Stancombe and Jade, of Larks and Bagley

319

children looking bored, and of Janna, as usual, smiling coyly up at Hengist.

When was Col Peters going to ease up?

Thank God the television coverage would be seen by millions more people than read the *Gazette*.

Most of our parents can't read anyway, Janna was shocked to find herself thinking. The rest of the press had followed Venturer's lead, photographing Kylie in her flowered dress: 'We thought Bagley would be stuck-up snobs, but they were really nice people.'

The *Guardian* had clearly dropped Sheena's piece on Stancombe, who'd be livid. They had however included a charming photo of the black children: Xav, Aysha and Feral, sending Aysha's proud but panic-stricken mother out to buy every copy in case her husband saw it on his return from Pakistan.

Only that most scurrilous of tabloids the *Scorpion* excelled itself by showing Cosmo's somewhat fuzzy pictures of the geography master's wife flashing her Brazilian as she descended from Stancombe's chopper and of 'Rough Trade Counter' on the back of the bus, which had a caption: 'This is what snooty Bagley really thought of Larks'. However, this hadn't stopped 'Toff Love', the caption on a picture of Kylie Rose, 'a 13-year-old single parent', breaking down social barriers with the Hon. Jack Waterlane behind a holly bush.

'Jack's lush,' enthused Kylie Rose . . .

Janna couldn't stop laughing. What would Hengist say? She was brought back to earth by a call from Crispin Thomas furiously cataloguing her iniquities. How could Janna have deserted her

320

post? One would have thought Nelson had gone ashore to frolic with Lady Hamilton during the Battle of Trafalgar.

'If you grant a handful of kids absurd privileges, the rest will act up.'

Janna left the telephone on her desk, made a cup of coffee, and when she picked it up again, Crispin was still snuffling.

'If Rod Hyde hadn't held the fort yesterday . . .'

Oh God, another text message was coming through. Janna steeled herself, but it was from Hengist.

'Hurrah for Toff Love. Ignore *Gazette*, coverage great and should take Sheena down a few square pegs. A bientot. H B-T.'

Trying to keep the silly grin off her face, Janna found Crispin still yakking: 'I'm surprised you have nothing to say to justify such a lapse. It will be top of the agenda at the governors' meeting next week.'

As Wally came in whistling Prokofiev One, Janna handed him a bottle of whisky.

'What's this for? I had a great time. The wife loved seeing us on TV and taped the programme. That Emlyn Davies is a smashing bloke. And that's a nice little dog. Is this Partner? Looks like a cross between a fox and a woodlouse. Come on, boy.'

Partner cowered in his basket.

Then Rowan raced in weighed down by Tesco carrier bags.

'How did it go? Lovely piece on Venturer; the kids looked so happy and you looked so pretty, and you were great, Wally. Oh! This must be Partner, isn't he adorable? Look at his sweet face. He must be part cairn, part Norfolk. Look at his poor bare tail, but I'm sure it'll grow back. Goodness he's sweet.'

Thus encouraged, Partner edged forward.

*   *   *

'We had a lovely day at Bagley Hall,' announced Janna at assembly. 'Later, we'll tell you about it and the wonderful things planned for the future. But first, I want to introduce a new member of Larks. I hope you'll be very kind to him; it's so hard starting late in the term.

'Many of you have been asking what happened to the little dog who nearly died when some cruel boys tied a rocket to his tail. The answer is he recovered, he's living with me in Wilmington and he's so clever, when I overslept this morning, he pulled the duvet off my bed to wake me up. But he gets frightened on his own during the day and howls, thinking he's been abandoned again. So he's going to come to school every day to be our mascot, bringing us luck. His name is Partner,' she added as Rowan carried him proudly up on to the stage and handed him over.

'I want you all to say "Howdy, Partner", like the cowboys.'

'Howdy, Partner,' roared the delighted children.

Partner quivered at such a big crowd, particularly when Janna carried him down the steps so Year Seven in the front row could stroke him. Then suddenly he caught sight of Paris, who had hugged him and so gently bathed his sore tail and, leaping down, he jumped into Paris's arms.

'Now we really know how much time Paris Alvaston spends at our Senior Team Leader's

322

cottage,' muttered Red Robbie, who was furious that Gloria had had such a lovely time in a capitalist playground yesterday.

'That remark should be withdrawn,' cried an outraged Cambola. She strode up to the piano. 'Now we will sing "All Things Bright and Beautiful", with special emphasis on the Lord God loving all creatures great and small.'

Cambola started playing. The children started singing, but had great difficulty carrying on when Partner put back his ginger head, like the fox in Aesop's fable, and howled until Miss Cambola rose from the piano and conducted him with her pencil, so he howled even louder and the singing broke up because everyone was laughing so much.

As a dog who could end assembly five minutes early, Partner's fame was assured.

36

Cara had only been off sick five minutes before a flood of Larks teachers, realizing how wonderful school was without her venomous demoralizing presence and unable to face the prospect of her return, handed in their notice. These included Adele, Robbie Rushton's deputy, who would now have no means of supporting two little children; Jessamy, Mike Pitts's teaching assistant; Gloria, the gymnast; Lydia and Lance, the newly qualified teachers; and, most surprisingly, Miss Basket, who, because no one else would employ her, everyone thought would ensure her pension by clinging on by her bitten fingernails to the end of time.

Lydia summed up the exodus:

'I love Larks and you, Janna, but I can't handle Cara any more. I feel sick with terror every morning. She's supposed to watch my teaching and encourage me, but I haven't had a page of notes since I've been here. And she punishes me by inciting her favourites to act up. Kitten Meadows stood with her hands on her hips and said, "You're just jealous because I'm hotter than you," then spat in my face. When I complained, Cara just laughed and said, "If you can't handle sassy girls!"

'We're supposed to go to the deputy head if we've got a problem with her, but as he's shagging her anyway, he'd just grass me up, then she'd murder me.

'I'm scared of her, Janna. Please let me leave at Christmas.'

'I'll see what I can do, but please reconsider.'

Janna felt bitterly ashamed that she hadn't protected poor Lydia, who'd been so plump and pretty when she'd joined the school, and was now a thin, pale, trembling wraith.

She must tackle Cara, but how?

It was the same at governors' meetings. Although Cara, as a teacher governor, left the room when staff, salary or financial matters were discussed, Stormin' Norman, like Mike Pitts, would report back any snide remarks and Cara would put in the stiletto.

Janna herself grew increasingly fearful as the obscene telephone calls continued. One night her tyres were let down; on another a circle of barbed wire rested against her windscreen.

Some people are terrified of snakes, others of spiders. Janna was terrified of madness. As an imaginative child often left alone at night when her mother went out cleaning, she'd lived in fear that the inhabitants of a nearby lunatic asylum would escape across the fields and come screaming and scrabbling at her bedroom window. Later, dotty Miss Havisham and Mr Rochester's first wife, imprisoned upstairs with her crazy mirthless laugh, had haunted Janna's nightmares. For years, she wouldn't touch apples in case they'd been poisoned by the evil queen in *Snow White*. Most frightening of all was the wicked witch in *The Wizard of Oz*, who, in her sudden appearances and wanton capacity for disruption, reminded her most of Cara.

Thank God for brave little Partner, curled up on her bed or at her feet. Janna longed to put on Dorothy's shiny red shoes, gather him up like Toto and escape down the Yellow Brick Road—but first she must stand up to the governors . . .

*   *   *

Cara in fact limped in a week later, flanked by Satan, Monster and sassy Kitten Meadows, and in time for the after-school governors' meeting. This was held in Cara's classroom, whose walls were covered with masks of everyone from Tony Blair to Maria Callas, gazing sightlessly down from the black walls. Blood-stained rubber knives, instead of scarlet anemones, stood in a blue vase on the table.

Cara looked so deathly pale and red-eyed, and her rasping voice was so pathetically muted, Janna wondered why she had ever been scared of her.

'That's green base and red eyeshadow,' muttered a passing Pearl scornfully.

Fear is the parent of cruelty, but also of sycophancy. Thus staff and pupils were so terrified that Cara, through her KGB system, would learn they had been slagging her off that she returned to a heroine's welcome of cards, flowers and bottles of wine.

There was also a full house at the governors' meeting.

Sir Hugo Betts had had a good lunch and was fighting sleep. Sol the undertaker had just had the satisfaction of burying a very rich local businessman. Cara was flanked by a solicitous Stormin' Norman and by Crispin, who was wearing dark glasses to hide a stye and flustering Miss Basket who, in the absence of Rowan at the dentist, was taking the minutes on her laptop and kept begging people to 'slow down please'. Basket was also terrified that Cara might have bugged Janna's office and found out why she was leaving.

Ashton Douglas was flipping distastefully through a pile of cuttings on the Bagley jaunt. Sir Hugo Betts put on a second pair of spectacles to admire Sheena's Brazilian. Russell Lambert, his mouth sinking at the corners like the mask of tragedy on the wall, exuded disapproval, particularly at Partner curled up on Janna's knee.

Ashton kicked off, deploring Janna's involvement in the trip to Bagley, 'against the advice and pwinciples of your colleagues and your Labour/Lib Dem county council, who you know are violently opposed to integwation. The result was an unprecedented outbweak of destruction and a lamentable pwess.'

'It was not lamentable, except for the *Gazette*,' protested Janna. 'I've had so many nice emails. It's been so good for the kids' morale.'

Support then came from an unexpected source.

'My Kylie had the most wonderful day of her life,' enthused Chantal Peck.

'We noticed,' said Stormin' Norman sourly.

'Sally Brett-Taylor was most gracious to Kylie Rose, encouraging her to persevere with her singing, because it's a flexible career for a single mother. Cosmo, Dame Hermione Harefield's son, also said Kylie's voice is remarkable. The day was a 'uge success.'

'Because your slag of a daughter got orf with an 'Ooray.' Stormin' Norman was brandishing her short umbrella like a baseball bat.

Chantal, however, decided to rise above this insult.

'Jack is a charmer,' she said icily. 'He's already

texted Kylie Rose seventeen times.'

'I'm sure he'd love you as a muvver-in-law,' snarled Stormin'.

'Ladies, ladies,' said Russell smoothly. 'Cara wishes to make a point.'

'I don't feel,' quavered Cara, 'that whoever planned this ill-judged trip appreciated the fragile egos of our students. Anarchy broke out because those left behind felt undervalued.'

' 'Ear, 'ear,' growled Stormin'.

'We have great plans for the future,' said Janna quickly, 'for a joint concert and a joint play next term. The theatre at Bagley is big enough for all our parents and children, so no one will feel excluded.'

'Except the Larks head of drama and English,' said Cara pathetically.

'Please slow down,' wailed Miss Basket.

'We can't spend an entire meeting discussing Bagley Hall and Larks,' said Ashton.

'I would like to register,' boomed Russell Lambert, 'that I found all the publicity so distasteful, I'm contemplating stepping down.'

Janna murmured:

'He, stepping down
By zigzag paths, and juts of pointed rock,
Came on the shining levels of the lake . . .'

Her thoughts were wandering. Odd that King Arthur and St Joseph, two of the most famous cuckolds in the world, were also regarded as the most noble of men.

'Janna,' said Ashton sharply.

'Sorry, I was miles away,' mumbled Janna, which

328

didn't help.

'We have decided to form a sub-committee to discuss the Larks–Bagley partnership,' went on Ashton.

'Why not a Government enquiry?' quipped Sol the undertaker, winking at Janna.

'Let us move on to the high level of truancy,' went on Russell . . .

'It's down ten per cent,' protested Janna.

'That's not enough.'

'Anyone like one of my choccy biccies?' said Cara, getting a packet out of her bag. 'So many presents and I got forty-two get-well cards.'

'No one's used to you ever taking time off,' gushed Miss Basket, blushing even redder as she met Janna's eye.

'Could we instead move on to wedundancy?' said Ashton.

As teacher governors were excluded from discussions about staff or financial matters, Russell asked Basket and Cara to leave.

'I can speak for all of us in saying how pleased we are you're back, Cara.'

'Hear, hear,' cried Miss Basket.

'Thank you,' whispered Cara.

Crispin leapt up to open the door for them, adding:

'Cara's a lovely woman, such a dedicated teacher.'

'I hope she hasn't come back too soon,' said Russell. 'She looks very pulled down.'

'Wedundancies,' said Ashton. 'I'll make notes now Miss Basket's gone. We've examined your budget situation, Janna. Your only hope is to instigate at least eight wedundancies.'

Janna, who was drawing a picture of Crispin as a pig in a trilby, replied that it was sorted.

Ashton looked up, startled.

'Nine people handed in their notice this week.'

'Whatever for?' said Russell.

Janna took a deep breath. She might as well be hung for a Sharpe as a lamb.

'They're all terrified of Cara.'

'Nonsense,' said Ashton.

'This is disgraceful,' exploded Russell. 'Look at all the cards and flowers greeting her return.'

'Those people were sucking up to her, as his minions fawn over Saddam Hussein. Cara shamelessly favours certain children over others.' Janna looked straight at Stormin' Norman. 'That's why they sent her cards.'

'These are very serious accusations,' said Ashton.

'And very serious transgressions. I have already given Cara three formal warnings for intimidating children, and made a note of numerous others. I also assumed that teacher governors left the room during human resources discussions, so that the rest of the board could talk off the record in the strictest confidence.'

'Of course,' said Russell heartily. 'Within these four walls.'

'I'd therefore like to reiterate that Cara Sharpe is poisoning our school.'

There was a squawk of a tape running out.

'Ha,' said Janna. 'So this meeting is being recorded.'

Pouncing on Stormin's bag, she whipped out a recorder and played it back.

' "Cara Sharpe is poisoning our school",' said the tape.

'I must have left it on by mistake,' puffed Stormin', for once discomforted.

'I'm sure,' said Janna. 'Just for the record, I'm keeping this.' Removing the tape, she dropped it into her bag. Then she turned furiously on Ashton and Russell. 'I don't understand you. Because of my ailing budget you demand redundancies. But when nine teachers hand in their notices, which will cost you nothing compared with the vast amount you'll have to fork out if you have to make people redundant, you don't seem remotely pleased. This saves money, which I thought was your top priority.'

'I agree,' said Sol. 'Janna's achieved what you wanted, cheaply and painlessly, so stop whingeing.'

'Hear, hear,' said Sir Hugo, waking up.

The meeting broke up in uproar.

Only after she had escaped did Janna start shivering. How long would it take Cara to get her revenge?

When she finally got home several hours later, the outside light came on to illuminate a front door daubed with red paint: 'Get out of Larkshire, cradle-snatching bitch'.

Far more dreadful, Partner was frantically sniffing at something on the step. It was a little black cat with its throat cut, its poor body still warm. The nutters were out to get her.

Running into the house, she rang Mags Gablecross and left a terrified, pleading message.

37

After a night with her four-poster shoved against the bedroom door, Janna was passionately relieved first thing to get a call from Chief Inspector Gablecross. He and Mags had been away meeting fellow in-laws and only just checked their messages. Could he pop in around eleven-thirty after break, when hopefully most staff and children would be in lessons?

Janna liked the Chief Inspector as much as when she first met him. The world immediately seemed a better and safer place. Face to face across her desk, rather than side by side at the Winter Gardens dinner, she noticed the shrewdness of his curly lashed green eyes. His rugby player's body, running not unpleasantly to fat, and his slow, soft, gentle voice, evoking the drinking of cider in pubs on the edge of fields of buttercups, reminded her a lot of Emlyn Davies.

And after Janna had reiterated how much she liked and admired Mags, and Gablecross had said how much he liked Partner, who was now chewing on a dried pig's ear, and didn't Janna think he was part dachshund, part corgi, Janna shut the door and told him everything from the daubed windscreen to the murdered cat.

'Cara should be having a rest period,' Janna said finally, 'but she's taking Nine E, which includes the Wolf Pack, because Lydia stayed at home. She's really conscientious but she couldn't hack it now Cara's back.'

Janna   was   badly   frightened,   observed

Gablecross, but fighting like a little terrier. He admired her guts.

'Could you show me round the school?'

The Chief Inspector had an even more dramatic effect on the children than Uncle Harley. The din in the corridors subsided as though a radio had been turned off. Pupils slid into classrooms. Guilty parties shot into the toilets. Satan Simmons leapt out of a window he'd just broken and set off bleeding like a pig down the drive.

Year Nine E were reading *The Mayor of Casterbridge*, which Paris thought was a fabulous book. Was it possible that his own father had sold him and his mother at a fair, and his mother, unable to support him, had left him on the children's home steps? He was touched Henshaw the Mayor loved Elizabeth-Jane just as much when he discovered she wasn't his natural daughter. Perhaps some father could one day love him. He also liked Hardy's pessimism. He'd have made a good *EastEnders* scriptwriter.

Paris, on the other hand, was churning inside. Lydia, who normally took this class, had thoughtlessly asked the pupils to write an essay about their family tree and bring in photos of their parents and themselves as babies.

Most of the children on the Shakespeare Estate hadn't seen their fathers for years, if ever. Cara was joyfully poised to skin Lydia alive for such gross insensitivity, but meanwhile she intended to have fun and with a cackle picked up Rocky's photograph.

'What a hideous baby you were.'

As Rocky's face fell like a chastised Rottweiler, the class tittered out of fear, rather than agreement.

'You were an even uglier baby, Feral,' went on Cara, 'and goodness me, where did your mother meet your father, Pearl?'

'In the dole queue,' said Pearl sulkily.

' 'Spect it's the only time they did meet,' taunted Satan. In the front row with Kitten Meadows, who'd had a row with Johnnie Fowler, he was egging Cara on. 'Pearl's father's inside.'

'And when my dad comes out, he'll get you if you don't stop fucking bugging me,' spat Pearl.

'Don't swear.' Cara turned with such venom, Pearl shrank away.

Cara had reached Paris. Beside him Graffi, stressed that he had a zit bigger than the Millennium Dome, was texting Milly, whom he was meeting for a first date after school. Paris had had a lousy week. He'd borrowed a copy of *Private Lives* from Bagley library without asking and last night, kids in the home had ripped it to pieces. Inside it had been signed 'To Hengist, love Noël'. He'd meant to give it back, but now no one would believe him. He wasn't sleeping because of Janna; he'd been watching her all week and knew she was unhappy. He'd hardly spoken to her since the Bagley trip, but he'd been taking Partner for walks round the school grounds.

Cara was poised for the kill. Kitten and Satan were grinning in anticipation.

'I see you've forgotten to bring in any photographs or produce an essay, Paris.' Then, when Paris didn't answer: 'Have you lost your tongue?'

'I don't have parents to write about,' he muttered.

'He don't know who they are and he hasn't got no photographs of himself as a baby nor a family tree,' protested Graffi furiously.

'How unfortunate,' drawled Cara, then cruelly intoned:

' "Rattle his bones over the stones; He's only a pauper, whom nobody owns!" '

Only a few grasped the significance of the lines. Fear of Cara inhibited even the Wolf Pack.

Cara detested Paris for his beauty, his brains and, most of all, for his adoration of Janna. She had seen his lovelorn looks and had pieced together torn-up notes in the bin. Stalking Janna herself, she'd had to be very careful not to be apprehended by him.

Gablecross and Janna had just slid into the classroom and witnessed Cara's narrow scarlet back quivering like a cobra poised to strike. At the sight of Gablecross, Feral edged towards the window.

'Where are you off to, Feral Jackson? Sit down,' screeched Cara. Then, turning back to Paris, with her mad laugh: 'I'm not surprised your mother didn't want to keep you. If you only had a fraction more charm . . . Still, I'm sure Janna is like a mother to you, or would you rather be her toyboy?'

Cara had lost it, evil seemed to gush out of her. The class edged away. Only Paris stood his ground. Janna was poised to move in, but Gablecross put his hand on her arm.

'Can't you give me an answer?' screamed Cara. 'You insolent lout.'

'Shut up,' yelled Paris. 'Janna's the loveliest woman in the world. You're just a jealous old bitch.'

335

Next moment, a mobile rang and Graffi snatched it up. His shoulders hunched in ecstasy: 'Milly, lovely!' As Cara swung round to silence him, he thrust out his palm in a lordly fashion: 'Talk to the hand, dearie.'

Paris made the mistake of laughing. Next moment Cara had whacked him so hard that she left a red handprint darkening on his face; then, as he ducked, balling his fists to strike her, she lashed at him again with the back of her hand. Unable to stay neutral a moment longer, Partner wriggled out of Janna's clutches and, yapping furiously, rushed forward to defend his friend.

'You fucking animal,' screamed Cara, snatching up a pair of scissors lying on the table and jabbing first at Partner, then at Paris.

'Put that down,' thundered Gablecross.

A heavy man but as quick on his feet as Feral's idol, Thierry Henry, he was across the room grabbing Cara's arms from behind and slapping on handcuffs.

'Let me go,' she screeched.

'Cara Sharpe, I am arresting you. You do not have to say anything, but . . .'

'Just like *The Bill*,' cried Kylie in ecstasy.

*　　　*　　　*

Janna called Russell Lambert.

'You'd better call an emergency governors' meeting. I've got rid of ten teachers now. I've just fired Cara Sharpe.'

*　　　*　　　*

336

'Hey ho, the witch is dead,' sang the children, racing along the corridors and round the playground and for once no one hushed them. By the afternoon, a raving mad Cara down at the police station had, between bouts of wild laughter, confessed to everything from graffitiing Janna's windscreen to leaving the murdered black cat outside Jubilee Cottage. By late afternoon the teachers, realizing Cara had really gone, started sidling into Janna's office, saying that, after a lot of heart-searching, they'd decided not to resign. Even arch red Robbie Rushton announced that he couldn't live with himself deserting a sinking ship.

Refraining from expressing doubt that anyone else could live with him, Janna took him and everyone else back, and then went out and got drunk with them all in the Ghost and Castle. Mike Pitts bought her a huge gin and orange, and confided that he actually approved of the Larks–Bagley partnership and it would be grand if they could get a football team up and running, then admitted he'd played once for Brentford.

Partner had a wonderful evening, picking up the general euphoria, being fed crisps and pork scratchings, sitting on the bar stool being fussed over as everyone discussed his possible parentage.

'He can take over from Cara as a teacher governor,' said Mags. 'Essential not to have a spy or a sneak.'

Partner dusted the bar stool with his increasingly plumey tail.

*   *   *

The only real resistance to Cara's sacking came

337

from Satan and Monster, who, revved up on crack and armed with crowbars the following morning, threatened Janna on her way to assembly. Partner, however, had barked so furiously before flying at Satan's ankles that both Satan and Monster had fled down the drive. Enough people witnessed this display of canine courage to secure Satan's exclusion and Monster's long-term suspension.

With Monster, Satan and Cara out of the way, children terrorized in the past came flooding back into school over the next few weeks, and attendance went up by twenty per cent.

Partner, who had acquired cult status by seeing off the forces of darkness, also proved a huge help in the battle against truancy. Each week, the class with the best attendance was rewarded with the task of looking after Partner for the next week. Partner adored children and, as long as Janna left her door open and he could pop back and check she was there, was quite happy. He was soon heading and pushing footballs around with his nose and delivering praise postcards, an idea Janna had picked up from Hengist, and certificates of merit. With one child holding one end of the skipping rope, and Charlie Topolski, who was in a wheelchair, holding the other, Partner learnt to skip. When he got tired, he would leap on to Charlie's knee, lick his cheek and curl up.

Because he had suffered himself, the little dog seemed to know instinctively how to comfort a lonely child. Bad readers grew in confidence when allowed to read to Partner. When a school photograph was taken, he took pride of place on Janna's knee.

38

Janna decided to postpone crossing the bridge of redundancies which, if it were anything like the bridge over the River Fleet in the rush hour, would take for ever. Right now she needed a head of English and drama.

In the past Janna had not felt confident enough to bring in her own people. Now Larks was so much happier, she felt justified in approaching Vicky Fairchild, an aptly named beauty of twenty-nine, who looked nearer sixteen. Vicky had long, dark hair, which fell in a thick fringe over melting, dark brown eyes and a pearly complexion, which grew more luminous with tiredness. She was incredibly slender, making the much shorter Janna feel like a bull terrier, and as a member of Janna's department at Redfords, had been an admirer and a huge support.

When Janna rang her to offer her head of drama, adding that as Vicky would have to give in her notice, she presumably couldn't start until the summer, Vicky instantly revealed she was leaving Redfords at Christmas.

'It was so horrible there without you, Jannie.' Then, in her sweet, breathy little girl's voice: 'And I haven't been well. Nothing serious.'

Vicky had also decided to leave because she'd planned to join her boyfriend, Matt, in Bermuda, but that hadn't worked out, so she'd simply adore to come to Larks.

'I love the Cotswolds and I've read all about you forming a partnership with Bagley—that's so cool,

I bet they've got a glorious theatre, and Hengist B-T is so inspirational. You've done so well, Jannie, you always know how to motivate people.'

'Larks is a very tough school,' confessed Janna.

'So was Redfords to start with. Oh Janna, thank you so, so much, it's such a compliment.'

The governors had been rather stuffy about the sacking of Cara—wasn't it rather a coincidence that Chief Inspector Gablecross had been in the building when one of Janna's favourites, Paris Alvaston, started acting up? Shouldn't Janna be advertising Cara's job? But the special interview panel of susceptible males—Sir Hugo, Sol the undertaker, Russell and Mike Pitts as deputy head—soon forgot their doubts when they clapped eyes on Vicky, glowing in a scarlet suit and long black boots as shiny as her hair.

'This is my dream job,' she told them. 'I really feel I can make a difference. A good drama production can unite an entire school, and raise their profile sky high in the area.'

'She was so interested in Larks,' said Russell Lambert, smoothing his pewter-grey hair, which, translated, meant that Vicky, briefed by Janna, knew Russell's name and occupation as head of the local planning committee and that the *Guardian* had once described him as 'Larks's personable chair'.

As part of the interview, Vicky had to be watched teaching a class. Janna craftily threw her to the Wolf Pack and troublemakers of Year Nine E. Thus Paris, Graffi, Feral and Johnnie sat in the front row, their dropped jaws resting on their trainers. Pearl, Kylie and even sassy Kitten Meadows were equally captivated as Vicky talked about the havoc caused by gang warfare and how Juliet had been let down by her parents and Friar Lawrence.

Then she showed them clips from the fights in the Leonardo di Caprio film, and suggested how brilliant it would be if Bagley and Larks did a joint *Romeo and Juliet* with Bagley as the Montagues and Larks as the Capulets.

'Wiv the Hon. Jack and Kylie Rose as Romeo and Juliet and both sets of parents going ballistic,' shouted Graffi to much laughter.

It was a happy, productive class. If Vicky could handle the Wolf Pack, reasoned the interview panel, she would take on anything, and promptly appointed her.

Effusive in her gratitude, Vicky floated off with Russell to meet Des Res, the smooth local estate agent who'd been so dismissive about Larks at the Winter Gardens dinner. Janna prayed Des wouldn't disillusion Vicky, but she rang ecstatically from the train.

'Des has found me a heavenly flat in the Close and we bumped into Ashton Douglas: such a darling. So is Des. What did you do to upset him, Jannie? I said I wouldn't hear a word against you.'

Lucky to have the kind of beauty that opened doors. Janna glanced at her increasingly lined face in her office mirror. She in turn was lucky to have a friend like Vicky to stick up for her.

'I'm so sad we didn't have more time to gossip,' went on Vicky. 'Everyone at Redfords is desperate to know how you're getting on.'

'How's Stew?' asked Janna, testing the emotional water.

'Sent his love. He's such a letch, pulled me on to

his knee at a party the other day, and he had this huge erection. I don't know how Beth puts up with him.'

Janna was surprised at the pain, as though a lovely Chippendale chair of her past had turned out to be a fake.

'I'm so excited about my new flat—and it's dirt cheap,' added Vicky.

*　　　*　　　*

Next day, Janna received a note through her letterbox at home from Des Res. He had several clients who'd be very interested in Jubilee Cottage, would she like a free valuation?

'Is this a hint?' wrote back Janna furiously. 'I'll give *you* a free assessment—you're an absolute shit.'

Having posted the letter, she got her hand stuck trying to retrieve it, and had to hang about until the postman came to open the pillar box.

As a result of Vicky's interview, it was decided that Bagley and Larks would stage a production of *Romeo and Juliet* during the spring term.

*　　　*　　　*

Christmas is the cruellest time for children in care. Bombarded constantly by images on television or in the high street of loving families and piles of gold-wrapped presents round glittering Christmas trees, aware that they have no parents or parents that can't look after them, the children rampage, rage, roar and weep at their loss. There is no refuge from their unhappiness.

342

Janna had tentatively suggested Paris should spend Christmas with her and Partner, with Aunt Lily and the Wolf Pack coming in on Christmas Day, but Paris had flatly refused, still mortified by Cara's cruel jibes about his ambition to become Janna's toyboy and terrified that, alone in the house, he might not be able to control his passion.

So Janna went to Yorkshire to stay with Auntie Glad and Paris remained at Oaktree Court, the sound and fury only redeemed by a navy blue sweater sent him by Janna, which he hid under his bed in case the other inmates nicked it, and by steeping himself in the beauty and sadness of *Romeo and Juliet*.

'Heaven is here,' he kept murmuring:

'Where Juliet/Janna lives, and every cat and
    dog
And little mouse, every unworthy thing,
Live here in heaven and may look on her;
    But Romeo/Paris may not.'

If he couldn't have Janna, at least let her be proud of him as Romeo.

39

Vicky arrived in January 2002, and cured truancy among boys almost overnight. Fathers suddenly seemed wildly keen to come in and paint classrooms. Rod Hyde, Ashton and Russell continually described Vicky as a breath of fresh air.

Janna was ashamed of feeling a little disconsolate. She knew her children at Larks were what mattered, but it would have been nice to have a man in her life, particularly as Hengist had been away and inattentive and even more particularly when Vicky came rushing into her office on a late, grey January afternoon, crying:

'Hengist Brett-Taylor has just dropped in and mistook me for one of the kids. He said girls at Larks were getting prettier and prettier, and isn't he drop-dead gorgeous?'

'So was Satan in *Paradise Lost*,' snapped Janna. Was she becoming a disagreeable old crone like Cara? 'Where is he?'

'Oh, he's gone. I said you were closeted with Ashton Douglas, so he said, "Rather Janna than me," and he'd ring you. So exciting we're starting casting *Romeo and Juliet* tomorrow.'

' "We?"' Janna tried to keep the indignation out of her voice.

'The drama departments: Jason Fenton and me. Emlyn Davies. And Hengist wants to have input.'

'So do I,' said Janna grimly.

*   *   *

The auditions took place in the General Bagley Room on a bitterly cold morning. Even with the play cut by nearly a half by Bagley's head of English, Piers Fleming, there were excellent parts not just for the two lovers but for Romeo's friends, Mercutio and Benvolio; Juliet's parents, Lord and Lady Capulet; Friar Lawrence; not to mention Juliet's volatile cousin, Tybalt, Prince of Cats; and Juliet's nurse.

Two hundred children had applied to take part but, as Year Ten and upwards would be occupied with GCSE and A level work through the spring term, it was decided to cast mostly from Year Nine, and name the production 'Cloud Nine'.

Determined Larks shouldn't let the side down, Janna, and Vicky to a lesser extent, had been giving Larks's pupils a crash course in the play and equipping them with speeches to learn or read out. Lit up by her subject, Janna inspired not just Paris, but many others to have a go.

Some had other motives. Kylie was anxious to snog the Hon. Jack again. Rocky went everywhere Kylie did. Pearl was desperate to do the make-up.

Feral wanted to see if Amber Lloyd-Foxe was as disturbing as he remembered. Graffi grasped any opportunity to see Milly. Aysha, forbidden by her heavy father, now back in England, to take part in such immoral frivolity, still longed to see Xavier again. Monster Norman, back in school but missing Satan Simmons and with a massive crush on Vicky, came along for the ride.

The judging panel, sitting at an oblong table armed with pens, notebooks and copies of the text, consisted of Emlyn, who'd been asked by Hengist to keep a lid on everything in case 'naughty little

345

Piers', head of English, went off at half cock. Or whole cock, reflected Emlyn, noticing the way Piers was snuggling up to Vicky, who was reeking of Trésor and ravishing in a raspberry-pink polo neck and short, tight black skirt. On Vicky's other side, whispering into her ear in an increasingly posh voice and looking very public school in a tweed jacket and dung-coloured cords, was Jason.

Piers and Jason had obviously bonded and would need some reining in, particularly where the budget was concerned, or they'd have David Linley designing Juliet's balcony and Stella McCartney her dresses. Beyond Piers was Janna; achingly aware she hadn't seen Hengist since the day of the balloon launch. He'd rung occasionally pleading overwork but now, grabbing the seat on her right, seemed unsettlingly enchanted to see her. Hengist was in fact eaten up with jealousy because his great rival and old boss David Hawkley, head of Fleetley, had been given a peerage in the New Year's Honours list, and been described in *The Times* that morning as the greatest headmaster of the twentieth/twenty-first century.

Hengist wanted to howl. Instead he stroked Partner, who was half asleep on Janna's knee, and said how he'd missed her and they must have lunch and catch up.

Pupils, meanwhile, hung around gossiping, waiting for the off. The Bagley Babes, Amber, Milly and Jade, all with ski tans paid for by Randal Stancombe, were sitting with Graffi, Feral, Paris, Kylie and Rocky. Jack Waterlane, Junior and Lando had parked themselves in the row behind, also inhabited by a sneering Cosmo, and Anatole the Russian, who was drinking neat vodka out of a

346

teacup.

As Dora Belvedon sidled in, Jade demanded:

'What are you doing here?'

'We were having sex education with Miss Sweet,' replied Dora. 'She was showing us how to roll condoms on to courgettes with the help of K-Y Jelly and got so embarrassed when Bianca asked her what fellatio was that she ran away and we got a free period. So Hengist said I could stay if I was extremely quiet.'

She plonked herself down between Cosmo and Anatole.

'You're incapable of being quiet,' spat Jade.

'Fellatio, fellatio, wherefore art thou fellatio,' sighed Cosmo, who wanted to conduct his beloved orchestra throughout the production but also to play the short, spectacular part of Tybalt.

Feral glanced up at a painting of rugby players leaping in the line-out to distract himself from Amber's thighs. Covered by barely six inches of fawn pleated skirt, they were utterly gorgeous.

'Silly using courgettes as willies,' went on Dora. 'We'll all get a shock when we discover the real thing's red, or pinkish, or purple. They're called zucchini in Italy, I believe.'

'Zucc orf,' said Paris, who'd been miles away in Verona.

To capture his Hooray Henry voice he'd been listening to a tape of Prince Charles; now he was trying to capture the nuances of Jack Waterlane and Lando France-Lynch's voices as they idly discussed snow polo.

'Christ, it's cold, throw another new boy on the fire,' grumbled Cosmo.

Outside, in sympathy, flakes of snow were

347

beginning to settle on General Bagley and his charger.

'All right'—Hengist helped himself to Vicky's tin of Quality Street—'let's get started, try and keep in alphabetical order. Kirsty, you're first.'

Kirsty Abbot, covered in spots and puppy fat, waddled on and delivered Juliet's speech: ' "Gallop apace, you fiery-footed steeds," ' as though she were taking the register at a primary school. Her audience tried not to laugh. Hengist let her run for sixty seconds.

'Thank you, Kirsty.'

'Useless,' scoffed Jade.

'I'd quite like to play Juliet. I learnt the part while I was skiing,' sighed Amber, 'hissing down the white mountains shouting: "Romeo, Romeo! wherefore art thou Romeo?" nearly setting off an avalanche.' She glanced at Feral under her lashes and yanked her skirt an inch higher.

'Paris Alvaston,' shouted Hengist.

I am Giovanni the lad, Paris was psyching himself up. I've gatecrashed the Capulets' ball, which is dripping with upmarket totty, including Rosaline, the beautiful cold bitch who's rejected me and is now wrapped round a rival. Suddenly I catch sight of little Juliet and realize everything I've felt before has been a mockery. When she leaves the party, I follow her, hanging around her garden, trampling on her father's plants.

As he walked to the centre of the room and turned, he could hear the thud of Partner's tail. For a few seconds he stood absolutely still, eyes shut as if in a trance, then, glancing up at the window, said as softly as the falling snow: ' "He jests at scars, that never felt a wound." '

And the room went still.

> 'But, soft! what light through yonder window
>   breaks?
> It is the east, and Juliet is the sun . . .
> See how she leans her cheek upon her hand!
> O! that I were a glove upon that hand,
> That I might touch that cheek.'

His voice was so filled with tenderness and longing, even Partner wagged his tail again. The only accompaniment was the tick of the clock. Paris then switched to the end of the play, when he discovered Juliet apparently dead in the Capulet tomb.

' "Eyes, look your last! Arms, take your last embrace!" '

Glancing at Janna, Hengist saw her face soaked in tears, and took her hand.

'We've got our Romeo,' he whispered.

As a burst of astonished clapping and foot-stamping greeted Paris's return to his seat, Feral turned to him in amazement.

'You was wicked, man.'

Graffi, Jack Waterlane and Lando thumped him on the back.

Cosmo, his sallow face alight with malice, was less impressed.

'Talk about Kev and Juliet,' he drawled. 'No wonder the Capulets were devastated their daughter had fallen for such a yob.'

'Shut up, Cosmo,' snapped Hengist.

Paris was unmoved.

'I can do it Hooray Henry, if you like.' Shoving one clenched fist into the palm of the other, talking through gritted teeth, he strolled back to the centre of the room. ' "But, sawft! what light through yonder window breaks?" ' and sounded so like Prince Charles, everyone howled with laughter.

Wriggling free, Partner scampered towards Paris, who gathered him up, burying his grin in Partner's fur.

'Well done, Paris,' called out Vicky. 'Those one-to-one rehearsals we've been doing have really paid off.'

A hit so early in the proceedings cheered everyone.

'Now we've got to find him a decent Juliet,' said Jason.

Next moment Alex Bruce rolled up, on whom Stancombe had been putting pressure.

'There's a certain young lady, Alex, who'd be devastated if she doesn't land the lead role in this production.'

Stancombe was threatening not to put up the umpteen million pounds to finance the science block. Alex didn't think he could swing his favourite Boffin Brooks to play Romeo, but he was determined Jade should get Juliet.

Walking into the General Bagley Room, he was furious to find Hengist, who'd claimed he was far too busy to show the Archbishop of some African state round the school, stuffing toffees and giggling with Janna Curtis.

Draining his teacup of vodka, Anatole's turn was next.

'He's got to have a decent part too,' murmured Hengist to Janna, 'so we get another jetload of caviar.'

Anatole was in fact very clever and loved Pushkin, Lermontov and Shakespeare as much as vodka and Marlboro Lights.

'I must give it some velly,' he announced and proceeded to make a wonderfully exuberant Mercutio, teasing Tybalt to fight a duel with him: ' "Tybalt, you rat-catcher, vill you valk?" '

Then, after Tybalt's sword had run him through, his audience, willing him to live, could feel his vitality ebbing away as he swore a plague on both Capulet and Montague houses.

Again, Janna fighting back tears, was hugged by an equally overjoyed Hengist.

'Darling, we've got our Mercutio, and vats of caviar. Anatole's father might even bring Mr Putin to the first night.'

Dora, who'd been given a mobile cum camera by Cosmo for Christmas, was taking pictures. Alex Bruce, not a fan of Anatole, had just bustled off when a heavily pregnant woman in a flowered smock, socks and Jesus sandals waddled in.

'Who's that?' hissed Graffi. 'She's about to pop.'

'Very appropriately she's called Poppet Bruce,' giggled Dora. 'That's Mr Fussy's wife. She is *so* pants. She teaches RE and never mentions poor Jesus. She's also nicknamed "Maternity *Won't* Leave" because she keeps having babies. Can you imagine sleeping with Mr Fussy that many times? Then everyone prays she'll never come back, but she always does. She's the worst person I know.'

'Worse than No-Joke Joan?' asked Amber, applying lip gloss.

'There'd be a photo finish,' said Dora darkly.

From his expression as Poppet approached the panel, looking eager, Hengist clearly felt the same

351

about her.

'Hope you don't mind my joining you,' she said. '*R and J* has such strong RE overtones with Friar Lawrence and an under-age marriage, I hope I may make suggestions.'

'You're welcome today,' said Hengist coolly, 'but too many cooks . . . I'd leave it to the production team.'

Poppet's lips tightened as she pressed her bulge against the table, waiting for someone to give her their seat. Terrified she might explode, Jason leapt to his feet.

'Come and sit down, Mrs Bruce.' Vicky patted Jason's chair. 'I'm Vicky Fairchild, Larks's head of drama. Of course we welcome input. We're planning to have Arab/Israeli overtones in the street fighting and put the play in modern dress with perhaps Friar Lawrence as a mullah.'

'Are we?' muttered Janna to Hengist, who muttered back: 'Friar Lawrence of Arabia.'

To Poppet's noisy approval and much clashing of bracelets, Boffin Brooks read two of Friar Lawrence's speeches in the high fluting voice of a curate at choral evensong.

'Excellent, excellent, Boffin, although I wish you'd read for Romeo.'

'Only with a recycled carrier bag over his head,' muttered Cosmo.

'Essential, in the bedroom scene and with the rise of STDs,' Poppet was now saying, 'that Romeo is shown to wear a condom.'

'And has a green courgette as a willy,' said Milly, 'which Friar Lawrence has grown in his garden.'

'Ah, here's Jade,' cried Boffin.

'Oh good,' said Poppet.

Jade Stancombe's legs were longer and her pleated skirt shorter even than Amber's; her cream silk shirt and blue cashmere jersey clung to her lovely rapacious body.

' "What's in a name? that which we call a rose By any other name would smell as sweet," ' began Jade, overacting appallingly.

Everyone tried not to giggle.

'She's dreadful,' whispered Dora.

' "Thou knowest the mask of night is on my face," ' went on Jade.

'And a whole lot of Clarins,' hissed Dora.

' "The more I give to thee, The more I have, for both are infinite," ' concluded Jade, rolling her eyes and clutching her cashmere bosom.

'Bravo, bravo! That was very convincing, Jade,' called out Poppet.

By contrast, Amber, with her hair piled up, her charming lascivious smile and air of insouciance, decided to go for Lady Capulet—'just for a laugh'—and was brilliant.

'You're booked,' called out Piers. 'Lady C was only twenty-seven.'

Emlyn wondered how long this was going to last. He had a two-hour period on Hitler and the Nazis and rugby practice for the first and second fifteen after that.

Ah, here was Feral. God, the boy was beautiful. There was a chorus of wolf whistles as he prowled in to audition for Tybalt, 'Prince of Cats', the furious playground bully who picks fights with everyone, who has comparatively few lines but huge impact on the play.

Coached by Paris until he was word perfect, not caring if he got the part, Feral kept exploding into violence:

> 'What, drawn, and talk of peace! I hate the
>   word,
> As I hate hell, all Montagues and thee:
> Have at thee, coward!'

He was booed, hissed, then cheered to the
stuccoed ceiling as he sauntered back, grinning, to
sit beside Amber.

Cosmo, whose heart was set on playing Tybalt,
was not amused.

'Why not give Cosmo Capulet?' Piers was
muttering across Janna to Hengist. 'He's the
biggest shit in the play, which figures, then Jack
Waterlane might just manage the Prince, if I cut his
lines to nothing.'

'Good idea,' said Hengist. 'Yes, Vicky?' as she
perched on the end of the table beside him.

'At the Capulet ball, why don't we get a
wonderful little dancer to play Romeo's ex-
girlfriend, Rosaline, and do a fantastically sexy
dance with Tybalt, if Feral gets the part—he's an
incredible dancer. Then, after being wildly jealous,
Paris takes one look at Juliet, and Rosaline is
forgotten. It makes the coup de foudre so much
more dramatic.'

That was my idea, thought Janna indignantly,
particularly when Hengist congratulated Vicky and
put forward little Bianca Campbell-Black, who was
being tipped as the next Darcey Bussell.

'Let's audition her. At least it would ensure
Rupert rolled up on the opening night.'

'Kylie could sing with the band at the ball,' went
on Vicky, 'she's got a lovely voice, and Cosmo's

354

Cosmonaughties must be the band.' She smiled winningly at Cosmo, who smouldered back. He must pull Vicky before the opening night.

Pearl, everyone agreed, would be in charge of make-up.

The auditions were nearly over.

Primrose Duddon of the huge boobs, who'd been taking a Grade 7 piano examination, was now making a pitch for the coveted comedy role of Juliet's nurse. Squawking, slapping her thighs, overacting worse than Jade, she reminded Janna of Sam Spink.

'Thank you, Primrose,' said Hengist after a minute.

They were down to the Ws and no one had been outstanding enough to play Juliet. They couldn't have Jade. Then Milly Walton wandered in. Like Amber, she'd only come along for a laugh and a chance to see Graffi. Her auburn curls were scraped back, her ski tan shiny and Graffi had kissed off all her lipstick in a nearby classroom.

' "My bounty is as boundless as the sea," ' she said thoughtfully. ' "My love as deep; the more I give to thee, The more I have, for both are infinite." '

Then she turned to Graffi and smiled and Graffi's shaggy black locks rose up on the back of his neck, and his toes turned over. Even Paris took his nose out of *The Iliad*.

Hengist turned to Janna, running the back of his hand down her cheek. 'That's our Juliet. Ruth, her mother, will be so pleased. She's always worried about overshadowing Milly.'

I can't help it, thought Janna, when he strokes me I have to purr.

355

Graffi, being Williams, was the last to go. He was still clapping Milly when a terrible thought struck him. If Paris got Romeo and Milly got Juliet, Paris would spend the whole play kissing and shagging her. Paris was much too good-looking. Graffi hated the thought of his woman making out with someone else.

He had been going to pitch for Benvolio but, nipping off into the nearby dining room, he grabbed a white damask napkin from the table laid for the African Archbishop, folded it into a triangle and wrapped it round his forehead, tying two ends behind his head. Then he grabbed a drying-up cloth from the kitchens, tying it round his waist. Leafing through the text, he found the place and bustled in as Juliet's nurse, the most irritating woman in literature, and brought the house down.

'The nurse in drag, why didn't we think of it?' said Hengist.

'We can cut a lot, but he's hilarious,' agreed Piers.

Then, after all the teasing and horseplay, Graffi's grief when he found his beloved Juliet apparently dead—the scene Primrose Duddon had dreadfully overplayed—was truly touching.

Hengist hugged Janna once more.

'Your boy's come good, darling.' Then, rising to his feet: 'Thank you very much, you all did very well. Think we've found some real stars. Go off and have lunch and we'll let you know.'

40

When the cast list was pinned on the noticeboards of both schools two days later, whoops of excitement and not a little jeering at Larks greeted the news that Paris would be playing Romeo; Feral, Tybalt; Graffi, the Nurse; and Kylie Rose both the Chorus and a blues singer at the Capulets' masked ball.

Janna was particularly gratified that Rocky had been cast as the Capulet heavy who bit his thumb (the Shakespearean equivalent of giving a middle finger) to the Montagues and Monster had landed the small, crucial part of the apothecary who sells deadly poison to Romeo, 'and probably will,' quipped Graffi. Monster was chuffed to bits at the prospect of his own chemist's, open on Sundays, with druggies hanging around. Other members of Year Nine would be filling in as members of the Watch, guards, street fighters, paparazzi and guests at the ball.

The casting over at Bagley caused more ructions. Primrose Duddon, much championed by Poppet and No-Joke Joan, was hopping that Graffi, not she, would be playing the Nurse.

'There are only four parts for young women in the play and the most characterful one's gone to a male student.'

Stancombe was outraged that Juliet had been given to Milly rather than Jade—and so was Jade, particularly when bloody Cosmo applauded the decision, claiming that by no stretch of the imagination or shrinking of the vagina could Jade

357

ever pass as a thirteen-year-old virgin.

Jade was, in fact, over Cosmo. Now it was Paris who robbed her of sleep. She detested indifference and loathed her fellow Bagley Babe Milly for landing the part and the chance to snog and more with Paris for the next two months, particularly as she herself had been cast as Lady Montague, Romeo's mother.

'And this play ain't *Oedipus Rex*,' mocked Cosmo.

Nor had Jade realized Lady Montague only had two lines.

After prolonged hysterics through splayed fingers, it was agreed she could swap with Amber and play the much longer and meatier part of Lady Capulet.

'Lady C was a sassy, glamorous woman in her late twenties,' Vicky explained to Jade. 'And as you're married to a rich peer, with a wedding and a funeral in the offing, there's scope for a fantastic wardrobe.'

Amber, who'd been bribed with a Joseph dress she could keep after the play, was only too happy to play Lady Montague instead, particularly since Pearl, now in charge of make-up, was threatening to add arsenic to the face powder of anyone who flirted with Feral.

Cosmo had been outraged only to be offered Capulet, rather than Tybalt, until he discovered subtleties and ironies in the part as Capulet changed from a kind, tolerant father and genial host to an evil bully. He was delighted that the Cosmonaughties would be playing at the Capulets' ball with Kylie as their lead singer. He intended to bill the school £1500 a night and as the group would be providing the music for a sizzling dance

358

routine performed by Feral and Bianca, Cosmo would be able to clock to the second the comings and goings of the divine Bianca.

Xavier, still terrified of Cosmo, and having learnt that Aysha's father had forbidden her to take part, had refused to get involved with the production. Everyone therefore was relieved Bianca was participating, which would at least ensure the presence of her crowd-pulling parents on the opening night.

'I can't wait to meet Rupert Campbell-Black,' gushed Vicky.

*   *   *

As soon as the play was cast Vicky, a genius at delegating—often a euphemism for extreme laziness—called a staff meeting to discuss what help she needed with the play.

The Larks art department was soon coaxed into designing scenery; Gloria into coaching Bianca and Feral in their dance routine; design and technology into producing costumes and props. Cambola was in cahoots with Cosmo over the music. Johnnie Fowler's father Gary, when sober, was an ace electrician and agreed to help with the lighting.

Once Gary Fowler was involved, other fathers felt impelled to follow suit. Most of them DIY experts, they were soon building and painting scenery, and their wives and girlfriends, having clocked Vicky and determined to keep an eye on their other halves, were giving a hand with costumes—over which there was fierce debate.

Anatole, who had sensational legs, wanted doublet and hose. This meant long skirts for the women, deduced Jade, which meant her even more sensational legs would be hidden, so she pushed for modern dress and won.

'Alex Bruce has a finger in every tart,' grumbled Anatole, who in the end was delighted to wear a Red Army mess jacket and tight black trousers with a red stripe down the side. Other boys in the cast wore paramilitary uniform: berets, peaked caps or red and white keffiyehs borrowed from fathers and masters. Chief Inspector Gablecross provided policemen's uniforms for the Watch. This meant more could be spent on female members of the cast.

Janna contented herself with giving lessons to Year Nine on the background of the play, pointing out its topicality; how innocent people were always caught up in the crossfire of war—particularly domestic violence.

' "Poor sacrifices of our enmity," Old Capulet called them, who'd caused a few in his time.'

Determined Larks would be word perfect, she also helped cast members learn their parts.

Rehearsals took place at Bagley every Tuesday and Wednesday after school from 4.00 to 5.30 p.m., and often in the lunch hour but only using the actors that were needed, which involved endless round trips for Wally.

Caught up in Vicky's enthusiasm, none of the teachers seemed to mind covering for her. Basket had a massive crush. Even Sam Spink was looking quite moony and presented Vicky with a pair of Piglet character socks, causing squeals of delight.

'Piglet is my most favourite character.'

Even though the school was a happier place, Janna herself was still ridiculously overstretched.

There was always some desperately crying child needing comfort over cigarette burns or cracked ribs. There was always some furious parent: 'My daughter was top in English last term, why isn't she playing Juliet?'

February brought incessant rain, pouring in through the roof on classes and on coursework, and the heating broke down. The classes not involved in the play were also very jealous. Janna tried to compensate by organizing trips to the ballet or ice skating or football, but she understood how they felt and found it hard to not feel jealous herself. Hengist, so adorable on casting day, had not been in touch since.

Vicky, on the other hand, flaunting those vogue words 'Transparency and Accountability', insisted on keeping her boss up to date with events, particularly late one evening, when she dropped in on a very cold, still-working Janna and announced:

' "My boys", as I call Emlyn, Piers and Jason, are working so hard. Hengist is constantly popping in to see if I'm OK and Sally Brett-Taylor is being so supportive. She's insisting on making Juliet's dress. We discussed it over a drink last night. Jade Stancombe's ordered a dress for the Capulet ball from Amanda Wakeley, which costs well into four figures, which made Ian Cartwright, the darling old bursar, frightfully uptight till I calmed him down.

'His wife Patience is a pet; she teaches riding at Bagley. His 'mistress of the horse', Hengist calls her, claiming Patience couldn't be anyone else's mistress because she's so plain, naughty man! But Patience has agreed to teach Paris to ride, so he can clatter up the gangway when he storms back from exile, believing Juliet's dead.'

'Paris is terrified of horses,' interrupted Janna icily. 'There's no way he should be forced to ride.'

Ignoring her, Vicky glanced over her shoulder:

'What are you wrestling with? Oh, figures. You ought to talk to Ian. Ian Cartwright. He'd be able to sort them out for you. He's been ringing round other independent bursars, checking their fees all week. I thought I might ask him and Patience to supper, and Hengist and Sally and Emlyn, of course. Emlyn is such a tower of strength. I hope you'll come too, Jannie. You ought to get out more, you look so tired.'

Stop patronizing me, Janna wanted to scream.

'I've no time for jaunts,' she snapped, turning back to her computer. 'Sorry, I must get on.'

The following week, however, Vicky forgot to book the bus for Year Ten's ice-skating trip. As a result, dreadful fights broke out. Not only were Year Nine having all the fun and the kudos, no one could organize anything for Year Ten.

When Janna summoned Vicky back from Bagley and bawled her out, Vicky sobbed and sobbed, rivalling the overflowing River Fleet, and fled into the dusk.

Arriving home from work around midnight, Janna was splashing up the path, lamenting yet again that rain had stopped stars, when Partner went into a frenzy of barking. Lily's cottage was in darkness. Catching sight of a huddled figure in the porch, Janna gasped with terror—had Cara escaped from prison?

'Who's there?'

She was overwhelmed with a divine smell of spring. It was a still-sobbing Vicky, thrusting out a huge bunch of narcissi.

'I'm so sorry to let you down, Jannie. I wanted you to be proud of me and put Larks on the map. I've been so thoughtless.'

So Janna opened a bottle and they ended up crying on each other's shoulders, and Vicky staying the night. But once again, as Janna made up a bed on the sofa, the goalposts changed.

'I never meant to make you jealous, Jannie. Has Hengist upset you? He can be so dismissive. Piers and Jason were saying only the other day, it's a shame you've had no input.'

Vicky looked so enchanting curled up under Janna's duvet, cuddling Janna's only hot-water bottle.

And I meant to slap you down for neglecting Year Ten and your tutor group, thought an exasperated Janna, and vowed once again to spend more time at Bagley.

*   *   *

But the following day, Ashton Douglas and Crispin Thomas summoned her to their plush S and C Services headquarters, overlooking an angry, grey and still rising River Fleet.

Even though the appointment was for midday, not a cup of coffee nor a drink was on offer. Janna's spirits were lowered by a huge wall chart, showing Larks at the bottom of the league tables of Larkshire schools.

Both men had big desks side by side. Crispin, who had gained another chin over Christmas and whose pink pullover had shrunk in the wash, was fussily arranging papers. Ashton, wafting his cloyingly sweet chloroform scent, his apple

363

blossom complexion flushed up by tropical central heating, had removed his jacket to flaunt his trim waistline.

S and C must be making a fortune, decided Janna, judging by the fuck-off lighting, the leather sofas in beiges and browns and the suede cushions to match suede cubes on which to rest your feet.

The pictures on the walls were even more impressive. The bunch of red tulips was certainly by Matthew Smith and the lookalike photograph of Beckham by Alison Jackson. Also blown up over the fireplace was the artwork for S and C's latest logo of a grown-up's hand on a child's back both propelling forward and comforting: a symbol of support and challenge, except the hand was placed a little too low. Janna shuddered.

Ashton was examining his very clean fingernails, the diamond set in the gold band on his third finger catching the light.

'This is wather embarrassing, but we feel you ought to spend less time at Bagley in future.'

Janna's bag tipped over, spilling out biros, lipstick, hairbrush, perfume, Bonios for Partner and diary on to the thick pale beige carpet.

'I've hardly been near the place,' she squeaked, dropping to the floor to claw back her belongings. 'I've been too busy.'

'Maybe.' Ashton sighed with pleasure. 'But I'm afwaid people are talking about you and Hengist.'

Retrieving a tampon from under Crispin's desk, Janna banged her head.

'I know you feel demonized by the *Gazette*,' went on Ashton, 'but you have a good fwiend in Col Peters. These are the pictures he refused to publish, and instead handed over to us.'

Playing the ace, Ashton produced out of his crocodile notecase a photograph of Janna in Hengist's arms, her cheek rammed against his, her eyes closed in ecstasy. She was wearing a dark blue shirt; a painting of leaping rugby players could be seen in the background.

'This is ridiculous,' she protested. 'This was at an audition surrounded by hundreds of teachers and children. Who took it, for heaven's sake?'

'We're not at liberty.'

'Well, I want to know. Hengist and I were knocked out—Paris Alvaston had just auditioned. We'd found our Romeo. You'll see how brilliant he is on the opening night.'

'Rather unbridled enthusiasm,' observed Crispin. God, he was loving this. 'Particularly when you put it beside this,' and pointed to another shot of Hengist's hand stroking Janna's cheek and then two cuttings of her smiling adoringly up at Hengist at the Winter Gardens civic dinner and on the air-balloon day.

'The cumulative effect is unfortunate,' said Ashton sympathetically. 'We understand. It's so easy for lonely unmarried women of a certain age to develop these cwushes. Hengist is very charismatic, but Sally Bwett-Taylor is such a good egg.'

'There is absolutely nothing between Hengist and me,' said Janna furiously, her face feeling as though it had just come out of the microwave. 'Head teachers have common problems and practice to discuss. Hengist has been genuinely kind and constructive.'

'In future I'd go to Wod Hyde,' urged Ashton. 'He is after all your official mentor. You don't want

365

tittle-tattle to sabotage the excellent work Larks's teachers are doing at Bagley. Vicky Fairchild is first class. Give her her head.'

'I am her Head,' spat Janna.

'No need to be facetious. Just leave Hengist alone.'

Blinded by tears, Janna fumbled her way out to the car park. Ironically, Hengist seemed to feel the same as S and C; he hadn't been in touch for weeks.

Partner, leaping on his hind legs, grinning and scrabbling in ecstasy, body shaken by frenziedly wagging tail, stopped her chucking herself into the swift-flowing river.

You're the only male in my life from now on, she vowed grimly. Vicky can get on with it.

41

Paris was missing Janna desperately. He had to be back in the children's home by eight and was thus denied any of the jolly after-rehearsal get-togethers. He'd invested so much in the play because he thought Janna would be there all the time. He longed to talk to her about his part. Vicky never listened and wanted to impose her own views. Graffi was so busy painting scenery, designing posters, camping it up as the Nurse and snogging Milly, he had abandoned Janna's mural which was nearly finished anyway, so the tea parties at Jubilee Cottage had been scrapped.

The Bagley Babes all fancied Paris like mad, but miffed he was always reading and wouldn't respond, they took the piss out of him instead. Milly was convinced he'd been put off by her costume, which was white muslin, high-waisted, sleeveless, with a buttercup-yellow sash like a little girl's party dress.

'It's so drippy. It's only because Sally Brett-Taylor's made it and Vicky's so far up her,' stormed Milly.

Sally in turn was charmed by Vicky, disloyally thinking how nice it would be to have a daughter with whom you could discuss girly things and who didn't always disagree. She had invited Vicky to supper with Emlyn the night Ireland thrashed Wales, and Emlyn, unable ever to envisage his country's rugby revival, arrived utterly legless. Hengist had had to drive him home before the crème brûlée and let him into his flat. Sally only just stopped herself unbuttoning to Vicky that Emlyn wasn't really the ideal son-in-law. Emlyn also seemed the only male in Bagley not besotted with Vicky. The bursar was making a complete idiot of himself hanging round the rehearsal rooms.

But, as February gave way to March, most of the cast were shaping up splendidly. Feral as Tybalt was an unexpected, if reluctant, star.

' "Why, uncle, 'tis a shame", such a crap line,' he grumbled to Paris.

'Think of Uncle Harley.'

'Everything he does is a shame,' shuddered Feral, then, launching back into his part: ' "To strike him dead, I hold it not a sin." '

He was gratified one of the highlights of the evening was going to be his dance with Bianca Campbell-Black at the Capulets' ball.

Normally football was Feral's passion. At every opportunity, down on the grass went the fleece, down twelve feet away went the school bag. Instantly a ball would be kicked between them. But, having agreed *Dirty Dancing* was their favourite film, Bianca and Feral practised their sexy Argentine tango routine, with Bianca rubbing her legs up Feral's, with increasing excitement.

After one particularly successful rehearsal, during which the room seemed to fill up with lustful schoolboys who should have been in lessons and an accompanying Cosmo broke two strings of his guitar, Feral sloped off for a quick game of football while Bianca returned to the changing rooms.

No one was about for her to chatter to—a great deprivation for Bianca. She was just wriggling out

368

of her sweaty leotard when she felt herself grabbed from behind.

'You shouldn't dance so sexily,' said a smoky, bitchy voice as hands crept over her little breasts.

It was Cosmo, who was very strong. Next moment, he'd yanked her against him, clamping her between his legs and bending over her shoulder, forced his lips down on hers.

'Lemme go.' A revolted Bianca, despite writhing like an eel, was unable from this angle to knee him in the groin, even when he plunged his tongue deep down her throat. Retching, gagging, she struggled harder.

Then she heard a crash as a bench was knocked over and Cosmo was dragged off and punched in the face, sending him toppling backwards into a rail of dresses. Feral then opened the window and, gathering Cosmo up, hurled him out on to Sally Brett-Taylor's precious bed of spotted hellebores.

'Keep your filthy hands off her,' he howled. Tugging the window shut, he turned to Bianca, who was struggling to replace her leotard. Seizing Jade Stancombe's big soft dark blue towel, Feral wrapped it round her frantically shuddering body.

'You OK, little darlin'?'

'Yes. No.' Fighting back the tears, Bianca rubbed the back of her hand across her bruised mouth again and again. Cosmo's tongue had been so disgustingly hard, wet and bobbly underneath, her mouth felt raped.

Feral put an arm round her, then, flourishing an imaginary sword with the other: ' "To strike him dead, I hold it not a sin." '

' "Why, uncle, 'tis a shame",' mumbled Bianca.

'It is too.' Feral felt so sorry for her. 'Let's go and

find your teddy bear.'

He tried to joke and Bianca had giggled through her tears, but he wanted to kill Cosmo. Bianca was only twelve, but holding her had released some highly unavuncular feelings in Feral.

He so wished Janna was here to advise him and steady the ship.

Vicky seemed to read his mind. As they were waiting in the drizzle for the minibus back to Larks, she could be heard grumbling to Cambola: 'I can't understand why Janna opted out of this production. When she was at Redfords, she never missed a rehearsal. I suppose she was there longer and felt closer to the pupils.'

Seeing the hurt in the children's faces, Cambola snapped that Janna was frantically busy.

'She was never too busy at Redfords,' said Vicky smugly.

*　　　*　　　*

Pearl, meanwhile, was taking her responsibility for make-up very seriously and had managed to persuade Paris to let her dye his pale eyelashes and apply dark brown eyeliner before he and Milly were photographed by Cosmo for Graffi's posters.

Cosmo would never forgive Feral, but he was enough of a perfectionist to want to get the best out of Paris and Milly. The results had an unearthly beauty, and posters of the star-crossed lovers were soon plastered all over Larkminster. Tickets designed by Graffi, with a dagger plunged into a bleeding heart, were also selling well.

Paris, as a result, was being teased rotten both at Larks and Oaktree Court, particularly when the inmates got hold of a poster, gave it golden ringlets and a scarlet rosebud mouth and scrawled 'Homo and Juliet, good on you, Woofter' underneath.

'You haven't arrived until you've been graffitied,' Graffi told him airily.

*   *   *

At the beginning of March, three weeks before the opening night, Year Nine and Bagley Lower Fifth had to decide what GCSE subjects they wanted to take in 2004. Ninety per cent opted to take drama with Vicky, almost as many as those who wanted to take history with Emlyn Davies. After such a vote of confidence, Vicky felt entitled to put pressure on Paris to gallop up the gangway to the stage and when he baulked, to suggest they use a stand-in.

'Cosmo, Lando, Junior, Jack Waterlane, all great riders, could put on your jacket and breeches, thunder up the gangway in the half-light, chuck their reins to Dora, jump across the orchestra on to the stage and exit right into Capulet's tomb. Next scene, which is the interior of Capulet's tomb, you barge in having reappropriated your clothes.'

'That would work,' mused Jason.

If Emlyn were here, Vicky wouldn't have dared, thought Paris, who was at breaking point.

'I'm not having a stand-in and I'm not doing this fucking play,' he snarled and walked out.

Dora caught up with him halfway down the drive and took his hand. 'Just come and meet Mrs Cartwright—the bursar's wife—she's lovely. They live in the Old Coach House, through the woods.'

The faded leaves on the path matched the brown ploughed fields; other fields were the same pale fawn as the sheep that had been grazing them. The woodland floor was turned emerald by wild garlic leaves.

Dora led a grey-faced, frantically trembling Paris into the yard, where hunters and polo ponies with clipped manes stared out over the bottle-green half-doors. A smell of leather and dung made him want to throw up.

'This is Mrs Cartwright,' said Dora. 'She's a brilliant horsewoman.'

Paris looked unenthusiastically at the big-boned, large-nosed maroon-complexioned woman in the clashing scarlet Puffa.

'Hello Paris,' brayed Patience Cartwright, holding out a rough mottled hand that had never seen a manicure. 'I hear you're a wonderful Romeo.'

Not only did she look like a horse, she sounded like one.

'I don't ride,' he said icily.

'This is Beluga,' said Dora. 'He's extremely kind and loves people, unlike Loofah, my pony'—she stroked the brown and white nose of a small skewbald leaning meanly out of the next box—'who doesn't.'

'The thing to do is to get on Beluga's back in the middle of the field for a few moments,' advised Patience, 'so if you fall orf it's nice and sawft.'

Paris quarter-smiled. At least he could bone up on his Hooray accent.

'Here's a carrot to sawften him up,' giggled Dora.

The saddle was very slippery and the ground below seemed miles down in Australia, but Beluga had a thick black mane to cling on to. Beluga was also lazy and devoted to Plover, Patience's mare,

372

and therefore quite happy plodding round the fields on a lead rein.

After days of downpour it was a wonderfully gentle, sunny day. Woodpeckers laughed inanely in trees already glowing russet, amethyst and warm brown with swelling buds; the singing birds exhorted him not to be frightened. Very gradually Paris unfroze; sweat dried on his pinched face.

'You're doing really well,' encouraged Patience. 'If ever you want him to stop, just pull very gently on the reins.'

A cock pheasant waddled across their path, showing off ginger, scarlet and bright green plumage and a neat white collar.

'The shooting season's over. Such a relief for him,' said Patience.

'Just like Boffin Brooks as Friar Lawrence,' observed Paris. 'Same silly beaky face and fussy walk.'

Patience brayed with laughter.

'Boffin's a little beast.' She lowered her voice furtively as though a passing rabbit might grass her up. 'He drives my husband Ian mad suggesting to Alex Bruce ways the school could economize. He'd have the stables turned into an IT suite, whatever that might be.'

'Can we go a bit faster?' asked Paris.

'Of course, if you're sure.'

Paris nodded, taking a firmer grip on Beluga's mane.

Patience bypassed the trot, which was bumpy, going straight into a much smoother canter up a green ride flanked with hazels. Paris gave a gasp of terror, but by the time they'd reached the gate on the crest of the hill, he'd settled into the rhythm.

'Can we canter back to the stables?' he asked twenty minutes later.

And they did.

Paris slid off, trembling violently, hanging on to Beluga as his legs collapsed like plasticene. 'Thanks, horse.'

'Awfully well done,' said Patience. 'You're really good with animals. Dora was saying how Elaine Brett-Taylor loves you.'

'Well done,' said Dora, who'd been up in the hayloft watching through binoculars. 'Looks as though you've ridden for ever.'

'Different ball game clattering up the gangway surrounded by a yelling audience,' grumbled Paris.

'We've got three weeks,' said Patience soothingly. 'Come and have a cup of tea.'

She led him into a messy kitchen, with bridles hanging from a clothes horse, plates and mugs still in the sink and ironing, reminding him of Janna's in-tray, rising to the ceiling.

'Christ!' Paris had caught sight of a photograph of a stunningly beautiful girl on the dresser.

'That's my sister, Emerald,' announced Dora, 'and to muddle you completely, she's Mrs Cartwright's daughter.'

How on earth could a dog like Patience give birth to something so exquisite, wondered Paris, then blushed when Patience read his mind and laughed.

'They always say the fairest flowers grow on the foulest dung heaps, but actually we adopted Emerald and when she sought out her natural mother, she turned out to be Dora's mother, Anthea.'

'The old tart,' chuntered Dora, 'having sex before marriage.'

'Dora,' reproved Patience, seeing Paris grinning.

'We adopted both Emerald and Sophy, who's a schoolmistress,' explained Patience, 'and longs to move to the country. She's a great friend of your headmistress, Janna Curtis. I keep hoping to see her at rehearsals so I can introduce myself and ask Janna to supper.'

Glancing out of the window towards Bagley, appreciating the extent and complexity of its spread of buildings, Paris felt himself flushing as he always did when Janna's name was mentioned.

'I must go,' said Dora wistfully. 'Joan's taking prep. Where's Northcliffe?'

'Our golden retriever,' Patience explained to Paris. 'Gone to work with Ian.'

'Cadbury's still living with the beagles,' sighed Dora. 'I wish he could live here.'

'Not sure if Northcliffe would like that, he's awfully territorial. I'll ask Ian.' Patience had taken off her red Puffa to reveal a purple knitted jersey on inside out.

After Dora had gone, she made very strong tea and toast and then surreptitiously scraped mould off some pear jelly entitled 'Poppet Bruce 2000', before discovering to her relief some chocolate spread and a coconut cake stuffed with glacé cherries.

'Were they very young when you adopted them?' asked Paris.

'*Very*, we were so lucky, and they've both got heavenly babas of their own now. It's so crucial for adopted people to have their first blood relation.'

Euphoric that he'd conquered his phobia of horses, Paris, over a second cup of tea and third slice of cake, found himself most

375

uncharacteristically unbuttoning to Patience about his fruitlessly advertising for a family.

'There was no takers. Guess I looked too likely to knife them in their beds.'

'That's horrible.' Patience looked as though she was going to cry. 'Anyone would feel privileged and overjoyed to have you for a son. Everyone thinks so highly of you at Bagley. Your Romeo is the talk of the staffroom.'

Paris shrugged.

'I do hope'—Patience blushed an even darker maroon—'you'll drop in and see us, like Dora does, even if you don't want to go on riding.'

Seeing Paris's eyes straying to a bookshelf crammed with poetry, much more thumbed than the cookery books, she explained: 'My husband loves poetry. Matthew Arnold's his favourite. I'm awfully badly read, but Arnold wrote a lovely poem called 'Sohrab and Rustum', which has a sweet horse in it called Ruksh who sheds real tears'— Patience's voice trembled—'when his master unknowingly slays his own son in battle. You must read it.'

'Horses cry when their masters die in the *Iliad*,' said Paris, reaching out his hand for more coconut cake, then pausing.

'Please have it,' begged Patience. 'We used to say whoever had the last piece got a handsome husband and a thousand a year, which wouldn't go very far these days.'

'I could use it,' said Paris.

'I do hope you'll have another go on Beluga. I think you're a natural.'

42

Gradually as March splashed into its third week and Bagley was lit up by daffodils, the excitement began to bite. Wally borrowed a lorry to transport props and scenery made by Larks parents, which included a four-poster painted with flowers for Juliet and a wrought-iron balcony: 'More suited to a Weybridge hacienda,' said Hengist, 'but perfect for sixteenth-century Verona.'

The dress rehearsal in front of pupils from both schools was scheduled for Wednesday evening; the big night for governors, parents and friends would take place on Thursday.

Larks participants spent Wednesday afternoon over at Bagley taking part in a dry run to fine-tune performances, scene shifts and lighting. Glimpses of Paris's naked back view would add excitement to the bedroom scenes. Johnnie Fowler, in charge of his dad's lighting, was determined to catch Paris full frontal.

Amber, meanwhile, was shouting at Alex Bruce:

'I'll pay for my own fucking dress, it was only five hundred pounds,' which is the difference between them and us, thought Graffi, who'd never been paid by Junior for Shining Sixpence's winnings.

All the cast were jittery and Vicky didn't help by ringing in with a migraine. 'So sorry, I've overdone things. I'll try and stagger in later.'

Emlyn took a deep breath and counted to ten.

'Right, let's get started. We all know this is a play about conflict rather than love.'

'Why can't Miss come in instead of Vicky?'

sighed Kylie.

The day continued full of spats.

Jade Stancombe, insisting on wearing four-inch heels, fell down the stairs. A waiter carrying full glasses of coloured water bumped into a bodyguard, soaking the stage, which resulted in Feral and Bianca nearly doing the splits in their tango. Juliet's bed collapsed during her night of passion with Romeo. Everyone burst out laughing when Feral's moustache fell off during a fight.

The instant Juliet's bed had been repaired and her wedding night resumed, Poppet Bruce marched in brandishing a packet of rainbow-coloured Durex.

'R and J are having underage sex; Paris must be publicly seen to be wearing a condom.'

'Surely that's wardrobe's department?' grinned Jason.

'The audience won't see him in the dark,' snarled Emlyn. 'Get out, Poppet.'

'That is not how you should address your deputy team leader's wife,' spluttered Poppet, then, as Emlyn rose to his mighty height, flounced out slamming the door.

'Romeo, Romeo,' sighed Milly, 'wherefore fart thou, Romeo,' producing more giggles.

'Shut up, Milly,' howled Emlyn.

Paris gritted his teeth. His ride up the aisle and his last impassioned speech were still to come.

' "The day is hot, the Capulets abroad . . ." ' Junior Lloyd-Foxe, who had the part of Benvolio, delivered his best and most ominous line.

Next moment, Feral and Cosmo were on the floor, howling, punching, clawing like tomcats.

'Take your hands off her, you sick bastard.'

378

'Don't give yourself airs, you fucking golliwog.'

'Don't black Cosmo's eyes,' begged Jason as Feral lunged and missed.

'Pack it in,' yelled Emlyn and, when they didn't, he emptied a dusty fire bucket over them. This, as they retreated, spluttering and swearing, did nothing to aid Paris's concentration.

Somehow he managed to gallop Beluga up to the orchestra pit and keep control when Cosmo, to spook the horse, deliberately launched the brass into a deafening tantivy. Chucking his reins to Dora, Paris managed to leap off without touching the floor, run up the plank laid across the pit and dive into Juliet's tomb to a round of applause.

'I don't need no fucking stand-in,' he hissed at Cosmo.

Now Juliet lay before him in her coffin and the half-light. He had just launched into his impassioned soliloquy about the colour still in her lovely face, when he realized Milly, bet by Amber, had slipped on a red Comic Relief nose, and raised a hand to hit her.

'Don't,' thundered Emlyn, so Paris swore at him, spat on the floor and stalked off the set.

'You stupid bitch,' yelled Emlyn. 'How dare you wind him up like that?'

'It was only a joke to loosen him up,' wailed Milly. 'It's not me he's kissing, it's Juliet. I'm fed up with pandering to him."Paris, Paris, don't upset Paris." What about my needs?'

Graffi, in his Nurse's costume, rushed on to the stage and flung his arms round Milly. 'There, there, lovely, it's OK. Don't bully her,' he shouted at Emlyn.

Milly was touched but rather wished her knight

in shining armour wasn't wearing drag and a grey granny wig.

'But soft what brick through yonder window breaks,' intoned Amber.

Although he was consistently bottom in maths, Jack Waterlane had worked out that between appearances on stage, he and Kylie had at least an hour unaccounted for. He had therefore whipped her into the biology lab and hung his red jacket on a skeleton, then they both froze as Poppet Bruce, exuding bossy bustle in her eco-monitor role, rushed by flicking off the lab lights and seemingly giving them her blessing.

*　　　*　　　*

'Gosh, we've just had underage sex,' sighed Jack as he lay in Kylie's arms. 'My father had to have sex before polo matches—relaxed him—'spect I'll win an Oscar now. I love you, Kylie Rose.'

'I love you, Jack,' said Kylie.

*　　　*　　　*

It was an hour to the dress rehearsal. No one could find Paris. He hadn't even been to make-up. Everyone was panicking.

'Sometimes he disappears on trains for days,' said Feral, then, turning on Amber and Milly: 'Why'd you wind him up, you stupid cows?'

*　　　*　　　*

Patience Cartwright found Paris in Beluga's box, throwing up into an empty water bucket, wiping his

380

face with hay from the rack. At first he wouldn't speak and carried on retching, but when Patience brought him a glass of water, he told her about the red nose, mumbling that he found it so hard without Janna.

'She got me into Shakespeare. Explained things. But she hasn't been to rehearsals for weeks, 'spect she's too busy.'

He slumped against Beluga, his face grey and defeated.

'She probably doesn't want to cramp Vicky's style.'

'Vicky's a stupid bitch.'

Patience felt ashamed at her elation; Ian was besotted with Vicky.

'You've got to be terrified to be any good,' she reassured Paris. 'I once competed at the Horse of the Year Show, and I was so worried about letting Bentley, my horse, down, I spent three hours in the lav. They had to drag me out and then we won our class. I crept into the rehearsal room the other day: you're miles the best in the cast. I'm sure Milly was trying to relax you.'

'I can't kiss her tasting of puke.'

'I always keep spare toothbrushes and toothpaste in case a pupil needs it, and Ian confiscated some peppermint chewing gum yesterday, you can have that.'

'You weren't just saying I was OK?'

He looked so forlorn and despairing, Patience longed to hug him. 'You'll be sensational.'

As soon as he'd gone, Patience called Emlyn. 'Paris is on his way back. I don't mean to interfere, but he needs Janna, he's so alone.'

The dress rehearsal was a great success. When the cheers and clapping finally died down, the cast yelled for Mr Davies: 'Attila! Attila! Attila!' They stamped their feet until, loose-limbed and bleary-eyed, Emlyn shambled on to the stage, where Graffi presented him with a big bottle of red, 'from Larks as a mark of our gratitude'.

'Mr Davies builds us up,' shouted Rocky. 'He puts the boot in, but he's always looking for fings to praise.'

'Why, thank you, Rocky.' Emlyn was touched. 'What about Miss Fairchild and Mr Fenton?'

'We've got fings for them tomorrow, but you do all the work,' said Pearl.

Emlyn was so tired, he would have loved to unwind over a few beers with his friend Artie Deverell, the head of modern languages. Instead he threw the bottle of red into his dirty Renault Estate and drove over to Larks where, although it was after eleven, lights were still blazing.

Inside he thought what a good job Janna was doing. The building might be falling down, but newly painted walls and noticeboards were covered in praise postcards, brightly coloured work and crammed with pictures of the children and their activities: a new baby brother yesterday, a birthday today. Along the corridor, *Romeo and Juliet* posters proudly flaunted yellow 'sold-out' stickers.

Janna was in her office, squealing with frustration as she tried to put back a cupboard, which, as a result of the damp, had fallen off the wall. Her fathers weren't as diligent about do-it-yourself when Vicky wasn't around.

Nor was putting back screws without a screwdriver very easy. 'Bugger, bugger, bugger,' yelled Janna, as a 50p piece slipped out of the groove. The handle of her tweezers had been no more successful.

Then she shrieked as a dark figure filled the doorway. Partner woke up, went berserk, then, recognizing Emlyn's soft Welsh accent, dragged his blue rug across the floor in welcome.

'Fucking cupboard.' Janna gave it a kick. 'How did it go?'

'Wonderfully. They all did so well. Your kids presented this to me.' He dumped the bottle of red on Janna's desk. 'Why don't you open it?'

Rootling round in Wally's toolbox, Emlyn then located four big screws and a box of matches. Putting matches in the holes to make them smaller, he banged in the screws with a hammer.

'That is so cool,' cried an amazed Janna as the cupboard stayed put.

'Can't beat a good screw.' Emlyn took the corkscrew from her.

Noticing the bags under his bloodshot eyes, she said apologetically, 'You must be shattered.'

'No more than you,' said Emlyn, noticing the bags under her bloodshot eyes.

'Why the hell do we teach?' asked Janna, getting two glasses out of a second cupboard.

Emlyn was reading the letter on her laptop.

'Dear Mrs Todd, I thought you'd be pleased that Charlie wrote a wonderful essay on Oliver Cromwell this morning.'

The wine was unbelievably disgusting. If they hadn't needed a drink so badly, Emlyn would have chucked it down the bog.

'I don't think Larks children have much pocket money,' said Janna defensively.

'It was a sweet thought.' Emlyn collapsed on the sofa which still bore Pearl's ink stain. Partner jumped on to his knee.

'Now tell me how it really went.'

When he'd finished, Emlyn said, 'You should have been there.'

'I'm coming tomorrow.'

'Not good enough. I'm told you were always in the thick of things at Redfords. Why have you backed off?'

'I'm frantic,' said Janna defensively.

'Everyone's frantic.'

'Everyone adores Vicky.' Janna tried not to sound bitter. 'I put people's backs up.'

'Vicky lacks your vision,' said Emlyn flatly, 'and she doesn't understand the play. Jason's been terrific, but it's you the kids love. They're dying to show you how far they've come, that they're carrying out your ideas—which Vicky claims are hers.'

'How was Paris?' A defiant, shame-faced Janna wanted to change the subject.

'All to pieces; nearly lost it. Amber, Milly and Jade are fed up they're getting no reaction from him. Why did you stop coming?'

Getting up, he looked at the school photograph. Hands shoved into his pockets, he showed off a surprisingly taut, high, beautiful bottom. He had terrific shoulders too and the bulldog face had charm if you liked bulldogs. Janna longed to throw herself into his arms and tell him how Ashton and Crispin had warned her off. Instead she said, 'I've got a school to save.'

Emlyn could see how reduced in bounce she was and longed to comfort her. In the old days he'd have taken her home for a joyful romp in bed. But there was the cool, white body of Oriana to consider. 'I have been faithful to thee, Cynara! in my fashion.'

Janna anyway was too vulnerable and too nice for half measures.

'Let's go and have supper,' he said instead. 'I know somewhere still open.'

'I've got far too much to do,' snapped Janna, 'but thanks all the same.'

'We all miss you,' said Emlyn as he went out. 'Particularly Paris.'

Returning to Jubilee Cottage, Janna and Partner wandered into the garden. The rain, at last, had stopped and the stars for the first time in days were scattered across the sky like a sweep of white daffodils.

'Give me my Romeo,' she cried out:

'And, when he shall die,
Take him and cut him out in little stars,
And he will make the face of heaven so fine
That all the world will be in love with night.'

Oh Hengist! Oh Emlyn! She was so lonely for love and a pair of arms round her.

Even though it was nearly midnight, she rang first Mr Blenchley and then Nadine, Paris's social worker.

'I've got a few spare tickets. It'd mean so much to Paris if you came along.'

43

Paris was gratified next day to get lots of cards, including one from Aunt Lily and another from Nadine, delivered to school by hand: 'So looking forward to seeing you tonight.' Normally she wasn't remotely interested in his academic progress, only his social welfare. There was even a card from the children in the home: 'Sorry we took the piss.'

Patience sent him a silver horseshoe and some chewing gum. Dora had bought him a fluffy black cat, which, entitled 'Dora's pussy', became the subject of much ribaldry. Cadbury sent him a good-lick card.

After last night's success, the cast were cheerful and over-excited.

'You've got to calm down,' Emlyn kept telling them.

It was a glorious evening, with the setting sun flaming the flooded playing fields below a vermilion and Cambridge-blue sky, which was considered a good omen, as the Montagues' uniform was flame red and the Capulets' pale blue.

All afternoon Pearl worked her magic on the cast, particularly Jade, who couldn't stop admiring herself in the mirror. Amber was less sanguine.

'Pearl's still convinced Feral's got the hots for me,' she whispered to Milly, 'but frankly he can't take his big eyes off Bianca C-B. So humiliating to be cuckolded by someone from the Lower Fourth.'

' "There's no trust, No faith, no honesty in men," ' sighed Milly.

Amber was not cast down. Both Eton and Radley boyfriends had sent her huge bunches of flowers and their undying love.

'I'd still like a night with Feral,' she confessed. 'Do you think Paris is gay?'

'That could explain it,' said Milly in delight. 'All the time he's fantasizing I'm Feral, not me. I still fancy him rotten.'

'One can't not,' agreed Amber.

'He stares and stares but it's to observe, not to lust. If Sally Bloody-Taylor hadn't forced me into such a prissy dress with that gross sash, I might have scored.'

*　　　*　　　*

Paris was shivering uncontrollably. Thank God he wore a flimsy white shirt in the first act, so the circles of sweat wouldn't show. Already he could hear strains of Tchaikovsky as the orchestra warmed up.

*　　　*　　　*

Emlyn was everywhere, calmly encouraging, dealing with last minute crises. 'No, the Prince can't wear gel, Jack, go and wash it out.'

As Mr Khan had shot off to Pakistan on business, Aysha had bravely applied to be a stage hand. Hearing the news from Bianca, Xavier Campbell-Black had applied as well. They had only been working with the cast for a week. Occasionally Xav's hand touched Aysha's as they shifted balconies, beds and coffins around. There were twenty scenes to be set up. They were both very nervous. Aysha looked more beautiful than ever in a shalwar kameez of midnight-blue silk.

Xav had avoided Cosmo and his minions since they tried to drown him in the bog. Now as he and Aysha made sure that Paris's plank was in place, stacked in a corner of the pit ready to form a bridge across the orchestra, Cosmo shouted nastily:

'Good thing you and Miss Khan are black, so the audience needn't see you when you're shifting scenes.'

Next moment, Feral had grabbed Cosmo's dark curls, holding a knife to his throat. 'Take that back,' he hissed.

'I'll have that.' Emlyn grabbed the knife. He also confiscated Anatole's vodka. 'You can get drunk after you're killed off.'

' "Why, uncle, 'tis a shame",' grumbled Anatole.

Jade had got forty-eight red roses from her father, and a huge bunch of pink lilies that she'd sent herself and made a lot of fuss wondering who they came from. Stancombe also sent yellow orchids to Milly. Milly's mother was not as biddable as Stancombe would have liked. He had wanted to arrive with her in the helicopter this evening, but perversely she insisted that, as a governor, she should make her own way.

'When's Hengist going to make me a governor?' grumbled Stancombe.

'When a vacancy occurs. No one resigns because meetings are such fun,' said Mrs Walton.

*　　　*　　　*

Mags Gablecross and Sally B-T were working flat

388

out on final alterations to costumes.

'Where's Vicky?' demanded Monster fretfully.

'Gone to the hairdresser's,' said Mags dryly. 'She felt the need to pamper herself before her big night.'

'I bought her these flowers,' protested Monster.

'How very thoughtful of you,' said Sally, recognizing five of her rare irises and the only spotted hellebores not squashed earlier by Cosmo. 'I'll put them in water for Vicky.'

Mrs Kamani, thrilled to be sent a ticket, had closed her newsagent's especially early and was now sitting in the second row next to Vicky's proud parents.

* * *

Janna crept into the dressing room, where everything seemed chaos. So many ravishing girls and boys. Whatever happened to spots and puppy fat? Such smooth flesh to make up, she thought wistfully, no crevasses for it to sink into.

Milly's streaked ponytail was being brushed out by Sally, before being put up with a white rose. Bianca Campbell-Black, watched surreptitiously by every boy in the room, was being zipped into her scarlet spangled dress.

Feral paced up and down, muttering, ' "Have at thee, coward!" ' He must remember to speak up.

* * *

'Who's coming tonight, apart from my mum?' asked Kylie as Pearl toned down her flushed post-orgasmic face.

'Press, parents, friends of the school.'

'Din't know we had any friends,' said Graffi.

' "Why Uncle, 'tis a shame",' muttered Feral.

'I'm going to throw up again,' said Paris.

'No you're not.' Hengist swept in resplendent in a beautifully cut pinstripe suit, sky-blue shirt and dark blue spotted tie. 'The audience are arriving. I want you all down in the General Bagley Room. Take the back stairs so no one sees you.'

On the way they passed props tables groaning with policemen's helmets, Sally's old scent bottles filled with coloured water for Monster's chemist shop, pots of rosemary, camomile and foxglove for Friar Lawrence's garden, phials of fake blood, retractable knives and pistols, which Emlyn constantly checked for the real thing.

Self-conscious yet astounded how newly beautiful Pearl had made so many of them, the cast took up their positions in rising tiers on three sides of a square. Amber and Jade had become glamorous society hostesses, Milly an innocent vast-eyed angel, towards whom even Paris felt a flicker of lust.

'I look almost as good as Mummy,' sighed Milly.

Graffi, aged up with wrinkles, parsnip-yellow bags under the eyes, a shaggy grey wig and a Norland Nurse's uniform, with a fob watch on his starched bosom, looked nearly fifty and decidedly unattractive. Milly loved him but she wished once again he looked as sexy as Feral who, with his lithe beautiful body encased in black, his amazing tawny eyes elongated to his temples and with a suggestion of ebony whisker, looked indeed the Prince of Cats. Paris had refused blusher or lipstick, but Pearl, with bronzing gel, had warmed his deathly pallor to the olive glow of an Old Master and defined his pale unblinking eyes with eyeliner and mascara. He looked drop dead gorgeous with his officer's peaked cap shoved on to the back of his head.

'I must not fancy Paris,' pleaded Milly.

Standing facing his young audience, Hengist smiled.

'You all look fantastic.' Then, sternly: 'But remember your job tonight is to entertain. Invite the audience on stage with you, invite them to become part of this amazing story. It's all about eye contact, even if you're a bad guy or one of the crowd—look out at the audience.

'Up until now, no one's given more than seventy-five per cent. Tonight I want one hundred and fifty per cent. It's already a great show. I want it to be a brilliant show. I want you to change what the audience feels about you. Your parents are out there, longing to be proud of you.'

Not for Paris, thought Janna in anguish.

'Stand up,' ordered Hengist.

As the children struggled to their feet, the girls swaying on their high heels, his voice became almost messianic:

'Shut your eyes. You are young, you are beautiful, you're energetic, you have ability and gifts. You have time to entertain.'

'Yeah, man.' Rocky punched the air with his fist.

Kylie suppressed a nervous giggle. Aysha was horrified to feel her hand creeping into Xav's, and nearly fainted when he squeezed it back.

'Make the audience want to be what you are,' Hengist's voice dropped seductively: 'Make them adore you. Your job is to break their hearts.'

Against the force of Hengist's personality, Feral wrenched open his eyes and caught Bianca gazing at him; then she smiled shyly. Feral was jolted, he must get a grip on himself. Quickly he looked away. Cosmo, intercepting this exchange, was determined to negate it.

'Good luck, God bless you all,' ended Hengist to a round of applause. Hovering at the back, glancing at the rapt, inspired faces of the children, Janna was reminded once again why he was head of one of the best schools in the country. He could have sent entire armies over the top.

And he looked so divine. The strong features, the ebony eyebrows, the high colour, the slicked-down hair already leaping upwards, the vitality tamed by the dark-grey establishment suit. An arrogant public-school shit, and yet, and yet . . .

'My only love sprung from my only hate', she thought helplessly, stepping out from behind a tier of seats, then leaping back as Pearl shouted, 'Miss, Miss,' and all the children took up the cry.

But Janna had fled, racing down the corridor, losing herself in the crowd gathering in the foyer outside the theatre. All round the walls were Cosmo's blown-up photographs of the cast. Janna swelled with pride. Paris, Feral and Kylie looked so beautiful.

Even more beautiful to the Larks parents was a splendid array of free drink. Two coachloads had been ferried over from the Shakespeare Estate by the heroic Wally and were fast losing their shyness. There was Pearl's mother and her very young lover, who didn't look capable of beating Pearl or anyone else up, and Chantal Peck in gold lurex and a high state of excitement, telling everyone she was a parent governor. Stormin' Norman, in a black trouser suit, had been spoiling for a fight, but her aggression evaporated when she saw the blow-up of Monster as the apothecary. The small stocky man with black curls and naughty laughing eyes, drinking red wine out of a pint mug, must be Dafydd Williams, Graffi's dad.

Out of loyalty to Vicky, but not bothering to change out of very casual clothes, Skunk Illingworth, Sam Spink, Robbie Rushton and Chally had overcome their loathing of private education enough to get stuck into Hengist's drink.

Bagley parents, however, were in the ascendancy.

'Darling darling, kiss kiss, yock yock, ha, ha ha, skiing, the Seychelles, the Caribbean, Egypt, Aspen, Florida, Klosters. Are you going to the Argentine Open? Must come over to kitchen sups,' to show they'd got a dining room. Listening to the confident yelling and exchange of proper names, Janna had forgotten how much she detested the upper middle classes.

It was still light outside; through the open windows, birds were competing with the orchestra. Chantal and Stormin' Norman were pointing out celebs.

'Look, there's Rupert Campbell-Black, ain't he beautiful?'

'Best owner-trainer in the country,' agreed Dafydd, 'and there's Billy Lloyd-Foxe,' as Amber's father, clutching two large whiskies, pushed his way through the throng.

'Never miss him on *Question of Sport*,' said Stormin'. ' 'Ello Billy, don't drink it all at once.'

Billy grinned back at them: 'I hate running out.'

Dafydd was over the moon and in turn helped

393

himself to two mugs of red.

'And there's Jupiter Belvedon, our Member,' squeaked Chantal. 'Evening, Jupe.'

Jupiter nodded coolly as he joined the group round Rupert Campbell-Black.

'Pity I didn't bring my autograph book,' sighed Chantal.

Such was Janna's paranoia, having been warned off by Ashton and Crispin and imagining everyone would be dubbing her a whore, that she was amazed so many parents hailed her.

'She's so nice, she's our head.'

Maybe all those home visits were paying off.

Randal Stancombe, hovering hopefully round the Campbell-Black clique, kissed Janna on both cheeks. Mrs Walton, ravishing as ever in a Lindka Cierach cream velvet suit, to which she had pinned a big pink rose, Calèche rising like morning mist from her ravine of a cleavage, rushed up and insisted she and Janna have lunch soon.

'I am so thrilled Milly's playing Juliet,' she whispered. 'Randal's livid that poisonous Jade didn't get it. Have you met Taggie Campbell-Black? She can't sleep for worrying Xav's going to move the wrong chair, or Bianca forget her dance steps.'

Janna smiled up at Taggie, who, slender as a young birch, with a dark cloud of hair, kind, silver-grey eyes and soft pink lips, seemed infinitely sweeter and more beautiful than Mrs Walton.

'I gather Bianca's champion,' she said. 'She's doing her dance with one of my most adorable pupils.'

'Is that Feral? Bianca chatters about him all day. Rupert's getting very jealous. But we're so pleased

Xav's got involved. Darling, you've met Janna,' Taggie called out to Rupert who, detesting school events, was cringing behind a pillar talking into two mobiles.

Peering out nervously, he waved at Janna.

'I've still got that sheepdog that fell on my head when I visited your school—much better behaved than my dogs.'

Absurdly flattered to be remembered, Janna was thanking him once again for sending *Gladiator* and the huge cheque, when she lost her audience as Rupert muttered, 'Oh God,' and shot behind his pillar again, as a large woman, outcleavaging Ruth Walton and with the wide innocent eyes of a doll, appeared in the doorway awaiting adulation.

'There's Dime Kiri,' shouted Stormin' Norman, who was well away. ' 'Ello Dime Kiri.'

'That ain't Dime Kiri,' chided Chantal as the large woman expanded like a bullfrog, 'that's Dime Hermy-own, stupid. 'Ello, Dime Hermy-own.'

'It's Dame Herm*i*one, Cosmo's mother, silly old bat. Hengist can't stand her,' said Ruth Walton with rare venom as Randal shot forward to kiss Dame Hermione's hand, determined to harpoon this great whale to open his hypermarket.

'Can I take your photograph, Miss Curtis?' said a shrill voice. It was Dora, ostensibly covering the play for the Bagley school mag. 'Oh bugger, here comes my mother, she's crazy about Rupert.'

'Christ!' Rupert had now disappeared round the other side of the pillar to avoid Lady Belvedon, a very slim pretty blonde, crying: 'Rupert, Rupert.'

'Did I hear Rupert's name?' cried Dame Hermione roguishly and, leaving Stancombe in mid-supermarket pitch, rushed off in pursuit.

Advanced on from right and left, Rupert bolted for the bar.

'Poor Rupert, he's so naughty,' laughed Taggie, then, lowering her voice: 'He can't stand Dame Hermione or Anthea Belvedon, but they're like cats and always crawl over people who are allergic to them.'

'Oh look, he's now been clobbered by Poppet Bruce,' giggled Dora. 'I expect she'll invite him to her workshop on behaviour management.'

Strains of Prokoviev's *Romeo and Juliet* were rising above the din of chat as the five-minute bell went.

'God, I loathe school plays,' grumbled Amber and Junior's mother, Janey, a blonde Fleet Street journalist who'd seen better days. 'This one's going to be even direr, since Bagley bonded with that grotty comprehensive . . .'

Ruth Walton laughed.

'This is the grotty comp's headmistress, Janna Curtis.'

'Oh dear,' said Janey, filling up Janna's glass from her brimming half-pint mug, 'I'm so sorry. You're much too pretty and young for a head. I'm covering this for the *Mail*. I'll say you're charismatic and deeply capable.' Then, as Uncle Harley sauntered in looking sleek and dangerous: 'Who's that utterly ravishing man covered in diamonds?'

'Some African prince,' said Janna slyly.

At least someone's come for Feral, she thought as she waved at Harley. She was also delighted Nadine and Mr Blenchley from Oaktree Court had showed up.

'Christ.' Rupert had joined them again.

'Hermione, Lady Belvedon and that ghastly Poppet: I thought the three witches came in *Macbeth*.'

There was an explosion of flashes as Hengist swept in with Anatole's father the Russian Minister and his glamorous wife, who was wearing a floor-length fur.

'It must have accounted for a hundred bears,' said Dora furiously, 'I'm going to blow her up.'

'I feel one has a duty to support these functions,' Lady Belvedon was telling Stancombe, then squawked as the long pink tongue of Elaine, the greyhound, relieved her of the vol-au-vent she was clutching.

The sixty-second bell was ringing imperiously. As everyone surged into the theatre, Taggie turned shyly to Janna.

'Good luck. I'm so sick with nerves for Bianca, I can't imagine what it would be like to worry about a whole school. You've done so well, Xav and Bianca have really taken to your Larks children.'

If only all posh people were like you, thought Janna, noticing Graffi's dad tucking a bottle of red wine inside his jacket.

'Thank you for helping our Graffi with his muriel,' said his wife.

'You must come and see it,' said Janna happily, then any joy was drained out of her as she saw the Tusk Force: Russell, Crispin, Rod Hyde and Ashton Douglas, in a dark purple smoking jacket, with an uncharacteristically adoring expression on his bland, pink face.

'Dame Hermione.' He seized both her hands. 'You were the most wonderful Elisabetta I ever saw. Pawis nineteen eighty-five.'

'You're very kind.' Hermione bowed gracefully. 'Perhaps you could rustle me up another glass of bubbly?'

'Indeed.' Ashton belted off.

'You're looking very iconic this evening, Dame Hermione,' snuffled fat Crispin.

'Where's Vicky?' asked Russell.

'Backstage.' Rod Hyde's voice thickened. 'The good general is always with his troops.'

Catapulted forward by the crowd, Janna couldn't avoid them.

'Good evening, gentlemen,' she said coolly.

They nodded back equally coolly.

'Good of you to turn up.'

'We felt we must support Vicky,' said Ashton.

Janna glanced at her ticket. 'I must find my seat.'

Next moment, a big warm hand grabbed hers. 'Gotcha,' said a familiar deep husky voice. 'Come and watch with me.'

'I'm sitting with Tim and Mags Gablecross,' shrieked Janna, aware of Ashton and Co's delighted disapproval and wriggling like a stray cat to escape.

'The Gablecrosses won't mind,' said Hengist. 'We started this together, I want to share it with you,' and he dragged her off to sit in the middle of the tenth row, making everyone move up.

'Sally's backstage, doing last-minute repairs,' he told Janna. 'Half our girls are so besotted with your Feral, the other half with your Paris. They've all had to have their costumes taken in.'

Oh God, thought Janna in panic as a flurry of 'Excuse me, sorry, excuse me' indicated that the Tusk Force had taken the seats directly behind her.

I haven't seen Hengist since I last saw you, Janna

398

wanted to scream at them, but then she thought defiantly: I don't care, I don't care. Maybe it's three glasses of wine on an empty stomach, but I still really adore him.

Giving her a slug of Courvoisier from a silver hipflask, Hengist introduced her to two masters on her right.

These were Artie Deverell, the handsome, languid, gentle head of modern languages, whom Mags Gablecross, who taught the same subject, had fallen in love with on balloon day, and Theo Graham, the bald and very wrinkled head of classics, revered for his translation of Euripides.

'I've got Jack Waterlane, Junior, Lando and Lubemir in my house,' whispered Artie. 'Theo's got Cosmo and Anatole, so we both have our crosses.'

The Russian Minister and his wife were seated on Hengist's left. Next moment, everyone jumped out of their skins as Dame Hermione started singing along to Prokofiev.

'Lurex tremendous,' murmured Hengist as Chantal Peck swept up to the front.

44

It was a wonderful theatre, stark and forbidding, with black brick walls forty feet high and black leather seats. Saxophones and clarinets glittered like jewels in the pit; pearly drum skins gleamed in the half-light.

The only prop in front of the crimson curtains was a big cardboard television with the screen cut out. As Prokofiev's menacing 'March of the Capulets' faded away, Kylie Rose appeared inside the now lit-up screen as a presenter.

' "Two households, both alaike in dignity . . ." '
She held up cards saying Bagley and Larks:

'In fair Verona, where we lay our scene.
From forth the fatal loins of these two foes
A pair of star-crossed lovers take their laife.'

'Christ,' muttered Rupert, 'she's been here half a term and she talks like Anthea Belvedon.'

Chantal was in ecstasy: Kylie looked so dignified.

Back creaked the crimson curtains to a howl of police sirens and a burst of clapping. Against Graffi's fantastic backdrop of mosques, tumbling twin towers, tower blocks and army barracks strangled by barbed wire was a street in Verona with an ice-cream van, AC Milan posters, a large bullet-pocked Shakespeare Estate sign, and a signpost saying 'Bagley 5 miles, City Centre ½ mile'. There was the Ghost and Castle and Mrs Kamani's newsagent's with a broken window.

Oh God, thought Janna, but, rising out of her

seat, she could see Mrs Kamani laughing. Revelling in the roars of applause, Janna forgot her nerves. This was no school production; it was slick, yet bursting with exuberance and passion. Larks's confidence had grown so much, they were as assured as their Bagley counterparts.

Here was Rocky lumbering out of the Ghost and Castle and turning on the Montagues.

' "No, sir, I do not bite my fumb at you, sir, but I bite my fumb, sir. When I have fought the men, I will be civil with the maids, and cut off their heads." '

' "The heads of the maids?" ' demanded Junior.

' "Ay, the heads of the maids or their maidenheads." ' Rocky leered round; the audience laughed.

Then Feral erupted on to the stage to huge cheers and boos.

' "What, drawn, and talk of peace! I hate the word," ' he spat, his fury scattering the Montagues, then paused.

Although the cast knew he'd dried, the audience thought it was terrific timing.

' "I hate the word," ' repeated Feral, recovering, ' "As I hate hell, all Montagues, and thee. Have at thee, coward!" ' And guns were flashing and blanks ringing out.

'That's Bianca's boyfriend,' whispered Taggie. 'Isn't he gorgeous?'

'Very black,' muttered back Rupert.

*   *   *

Paris stood apart in the wings, psyching himself up, mindlessly chewing gum. I am Romeo; I am in

Verona; I am empowered; I am lovesick for a woman who hardly knows I exist. *Plus ça change*, he thought bitterly, I am about to crash a ball and fall in love for the first and last time in my life.

'Good luck, Paris.' Vicky's clap on the back nearly shot him on to the stage. 'Remember to speak up.'

* * *

Roars of applause greeted each new set, particularly the Capulets' ballroom with long-legged beauties in masks and paparazzi hiding, like Rupert, behind every pillar.

'That's my Jade in cerise,' said Stancombe loudly to Dame Hermione.

'That's my Cosmo playing Lord Capulet in a navy military jacket,' said Hermione even more loudly.

'Shut up,' said Janna.

'Don't wepwove Dame Hermione,' hissed a horrified Ashton.

Cosmo, having played the genial host, whipped off his jacket and joined the Cosmonaughties and Kylie Rose in a number he'd composed called 'Cocks and Rubbers', the words of which were fortunately obscured by the din of the band. Looking at Cosmo's pale dangerous face, ebony curls flopping maniacally as he lashed his guitar, Janna thought: That is one whole lot of gorgeous trouble.

Then the stage cleared for Feral and Bianca's tango. Never taking their eyes off each other, talking through their bodies as they danced, their red-hot passion branded the floorboards. Rupert, woken by his wife just in time to watch them, led the bravoes and thunderous applause. This resulted in two encores, which broke the mood for Paris's big entrance.

'Oh poor boy,' muttered Janna in anguish as the applause petered out.

'He'll be OK,' whispered Hengist.

And Janna moved her body against his so the comforting hand he'd laid on top of hers couldn't be seen from behind by Ashton and Crispin. Any minute, she imagined Crispin's fourth chin resting on her shoulder so he could peep over.

Despite a balloon bursting and Rocky now dressed as a waiter nudging him in the back, saying hoarsely: 'Nibbles anyone?' Paris remained motionless, waiting until he'd got everyone's attention, gazing in wonder at the young girl in white muslin standing with the shy dignity of the daughter of the house at the foot of the stairs.

Pausing for five seconds on that first ' "Oh!" ' then, glancing up at the flambeaux flickering round the room, he murmured: ' "She doth teach the torches to burn bright!" '

'Christ,' murmured Theo and Artie.

I must have that boy at Bagley, thought Hengist.

Offered another swig of Courvoisier from his flask, Janna shook her head, refusing to be distracted for a second. As Paris ended his speech, vowing he'd never seen true beauty till this night, you could have heard a pin and also the jaw of Dora Belvedon drop.

At the moment Paris fell in love with his Juliet, Dora felt herself blasted by similar lightning, as if she was seeing Paris for the first time, and he had become as beautiful, remote and beyond her reach as a stained-glass saint in the chapel.

403

He was even more heartbreaking in the balcony scene. Cosmo had given her five rolls of film to capture misbehaviour to flog to the nationals. Dora used them all on Paris. Even when Anatole and Feral were being killed off, she could only think of him. The wound made by Cupid's arrow was like the one in Mercutio's side.

' "Not so deep as a well, nor so wide as a church door, but 'tis enough, 'twill serve." '

Dora moaned in terror. She had lost control of her life.

*   *   *

In the dark beside Hengist, Janna had never been prouder or happier, breathing in lemon aftershave, rejoicing as his shout of laughter and the thunderclap of his big hands set off the rest of the audience.

In the interval, reality reasserted itself. Janna resisted going backstage, terrified of intruding. She'd lost so much confidence. She'd just found Tim and Mags and a large glass of wine, when Vicky emerged to hearty cheering from the Tusk Force.

She looked enchanting in jeans and an old petrol-blue jersey, her hair in a ponytail, make-up lightly but carefully applied. Janna was ashamed to find herself wondering if Vicky had got Pearl to add the smudge on her cheek and the violet shadows beneath her eyes.

'So sorry I'm not dressed, everyone,' she cried, 'it's hard to rush round backstage in high heels and glad rags. Is it all right? I'm so close to it!'

The Tusk Force, except for Crispin who had a

404

mouth full of cocktail sausages, assured her it was simply wonderful.

Janna steeled herself to invade the ring of admirers. 'Brilliant, Vicky, congratulations.'

'Your productions were so wonderful at Redfords'—Vicky hugged Janna—'I so wanted not to let you down.'

'No danger of that,' said Ashton, 'Pawis Alvaston is headed for stardom, I would say.'

'I must rush and have a word with Mummy and Daddy in the auditorium.'

'I hope you'll bring them to the party later,' said a passing Hengist, 'they must be very proud.'

*   *   *

Even with Feral and Anatole killed off, the second half was full of incident. Boffin Brooks had surreptitiously put back the lines cut out of his long speeches as the Friar, and the audience started slow handclapping.

Johnnie Fowler-Upper, as he was now known, had a heavenly time in the bedroom scene, lighting up Juliet's Barbie dolls and Justin Timberlake posters, the Hon. Jack and Kylie snogging illicitly in another corner of the stage, Milly's boobs twice, Paris nude three times, the beauty of his slender wide-shouldered body causing several masters and Ashton to drop their binoculars.

'Very tasteful and dignified,' cried Chantal, seizing Hermione's opera glasses. 'May word, what a botty.'

Hoots of laughter greeted Monster's chemist shop offering Durex at £10 and Viagra at 50p. The mood was brought back on course by Cosmo, no

405

longer the brutal father, but deranged with grief over his daughter. ' "Death lies on her, like an untimely frost Upon the sweetest flower of all the field." '

Then, not on stage until the next act, Cosmo belted off to conduct the orchestra as they broke into galloping music. Suddenly the audience was startled by a clatter of hooves, the doors flew open and Paris thundered up the gangway. Unfazed by the screams and cheers, Beluga reached the pit and slithered to a halt, but as Paris chucked his reins to a starry-eyed, blushing Dora, he realized someone—no doubt Cosmo—had removed his plank.

Should he jump off and race round backstage, which would wreck the momentum, or risk falling into the pit? He chose the latter and scrambled on to Beluga's slippery saddle.

'Careful,' cried Dora in anguish as he took a massive leap, crashing on to the ill-lit stage, struggling to his feet before disappearing into the Capulets' mausoleum.

'Oh, my brave lad,' gasped Janna.

Even when Paris launched into the 'Eyes, look your last! Arms, take your last embrace!' speech and someone yelled: 'She's not dead yet, you berk,' he held the mood.

Tears were pouring down Janna's face and even Rupert was blowing his nose on Taggie's paper handkerchief as Paris drank purple flavoured water out of Sally's scent bottle, which had once contained Beautiful, and collapsed on Milly, gasping:

' "Thus with a kiss, I die",' and did.

'Well done,' whispered Milly, 'you've made it.'

406

45

The cast were called back again and again—all beaming—except Paris, who looked drained and utterly shell-shocked, but who got the biggest cheer of the night every time he took a bow.

My boy, thought Janna in ecstasy, and her heart nearly burst as Feral and Bianca bounded on hand in hand and slid into a ten-second tango routine, with Feral arching Bianca back until her black ringlets touched the floor, to stampings and cries of, 'More, more.'

Emlyn ensured that there was thunderous applause for every participant from Pearl for her make-up, Graffi for his sets, and Johnnie Fowler for his lighting:

'You should work in a strip club, Johnnie.'

The stagehands filed on until everyone had clapped their hands raw. But at the first pause, Ashton and Rod Hyde called out: 'Director!'

Whereupon the cast all put on their red noses and Primrose Duddon made a glowing breathy speech, handing out bottles to Emlyn, Jason, Sally Brett-Taylor, Mags and Cambola to thank them for all their hard work. Wally was also praised for being a tower of strength and ferrying everyone about in the wonderful Randal Stancombe bus. Wally was then presented with the definitive book on bell-ringing.

'But most importantly'—even Primrose had a crush on Vicky—'I'd like to thank our wonderful director, Vicky Fairchild.'

Everyone stamped and yelled as Vicky ran on,

accepted a vast bunch of pink roses and launched into an orgy of gratitude, for the wonderful chance she'd been given, for the children and teachers at Bagley and Larks, 'and particularly'—dimple, dimple—'Hengist and Sally for making us so welcome and for all my dear friends at Larks for covering for me. I know I've played hookey a lot but I was so anxious to make a difference.

'And I'd like to thank dear Ashton and Crispin, at Support and Challenge, and dear Russell and all the governors, for being so supportive, and my parents who've come all the way from Harrogate.'

Audience and cast were getting restless. Cosmo, if he hadn't been trapped on stage, would have started up the orchestra.

'Oh come on, Vicky,' muttered Janna.

'Hush.' Hengist patted her arm. 'Let the little poppet enjoy her moment of glory.'

'If you'll just bear with me,' twinkled Vicky.

'Anytime you like, darlin',' yelled Graffi's father, who after the interval had smuggled in an entire bottle of champagne.

Vicky giggled enchantingly.

But Rocky had had enough. Shambling in front of Vicky, he raised a huge red hand. 'And I'd like to fank Miss Curtis, Janna, for believing in us, and making us feel we could do fings and for turning our school round,' he shouted.

This was greeted with cheers, Tarzan howls and fists punched in the air by both Larks and Bagley.

'Get that nutter off the stage,' howled Ashton.

'I was just coming to Janna,' said Vicky tartly.

*　　　*　　　*

408

With all the cuts, the play had lasted only ninety minutes, but it felt like midnight as Janna fought her way backstage to embrace and congratulate a euphoric cast in various states of undress.

'I am right proud. I never believed in a million years you could do so brilliantly.'

In his purple-stained shirt, a burning-hot Paris trembled as she hugged him, but couldn't speak or smile. His head was still in Juliet's tomb, but he was gratified that Nadine and Mr Blenchley, both of whom he loathed, rolled up to congratulate him at the same time as Patience, who in her raucous voice told them how bravely he'd overcome his terror of horses and even more brilliantly circumnavigated the missing plank.

'Plank's been relocated on his shoulder,' murmured Cosmo who, nevertheless, was feeling vulnerable. Judging by the way Feral and Graffi, still in his nurse's uniform, kept scowling in his direction, they were planning revenge.

Cosmo had lost his guards. However much he snapped his fingers, Anatole and Lubemir were ignoring him. Back in the General Bagley Room, where a splendid party was under way, they were happily getting drunk with the opposition.

' "Tybalt, you rat-catcher, vill you valk," ' said Anatole for the hundredth time.

Feral grinned, making a feint with a bread knife.

'We can't stop them drinking after such a magnificent performance,' Sally Brett-Taylor was telling Janna as big bowls of lasagne and sticks of bread were placed on a side table. 'But let's at least give them plenty of blotting paper.'

'An Italian dish—appropriate for *Romeo and Juliet*,' Boffin was saying pompously. 'Although at the Capulets' ball they would probably have eaten boar.'

'Unlike us who have to listen to one,' said Anatole, sprinkling Parmesan over Boffin's hair.

Paris, having survived his ride up the aisle, would have liked to retreat to Beluga's stable, thank the kind horse and relive with him every moment of the play. As it was, when he slunk into the party, everyone wanted a piece of him. With such a bone structure, what did it matter if he was monosyllabic?

'Cosmo will invite you back to River House for the weekend,' gushed Dame Hermione.

Cosmo, flipping through the film in Dora's camera, was enraged to find only pictures of Paris.

'They'll be worth a fortune when he gets an Oscar,' protested Dora.

'We need cash now,' snarled Cosmo.

Cosmo was right, thought Dora in panic. How could she support Cadbury or Loofah if she didn't sell stories? What had become of her? She normally had three helpings of lasagne; now she couldn't eat a thing. She couldn't take her eyes off Paris. He was as beautiful as the wild cherry blossom floodlit outside the window. She longed to tell him how wonderful he'd been, but the words stuck in her throat. The hurt was dreadful.

A record player was pounding out music from *Grease*. Amber and Pearl, sharing a surreptitious spliff and a bottle of white, were drowning their sorrows.

'We've lucked out there,' observed Amber as Feral and Bianca, unspeaking, making love with their eyes, danced on and on.

'She's only twelve,' snapped Pearl.

' "Younger than she are happy mothers made",' quipped Amber.

Aysha had gone home. A dazed, deliriously happy Xav gazed out of the window, breathing in the scent of Sally's narcissi, as sweet and delicate as Aysha, who had held his hand.

Janna moved from actor to parent to teacher to technician, praising and thanking. Not realizing Cosmo had been instrumental in Paris not walking the plank, she thanked him too.

She had a lovely chat with Theo Graham and Artie Deverell. Theo seemed keen on teaching Paris Latin and Greek, and quoted Keats about feeling 'like some watcher of the skies When a new planet swims into his ken'.

Artie seemed equally keen to teach Paris modern languages.

'That boy is separate,' he said. 'You can't watch anyone else when he's on stage.'

'Or off it,' sighed Theo.

Kylie unplugged herself for a second from Jack Waterlane's embrace to ask Janna, 'People aren't just saying Larks did good, miss, because we didn't fight or trash anyfing?'

'You weren't good,' said Janna, then, as Kylie's face fell: 'You were utterly sensational.'

'Better'n Redfords?'

'A million times,' said Janna truthfully.

She was pleased when Emlyn, who'd been clearing up the stage, hove into sight clutching a large whisky and asking if she'd had anything to eat.

'Yes,' lied Janna. 'You were the real star. That play was only brilliant because you held everything together.'

'Not for much longer. The Wolf Pack are spoiling for a punch-up.'

'We'd better get them home,' said Janna. 'I'll alert Wally.'

On the way, she was accosted by Stormin' Norman, very drunk and singing Vicky's praises. 'Vicks realized Martin was visually and aurally impaired, put him in the front row and his school work's gone from strengf to strengf.'

Next Janna passed Vicky, surrounded by more admirers than Paris.

'If I had had my way,' she was telling Randal Stancombe, 'your Jade would have been Juliet.' Meeting Janna's eyes, she blushed. 'Well, Jannie, are you proud of us?'

To conceal her galloping disillusionment, Janna was shocked by her own effusiveness. 'It was all great. You did so well.'

'Send us Victoria, Sweetie and Gloria, Long to reign over us,' sang a drunken Lando and Junior.

'It was priceless,' said Vicky, dimpling again. 'Anatole insisted on introducing me to his father, who asked me what I taught. Quick as a flash, dear Anatole said: "She teaches the torches to burn bright, Dad." Wasn't that darling? I must tell Hengist.'

'Hengist has gone,' said Alex Bruce sourly. 'Pushed off to dinner at Head House with the Russian Minister, Rupert and Jupiter. He wouldn't waste time bothering with riff-raff like us.'

Vicky's lips tightened. Janna felt wiped out with tiredness and wondered if it would be letting the side down to go home, but first she must find Wally.

In her search, she bumped into Jason,

412

congratulated him warmly and asked how he was getting on.

'Bloody tiring. I like the work, but you're on call twenty-four hours a day. You can't bunk off at three-thirty like we did at Larks. Thank God it's the end of term.'

'Thank you for working so hard on the play.'

Jason glanced back at Vicky still holding court.

'Come back, Cara,' he said acidly, 'all is forgiven.'

Janna gave a gasp. 'Then I'm not imagining things?'

'You are not. Nothing sucks like success. You turned Larks round. You made the kids understand the play. I know how much Emlyn, Piers and I put in, and how lazy little Vicky has claimed credit for everything. She thanks too much; such women are dangerous ... And she's after Emlyn.'

'Oh dear.' Janna loathed that. 'He's much too nice.'

'But lonely without Oriana. You two should have dinner.'

Outside, Janna met Patience and thanked her for befriending Paris.

'We love him.' Patience lowered her donkey bray as Nadine and Mr Blenchley went down the steps: 'I just wish we could get him out of that horrible children's home.'

'Oh, so do I.'

'He's such a gentle soul.'

As they spoke, the fist of the gentle soul powered into Little Cosmo's jaw, sending him flying across an empty dining room. Scrambling to his feet in terror, Cosmo managed to leap out of a nearby window, landing this time on Sally's beloved white

413

narcissi and budding crown imperials, followed by a yelling Paris, Feral and Graffi, only slightly impeded by his nurse's costume.

They were all beating the hell out of Cosmo and the crown imperials when Emlyn and the guards of the Russian Minister rolled up, yanking them off by their shirts.

'Lemme go, you fuckers,' howled Paris, escaping back into the fray. 'Lemme get at you, you fucker. How dare you move that plank?'

'How dare you grope my woman?' yelled Feral, also wriggling free.

'Lemme get at him,' bawled Graffi, fob watch and white cap flying.

'Let's all get at him,' shouted the Chinless Wanderers, leaping out of the window and pitching in.

'Stop it,' bellowed Emlyn, hauling Graffi off by the starched white collar of his costume, then, launching into Welsh: 'Back off. Your da's drunk, I need your help to carry him on to the coach before he throws up.'

Swearing and spitting, Graffi backed off.

*   *   *

It was a very warm night. No one could explain why Cosmo was discovered in the flower bed next morning with bruising and mild concussion, but otherwise unhurt, which was more than could be said for Sally's beloved narcissi, trillium grandiflora and crown imperials. Thanks to Emlyn and the Minister's guards, none of this reached the press, which, as a result, was excellent.

Venturer had filmed the whole production, five

414

minutes of which was aired, including Paris's gallop up the gangway and the tango of Feral and Bianca, whose father was, after all, a Venturer director.

46

Mrs Kamani was so pleased to be invited and featured in *Romeo and Juliet*, she gave every Larks child an Easter egg. Janna organized a treasure hunt around the grounds, but she continually had to replace eggs, because they kept being tracked down and gobbled up by Partner.

Everyone had a wonderful time, as did Hengist and Sally, who spent Easter with Anatole's family in Russia.

'We had a treasure hunt for Fabergé eggs,' laughed Sally. 'Hengist and I found one each. Simply heavenly.'

All of which was too much for poor Alex Bruce, still festering over Hengist's lack of concern over Poppet's smashed figurine and being excluded from Hengist's private party after *Romeo and Juliet*, particularly when he discovered that feline smoothie Artie Deverell had been invited.

Then Emlyn Davies, who never showed any respect, announced that as he'd been working all hours on the play, he intended to take two days off to play golf and go racing.

It was high time, decided Alex, to impose some discipline. Staff therefore returned for the summer to find glass panels fitted into their classroom doors so Alex could monitor their lessons.

Theo Graham, head of classics, led the mutiny, promptly hanging his old tweed coat over the panel.

Alex then emailed all staff saying he would be monitoring random classes. Again, Theo led the resistance.

'I've been teaching for nearly forty years; no one's sitting in on my lessons.'

'Well, at least submit a plan for each lesson,' persisted Alex. 'This is required practice in the maintained sector.'

'I don't care, my lesson plans are in here.' Theo tapped his bald head. 'I don't need to write them down.'

Alex was furious and later in April, when Hengist went to America (ostensibly to attend a conference of heads; actually to join Jupiter in talking up their New Reform Party, as it was now officially known, to American senators), Alex decided to introduce daily staff meetings before chapel to discuss targets. This caused uproar.

On the first day only Alex's supporters—Joan Johnson and Biffo Rudge, head of maths—arrived on time: Biffo, because he wanted to seize the most comfortable big brown velvet armchair; Joan, big, meaty, dominating, because she believed in targets. Both she and Biffo rolled up armed with clipboards.

Miss Sweet, sex educator and undermatron of Boudicca, also arrived on time because she was terrified of Joan, as did little Miss Wormley, who was feeling sick at the mid-morning prospect of initiating Amber, Cosmo *et alii* into the erotic subtleties of 'The Love Song of J. Alfred Prufrock'.

The view from the staffroom was already causing controversy. It looked north-west over the shoulder of General Bagley and his charger down the long lime walk, which was just opening into palest acid-green leaf, to the golf course and woods beyond. It was a view which had restored the sanity of many a staff member since the mid nineteenth century, but which was now under threat because Alex Bruce was applying for planning permission to build on this site a new Science Emporium, financed by Randal Stancombe.

Hengist, who would have gone berserk if Alex had threatened a twig on his beloved Badger's Retreat, was comparatively indifferent to the positioning of the new Science Emporium—it had to go somewhere, preferably as far as possible from his office, which faced east, or from Head House, which was tucked away on the other bosky side of the campus, facing south.

And if push came to shove, General Bagley could always be relocated to the lawn below Hengist's office, where more people could admire him. He'd enjoy watching rugger and cricket far more than rats being dissected, and he'd be facing the East and India, where his great career had been carved out.

Alex and Poppet thought General Bagley, who'd won glory at the Battle of Plassey and wreaking vengeance after the Black Hole of Calcutta, was a dreadful old Empire-builder and wanted to get rid of his sculpture altogether.

From eight thirty-five, on the morning of Alex's first meeting, other staff drifted in, grumbling about having no time to walk their dogs, ostentatiously carrying on marking work and preparing lessons. Theo Graham, having scowled at Biffo for pinching the only chair which eased his bad back, perched on the window seat, reading a handful of Paris's poems sent him by Janna. They were very good, particularly one about a dandelion clock, glittering silver then puffed away to decide men's fates. Will she accept my proposal, will I get this job, will I get into Cambridge, is this cancer malignant, it is, it isn't, it is, it isn't. Thank God. My life will go on, but not the dandelion stalk, all its silken feathers flown, given no life in water after such a momentous forecast, chucked down to die on the dusty road.

'Have a look at this.' Theo handed the poem to Artie Deverell who'd just wandered in in a dark blue silk dressing gown, carrying a cup of black coffee, and who, putting the poem in his pocket, stretched out on the staffroom sofa and went back to sleep.

The room was almost full up, so Alex proceeded to involve the staff in a brainstorming session.

'Where d'you think you'll be in five years' time, Theo?'

'In a coffin, with any luck,' growled Theo.

'Don't be fatuous,' snapped Alex.

A disturbance was then created by Emlyn strolling in, still in pyjamas, eating a bowl of cornflakes and reading the *Sun*.

'We're trying to discuss targets and aims, Emlyn,' Alex told him icily. 'Tell us, if you please, the most important ingredient in your teaching plan.'

'A bullet-proof vest,' said Emlyn. 'Crucial for anyone who teaches Cosmo and Anatole.'

'And what is your goal when teaching the Lower Fifths?'

'To get out alive,' grunted Emlyn, not looking up from page three.

'Try to be serious.' Alex was fast losing patience. 'What is the most satisfying part of your lesson?'

'A large gin and tonic afterwards,' snapped back Emlyn.

419

'And the worst thing about Bagley Hall?' asked Alex through gritted teeth.

'Answering bloody stupid questions like this.'

'And the best?'

'Playing golf and getting wasted with Artie.' Emlyn blew a kiss to the sleeping Mr Deverell.

Alex was beside himself, particularly as Mrs Axford, the school cook, chose that moment to march in:

'Here's your sausage sandwich, Emlyn.'

Emlyn smiled sweetly up at her. 'Thanks so much, lovely.'

'Now we all know why you are so fat, Emlyn,' exploded Alex.

'No we don't,' said Emlyn amiably. 'It's because every time your wife takes me to bed she gives me a biscuit.'

The meeting broke up in disarray and howls of laughter.

The next day, Hengist flew back from America and enraged Alex Bruce by cancelling the meetings, adding they were the stupidest idea he'd ever heard and that good housemasters should be looking after their houses at that hour.

*   *   *

Hengist then embarked on the poaching of Paris Alvaston and the possibility of offering him a free place at Bagley in the Michaelmas term. In this he was much encouraged by the governors, who'd been entranced by *Romeo and Juliet*, and by the number of masters pixillated by Paris's white beauty, in particular Theo Graham and Artie Deverell, who were also impressed by Paris's

420

poems.

Hengist, whose motives were invariably mixed, also wanted to take on a boy who would outshine Alex's favourite, Boffin Brooks, and scupper No-Joke Joan's smug prediction that her girls would soon be outstripping his boys. David Hawkley had also been the subject of a flattering *Sunday Times* profile, and since the death of Mungo from meningitis and with Oriana constantly abroad, Hengist's longing for a son had increased.

Towards the end of the month, therefore, a secret afternoon meeting was held in the tranquillity of Head House to discuss the logistics of Paris's transfer.

Sitting round the highly polished dining-room table, admiring the bottle-green jungle wallpaper and Emma Sergeant's painting of Hengist's legendary drop goal, were Ian Cartwright, the bursar, Crispin Thomas, representing S and C, Nadine, Paris's social worker, Mr Blenchley, who managed Oaktree Court, Janna, who was spitting with Hengist for trying to poach her star pupil, and Hengist himself, who'd been playing tennis and was wearing a dark blue fleece, white shorts and trainers and showing off irritatingly good, already brown, legs.

It was a warm, muggy afternoon; a robin sang in a bronze poplar tree; the cuckoo called from a nearby ash grove; young cow parsley leaves and the emerald-green plumage of the wild garlic spilt in jubilation over shaven green lawns. Beyond, in the park, acid-green domes of young trees rose against a navy-blue cloud, from which fell fringes of rain.

Sally had provided a sumptuous tea of cucumber

and tomato sandwiches, a chocolate cake, warm from the oven and thickly spread with butter icing, and Earl Grey in a glittering Georgian silver teapot.

'Who's going to be mother?' snuffled Crispin.

'Who better than you?' mocked Hengist.

Nadine hastily grabbed the teapot. 'I will.'

The next question was who was going to be mother and father to Paris. Having poured out and piled up her plate, Nadine, who was wearing a black trouser suit which couldn't disguise thighs fatter than duffel bags and who, with her short curly fringe, glassy, expressionless eyes and long face, looked like a badly stuffed sheep, proceeded to consult her notes.

She reported that since *Romeo and Juliet*, Paris had had a rough time at Oaktree Court.

'He's too strong to be beaten up, but the inmates have ganged up and trashed his room, torn up his homework, shoved his books, many of them from Bagley library, down the toilet, stolen his school bag and thrown his denim jacket, which you gave him for his birthday, Janna'—Janna blushed as Crispin raised an eyebrow—'into the boiler.

'As a result, Paris's behaviour has been very challenging. Last week he nearly strangled a boy who ran off with a snow fountain of the Eiffel Tower, the only gift left him by his birth mother.'

'If he moved to Bagley,' continued Nadine in her sing-song voice, helping herself to another tomato sandwich, 'conflict at Oaktree Court would escalate and he would be subject to peer pressure on two fronts. We therefore feel that if he were to go to Bagley, he should leave the care home and be fostered. Over to you, Gordon.'

In his shiny grey suit, with his brutal pasty face, nicotine-stained hands and dirty nails, Mr Blenchley looked both seedy and sinister. He had reached an age when his black and silver stubble merely gave the impression he had forgotten to shave. Hengist, Janna and Ian Cartwright shuddered collectively.

Mr Blenchley then said in his thick, clogged voice that he'd be extremely sorry to lose Paris.

'The lad's been with us for nearly four years; reckon we can congratulate ourselves. Before that he had over twenty placements. In some ways a difficult boy, inscrutable, but very able, needs challenging.'

Mr Blenchley was in fact desperate to get shot of Paris. In the past, the lad had been too terrified of being parted from his friends at Larks, the only family he knew, to blow any whistles. But at five foot nine, whippy and well muscled, Paris could no longer be intimidated into accepting that doors stealthily sliding over nylon carpets and creaking floorboards in the dead of night were the work of ghosts—or that predatory fingers creeping inside pyjama trousers and under little nightdresses were figments of the imagination.

'It costs fourteen hundred pounds a week to keep you at Oaktree Court, you ungrateful little shit,' he had shouted at Paris that very morning.

To which Paris had shouted back, 'Give me the fucking money then.'

'What we feel Paris needs,' chipped in Nadine, 'is a sympathetic foster family, a middle-aged couple whose kids perhaps have grown up. It will be challenging, coming from an institution, however admirable, and a maintained school like Larks, then mixing with the protected, privileged students at Bagley. Paris gets ten pounds a month clothes allowance.'

'Jade Stancombe gets about a thousand,' sighed Hengist.

Janna gazed out into the park at the young green trees in their little wooden playpens. Even trees that soared twenty-five feet still retained their wooden cages. Paris would have no such protection.

'Children of Paris's age seldom find a home,' said Crispin, who'd been too busy filling his face to contribute to the debate, 'because potential adopters think they're too damaged.'

'Paris isn't damaged,' cried Janna in outrage. 'He's a sweet boy, so kind to the little ones and intensely loyal to his friends.' Then, as hateful Crispin smirked again, she went on: 'It would be like trapping a skylark to send him to Bagley, away from Feral and Graffi. What he needs is love and some kind of permanence.'

'I agree,' said Nadine. 'Ideally Paris Alvaston needs a forever family to facilitate the adjustment.'

Hengist had put his chocolate butter icing on the side of his plate. Was he watching his figure or keeping the best bit till last? He kept glancing across the table trying to make Janna laugh each time Nadine murdered the English language, but she refused to meet his eye. She was unable to forgive him for not consulting her before offering Paris a place or for looking so revoltingly sexy in those shorts that she wanted him to drag her upstairs and shag her insensible.

And yet, and yet, however much she loathed the idea of private education, she had to recognize

Bagley would give Paris a step up the ladder that Larks never could. But if Oaktree Court had given him such hell for getting posh, surely Bagley would roast him for being a yob?

If only she could foster him herself and provide him with a haven at weekends, half-term and during the holidays. Then she'd have someone to love and to cherish; they'd have such fun together.

But I'm too busy, she thought despairingly.

The spring holidays might never have been. The dark circles were back under her bloodshot eyes. She had 400 kids, 399 if Paris went to Bagley, and a school to save.

'You haven't had any cake.' Ian Cartwright, silly old blimp, was about to slide the last piece on to her plate. 'It's awfully good.'

Janna shook her head. She didn't want anything from Bagley. As the meeting roved on over pros and cons, she fought sleep, finally nodding off only to wake with a start, crying, 'Bagley won't hurt Paris, will they?' making the others stare at her in amazement.

Fortunately, at that moment, Sally Brett-Taylor wandered in, rivalling the spring's freshness in a pale-green cashmere jumper, asking if the teapot needed more hot water and discreetly giving Hengist an escape route by reminding him his next appointment was waiting. Everyone gathered up their papers.

'To sum up,' snuffled Crispin, licking chocolate icing off his fingers, 'unless we can find a foster family for Paris, you wouldn't recommend a move to Bagley.'

'That's right,' said Nadine. 'I think the contrast would be too extreme.'

'Beautiful garden, Mrs Brett-Taylor,' said Mr Blenchley, gazing out on Sally's riot of tulips, irises and fritillaries. 'Do you have a sprinkler system?'

'I prefer to water plants myself.' Sally smiled. 'That way you get to know them individually.'

Like my children, thought Janna. Why did everything at the moment make her cry?

47

Hengist returned from Rutminster Cathedral, where the school choir had been singing at Evensong, around nine. On the bus home he had sat next to Dora Belvedon, who, having somehow discovered the meeting had taken place, was desperate for Paris to come to Bagley.

'Just think, he'll mention you and Bagley one day in his acceptance speech at the Oscars.'

Hengist was greeted by a squirming, pirouetting Elaine, who left white hairs all over the trousers of his dark suit, the jacket of which Hengist hung on the banisters before removing his tie and pouring himself a large whisky.

He found Sally at the drawing-room piano playing the beautiful second movement of Schubert's D Major Sonata, which was slower and easier than the first. Only holding up her cheek to be kissed, she didn't stop. Hengist slumped on the sofa with Elaine to listen, watching the lamplight falling on his wife's pale hair, on Mungo's photograph and on a big bunch of white tulips, which shed petals each time she played more vigorously.

Swearing under her breath at the occasional wrong note in the difficult cross rhythms and vowing to set aside time to practise in the future, Sally reached the end.

'How would you feel about adopting Paris Alvaston?' asked Hengist.

Sally looked down at her hands, closed the music and shut the piano with a snap.

427

'Or, for a start, fostering him?'

'Not fair to him,' said Sally, with unexpected harshness. 'He'll be conspicuous enough coming from Larks; imagine being the head's son.'

'Easier than if he was our actual child. No one could blame him for my cringe-making idiosyncrasies. Nor would he be upset by other children slagging us off.'

Rising and crossing the room, he massaged Sally's rigid shoulders for a moment, then slid his hands down inside her pale-green jersey, which had been washed in Lux so many times.

'We don't have the time,' said Sally angrily. 'You want Fleetley, the Ministry of Education; you want to write. You have eight hundred children and an army of staff. You're always away and poor Elaine doesn't get enough walks.'

Elaine thumped her bony tail in agreement.

'Paris deserves better,' she went on. 'He needs time, individual attention and a live-in father.' And I don't see enough of you, she nearly added.

As his hands crept downwards, she willed her nipples not to respond. He had such a hold over her.

'It'd only be the holidays, half-terms and weekends,' protested Hengist. 'Give Oriana a bit of competition—a sibling to rival. She might come home more often.'

'Why did she stay away so much in the first place?' At heart, Sally felt she had failed as a mother to the absentee Oriana. Why should she fare any better with Paris?

'The voice of reason,' said Hengist irritably. 'He's such a lovely boy and such a potential star. I could bask in his reflected glory in my dotage.'

As his hands slid over her breasts, he felt the nipples hardening, and Sally felt liquid ripples between her legs.

'I was thinking of you,' whispered Hengist. 'You can always make time. Those geeks today had never eaten anything like your chocolate cake.'

'Janna and Ian Cartwright aren't geeks,' protested Sally, 'although she was looking awfully peaky, poor child.'

'Paris would be company. Mungo—' he began.

'Don't,' gasped Sally. The pain was still unbearable.

'Sorry. I just can't bear the thought of the poor boy being abandoned to that grotesque Blenchley, who I'm sure's a paedophile. His nails looked as though they were steeped in dried blood. Did you know that twenty-five per cent of the homeless are care leavers who've been cast out on the world?'

'Stop it.' Sally clapped her hands to her ears. 'I'll think about it.'

'Elaine loves Paris.' Hengist's hand slipped under the waistband of her skirt, over her flat stomach, to lose itself in warm flesh. 'I'm going to ring Mrs Axford and tell her to wait dinner half an hour.'

*   *   *

Despite his brusque, bossy exterior, Ian Cartwright liked children and, as a fine cricketer and rugby player, had always wanted a son. Since his adopted daughters Emerald and Sophy had married and had their own children, the house had seemed very empty.

Arriving home from the meeting, he could smell shepherd's pie, made from the remains of the cold meat from Sunday's shoulder of lamb. If one carved narrow slices, there was always plenty over. He found Patience crimson in the face, reading *Horse & Hound* as she spread mashed potato over the lamb.

'Good day?' she asked.

'Interesting.' Ian poured them both a glass from the bottle of red with which she was jazzing up the mince. 'Hengist wants to offer a free place to Paris Alvaston.'

'That's wonderful.' Patience tested the broccoli with a fork. 'How brilliant of Hengist.'

'Paris is having a bloody time at the children's home. They're looking for a family to foster him.'

'Oh, poor boy. If only we weren't so old.'

'We may not be. They want an older couple, who, if it worked, might consider adopting him to bridge the gap when he'd normally leave care and be chucked out on the streets.'

Out of the window, Ian could see Northcliffe, the golden retriever who had a tendency to go walkabout round the campus, cantering back across the fields, pausing to pick up a twig as a peace offering.

'Social services won't let him come to Bagley unless they can find someone. "Family find" is the awful expression.'

'Oh, Ian.' Patience sat down. 'Are you sure? We've only just got ourselves sorted.'

'You mean clawed our way back from financial ruin,' said Ian with a mirthless laugh. 'I won't be so stupid again.'

'I'd love to give it a try,' mused Patience. 'Dora simply adores him, so does Northcliffe. But I'm sure he'd find us too square. I don't know anything about Liverpool or pop music or Larkminster Rovers or computers.'

'Why don't we ask him?' said Ian.

They were brought back to earth by the smell of burnt broccoli.

*   *   *

First thing, Ian rang Nadine, who dropped in later in the day and was most enthusiastic.

'Paris loves coming to you. Your daughters and their kids visit often, so he'd have an extended family. You've been cleared by the Criminal Records Bureau; you've experienced the ups and downs of adoption. It could take several months, however, because you'd have to go on a course and undergo some counselling and some extensive interviews, I'm afraid.'

'We've been there. Last time they kept asking about our sex lives,' brayed Patience. 'We're a bit past that now.'

Ian frowned. 'I'm sure Nadine doesn't want to hear about that.'

'Paris's behaviour will probably be very challenging,' said Nadine. 'Looked-after kids invariably test their carers to the limit, just to prove they really care.'

'Just like rescued dogs,' said Patience happily. 'I must start reading the football reports.'

*   *   *

'I can't bear to think of poor Paris trapped in that children's home with that repellent man,' announced Sally the following evening. 'I'm sure

431

we could make time.'

'Too late,' said Hengist, almost accusingly. 'Fools have rushed in. Ian and Patience have offered. They've got to undergo loads of ghastly trials, like the labours of Hercules. But Nadine is taking Paris to "meet with" them shortly. "None but the brave deserves the fair",' he added bitterly and Sally felt reproached.

*   *   *

News of the poaching of Paris flashed round the staffroom.

'Just like a feminist version of the Trojan Wars,' sighed Artie Deverell. 'Lucky, lucky Cartwrights, but bags I be Helen of Troy.'

Dora was in ecstasy:

'I'll come and help you dirty up your house,' she told Patience. 'Social workers don't like prospective foster homes to be too pristine.'

48

The first meeting with the Cartwrights was excruciatingly embarrassing. Paris had only had mugs of tea in the kitchen before, but this time Patience had put on a skirt and make-up and heels she had great difficulty walking in, and had plunged into a drawing-room rat race of best china, silver, bread and butter and strawberry jam and 'Would you like milk, sugar, lemon or another slice of walnut cake?' all to be balanced on one's knees or the cat-shredded arm of a chair.

The drawing room, like Lily Hamilton's, seemed overcrowded with dark furniture, suggesting departure from a much larger house. Every shelf and table was crowded with ornaments or yellowing silver or blossom from the pink cherry outside rammed into vases.

Paris wished Ian and Nadine would bugger off and he could sort things out with Patience. Hitherto he'd only seen Ian flitting round Bagley being bossy about overspending and drooling over Vicky Fairchild. He seemed very old and straight, smelt like Mike Pitts of peppermint and stiff whiskies and kept barking, 'Mind out,' as Northcliffe's plumy tail endangered a precious teacup. He was like Captain Mainwaring in *Dad's Army*; Paris couldn't imagine him wearing jeans or taking him to McDonald's.

'I'm afraid it's bought,' confessed Patience when Nadine congratulated her on her walnut cake. 'I'm not much of a cook.'

Anything would be better than Oaktree Court,

433

thought Paris, where, as if Nigella and Jamie Oliver had never existed, Auntie Sylvia boiled mince, diced carrots and onion in water until they were cooked and turned cod the grey of the ancient pair of knickers, almost divorced from its elastic, which a wagging, singing Northcliffe had just laid at Nadine's big feet.

'Oh Northie,' giggled Patience, grabbing the pants and shoving them under a cushion.

'The most important thing is to hold back and listen,' Nadine had urged Patience, who, however, came from a generation and class who regarded it as a crime not to keep conversation going, however inane, and proceeded to do so.

How the hell was he going to put up with a lifetime of this, wondered Paris. If only he could turn on the television and watch Chelsea play Liverpool.

'This is our granddaughter, Dulcie,' said Patience, picking up a photograph of an adorable child with blond curls. 'She's a darling.'

Paris loved children. The best part of the home had always been making up games and stories for the littlest ones and comforting them when they cried. A few years ago, abuse had been rife; now the pendulum had swung. No careworker was ever on for more than forty-eight hours and the majority were so terrified of being accused of abuse, they wouldn't even take on to their lap a child who'd grazed a knee or been torn away from its parents. Desolation ruled. And if you dared complain of past abuse, you'd be bombarded by social workers, counsellors and therapists, prising you open, gouging out your secrets. Easier to trust no one and keep your trap shut.

There was another long pause.

'Our daughters Emerald and Sophy both married painters,' announced Patience, to explain the large, strange pictures rubbing shoulders with the hunting prints and landscapes on the walls.

'You were in the army, Colonel Cartwright,' accused Nadine, pointing to an oil of a lot of screaming women being mown down by a firing squad and their blood watering the young barley. 'Is this your taste?'

'Certainly not. It was painted by my son-in-law. He's actually a war artist, with work in the Tate.'

'You mustn't be so defensive,' chided Nadine.

Ian turned purple.

'Emerald's a sculptor,' said Patience quickly. 'She made me this adorable little maquette of Northcliffe for my birthday. You can almost see his tail wagging.'

'How old were they when you adopted Emerald and Sophy?'

'Just babies.' Patience reached for more photographs.

Those children had clearly inspired love, reflected Paris. Could he do the same? He was terrified they'd discover, beneath his cool, that he was as needy and desperate to escape as those mongrels pathetically scrabbling at the bars in a dog's home.

'We've got to go through some gruelling interviews,' Patience told him. 'We won't know if we're suitable as parents until August, which is a bore, but more importantly you might hate the thought of living with us.' She tried to stop her voice shaking.

Out in the yard a horse neighed, calling out to its

435

stable mate who'd been taken out for a ride.

'Dunno,' muttered Paris, pulling at a piece of cotton on his chair and releasing an avalanche of horsehair. 'Oh shit.'

'Paris, that's not very nice,' reproved Nadine.

Shut up, Paris wanted to scream, because he didn't know what to say, and was even more terrified that if they found out about his red-haze temper, his light fingers, his capacity for demolition, that he occasionally wet the bed, and was racked by fearful, screaming nightmares, they'd chuck him out after a week, a care leaver destined for homelessness.

'We'd so love you to come and live with us,' stammered Patience, missing the cup as she topped up Nadine's tea. 'But first you must get to know us.'

'That's enough,' snapped Ian. 'Let Paris make up his own mind; there's no hurry.'

'You will come and see us next week?' persisted Patience.

'For Christ's sake,' exploded Ian.

Oh God, they'll reject Ian and me because we don't get on, thought Patience in panic.

'Careful not to invade Paris's personal space,' reproved Nadine.

Paris scowled round at her. 'I can go if I like,' he said curtly.

*   *   *

The following Saturday, they asked Paris if he'd like to go to the cinema, but he said he'd prefer to muck about at home, and spent a couple of hours looking at Ian's military collection, which contained pieces of shrapnel, shells and bullets, and even a bit of marble from Hitler's desk.

'Rupert Brooke and I were at the same school,' volunteered Ian and, secretly thrilled by Paris's interest, presented him with a paperback of First World War poems.

Later, as the evenings were drawing out, Patience took him out to watch the Bagley herd being milked and took a picture of him with Ian and Northcliffe.

*   *   *

Paris's next visit was a disaster. Examining the photographs of beautiful Emerald in the drawing room, he knocked off and smashed the maquette she had modelled of Northcliffe. In terror, he shoved the pieces under the sofa, but missed the tail, which had fallen on a rug.

'I'd better go,' he told Patience, edging towards the door.

'You haven't had any tea—I've got Cornish pasties and chips.'

'Don't want anything.'

'I'll drive you back.'

'I want to walk.'

'Oh look, Northcliffe's tail's fallen off again. I must stick it back.' When she found the other pieces under the sofa, her face fell, then she smiled. 'Doesn't matter, I'm sure Emo can make me another one. I'm always breaking things. I smashed a vase this morning.'

Paris flared up:

'Why aren't you mad at me? You must be, you loved that dog.'

'It's only an ornament that's broken—not a promise or a heart.'

'Oh, for Christ's sake.' Paris stormed out and, crying helplessly, ran all the six miles back to Oaktree Court.

Two days later, he received a letter from Patience.

'Please come to tea next Saturday. Longing to see you.'

It wasn't natural to be so forgiving.

*   *   *

Nadine dropped him off, jollying him along, interrogating him all the way, as though she were forcibly opening an oyster with a chisel. He didn't tell her he was only intending to stay five minutes. Working himself into a rage, heart crashing, his breath coming in great gasps, he marched into an empty kitchen, rehearsing his speech: 'Look, it's not going to work. I want to chuck the whole thing: I can't handle Bagley and sod Hengist and Theo Graham and fucking Homer and Virgil.

'Get out the way,' he yelled, aiming a kick as Northcliffe, carrying a feather duster, bounded towards him in delight.

He was about to sweep all Patience's recipe books on to the floor, and then start smashing plates and mugs so they'd definitely never want to see him again, when he caught sight of his own photographs in a silver frame on the dresser: one of him with Northcliffe, another of him as Romeo. Yet another of him, with Dora and Beluga, Romeo's fiery steed, had been put in a big frame beside pictures of Emerald and Sophy.

Paris blushed and blushed, a huge smile spreading over his face, as Patience bustled in:

'Oh, hello, Paris.' Then, catching sight of the photographs, she added humbly: 'We hope you don't think we're jumping the gun.'

Paris kicked the kitchen table and shook his head.

'It's fine.'

'Thank goodness. Plover's sister's about to foal, the vet's on his way, I thought you might like to help.'

'OK.' Paris then screwed up courage to ask how the interviews were going.

'Pretty well,' said Patience, putting on her red Puffa. 'They do ask extraordinary questions. If normal couples went through such hassle, they'd never have children. But it's all worth it,' she added hastily.

After the foal had been born, all covered in blood and gore, the vet and Patience had shared a bottle of white wine with Paris and congratulated him on having such a calming effect on the frightened mare. When Nadine rolled up, Patience hastily dropped the bottle in the bin.

As he was leaving, she shouted he'd left his jacket, and as she picked it up from the kitchen chair, a photograph of her and Ian fluttered out.

'Must have picked it up by mistake,' muttered Paris. 'No, that's a lie, I wanted one until I moved in, like.'

'Keep it,' said an enraptured Patience.

Watching him go off into the hazy blue evening, Patience hugged herself. Until he moved in, like. She ran to the gate to wave him off.

Back at the home, Paris hid the photo between

439

his under-blanket and the mattress, because he didn't seem to be wetting the bed any more and because Patience and Ian were pretty old and ugly, and he couldn't bear the other kids taking the piss or, even worse, tearing up the photo.

*   *   *

As bursars work extremely hard, Paris saw more of Patience than Ian, who was nervous but determined things should work.

'What'm I supposed to call you?' Paris asked him on the next visit.

'You could call me "Colonel Cartwright", but that's a bit formal, and "Uncle" is silly because I'm not. Would it be OK, if we pass the tests, to describe you as "Paris, our foster son", which would be true, then if things go very well, we can drop the foster.'

'That's good,' agreed Paris. 'I'll call you Mr Ian, if that's OK.'

'Good start,' said Ian.

'As we know each other better, you can call me Patience.'

Paris really smiled for the first time.

'Going to need a lot, if you're taking me on.'

'Next week, why don't we go to IKEA and choose some stuff for your room?' Treading on eggshells, trying not to presume, she added hastily: 'If we don't pass the test, you can always use the room when you come and stay.'

49

In the middle of May, when Bagley was looking at its most seductive, with the setting sun warming the golden stone, cow parsley lacing the endless pitches and the trees still in their radiant young, green beauty, Hengist formally offered Paris a place.

On the wall of Hengist's study, Paris was intensely flattered to see, alongside other triumphs, a framed photograph of himself as Romeo. Then Hengist had added he was also offering a boarding place to Feral, so he and Paris needn't be parted, and when Paris accepted, trying to keep the excitement out of his voice and face, Hengist offered him a glass of champagne to celebrate.

'Patience and Ian are a super couple.' Hengist sat down on the dark red Paisley window seat beside a reclining Elaine, and beckoned Paris to join them. 'A super couple, salt of the earth, although one's not, according to Poppet Bruce, supposed to have salt in anything these days. You'll have fun when their daughters come down—Emerald is stunning—and with young Dora hanging around and lots of horses and a charming dog. But if you find it hard to discuss things with them, speak instead to Theo Graham, who's going to be your new housemaster. Beneath the rather crusty exterior Theo's a sweet man.

'But if you ever think of running away from Bagley'—Hengist was lovingly smoothing Elaine's white, velvet ears—'I want you to promise to pop in on Sally and me first, and we'll give you some sandwiches and a can of Coke for the journey. Give me your hand and your promise,' and his big suntanned hand enveloped Paris's, which was almost as white and slender as Elaine's.

Paris promised. He'd never met anyone as charismatic as Hengist. The thick, dark hair, olive skin, heavy-lidded eyes, beautiful clothes, the element of danger, the desire not exactly to corrupt but to stir up and subvert reminded him so much of Lord Henry Wotton in *The Portrait of Dorian Gray*. The same sweet, seductive scent of lilac, so memorable in the book, was now drifting in through the window, overpowering the clean, healthy, soapy smell of hawthorn.

Paris had been jealous of Hengist in the past, because Janna smelt so lovely and always seemed to be laughing when Hengist was around. Paris still thought and dreamt of her constantly. At the end of term, they would be split up, but at least before that, at the end of June, she would be coming on the geography field trip, when Larks and Bagley would be taking off together for Wales, and he might slay a dragon for her. He was very proud Hengist had chosen him, and with Feral by his side, he could face anything.

Hengist, predictably, was not just enlisting Feral entirely for Paris's benefit. As a dazzling athlete, who'd really profit from decent coaching and pitches, Feral would bring glory to Bagley. Nor could Hengist resist unsettling that pompous ass Biffo Rudge by installing a gloriously priapic black boy in his house.

Alas, the next day, Feral was summoned off the cricket field, having just been bowled after knocking up a useful fifty in twenty minutes, and flabbergasted Hengist by turning down his offer of a place.

'Kind of you, man, but I don't like the thought of being locked up in the evening.'

He didn't add that he was worried his family would fall apart if he wasn't there to hold it together.

' "Why, uncle, 'tis a shame",' said Paris when he heard the news. Although devastated by Feral's refusal, he wasn't prepared to betray regret or try and talk him round.

'As I'm locked up already, I might as well accept a more upmarket gaol.'

Nor was everyone pleased about Paris going to Bagley. Joan Johnson thought free places should have been offered to clever Aysha, or Kylie for her pretty voice, or Pearl for her artistic skills.

And if the masters at Bagley were excited, the staff at Larks were outraged that Paris would be thrown to the wolves of private education.

Emerald and Sophy Belvedon, who liked to dump their own children on Granny Patience whenever they needed a break, also expressed doubts.

'He'll be bringing his rough friends home and breaking the place up. He's already smashed my maquette of Northcliffe,' raged Emerald. 'And I hope Daddy's not going to get any silly ideas like Jupiter about sons inheriting everything.'

Sophy was more worried that teenagers were wildly expensive and that her parents had just got straight financially after Ian going bankrupt in the nineties.

Janna, meanwhile, had not made it up with Hengist. Ringing up to ask her to lunch, he received an earful, but refused to admit he'd pulled a fast one by poaching Paris.

'Darling, from the moment we met at La Perdrix d'Or, you kept telling me how wonderfully clever Paris was, thrusting his poems and essays at me, saying he needed to escape from the poverty trap. I honestly thought that was what you wanted.'

'Oh, go to hell.' Janna slammed down the telephone.

She was having a very tough summer. The GCSEs loomed and unless their results improved, they would again be branded one of the worst schools in the West. Exams also meant the gym would be out of action, so the children couldn't work off any energy. The Wolf Pack were demoralized and acting up because Paris was leaving. Half the staff were moonlighting and exhausted and tetchy, after four or five hours marking GCSE papers every night.

After the good publicity generated by *Romeo and Juliet*, many parents had put Larks as their first choice. Then the wretched council had changed the bus route, which meant buses no longer stopped outside the school gates and parents, worried about kidnapping and sexual abuse, changed their minds.

One step forward, one step back.

But despite not a week passing without a slagging off in the *Gazette*, Janna felt the school was steadily improving. Thanks to frequent visits from Gablecross's constabulary, there was much less fighting in the playground or in the corridors. Teachers were mostly able to teach. Mrs Kamani no longer complained of shoplifting and rowdy behaviour. Even Miss Miserden, the old biddy who lived at the bottom of the drive, stopped grumbling about Feral's football after Graffi rescued her cat Scamp from the top branch of a pear tree. The children had also been on some terrific jaunts to the seaside, to the Blackpool illuminations, to Longleat and the London Eye. A production of *Oliver!* was planned for next term.

Vicky, who would direct it, was not enjoying the summer term as much as her spring one. She couldn't slope off to Bagley all the time and had to face up to the rough and tumble of Larks.

In the last week in May, in the middle of the GCSEs, having gained Mike Pitts's permission and claiming it was 'vital for her professional development', Vicky sloped off for two days at a National Theatre workshop.

In her absence, Janna discovered a shambles of homework unmarked and work unset. Worse still, Vicky was hardly engaging with her tutor group, with the result that one girl was being so badly bullied, she tried to hang herself with a pair of tights during break.

Janna, who had already received a warning from the girl's mother, had ordered Vicky to sort it out. Vicky had clearly done nothing.

Bitter shame that she herself hadn't prevented it fuelled Janna's anger. Vicky was due back on the Wednesday morning before half-term, then rang in to tell Rowan her train had broken down and she wouldn't be back till after lunch.

She had eventually floated in around two-forty-

445

five, Little Miss Demure in a navy blue suit, with her shining clean hair drawn into a neat bun, pale cheeks flushed, wafting Trésor. Immediately, she started wittering on about 'cutting-edge productions' and 'unique opportunities to discover my own creativity'.

Janna let her run, then let rip, epitomizing every cliché about redheads and fiery tempers. Partner shot under the sofa.

'I trusted you, Vicky. How dare you bunk off like this? Year Eight is totally under-rehearsed for their play on Parents' Day. Year Eleven can't quote a single line from *A View from the Bridge* and they've got Eng. lit. tomorrow. You left no lesson plans for this morning.'

'I rang in,' bridled Vicky.

'You should have come back. Lottie Hargreaves, one of your tutor group, tried to hang herself. We've had the police here all morning. I told you to keep an eye on her. You've let me down!'

'And you've let me down,' shouted back Vicky. 'You never warned me this school was completely out of control. A parent slapped my face the other day.'

'Why didn't you report it?'

'I didn't want to sneak.' Vicky burst into tears and fled.

Overnight, Janna cooled down. The fact remained she needed Vicky. Whatever her limitations, she had reduced truancy among the boys, and with so many children taking drama and English GCSEs next year because of her, Janna couldn't really sack her. She'd better call her in first thing, before she caused too much havoc.

She was greeted on the morrow by a furious

Rowan.

'You're not going to like this.'

It was a letter from Bagley's personnel department asking for a reference for Vicky who had applied for a job teaching English and drama. Janna flipped and rang Hengist who, as Painswick had gone to the dentist, picked up the telephone. Bruckner's Eight was on fortissimo. Hengist only turned it down fractionally and when Janna started screaming at him, became quite sharp. Education was a free-for-all. Vicky was entitled to work where she wanted. As long as her notice was in by 31 May, which was tomorrow, she could start in the autumn.

'Anyway, I can't see why you're making such a fuss. You seemed pretty anxious to be shot of the poor child yesterday. I also wanted to make things easy for Paris,' he went on, even more infuriatingly, 'who will feel happier if he's acquainted with a member of staff.'

Out of the window, Janna could see a Year Eleven pupil so deep in last-minute revision, she bumped into an oak tree.

' "All my pretty chickens and their dam, At one fell swoop?" ' she said tonelessly. 'How dare you poach my staff and pupils without asking?'

'Because I knew you'd try and stop me,' said Hengist unrepentantly.

'Vicky has ensured three-quarters of Year Ten will be taking drama GCSE next year.'

'That's great. We can hold joint Larks–Bagley classes. Means I'll see more of you.'

After that, Janna's shouting could be heard all over Larks, and Partner took refuge in Rowan's office.

447

'I'm not going to talk to you until you cool down,' said Hengist and hung up.

'We're well shot of her, she's an applause junkie and a dozy bitch,' said Rowan, rushing in with a box of tissues and a cup of black coffee laced with brandy. 'Give her a good reference to show you're magnanimous. Lord Brett-Taylor can pick up the pieces when she fucks up.'

'Rowan,' said Janna in awe, 'I've never heard you swear before.'

Janna's magnanimity was sorely tested when she and Vicky met.

'I'm tired of sticking up for you, Jannie.'

'Who first approached you?' asked Janna numbly.

'I don't remember, but Hengist, Emlyn and nice Alex Bruce, such a sweetie, all suggested I'd be an asset to Bagley, and frankly'—Vicky smiled helplessly—'Hengist is so charismatic, I can't resist the chance of working with him. And if I can ease Paris's transition and Hengist believes I can . . .' Then, misinterpreting the anguish on Janna's face: 'But don't worry, I won't let you down over the geography field trip. Emlyn's going and Hengist even said he might drop in. He's arranged for us to stay in some Welsh stately castle. I can't wait.'

Vicky didn't add that she herself had applied for the job, and at her first interview over lunch with Hengist on Wednesday, had presented him with a rare work on rugby football or that yesterday, after Janna had carpeted her, she had driven over to Bagley and sobbed on Alex's narrow shoulder, telling him:

'Larks is out of control: a Year Nine boy tried to rape me' (mild lunge from Monster) 'and I was

448

punched by a parent' (mild lunge from a mother whose husband Vicky had inveigled into Larks to paint cupboards).

'I loved Jannie so much in Yorkshire,' Vicky had continued to sob. 'She was such fun. Now she seems to have lost her creativity. She's so hard now.'

Dora Belvedon, busy weeding up wallflowers under the window, heard everything, which the following day appeared in the *Gazette* as 'Star teacher and pupil to leave Larks'.

Red Robbie, who'd been hoping to get his leg over Vicky on the geography field trip, was so shocked by her defection to an independent, he flatly refused to go.

Janna also received lots of flak.

'Just learnt of your tragic loss,' emailed Rod Hyde, 'you must try and hang on to your good staff.'

'I don't know what we'll do without our little Vicky to bring sunshine into our life,' moaned Basket.

Monster proceeded to trash the drama department.

I'm just jealous of Vicky having constant access to Hengist and Paris, thought Janna in despair. She wished she could pour her heart out to Emlyn, but he'd taken the opportunity of half-term to fly to Afghanistan to see Oriana.

Janna spent most of the break sobbing for her mother. She had to face up to the fact that hard work cannot blot out loneliness for ever.

The only positive thing she did was to telephone her friend Sophy Belvedon. Sophy was Ian and Patience's daughter, married to Alizarin, the

449

brother of Jupiter, Dora and Dicky. Sophy was also an English and drama teacher, with whom Janna had worked in Yorkshire, who now lived in London.

Sophy was her usual cheerful, adorable self.

'It's so lovely to hear from you. Mum says you're making a brilliant job of Larks. It must be so beautiful down there now.'

'How's Dulcie?' asked Janna. 'She must be nearly eighteen months now.'

'She's heaven, but I'm not sure being a full-time mother's quite me. I'm so turning into a cabbage, leaves are sprouting out of my head. I'm sure some German's going to make me into sauerkraut.'

'You don't want a job, do you?'

'God, I'd love one.'

'Head of English and drama in the autumn.'

'Oh yes, yes please.'

'It's a pretty rough school.'

'Couldn't be rougher than London. Someone chucked a brick through our drawing-room window yesterday. We could get an au pair or perhaps Mum could look after Dulcie during the day. Might put her and Dad off their latest mad project of fostering a looked-after kid of fourteen.'

*   *   *

Alex Bruce, while delighted by the annexing of Vicky, bitterly regretted that Hengist's ability to poach clever children and staff was only equalled by his irrational refusal to boot out the stupid children of his friends.

The Chinless Wanderers: Lando, Jack and Junior, although dazzling at games, were predicted to get straight Us in their GCSE exams in two years' time. Xavier Campbell-Black bumped sulkily along the bottom of the class and his sister Bianca, even more intellectually challenged, had recently revealed that she didn't know on which side Hitler fought in the last war.

Alex was anxious to single out any pupils on the Grade C/D borderline and give them early coaching. Anyone below that level would endanger Bagley's place in the league tables and should be asked to leave.

'Bianca will stay,' said Hengist firmly. 'She's destined to be the next Darcey Bussell. Screw the league tables. We must cultivate individual excellence.'

'You said you wanted to beat Fleetley and ward off any challenge from St Jimmy's.'

'Maybe I did. The secret of greatness is to admit one is in the wrong.'

Hengist's inconsistency drove Alex crackers.

'Thank God this school is in a safe pair of hands,' he told Miss Painswick.

'Thank God for a handy pair of safes,' smirked Little Cosmo, as he and Lubemir cracked the combination of the safe in the school office, photostatted the 2002 GCSE and A level papers stored inside and flogged them for five hundred pounds a go to needy candidates.

'We need never work again,' crowed Cosmo, 'and we're doing our bit for Bagley by ensuring it does really well in the league tables.'

Having insinuated himself as a regular in the school office by plying Miss Painswick with chocolates and Dame Hermione's latest CDs, Cosmo also overheard Alex chuntering over

Bianca's lack of intellect.

After his success at photographing the stars of *Romeo and Juliet*, Cosmo had been asked to do the pictures for the school prospectus and achieved an excellent multicultural mix by putting Anatole, Lubemir, Nordic blonde Amber and Bianca on the cover. No one could sack Bianca if she was in the prospectus.

Cosmo also found the proofs of the prospectus on Painswick's computer and added 'binge-drinking, buggery and Bruce-baiting' to the list of pupils' favourite activities. Fortunately this was picked up and deleted by an amused Hengist.

Alex also had to accept the fact that during Wimbledon, which coincided with the last fortnight of term, Hengist would be virtually incommunicado, claiming to be writing a crucial piece for *The Times*, when all you could hear was the thwack of tennis balls and the rattle of applause.

This year, Anatole's father dropped in for 'an important meeting' and to thwack and rattle were added the chink of bottles and roars of laughter as he and Hengist enjoyed the dazzling Miss Kournikova in the first round.

Hengist fiddled, while Alex burnt with resentment.

50

Field trips are very hard work and enmeshed in red tape, so once Red Robbie refused to go as a matter of principle, the rest of Larks's staff were only too glad to use their disapproval of the private sector as an excuse to opt out. Anyway, they were far too busy marking exams and writing reports.

So Janna buried her pride and pleaded with Robbie to change his mind: 'Next term Year Nine will begin their two-year GCSE course. This trip will whet their appetite not just for geography but for history and English. There are wonderful activities planned. They'll learn self-esteem and the ability to relate to people of a different background.'

Robbie had folded his arms and gazed mutinously up at the damp patch in the ceiling, until Janna lost it.

'You're just terrified of being shown up because Rufus Anderson's such a brilliant head of geography.'

This caused a rumpus, with the senior staff blanking Janna and Sam Spink marching in accusing Janna of humiliating Robbie.

'Good,' snapped Janna.

So in the end, Janna only had Vicky who, having sworn she wouldn't let Janna down, couldn't back out, and Gloria who had a crush on Emlyn, and Skunk Illingworth who would do anything for a freebie and who also had a crush on Vicky, and Cambola who was always game for a jaunt. Mags would have come but her new grandchild was about to be born and the ever dependable Wally had his son, Ben, home on leave.

Batting for Bagley were Rufus and a couple of his young geography teachers, No-Joke Joan who also had a crush on Vicky and didn't want to let any of her young women loose unchaperoned with Cosmo and all those dreadful Larks youths around, and, of course, Emlyn.

As Paris was moving to Bagley, it was felt the field trip would be a good way for him to bond with future form-mates. He was already enduring endless flak at Oaktree Court and at Larks for becoming a stuck-up snob, and as social services hadn't yet confirmed Patience and Ian as his foster parents, it was a time of deep uncertainty.

Paris refused again to betray how gutted he was that Feral—and Graffi as well—had refused to join him on the field trip. Graffi's father was off sick and heavily on the booze again; Feral's domestic life was always shadowy; but both boys were needed at home. Both vowed, as a band of brothers, they would always be friends of Paris, but he knew it would never be the same.

Without the other two he also felt less sanguine about protecting himself against Cosmo and his bodyguards. The female remnants of the Wolf Pack were unlikely to provide support. Pearl would probably go off like a firecracker. Kylie had not only persuaded Chantal to look after Cameron while they were away, but, at the prospect of Kylie becoming the future Lady Waterlane, to also bankroll a snazzy new wardrobe. This included a glamorous dress because everyone had been told to bring something 'eveningy' for a mystery destination on the last night of the trip.

Paris, fretting about his lack of wardrobe, was extremely touched when Ian took him aside and gave him sixty pounds, gruffly bidding him not to spend it all at once. Carrying this out to the letter, Paris nicked some T-shirts and trainers and sauntered out of Gap in unpaid-for dark-grey jeans, which he promptly slashed across the knees and thighs to age them up.

*   *   *

On the morning of departure, Janna was drying her hair when Emlyn rang and said he was dreadfully sorry, he couldn't make the trip. Whereupon Janna, mostly from disappointment and because Emlyn was the only person who could control this mob, lost her temper and bawled him out.

As she paused for breath, Emlyn repeated how sorry he was but that his father had died in the night, from lungs wrecked by a life down the mines, and he was on his way home to Wales to look after his mother and organize the funeral.

A mortified Janna was frantically apologizing when Emlyn displayed a flicker of his old self:

'Now the even worse news. Biffo Rudge has been press-ganged into going in my place. He'll be as anxious to chaperone his boys as Joan is. I'm sorry, lovely, I'll buy you dinner when I get back.'

'I'm the one who's sorry,' wailed Janna, 'I know how you loved him.'

*   *   *

The weather was hot and jungly. The journey in

three coaches seemed to take forever. Paris read *Le Rouge et Le Noir*; Rocky the *Mirror* with one finger; Cosmo read the score of *Harold in Italy*; Jade and Milly read each other's palms; Boffin read *A Brief History of Time* and, as litter monitor, bawled out everyone for dropping sweet papers. Amber read text messages from admiring boyfriends; Kylie, who felt sick on buses, tried to look at the pictures in *Hello!* and had to stop near St Jimmy's on the outskirts of Larkminster to throw up.

'You don't think she's up the duff again?' Pearl murmured to Paris.

Whereupon Rocky, realizing he'd left behind his Ritalin, leapt into the driver's seat and drove the bus back to Larks to collect it. Everyone was too petrified of a Ritalinless Rocky to stop him. When the outraged bus driver took over on the second journey, it was noticed how many desirable residences Randal Stancombe was building within the catchment area of Rod Hyde's school.

'These are the sorts of houses you can afford if you don't have to fork out for school fees,' observed Cosmo nastily.

*   *   *

Before leaving, both schools had received individual pep talks on the importance of good behaviour and overcoming the traditional animosities which divide private and state schools.

Cosmo, cash rich from flogging exam papers, had listened in amusement. He liked Emlyn, but they would be much freer without him. Biffo couldn't control an ant. Cosmo had packed a first-aid kit of vodka, brandy, cocaine, grass, Alka-Seltzer, a hundred condoms, the morning-after pill and amyl nitrate, and had had a bet with Anatole that he'd pull both Gloria and Vicky by the end of the trip.

He also fancied a threesome with Milly and Amber, was going to bully Xavier to a jelly and unsettle Paris, to whom he intended to give a rough ride next term, particularly as the Bagley Babes had just announced that, in the absence of Feral and Graffi, their target on the trip was to pull Paris.

As the coaches moved into open country, Cosmo proceeded to ring up Dora, ordering her at pain of death not to forget to water his marijuana plants— not that they would need it, as rain was now chucking itself like lover's gravel against the bus window.

Poor little Dora, being ordered around by a pig like Cosmo, thought an indignant Pearl, who was sitting across the gangway. Pearl was utterly miserable; her little stepbrother was teething and her mother had discovered fifteen pounds missing from her bag, which Pearl had nicked to pay for a long-sleeved olive-green T-shirt from New Look. This had meant her mother's toyboy couldn't go to the pub, whereupon her mother had hit Pearl and screamed that 'she could bleedin' leave home if there was any more trouble'.

The long sleeves had been needed to cover Pearl's arms, which she'd attacked with a razor and which now throbbed unbearably. Cosmo smiled evilly across at her. He was vile but dead sexy, with his night-dark eyes and his satanic pirate's smile.

Down the bus, Biffo Rudge, noisily crunching an apple as sulphuric farts ruffled his long khaki shorts, was sharing a seat with a pile of Lower Fifth reports.

Cosmo proceeded to convulse pupils from both schools by holding up behind Biffo's seat the air freshener from the lavatory. As the bus crossed over into Herefordshire, plunging into thick forest with glimpses of silver rivers gleaming in the valleys below, Biffo fell asleep. Whereupon Cosmo seized the pile of reports, found his own and wrote 'towering genius' and 'undeniably brilliant' all over it. Buoyed up by the mounting mirth of his audience, Cosmo dug out Boffin's report and scribbled 'deeply irritating', 'unimaginative' and 'stupid twat' all over it, before crying, 'You dropped this, sir,' as Biffo woke up.

At the back of the coach, Vicky had palled up very pointedly with Gloria: 'Such a relief to have someone fun and my age on the trip.'

Now they whispered and played silly games: 'In ten seconds—who would you rather go to bed with, Biffo or Skunk?' followed by squeals of laughter.

Occasionally they cast covetous eyes at Rufus, head of geography, but he was too busy calling his wife and mother, who was looking after the children, even to notice them.

As Cambola was in another coach, Janna was forced to sit with Joan who, despite taking up most of the seat, insisted on clamping a beefy thigh against Janna's.

'All my Lower Fifth students have opted for triple science,' she announced, adding that she was off to a conference in Atlanta at the end of term. 'I'm giving a paper on the Place of the Runner Bean in Teaching Genetics,' she boomed. 'The runner bean is the perfect plant to illustrate multiple

458

pregnancies.'

'Why not Kylie Rose?' murmured Amber to Milly. 'Did you know, Joan rejected seventeen possible gardeners provided by the bursar this week because none of them was ugly enough for us not to jump on him?'

*   *   *

Despite a desire to get off with the opposite sex, Janna noticed a look of relief on the Larks girls' faces when, after an interminable drive, they discovered they would be sleeping in one youth hostel near a river on the edge of a wood, while the boys would be housed four miles away in another.

'Thank goodness,' said Primrose Duddon, 'boys always gobble up all the food.'

In fact the food was awful, spag bol full of gristle, vegetables boiled into abdication and great blocks of jam roly-poly.

'Talk about Calorie Towers,' grumbled Amber.

After supper, if you could call it that, the rain stopped so they dried off the benches outside and Joan brought out her guitar and, led by Cambola, they sang round a dispirited camp fire.

'To think I got myself sacked from the Brownies to end up here,' muttered Amber. 'I need a drink.'

'You'll get cocoa at ten o'clock,' said Joan tartly.

At ten-fifteen, she went round with a basket confiscating mobiles. 'You've all got a long day tomorrow.'

So the Bagley Babes unearthed their second mobiles and rang their boyfriends.

'If anyone tries to escape,' boomed Joan as she marched up and down the rows of beds, 'there'll be trouble.'

'I don't know why we came on this jaunt,' moaned Milly. 'Tomorrow we'll start digging a tunnel.'

As the lights were turned off and everyone stretched out on their hard beds, Kylie, who'd thought by now she'd be curled up with the Hon. Jack, started to cry that she was missing Cameron and Chantal.

'I miss my dog and my horse more than my parents or even my boyfriend,' said Amber, which made Kylie cry even louder, so Jade pelted her with pillows.

*   *   *

For the staff, Janna noted nervously that there were a double and three single rooms.

Joan looked warmly at Vicky. 'I'm happy to share.'

'No, no. You deserve the privilege of a room of your own,' Vicky simpered. 'Gloria and I don't at all mind bunking up.'

Janna, who had watched the girls' faces during that dismal dinner, prayed things would improve tomorrow. Hearing sobs, she went into the dormitory and sitting down on Kylie's bed, patted her heaving shoulder.

'Shall I tell you a story?'

'Please, miss.'

' "O, young Lochinvar is come out of the west, Through all the wide Border his steed was the best",' began Janna in her sweet, soft voice, which in the dark sounded like that of a young girl.

She can't be more than early thirties, thought

Amber. It was such a good story, she managed to stay awake to the very end.

51

Things did get better.

'The students have bonded so well that the teachers are redundant,' Skunk Illingworth announced the following evening, froth gathering on his moustache like snow on a blackthorn hedge as he downed a pint of real ale.

He, Biffo and Rufus had sloped off to the local pub, leaving the pupils happy to write up their field notes because, thanks to Bagley's head of geography, they had discovered geography could be really interesting. Rufus, red-blond hair flopping, bony freckled face alight, had charged round Herefordshire, a piece of rock in one hand, a hammer in the other, book open in the grass, explaining the mysteries of the natural world to his enraptured listeners.

Earlier in the day, one group, including Paris, Boffin and Kylie, had carried out a tourist survey in a neighbouring forest. Unfortunately, on a dripping Wednesday morning, there was only a handful of tourists, who got fed up being repeatedly asked the same question. Kylie had even disturbed a couple in flagrante in the maturing bracken.

'When I asked Mr and Mrs Brown from Scunthorpe whether they had travelled here by train, coach or bicycle,' she was now writing in her round, careful hand, 'they told me to f— off.'

Everyone had then piled into the coaches and moved on to the next location, the source of the Fleet, which here was an eight-foot-wide brook, but which swelled into a great river as it passed Bagley, curled round Larkminster and Larks, then flowed on into Rutshire, past Cosmo's mother's house, through Lando France-Lynch's father's land, then skirting Xav's father's land in Gloucestershire.

If I could only climb into a boat and row home, thought Xav, who, that morning, had been punched very hard by Lubemir.

'Each group was allocated a section of the river,' wrote Primrose Duddon in a red and mauve striped notebook. 'We had to test our hypothesis on a "meander", which means the river bending several times, and on a "riffle", which is a fast-flowing, straight section. We rolled up a piece of tin foil, then checked how fast it floated down river.'

Pearl had kicked off her shoes and watched the ball of foil. It was snagged by tawny rushes, then floated on through the brown peaty water. Then she had collapsed on the warm wet grass, waiting for a teacher to tell her to get up. She was about to turn on her stopwatch and see how fast another ball of foil was floating down the far bank, when she felt a hand, as warm as the sun, on her bare legs.

'This is a "riffle",' murmured Cosmo as he ran his hand slowly up her bare legs, roving over her bottom, gently exploring in and out of her shorts. 'And this is definitely a "meander".'

He then lay down beside her on the bank, wickedly squinting sideways at her, stroking her rainbow hair, kissing her forehead, burying his tongue in her ear, murmuring endearments in Italian, his night-dark eyes blotting out the sun. As

463

she turned her head towards him, he kissed her, slowly sucking each lip, then dividing them with his tongue.

A roar of rage interrupted Pearl's moment of bliss.

'Cosmo Rannaldini. Stop that at once.' Then the roar diminished as Joan realized Cosmo was only molesting a Larks student. 'But stop it all the same. You're supposed to be testing the velocity of the river, not the speed of your seduction technique.'

Pearl couldn't wait to tell Kylie.

'Cosmo snogged me. He is so brilliant, my knees gave way and I was lying down.'

*   *   *

The Chinless Wanderers, who weren't remotely interested in riffles and who regarded rivers as places in which you caught salmon or retrieved polo balls, were smoking and listening to the test match. Further down the bank Paris read *Le Rouge et Le Noir*, totally engrossed in Julien Sorel's seduction of the beautiful, much older Madame de Renal leading to passionate mutual love—maybe Janna wasn't such an impossibility.

He had bonded least of the Larks contingent. He was sick of Bagley chat about gap years in Argentina and their parents' splitting up. There was also something sickening about the country, he thought, or the evils man imposed on it. Last year, he'd been haunted by the funeral pyres burning innocent sheep and cattle.

This year it was the rabbits lying in the footpath dying from myxomatosis, desperately trying to crawl away as their bulging eyes were pecked out

464

by huge killer gulls. The girls screamed in horror; Paris turned away retching; Jack Waterlane picked up a log and put one rabbit out of its misery, then another, then another, shouting at the gulls before returning to put a comforting arm round a sobbing Kylie.

Jack wasn't quite such a prat as he seemed, decided Paris.

The gulls were a symbol of the way Cosmo pecked away at Xavier and himself, if given a chance.

Before supper that evening, Paris wandered off from the hostel into the wood to read in peace. Hearing raised voices, he was about to sidle to the right, when he clocked Lubemir's very distinctive accent: 'Fetch eet, black sheet.'

Edging forward through the green curtain of a willow, Paris found a clearing in which Cosmo and Lubemir were playing football. To the left, like an enemy ambush, lurked a huge bed of nettles, giving off a rank, bitter smell as the still hot evening sun burnt off the rain. Beside them stood Xav, fat, hunched, terrified, as Cosmo powered the ball into the nettles.

'Pick it up, black shit.'

Desperate to avoid a beating, wincing from the stings, Xav plunged in and picked up the ball, only for Lubemir to boot it back again. 'Fetch eet, you fat creep.'

For a moment defiance flared: 'Why should I?'

'Because your black skin's too rhinoceros-like to feel stings. Pick it up,' demanded Cosmo.

Paris strolled into the clearing. 'Get it your fucking self.'

'Don't speak to me like that, yob,' said Lubemir

465

insolently.

Paris dropped *Le Rouge et Le Noir*. A second later, his right hook had sent Lubemir flying into the nettles.

Bellowing at the pain, Lubemir yelled, 'Get heem,' to Cosmo.

Cosmo, however, who believed guards should guard themselves, was examining his nails.

Turning on Cosmo, Paris grabbed him by his bright blue Ralph Lauren shirt.

'Want to make the same journey?' he hissed, yanking Cosmo towards the nettles. 'I thought not. Well, fucking lay off Xav.'

Picking up *Le Rouge et Le Noir*, he stalked back to the hostel, with Xav panting to keep up.

'Thanks very, very much.'

' 'S OK. Cosmo's a wimp if you face up to him.'

Xav didn't believe him, but he felt a little better.

*   *   *

'Dear Mum,' wrote Kylie, another twenty-four hours later:

> We're having a brilliant time. We've been clay-pigeon shooting, rock climbing and we cycled to a museum. We've also been to an art gallery, which Graffi would have loved. Everyone friendly—Bagley really nice, Jack gorgeous. We write up our notes in the evening when the teachers go to the pub, so we can get out the booze and the weed. Today some kids went riding. Cosmo raced his horse up behind Paris's and made it bolt. Paris fell off.

Paris hadn't any parents to write to. He'd started a card of a red dragon's tongue, symbol of the Welsh language, to Patience and Ian, then, not knowing how to address them on the envelope and deciding it was counting chickens, had torn it up. His head ached after his fall; if only he was with Janna in the pub.

Janna enjoyed these pub sessions, discussing the children, comparing state and private school practice.

'We work much harder in the independent sector,' moaned one of Rufus's young geography teachers. 'At least you lot can work at home. We're on call twenty-four hours a day and most weekends.'

'You have loads longer holidays and we've got so many teachers off with stress,' said Gloria, returning with another bottle. 'The ones who aren't work ten times as hard.'

'Hengist doesn't believe in stress or "generalized anxiety" as it's now known.' Rufus shook his head. 'He expects people to come in every day.'

'Except for himself,' grumbled Biffo.

'You won't be able to run to your union when you join us next term,' Joan teased an increasingly alarmed Vicky.

'Hengist is a despot,' complained Biffo. 'When Emlyn had to pull out, he virtually ordered me to take his place.'

'Poor Emlyn, his father's being buried tomorrow.' Janna found that he was seldom far from her thoughts. She kept wanting to call and comfort him, but felt it would be intrusive. She had arranged a wreath and a card of sympathy signed

467

by everyone on the trip.

'Hengist is driving down to Wales for the funeral—to show support,' said Joan dismissively.

'And distribute largesse. The great international in a Welsh rugger town,' said Biffo even more dismissively.

'I think it's lovely of Hengist to go,' protested Janna. 'Emlyn adores him. He is Emlyn's future father-in-law and it'll mean a huge amount to the family.'

'Hengist's probably rather relieved Sally won't have to walk down the aisle on the arm of Emlyn's dad,' observed Joan. 'He's a crashing snob.'

'He is not,' said Janna furiously. 'Hengist gets on with people from all backgrounds.'

'Hark at you defending him,' simpered Vicky. 'I thought the two of you had fallen out.'

*   *   *

Paris had spent Ian's sixty pounds on a pair of shorts, a Prussian-blue shirt and a Liverpool baseball cap, which someone had nicked. As a result, on the third day he got too much sun canoeing. On the way back to the hostel, he started feeling horribly sick and sweaty; his head, after yesterday's fall, ached abominably. Stepping down from the bus, his legs buckled and he fainted.

He came round to find himself on the grass under a spreading chestnut tree, with a rolled towel under his head and Janna fussing over him, and thought he'd gone to heaven. As the bus had drawn up nearer Calorie Towers than the boys' hostel, he was moved to Janna's bed and a doctor summoned, who diagnosed sunstroke.

'With a fair skin like yours, you should never go out without a hat. Realistically you should go home.'

But with Janna holding his hand, mopping his forehead with her own pale blue flannel and looking down with such concern, Paris definitely wanted to stay.

'Perhaps it's better if you're not moved.' The doctor turned to Janna. 'As long as you can keep him cool and quiet?'

'He can sleep in my bed,' said Janna. 'I'm so sorry, love.' She squeezed Paris's hand. 'I should have noticed you weren't wearing a hat.'

She had been swimming and was still in a sopping-wet primrose-yellow bikini, through which goose pimples were protruding like bubble wrap.

'Get something warm on,' advised the doctor, looking admiringly at her speckled body, 'you've had a shock. Don't want you getting a chill.'

Peel off that bikini in here, thought Paris longingly and said:

'I can't take your room.'

'You certainly can and I'm not leaving you either.'

*   *   *

Paris, for the first time in his life, knew the bliss of being cosseted. The Bagley Babes nipped down to the greengrocer's and brought him strawberries and raspberries. Vicky rolled up with lemon sorbet, Gloria with a melon. Paris was embarrassed, yet touched they were so worried. Even Lubemir and Anatole sent apologies and the Chinless Wanderers promised to get him a better horse next time. Finally, Xav shuffled in and offered Paris his mobile.

'You might want to ring someone. No one except my mother rings me.'

'I'll ring you.'

Xav grinned. 'You can't if I haven't got a mobile.' Then, staring at the floor and kicking a table: 'Thanks for sticking up for me. I'm really glad you're coming to Bagley next term.'

Shyly, they exchanged a high five.

*　　*　　*

Having shooed everyone out, Janna gazed out of the window across the river. She could see thirty or so red and white cows standing together, whisking flies off each other's faces. That's what a good school should be, she thought wistfully, everyone protecting each other.

Despite another deluge, it was still terribly hot. Paris was getting drowsy. As she leant over to straighten his pillow, he could feel the smooth firmness, like almost ripe plums, of her breasts. Soaking the blue flannel in iced water, she trickled it over his forehead, shoulders and chest, like a caress.

'Please don't go away, read to me.'

Janna picked up Matthew Arnold, which had fallen out of his shorts pocket. 'To Paris with love from Patience and Ian', she read on the flyleaf and felt happier that they were kind, educated people who would look after him. She read:

'But the majestic river floated on,
Out of the mist and hum of that low land,

470

Into the frosty starlight, and there moved,
Rejoicing, through the hushed Chorasmian
     waste,
Under the solitary moon; he flowed
Right for the polar star . . .'

'I wonder if he was a riffle or a meander,' mumbled Paris.

He could smell Janna's scent on her sheets. On the table were bottles: magic potions to make her even more beautiful. Gradually Janna's soft, young voice merged with the rain-swollen stream pouring into the river outside. He was asleep.

Oh, the length of those blond lashes. Not wanting him to catch cold, Janna pulled the blanket over him and couldn't resist bending over and dropping a kiss on his damp forehead.

'Good night, sweet Arctic Prince.' If only she'd been able to adopt him.

Paris opened his eyes a millimetre, next moment a tentacle hand had closed round her neck.

'Get away with you,' she protested.

Lifting his head, dizzy this time with longing, Paris kissed her. For a second her lips went rigid, then they relaxed and opened and kissed him back. Then she seemed to shake herself, prised away his hand and laid it on his chest.

'You're delirious,' she told him firmly. 'I must check on everyone else and find myself somewhere to sleep.'

'I love you, miss,' called out Paris, as he drifted into sleep.

52

'You've got to be better by tonight,' Jade Stancombe told Paris next morning as she dropped a box of white chocolates on to his bed. 'We're off to our mystery destination.'

She was followed by Cosmo, who'd clocked the burgeoning friendship between Xav and Paris and, wanting to punish Xav further, decided to take Paris away from him. Cosmo therefore rolled up with mangoes, peaches and Paris's baseball cap, which he claimed he'd found down the seat of a bus.

'But that won't keep the sun off back and front though, like this will,' and he plonked a panama on Paris's head.

'I don't want your fucking hat.'

'You will when you see how much it suits you.'

Paris was about to chuck it in the bin when Janna walked in: 'Oh Paris, you look gorgeous.'

'Just like Jude Law,' agreed Cosmo.

So Paris kept it.

*   *   *

Pearl was terribly excited.

'If you make me up for the mystery party this evening,' Jade had told her, 'you can borrow and keep one of my dresses.'

Then, when Pearl said she hadn't brought much make-up, Jade suggested they buy some in Hereford and proceeded to spend £300, also splashing out £550 on an aquamarine and diamond ring.

'I've brought a nice blue wraparound cardigan with me. You can have that too, Pearl, if you do my hair as well.'

It didn't look as though anyone would need cardigans: the weather was getting steadily hotter and muggier; huge white clouds rose like whipped cream on the horizon.

Terrified of being sent home, Paris kept telling everyone how much better he felt.

'You can come,' said Janna, 'if you take it really easy and keep that hat on.'

The panama was almost unbearably becoming. With the brim over his nose, he could have drifted out of *Brideshead* or *The Great Gatsby*.

But I'm Julien Sorel, he told himself. When I'm sixty, Janna'll be eighty, not a huge gap. Anyway, with her hair in a ponytail and freckles joining up on her face, she looked about fourteen.

*　　　　*　　　　*

As the coaches splashed through huge puddles, they seemed to be galloping back in time. Meadowsweet overran the emerald-green meadows, brown rivers struggled through great tangles of water lilies and dense primeval forests swarmed down the hills.

'That's a riffle, that's a meander,' yelled the children.

'God it's hot, are you OK, Paris?' asked the girls repeatedly.

Joan, the eternal chaperone, marched up and down the coach in search of bad behaviour. Boffin, still engrossed in *A Brief History of Time*, hummed a Bach prelude in a reedy tenor.

'Prince Harry's been done for drink driving,' said Amber, drinking Bourbon out of a Coke bottle, 'he's my hero.'

'Pity he's got a girlfriend,' sighed Milly. 'Boffin Brooks tried to snog me this morning. He must have month-old pilchards lodged in his brace. Where d'you think we're going tonight? It's so exciting.'

Jade stretched out long, newly bronzed and waxed legs.

'Good book?' she asked Paris.

'Very,' said Paris, not looking up.

Rufus was telling Kylie about whales.

'They'll be extinct quite soon.'

'That's really sad.' Kylie's big eyes filled with tears. 'Just like the dildo.'

Pearl had been sad too on the trip to Hereford because Cosmo had gone off in another coach with Vicky. Now he was back sitting beside her, reading *Classical Music* magazine, smiling wickedly, caressing the outside curve of her breast with his little finger.

And so, after four nights of rigorously enforced celibacy, the coaches rolled over the border into Wales. Biffo Rudge sat at the front, directing the driver.

'Here we are,' he shouted as they rounded the corner. On the other side of a wide river, hazily reflected in its water like a forgotten child's fortress, stood Castle Gafellyn against the darkening green trees.

As they crossed the river and drove through huge wrought-iron gates, flanked by rampant lions, they saw that the stern grey walls ahead were softened by rambling pink roses and pale blue hydrangeas.

'Castle Gafellyn was a most important military outpost,' read Biffo from Emlyn's notes. 'An early owner burnt it down to stop it falling into the predatory hands of the English.' He pointed to a square green field framed by crumbling stone walls. 'This was the enclosure into which livestock was herded at night to protect it from the wolves.'

'Sounds just like us,' said Pearl, sticking her tongue out at Cosmo.

I'll teach you, he thought.

'This is the sort of property in which the Macbeths might have resided,' announced Boffin, 'repelling other warlords and of course the English.'

The moat circling the castle was as green, still and smooth as mint jelly; all around dark forest encroached like stealthily invading armies. Like Burnham Wood advancing on Dunsinane, thought Paris, glancing at Janna, whose eyes were wide, her hands clasped in excitement like a child at her first pantomime. She deserved some fun; if only he could provide it.

Once inside, the children swarmed about, peering out through narrow, vertical windows, racing up winding stone staircases leading to turrets. Tapestries, swords and armour covered the walls. Meissen and Ming softened every alcove.

The owner, smooth, pewter-grey-haired, butterscotch-tanned, roving-eyed, was a childhood friend of Hengist called Bertie Wallace, who seemed deeply amused by the whole invasion.

'When one's ancestors have been accustomed to invading English hordes, Larks and Bagley seem very small beer,' he observed dryly as the children

475

fell on tomato sandwiches and rainbow cake.

'It would have been fun to dine in the great hall, but it's so hot, I thought you'd prefer the garden room which opens on to the terrace. Hengist used to stay here as a child,' he told the somewhat awestruck teachers. 'His parents were friends of my parents who sold the place to pay death duties. My wife and I bought it back and are planning to turn it into an hotel, but first it's got to be extensively rebuilt and redecorated. Then I read about Larks joining forces with Bagley and thought you might like to stay here as a climax'—he smiled knowingly at Janna—'to your trip.'

'You are so kind,' stammered Janna. 'What a treat. The kids have behaved very well so far. I hope they don't get carried away.'

'In olden days, castles like this would have had rushes and meadowsweet all over the floor instead of carpets,' pronounced Boffin.

A flurry of notes and a burst of *Rigoletto* indicated that Cambola had found the piano. Shrieks of joy echoed round the garden as the children discovered a croquet lawn and the swimming pool, a rippling turquoise expanse of water, framed by limes in sweet scented flower, heavy with the murmuring of bees.

'We can go skinny-dipping later,' purred Amber.

'Or fatty-dipping, in Xavier's case,' said Cosmo evilly.

Bertie, soft-voiced and rakish, was decidedly attractive. Janna could imagine him and Hengist getting up to all sorts of tricks and because he was Hengist's friend, she wanted to make a good impression.

'I cannot think of a more wonderful end to our

trip. And it will really help them to relate to history and Macbeth. "This castle hath a pleasant seat; the air Nimbly and sweetly recommends itself Unto our gentle senses",' she quoted happily.

' "This guest of summer, The temple-haunting martlet, does approve By his lov'd mansionry that the heaven's breath Smells wooingly here",' quoted back Bertie. 'I used to be an actor. Hengist told me I'd like you.'

Janna squirmed with pleasure.

A smell of mint was drifting from the kitchen.

'We've got smoked salmon, duck and puds. Do you think they'll like that?'

'Adore it, that's absolutely perfect. Thank you, particularly'—she thought of Calorie Towers—'after the food they've been having.'

'I'm sorry I won't be with you,' said Bertie. 'A friend's having a dinner party five miles away, so after the servants have served up your dinner and it's mostly cold, I hope you'll forgive me if I hijack them to help my friend. They can clear up first thing. You'll probably feel freer on your own.'

'You're awfully trusting.'

Vicky and Gloria, who, seeing Bertie, had raced to their rooms to tart up, now drifted in.

'What a lovely property,' gushed Vicky.

'I could say the same for you two,' quipped Bertie. 'What amazing taste Hengist has in women.'

'We're expecting him later,' said Vicky. 'Oh, tomato sarnies, how yummy. I've just checked on Paris, Janna, he seems OK.'

Calm down, Janna told herself fiercely. What if Hengist was rolling up just to pull Vicky, who would wear something amazing tonight? 'You are old, Father William.'

*   *   *

Janna's room, at the end of a long corridor, was tauntingly romantic. The big four-poster with deep blue curtains embroidered with silver stars needed only a handsome prince. Other delights included a pale yellow Chinese screen, painted with narrow-eyed warriors, a bottle of champagne in ice and a dapple-grey rocking horse with a rose-red saddle. On the wall was a tapestry of Diana the huntress, her chariot drawn by a purposeful stag who looked very like Joan. Joan, putting an arm round Janna's waist this morning, had definitely slid a hand upwards to grab a breast.

Janna and Joan: perhaps that was her destiny. Collapsing on the bed, she noticed even the blanket had a coat of arms, a golden ram with a motto, 'Fidelis et Constans'. 'An Atkinson Blanket, made in England', said the label. Janna Curtis, made in Wales. Hengist was on the way. Would he be faithful and constant to Sally? She liked Sally so much; how hideous it would be if Hengist were to cheat on her with Vicky.

*   *   *

In another part of the castle, Cosmo, who intended to enjoy his evening, was lacing the fruit cup with vodka and brandy. By studying the guidebook, he had located, ten miles away, a renowned observatory with some adjoining historic troglodyte caves. His suggestion that Skunk and Biffo should give them a ring had resulted in both

478

of them, plus Boffin and Rufus's two minions, being invited to supper to view some rare eclipse and visit the troglodyte caves.

Cosmo had also arranged for his mother to invite Joan and Cambola to *Ariadne auf Naxos* in which she was singing in Cardiff, which would occupy them for several hours.

Rufus should have stayed at the castle too, but getting no answer from his wife Sheena on her mobile or at home, where she should have been with the children, he had panicked and decided to miss dinner and slope home for the evening.

Situation excellent, which meant only Janna, Vicky and Gloria left in charge. If Hengist did show up, reflected Cosmo, Janna would be oblivious to everything else, so his plan to seduce Vicky and Gloria looked feasible.

Cosmo emptied another bottle of vodka into the fruit cup.

53

Before dinner everyone met on the terrace. The pupils in particular were amazed how unfamiliar and glamorous they looked in their party dresses. Jade, made up by Pearl, in a clinging white dress slashed to the waist from top and bottom, showing off St Tropez tan applied by Pearl, her hair plaited and threaded with flowers by Pearl, looked over the top but sensational.

Pearl glowed like a pearl, her normally pinched, sharp, pale little face softened and flushed by sun, love and Jade's flowered dress and pale blue wraparound cardigan.

'Designer clothes are certainly worf the price,' she admitted.

'Because I've got designs on you,' said Cosmo, patting her bottom.

Janna had washed and curled her hair, oiled her body and hidden sleepless nights with a lot of eye make-up. In her bronze speckled dress, which moulded her body and merged with her freckles, she looked like the Little Mermaid.

The children thought she looked stunning, but not as stunning as Vicky, who wore flamingo pink and who, perhaps trying to appear sophisticated for Hengist, had piled up and knotted a pink rose into her dark hair.

Everyone was agreeing they were having a fantastic time, when Bertie Wallace wandered in with a call for Joan Johnson.

'She's gone to the opera,' said Janna.

'It's Hengist.'

'I'll take it.' Vicky grabbed the cordless. 'Hengist, this place is a-mazing. Thank you so much. The kids are ecstatic. You stayed here as a child, Bertie told us. Are you coming over? Oh, what a shame. Of course, I understand. Research is all. Tintern Abbey. My favourite poem: "That time is past, And all its aching joys are now no more, And dizzy raptures."

'OK, I'll give your love to everyone,' and after a pause: 'Mmm, me too.' Catching sight of Janna's anguished face she added, 'Do you want a word with Janna?' who shook her head frantically. 'OK, thanks for ringing, enjoy your evening.' She handed the cordless back to Bertie. 'Hengist isn't coming, what a pity. He's staying near Tintern Abbey doing some research.'

' "Why, uncle, 'tis a shame",' murmured Anatole.

'Bloody isn't,' murmured back Cosmo. 'When the cat goes arty, the mice begin to party.'

'Where's Tintin Abbey?' asked the Hon. Jack. 'I always liked Tintin.'

'Have a drink,' said Cosmo, handing Janna a huge glass of fruit cup.

How even more amusing to seduce Miss Curtis, who didn't dwarf him and who was looking unusually tempting. Now that really would crucify Master Alvaston.

Fucking Hengist! Paris, also watching Janna, was aware of a dimmer switch turning off the glow in her face. If only he could comfort her.

The sun at thirty degrees was reddening the castle walls; a short shower of rain had scattered pink rose petals over the grass. Delphinium and campanula rose in blue and violet spires. A most heavenly smell of roasting duck mingled with the sweet, heady scent of lime blossom and philadelphus. Vicky and Gloria, succumbing to laced fruit cup and Anatole's deep-voiced blandishments, were getting noisy and sillier.

'I'm dreadfully sorry,' whispered Janna, 'I've got an absolutely blinding headache—a migraine actually. They come on suddenly, I can't see out of one eye.'

'I had one on the opening night of *Romeo and Juliet*,' cried Vicky, 'it was all I could do to stagger in. Poor you. Gloria and I'll hold the fort—or rather the castle.'

Everyone was very solicitous.

'Go and lie down, miss, come back when you feel better.'

'Shall I bring you some iced water?'

Janna could see secret relief in many faces. Without her, joy would be truly unconfined. Paris insisted on accompanying her back to her room.

Let me stay, he wanted to beg. I'll lie down beside you and stroke your forehead as you did mine yesterday.

'Too much sun,' mumbled Janna.

'Do you need a doctor?'

'I'm fine. You go and have fun. I'll probably join you again in half an hour.'

'Sure you're OK?'

The intensity in his face alarmed her. She shouldn't have led him on yesterday. She'd only just managed to shut the door on him and bolt it when the tears poured forth. She was overwhelmed with despair at not seeing Hengist and shock that she could no longer conceal the fact she was hopelessly in love with him.

But what the hell was she playing at? Hengist was

a married man, no doubt as faithful and constant to sweet Sally as the Atkinson blanket into which she was sobbing. He was also out of her league. She'd tried to cross the class barriers and found, as the Little Mermaid had when she tried to walk on shore, that she was treading on knives.

Then an imperious knock on the door sent her through the roof. It must be Paris back again. She should never have kissed him, but he'd looked so adorable. The knock became a tantivy. Nervously she opened the door a centimetre, but found the shadowy landing was deserted—perhaps it was the Gafellyn ghost.

The banging had become more insistent, coming from the far side of the room. Padding over the flagstones, she found a bottle-green wool curtain and behind it a rounded Norman door, buckling on its hinges. Oh God, was it Joan or raffish Bertie?

Someone was declaiming the Porter's speech in a strong Welsh accent. ' "Knock, knock, knock . . ." '

Janna opened this second door an inch, breathed in lemon aftershave and almost fainted as the door was thrust open, nearly concussing her. In the dim light she slowly made out a faded Prussian-blue shirt, a sunburnt throat, and eyes, slittier with laughter than the Chinese Warriors. It was Hengist. Ducking his head, he powered his way into the room and pulled her into his arms.

'I thought you were staying near Tintern Abbey.'

'I was, but I couldn't bear the thought of all those aching joys being past. I suddenly wanted a dizzy rapture.'

'I thought you fancied Vicky,' sobbed Janna.

She was so small in her bare feet, Hengist had to pull her chin upwards in order to smile down into

483

her reproachful, bewildered, tearful, mascara-stained face.

'Dear God,' he said, 'from the beginning you've been the one I wanted, the object of my desire.' And when he drew her against him, he was like a great, warm, solid wall; where his shirt was unbuttoned, she felt the burning heat of his body and was shaken by the relentless pounding of his heart.

Then his beautiful, wilful mouth swooped down on hers and she no longer doubted his passion as he kissed her on and on, his big hands closing round her small waist, then moving upwards to caress her high bouncy breasts, then moving down to cup her equally bouncy bottom. Finally, gasping for breath, he buried his face in her clean, silky curls.

'You utterly gorgeous child. Christ, I've fought this.' Then, laughing half ruefully: 'This is an awfully big adventure weekend.'

Janna escaped and paced round the room, heart battling with her head.

'How did you get in here?'

'By a secret passage. It comes out on the edge of the woods. Bertie and I were at school together; I used to stay in the holidays. I can get into every room in this castle.'

'And probably did,' snapped Janna, raging with insecurity, frightened her legs wouldn't hold her any more. 'I cannot believe this.'

'You soon will.' Hengist swiftly unzipped her speckled dress, unhooked her bra, then, gathering her up, dropped her on the blue and silver patchwork quilt.

'We can't,' stammered Janna. 'Sally? The party?

How did you know I was here?'

'I tried to ring you but your mobile was switched off. Bertie said you'd sloped off with a headache. You have the sweetest body, look at those adorable boobs.'

Lying down beside her, he swept back her hair, kissed her forehead and little snub nose, then her lips again, then her nipples, slowly, luxuriously, sensuously. The hand creeping lazily between her legs was so sure.

'Down comes the drawbridge,' he murmured, pulling off her knickers.

In turn he smelt so clean and healthy, and his face was so smooth and newly shaven—Janna was so used to beards and grating stubble—his glorious broad-shouldered body so powerful, his hair so springy yet silky. As he stroked and fingered her, leaving her quivering with longing, he made no attempt to undress himself.

'I really like Sally,' muttered Janna.

'Hush. Sally's my problem.'

As he drew her into a fairy-tale world inside the star-spangled blue curtains, any principle fled. Through the narrow window, she could see Venus, a glittering silver medal pinned on the deepening blue breast of the night.

'You do want this, darling?' Hengist's hand was roving further afield.

'Oh please, yes,' Janna gasped. 'I'm stunned, that's all. I didn't realize it was an option. I haven't slept with anyone since Stew.'

'I should hope not—you were saving yourself for me.'

'I'm out of practice.'

'We must exchange best practice,' murmured

485

Hengist, spitting on his fingers, finding her clitoris, caressing so gently and expertly.

'I'll give you best practice,' cried a fired-up Janna.

Wriggling out of his embrace, she took over, shoving Hengist back on the bed. Removing his loafers, kissing his bare feet, swiftly unbuttoning his shirt, kissing the dark brown tuft of chest hair, she licked his nipples and his belly button as she undid his belt and unzipped and removed his trousers. For a moment his red check boxer shorts were pegged by a splendidly excited cock, then he eased free and was divinely naked beneath her.

Clambering over his body like a squirrel, she kissed, caressed, sucked and licked until he was moaning in delight.

'For a head, Miss Curtis, you give exquisite head. Aaah . . .' Reaching down, he grabbed her waist and, pulling her up the bed, plunged his splendid rock-hard penis up inside her, which she had no problem accepting in full because she was so bubbling over with excitement.

'Aaah,' groaned Hengist again as her muscles gripped and released him, squeezing and coaxing, 'like the Bourbons, you've forgotten nothing. I'm going to be so selfish, darling, I cannot hold out a second longer, you'll have to catch the next bus. Oh, my Christ,' he shouted, 'here comes the drop goal,' and exploded inside her.

For an age it seemed, they lay giggling and in shared ecstasy.

'Hang out our banners on the outward walls; The cry is still, "he comes",' sighed Hengist. 'Oh my darling. That was even better than scoring at Twickenham.'

As he turned to kiss her, she was made happier by the intense happiness on his face.

'Now, I'm going to make you come lots,' he whispered. And he did.

Time stopped—fantastic, mind-blowing sex blotting out everything.

*   *   *

Under a weeping willow, whose leaves caressed her far more tenderly, Pearl was seduced by Cosmo, a coupling as brutal and perfunctory as Janna's had been ecstatic.

Retreating into the castle to wash, Pearl reflected it was a shame Cosmo had used a condom or she might have fallen pregnant and qualified for a free flat. At least Cosmo had said he loved her. She hoped Jade wouldn't be angry her wraparound cardigan had been torn.

54

After a glorious dinner, the plates had been stacked and everyone had drifted into the garden to dance under the stars, to snog in the bushes and, because it was such a hot, muggy night, to strip off and leap into the pool. Vicky and Gloria were far too drunk and giggly to worry that it was too soon after dinner to swim.

The scent of philadelphus and lime flower grew headier; more moths dived like kamikaze pilots into the lights round the pool; Jack and Kylie had retreated to the shrubbery; Lando and Junior were playing croquet, trying to hit each other's ankles.

Bertie, who'd gone off to see his mistress, had no intention of returning before dawn.

Paris, wearing just shorts, lay on the grass, admiring the stars; Venus was setting. Above him, the constellation Hercules, arms outstretched, mighty thighs apart, wrestled with his labours. Paris was worried about Janna; she'd been gone three hours. He decided to check her room.

He would have liked to clean his teeth, but someone had nicked his toothbrush. Returning to the dining room, he grabbed and bit into a Granny Smith, poured Janna a glass of orange juice loaded with ice, and set out. Normally at this hour, he'd be confined to his room at Oaktree Court, and he luxuriated in the cold dew beneath his feet and the night air warm on his bare shoulders.

Gradually the screams and shouts round the pool receded. In the moat below, the water-lily leaves gleamed like armour; to the right loomed the castle. Janna's lights were turned off; she must be asleep. O, that he were the pillow beneath her head.

Then he froze as a man appeared at her window, naked to the waist with a magnificent chest and heroic head thrown back, smiling triumphantly and stretching his arms in ecstasy. Not Hercules down from the skies—but Hengist. Then he turned and was engulfed once more in the darkness of the room.

Paris slumped against the castle, body drenched in sweat, heart crashing, ice frantically clattering against the glass in his hand. The whore, the slag! How could she? Women complained of headaches when they didn't want sex—and she'd kissed him first yesterday and not gone into a flurry of outrage, but had parted her lips when he'd kissed her back.

Paris gave a howl and hurled the glass against the wall. Bagley and Larks—'a plague on both your houses'. In a daze, he staggered back into the castle, heading for the bar. Grabbing a bottle of vodka, he filled a half-pint glass, splashed bitter lemon on the top and downed it in one, then downed a second, spluttering:

'The bitch, the slag.'

Picking up a patterned orange Chinese vase cringing in an alcove, he hurled it against a big gilt mirror, splintering them both. A Tang dog flew out of the window. Gathering up a mahogany side table, Paris hurled it at the bar, smashing glasses, bottles, then swept more glasses on to the floor.

'Fucking slag.'

A bamboo plant had taken off, crashing down on to the keys of the piano, as Rocky wandered in, his mad bull's face crimson, his red curls askew, a bottle of Grand Marnier in his hand.

'What yer doing, man?'

'Wrecking this pervy nob's castle.'

'Right,' yelled Rocky, picking up a large flower arrangement and hurling it against a tallboy. Then he ran into the dining room and started on the debris of duck carcasses and bowls of potatoes and raspberries stacked on the sideboard. There was a sickening crunch as a pile of Rockingham plates fell to the floor. Like Duncan's blood, summer pudding was soon dripping down the pale blue Chinese wallpaper.

Outside, the music was too loud and the dancers and swimmers having too much fun to notice. Someone had found a big yellow ball and Lando and Junior were playing water polo.

Telling herself that first sex with a guy was never very good, still sore from Cosmo's cavalier seeing-to, Pearl wandered back to the party, pausing in horror to see her new boyfriend ferociously snogging Vicky Fairchild, his hand unzipping her flamingo-pink dress.

Going over, Pearl tapped him on the shoulder:

'D'you mind?'

'Piss off,' said Cosmo, with such venom that Pearl shrank away, looking desperately round for someone to tell, but everyone was snogging or swimming.

Running down a grassy path, she bumped into a reeling, half-dressed Jade, who asked:

'Where in hell's Paris?'

'Dunno. Cosmo's a fucking bastard.'

Jade stopped, swaying in her tracks, smiling cruelly.

'What have you and Cosmo been a-doing of? He just texted me.' Jade unearthed her mobile from her bra and held it out.

'Mission acc-come-plished pearls a slag', read Pearl and gave a shriek of rage. 'The bastard. He said he loved me, that I was the biggest fing in his life.'

'You might have been five seconds before he shagged you. Cosmo doesn't let grass grow under his feet, only in window boxes.'

Next moment, Pearl heard the distinctive double beat of a message on her own mobile and read: 'Sorry its over cosmo'.

'Wot dyou mean', texted back Pearl.

'Thanks for terrific sex shame youve just become my X', came back the reply.

'Bstrd how am I supposed to handle this', Pearl replied.

'Ask joan for alka seltzer. now fuck off', texted Cosmo.

*   *   *

Leaving the castle ransacked, Paris found everyone skinny-dipping in the pool. He felt like Actaeon spying on Diana and her nymphs.

A naked Vicky, whose hair had come down, was giggling hysterically and pretending to swim away from Cosmo, who'd just returned from texting. Yanking her back by her hair, Cosmo's hands closed over her breasts.

Very drunk, Paris laboriously undid his belt and stepped out of his shorts. The Bagley Babes, frolicking like Rhine Maidens, gasped as he paused, sleek, white and beautiful. Actaeon had become a moon-blanched Endymion. The only flaw was the tattoo of the Eiffel Tower on his shoulder.

'Jesus,' said Amber.

Letting go of Vicky, leaving her dog-paddling frantically in the deep end, Cosmo scrambled out of the pool, grabbed his camera from his jeans and took a roll of film.

Paris, a glass of neat vodka in his hand, stood gazing into the pool in despair and loathing, then wandered off. After two attempts, a naked Jade managed to struggle out of the pool and ran after him.

'Paris, make love to me,' she called out.

'Fuck off.'

'How come you're so mean to me?'

'Because you're a bitch.'

When Jade slapped his face, Paris slapped her back, then, grabbing her arm, pulled her behind the changing rooms into the shrubbery. He shoved her on the grass and fell on top of her, yelling in pain as her hand clamped around his sunburnt neck, pulling him down to kiss her. Her lovely sleek body writhed beneath his. Her eyes were glazed with lust and booze, Pearl's so carefully applied make-up streaked by water. The coupling, like Cosmo and Pearl's, was violent, fierce, messy and meaningless. The moment it was over, Paris pulled out and walked off.

Bumping into his friend, Pearl, who sobbed hysterically that Cosmo had dumped her by text and told the entire party, he could only say: 'You shouldn't go with trash: sorry, I wish I cared.'

Five minutes later, Pearl stumbled over Jade, passed out on the grass, puked-up raspberries and cream gleaming like blood in the moonlight. Jade was so far gone, she didn't even stir when Pearl produced a kitchen knife and sawed off her twelve-inch plait, threaded with flowers. Then Pearl attacked her own wrist, gasping at the pain and joy of release.

Amber, wet from the pool, caught up with Paris.

'What goings on, Mr Alvaston.'

So Paris pulled her into his arms and shut up her patrician babble by kissing her. He didn't care any more.

'I like you,' he told Amber.

'And I like you.'

It was like being serviced by a unicorn, Amber reflected hazily, or a statue half come to life. Paris's face was dead, devoid of any tenderness. At one moment he called her 'Janna', at another his features seemed about to disintegrate in tears, then set like stone again.

'Oh Christ, oh Christ.'

It was not, as you might say, satisfactory. At least he said 'thank you' as he got to his feet and wandered off.

If he found Milly, thought Paris, he could chalk up a Bagley Babe hat-trick, as Feral had always wanted to do. God, he missed Feral; only Feral would have understood his agony. Then he heard the sound of sobbing. It was Xavier, slumped on a bench, head in his hands, an empty bottle of rum beside him.

'Dad'll never be proud of me. I failed to pull Jade and why haven't I got the guts to kill Cosmo?'

'I'm sorry. I can't help you,' said Paris.

493

55

Joan and Cambola sang tunes from *Ariadne* all the way home, putting down the hood of the convertible Joan had hired so they could admire the stars. Dame Hermione had been wonderfully gracious and invited them back to her hotel for a cold supper of chicken gelé, wild berries, white chocolate sauce and Pouilly-Fumé. When Miss Cambola had pointed out Cosmo's musical genius, Hermione had replied that Cosmo was 'such a kind boy and very, very sensitive'.

'He gets that from you,' suggested Cambola.

'Indeed.' Hermione bowed her head, then, turning her big, brown eyes on an excited Joan: 'High-spirited maybe, but genius must be untamed.'

It had been after midnight when they'd left Cardiff and her presence.

Overhead, Draco the Dragon, not Welsh this time, had been joined by the Swan and the Lyre, on which Joan would have loved to serenade Dame Hermione. Wild honeysuckle and elderflower bashed in the narrow lanes by her car released a sweet yet disturbingly acrid, sexy smell. The night air was a pashmina round their shoulders. The roads were quiet. Joan took Cambola's hand. They agreed that Skunk and Biffo would have been home hours ago and that Janna was a sensible young woman to leave in charge.

'Janna is like Toscanini,' mused Cambola, 'many wrong things, but redeemed by so much passion and vitality.'

As they drove towards the castle, they heard sounds of revelry by night. Striding down to the pool, Joan's first reaction was delight to see such charming young women frolicking naked in the pool. But her delight turned to horror when she realized they were not only her girls, but Vicky and Gloria also stripped off and extremely the worse for wear. Vicky was wrapped round Anatole, and Gloria snogging unashamedly in the shallow end with Hermione's 'very, very sensitive' little son, who, when Joan bellowed with rage for everyone to stop, gave her a V-sign.

Not making a great deal of potential deputy headway, Joan marched inside to be greeted by devastation. Summer pudding had incarnadined the exquisite blue wallpaper, a glazed brown duck carcass had nested in the chandelier. Empty alcoves reproached her. A raspberry pavlova had been rammed, like a custard pie, into the face of a replica of Michelangelo's David.

Bellowing with rage, blowing her whistle, crunching on smashed Meissen, Ming and Venetian glass, Joan stormed upstairs to find doors ajar and the beds of Jade, Milly and Amber empty. Primrose Duddon wasn't in her room either, nor were Kylie, Pearl or Kitten Meadows.

Red and more fiery than any Welsh dragon, Joan hammered on Janna's door.

'Kerist'—Hengist leapt out of bed—'it's that porter from Macbeth again. How time flies when you're really enjoying yourself.'

'The moon's gone, get on the balcony,' hissed Janna, kicking his Prussian-blue shirt and white trousers under the bed.

Wrapping herself in a towel for a second time

that evening, she opened her door an inch and again was nearly concussed as it was thrust open to reveal Joan bellowing like a Herefordshire bull. Hastily, Janna leapt backwards, aware she must reek of Hengist, his fingerprints luminous on her quivering, sated body.

'How could you let this happen? Downstairs has been totally wrecked. Students and teachers are frolicking naked in the pool. None of my students are in their rooms. As duty officer you're totally to blame.'

Retreating further from a fountain of spit, Janna mumbled she'd been struck down by migraine.

'The worst ever. I lay down for half an hour before dinner; I must have dropped off.'

'Well, get dressed at once,' thundered Joan, 'your students aren't in their beds either.'

Turning, Janna caught a glimpse of the rocking horse, hooded like a prisoner by Hengist's underpants and, fighting laughter, slammed the door and locked it. Equally weak with laughter, Hengist slid in from the balcony.

'Oh dear,' he sighed, 'but quite inevitable after segregating them in separate youth hostels all week. I don't expect they've come to much harm. And quite frankly, that was so miraculous, darling, nothing else matters. I suppose I'd better beat it.'

He was buttoning up his shirt and pausing to kiss Janna, when his mobile rang. It was Joan covering her tracks.

'Sorry to wake you, headmaster, just to alert you that anarchy has broken out at Castle Gafellyn. Janna Curtis was left in charge but deserted her post, claiming a headache. Both Vicky and Gloria are drunk and incapable. Half our students are missing.'

'And where were you and Biffo and Rufus whilst all this was happening?' asked Hengist icily. 'You went to the opera in Cardiff?' After a pause: 'Biffo and Skunk and Boffin went to some troglodyte caves? Surely that was taking coals to Newcastle? Well, you should all have bloody well been there.'

Then, after another long pause: 'Bertie's an old friend and very reasonable. I'm sure the bracelet will turn up.' Reaching out for Janna's pubes, he pulled her towards him, sliding his hand between her legs. 'Try to limit the damage. You've got yourself into this mess; don't call the police. I'm at Tintern Abbey and over the limit, or I'd drive straight over.'

Switching off his mobile, he kissed Janna lingeringly.

'I'd better scarper or we'll both be in trouble. Stick to the migraine story. Joan hasn't got a hairy leg to stand on.'

His feet groped around for his loafers.

'Where are you going?'

'Back down the secret passage. It comes out at the edge of Hanging Wood quarter of a mile away; my car's hidden in the trees. I utterly adore you, that was the best fuck I've ever had.'

'I feel drunk,' sighed Janna, 'and I haven't had a drop.'

'I'll call you,' said Hengist and was gone.

Groggily, Janna dressed. She couldn't stop giggling. She was no doubt about to be sacked, but she didn't care.

I love Hengist, Hengist loves me and two heads are definitely better in bed than one.

     *   *   *

Joan meanwhile had stepped over a supine Rocky on the landing, located Lando France-Lynch watching polo on Sky and finally tracked down an orgy in Jack Waterlane's bedroom. Here she found Johnnie Fowler, Monster Norman, Jack, Kylie, Kitten, Junior, Amber, Milly, Cosmo and Anatole, who she'd last seen behaving abominably in the pool, and oh horrors, Primrose Duddon, among the writhing bodies.

Inspired by an internationally prize-winning installation entitled 'Shagpile', which showed models of naked men piled on top of and plugged into each other like Lego, the geography trip participants were trying to create a replica of fornicating bodies.

'Vaitress,' shouted Anatole, falling off the pile and waving an empty vodka bottle at Joan, 'can you get us another drink?'

'How dare you?' thundered Joan.

'Come and join our team-building exercise, miss.' Johnnie Fowler took a hand off Amber's left breast and patted the bed.

'Stop it, all of you, what the hell d'you think you're doing?'

'Don't swear, miss,' giggled Kitten from the middle of the pile.

'You told us to overcome traditional animosities and bond with Larks,' panted Junior, 'and what better way of doing it?' He kissed Kitten's shoulder. 'You beautiful thing.'

'Help,' shrieked Kylie, bucking frantically then collapsing on top of Jack, 'I'm overcoming.'

'Have you seen the state of downstairs?' yelled

498

Joan. 'Thousands of pounds' worth of damage has been done.'

'Not by us,' chorused Shagpile II.

Drawing a dick the length of a conger eel out of a glassy-eyed Milly, Cosmo said chattily, 'Could have been Rocky. He was trashing the place as I passed, probably forgot to take his Ritalin.'

Downstairs, amid the debris, Cambola had swept earth from the hurled bamboo plant off the piano keys and, armed with a large brandy, was singing along as she picked out tunes from *Ariadne*.

Paris, having shed his shorts earlier, couldn't find them. Suspecting Cosmo, he nicked a pair marked Anatole Rostov from the Cosmonaughties' bedroom. Anatole wouldn't miss them; he'd brought six other pairs. Wandering into the garden, overwhelmed by vodka, despair and loveless sex, Paris passed Joan having a squawking match with Vicky.

'You will certainly lose your job, young lady.'

'Doesn't matter, I've got another one to go to.'

'Don't be too sure of that.'

Driven out of Jack's bedroom, Shagpile II were indulging in another shrieking stint of skinny-dipping. Reaching the pool, Paris stopped in his tracks to find Janna counting heads. As though nothing had happened, she turned and smiled at him.

'Oh, there you are. Are you OK?'

Paris was about to shout that she was a fucking slag, when he caught sight of a body in the shallow end, deathly pale even in the moonlight, hair streaming, stick legs askew, and realized it was Pearl surrounded by a flickering halo of blood. At first he thought she must have started her period and to save her humiliation looked round for a towel. Then he realized the blood was gushing from her wrists and, leaping into the water, he dragged her to the side. Hoisting her on to the flagstones, he yelled: 'Quick, she's cut herself.'

Janna rushed forward.

'Oh, poor child. Ring for an ambulance.' Crouching down, she put an ear to Pearl's chest. 'She's breathing, but unconscious, and terribly cold.'

Miss Cambola came running into the garden. 'We must make a tourniquet.' Tearing off her orange and black scarf, she wound it round and round Pearl's arm. 'Put your finger on the knot,' she ordered Paris. Then, turning to Janna: 'We must get her straight to hospital for a blood transfusion. If we meet the ambulance coming the other way, at least we save time.'

'I'll drive, I haven't been drinking,' said Janna. 'What the hell happened?' she asked as a suddenly sobered-up Amber, Junior and Paris helped her and Cambola carry Pearl to Joan's convertible.

'Fucking Cosmo. Shagged her, texted everyone to say she was a slag, then dumped her by text,' said Amber.

*   *   *

Jade, back in her bedroom, was calling her father. 'Daddy, Daddy, I'm having a horrible time. Paris Alvaston tried to rape me, he came on so strong and I didn't want to reject him because he's a yob and Xavier Campbell-Black tried to rape me too. I didn't want to be unkind, but he was drunk and went at me like an animal. I had to knee him in the

500

balls. And, oh Daddy, someone's cut off all my hair, I look hideous. Everyone's drunk; all the teachers are shagging and skinny-dipping.'

'Calm down, princess. Who's in charge?'

'Joan but she bunked off with Cambola to hear Cosmo's mum in some opera and Skunk and Biffo went to look at some lousy eclipse and Rufus's gone home, he thinks his wife's bunked off.'

'Who's in charge?'

'Janna, but she bunked off to bed and now she's taken some girl who's slashed her wrists to hospital. We're staying in such a lovely old castle and Rocky's gone berserk and broken the place up. Everything's out of control. My diamond bracelet's been nicked and oh, my hair, Daddy.'

'Did anyone actually rape you, princess?'

'No, but they tried.'

'Go to bed and I'll fly down and collect you first thing.'

Stancombe came off the telephone and turned to Rufus's wife, Sheena, stretched out beside him on black satin sheets.

'Mission accomplished,' he said triumphantly. 'There's no way the blessed Janna and Larks will survive this disaster.'

*　　　*　　　*

'The pupils have bonded so well,' mocked Cosmo as, back in their bedroom, he and Lubemir heated up an electric kettle to light their spliffs on the element, 'that the teachers felt redundant and soon will be declared so.'

'I wonder how the Lower Sixth are getting on with their tour of the battlefields,' pondered

Lubemir.

'Ought to start by studying the one downstairs,' said Cosmo.

·*   *   *

Alex and Poppet Bruce had spent the day walking in Wales. They had booked into a nearby hotel but, seeing lights still on in the castle, decided to drop in to see Biffo, Skunk, Joan and dear little Vicky and enjoy some free drink.

They found Joan in a state of shock. Desperately guarding her position, fulminating to hide her guilt she had been skiving, she whisked them as quickly as possible out into the garden.

'Where are the students?' asked Alex.

'In their beds.'

'What on earth happened?' asked Poppet, who loved trouble.

'A young woman, Pearl Smith, slashed her wrists. Janna Curtis has rushed her to Casualty. I've been trying to ring Pearl's emergency contact number in Larkminster, but the telephone appears to be cut off.'

'Why did she try to end her life?' pressed Poppet.

'Oh, some love affair,' replied Joan. Dame Hermione would never forgive her if she shopped Cosmo. Anxious to get off the subject: 'And Jade Stancombe has behaved in a most reprehensible way. She was observed in flagrante with both Paris Alvaston and Xavier Campbell-Black. She must be excluded.'

Alex Bruce turned pale.

'We can't exclude Jade. We'd jeopardize our Science Emporium. Stancombe's been supportive

502

when we've fired anyone else's kids, but he wouldn't like it if we excluded Jade. We must limit the damage. Don't call the police or the parents or the ambulance.'

'Janna Curtis insisted on taking Pearl to hospital,' said Joan.

'Well, I suppose Pearl is her responsibility.'

At that moment Biffo and Skunk strode in, laughing heartily.

'Alex, Poppet, how good to see you. We've seen the most dramatic eclipse,' said Biffo. Then, lest Alex should think they'd been skiving, he added that they'd taken Boffin, Alex's favourite pupil with them. 'He couldn't believe his eyes. We've packed him off to bed. No doubt he'll debrief you tomorrow, Alex. I could do with a Scotch, couldn't you, Skunk?'

Joan was just debriefing them about the last six hours, heaping blame on Janna, when Bertie Wallace, hot from his mistress, walked in, whereupon Joan heaped blame on Rocky.

'Quite an achievement,' said Bertie, surveying the devastation. 'Rocky should get a job with the council demolishing old buildings. Fortunately for me, this house is in my wife's name. I doubt if she'll be quite so sanguine, but I expect it's insured.'

Janna rang Joan from the hospital. Pearl, thank God, was out of danger. They had given her stitches and a blood transfusion. She was conscious and Janna had spoken to her. Then she asked if she could have a quick word with Paris.

'I know he's worried.'

Even though it was nearly three a.m., Paris was awake, lying on top of his duvet, gazing at the ceiling. He took the telephone into a deserted bedroom.

'I thought you'd like to know Pearl's going to be OK and you probably saved her life.' Then, when Paris didn't answer: 'She's all right, Paris.'

'You're fucking not.'

'I beg your pardon?'

'If you hadn't sloped off to bed with a made-up headache and Hengist Fucking Brett-Taylor, none of this would have happened, you dirty bitch.'

'What are you talking about?'

'I saw Hengist at your window, stripped off and flaunting his six-pack, you fucking slag.'

'Oh Paris,' pleaded Janna in horror, but he had hung up.

56

Bagley pupils who'd been on the field trip were gated until the end of term, which was only a few days away. As Dora Belvedon had not been among the participants, it fell to Sheena Anderson to sell the story of 'Toff School in Mass Orgy', complete with gory details of skinny-dipping, group sex, trashing of our precious heritage and, finally, of a young woman nearly dying from a suicide attempt.

The person who carried the can was Janna. She was the only head on the trip, and the catastrophe had occurred when she was in charge. She had let the maintained sector down. Hengist was very sympathetic to her plight and had bollocked his staff for leaving her exposed, but he was not prepared, 'for both our sakes, darling', to reveal his part in distracting Janna during the evening.

Parents were fortunately mollified by magnificent exam results released in August, in which Bagley, helped no doubt by Cosmo's leaked papers, had drawn away from St Jimmy's and edged towards Fleetley.

Larks did infinitely better than the previous year: up from four per cent to ten per cent of the pupils getting the requisite five A–C grades known as the Magic Five, but they were still near the bottom of the Larkshire league. Any satisfaction was doused by Ashton Douglas's call.

'Vewy disappointing wesults, Janna. We'll need a post-mortem on these and the geography field trip.'

On the credit side, Pearl bounced back quickly—

cheered by all the sympathy and by a large bunch of pink roses on Dame Hermione's account, plus a card from her 'very sensitive' little son saying: 'Sorry, I was a rat. Love, Cosmo.'

Remembering how she had smashed Janna's Staffordshire cow, Pearl organized a whip-round from both Bagley and Larks children who'd been on the field trip and raised enough money to buy an even prettier Herefordshire cow from Larkminster Antiques.

'Miss loves cows.'

'She don't love Chally or Basket or Spink or Joan,' grumbled Graffi, but he designed a beautiful card, saying 'You're a star' in gold and purple sequins and everyone signed it and wrote fond messages inside apologizing that the trip had gone pear-shaped, but insisting they had had the best time ever, and thanking her for all her kindness.

Janna, overwhelmed, stroked the spotted red and white cow, and blushed and wept with joy over the card. Only after she'd read it half a dozen times did she notice Paris's name was missing.

When asked, Pearl had also blushed. 'Paris gets funny.'

I doubt it, thought Janna.

Paris had blanked her for the rest of the term and when she'd given him a lovely edition of Housman's poems as a leaving present, had just put it back on her desk. How would he treat Hengist, she wondered, when he got to Bagley?

Paris had also fallen out with Feral who, resentful the field trip had been a riot, grew crosser when Paris refused to debrief him and Graffi.

'Did you shag Amber and Jade?'

'Fuck off.'

'Did you shag Vicky or Gloria? Did you shag Miss?'

'I don't want to talk about it.'

Feral then queried the wisdom of moving in with Ian and Patience. 'Be careful, man. People only foster in order to abuse. That Ian looks a fascist perv and she's an ugly cow. I suppose you can always phone Childline.'

Paris, fuelled by rage, misery and apprehension, hit Feral across the playground. The fight went to ten rounds and was not made up. Once again, longing for his lost mother overcame Paris. Two days before the end of term, he vanished, taking to the trains to find her. After two days of panic, social services in Larkminster received a call from a stationmaster in Land's End saying Paris was stopping the night with him and his wife, but would be put on the train back to Birmingham tomorrow. Seeing Nadine's stuffed-sheep face on the platform at New Street, however, beside grim bully Blenchley and Crispin snuffling in disapproval, Paris jumped trains and went off to Edinburgh.

'Children dumped by their mothers never stop looking for them,' said Nadine, which hardly helped a desperately nervous Patience.

So Paris never said goodbye to Larks, even when he was safely returned to Oaktree Court and started packing up his few belongings in the expectation of moving to the Cartwrights. Janna felt wiped out by guilt. She should have levelled with both Patience and Nadine that Paris had only been thrown off course and was likely to act up appallingly because he'd been let down by yet another mother figure.

'I needn't say I was in bed with you,' she begged

507

Hengist, when he visited Jubilee Cottage after the field trip. 'I can just say some lover rolled up.'

'You're in enough trouble as it is,' said Hengist firmly. 'Some bloody counsellor will worm it out of Paris and then we'll be really in the shit. We deserve a little happiness. It's going to be difficult enough to see each other as it is.'

So, just as Paris felt horribly guilty but let Rocky take the rap for trashing Gafellyn Castle, Janna also kept quiet. Hengist had bewitched her, as blindingly dazzling as low winter sun reflected in icy puddles. She found it impossible not to revel in such unfamiliar happiness.

Throughout the long, hot summer, she was amazed and gratified how often he managed to see her. Luckily, hers was the last cottage in the village, with no house opposite, and Lily's wise sapphire-blue eyes were too short-sighted to recognize Hengist when he crept in during darkening evenings, wearing a confiscated baseball cap, shades and shoes wet from the increasingly heavy dews.

He frequently rolled up with one of Elaine's Bonios for Partner, who, instead of barking, whimpered and wriggled his little body with joy.

When Hengist was unable to see her, he rang, having learnt from his pupils to acquire a second pay-as-you-go mobile so Painswick couldn't trace his calls. He wouldn't, however, write to Janna when he was away. 'Too risky. I trust you, darling, but not the press.' Instead he gave her poetry books with pages marked:

Ah, love, let us be true
To one another! For the world, which seems

To lie before us like a land of dreams,
So various, so beautiful, so new . . .

'I feel dreadfully guilty about Sally,' Janna told him repeatedly, but Hengist always claimed that was his department.

'I'm not going to lie and say Sally doesn't understand me or sleep with me or love me as I love her. But this is so utterly divine . . .' He buried his lips in Janna's freckled shoulder. 'That's why we must be so careful not to get caught.'

Lovers, like Stew in the past, had refused to say they loved her. Hengist said it all the time. The downside—like jesting Pilate—was that he could never stay for more than an hour or two.

They were in bed one early August afternoon when a naked Janna glanced out of the window and shot back as Alex Bruce jogged by, head held high, spectacles misting up, showing off a spare figure and skinny legs.

'D'you think he's spying?'

'No, determined to win the school steeplechase.'

'When's that?'

'Last Sunday in September. It's Biffo's baby, both staff and pupils take part in a six-mile run round Bagley village and the surrounding countryside. Excellent way of giving unfit masters coronaries. Biffo takes it incredibly seriously. Alex is a lousy games player—can't see a ball—so he's desperate to triumph at cross country. Robot the Bruce. I must keep Paris away from his deplorable wife, Poppet, who'd love to counsel our guilty secret out of him. Anyway, I can think of better ways of keeping fit.' He pulled Janna on top of him.

Hengist was as generous with presents as with his

affections: Ralph Lauren shirts; a dusty pink cashmere twinset; a topaz brooch and matching earrings; a little Staffordshire dog; a CD of *Beatrice and Benedict*, Berlioz's lovely opera based on *Much Ado*, because Janna reminded him of the mettlesome lippy Beatrice; a watercolour by Emily Patrick; endless books he'd loved that he hoped she'd enjoy.

Janna was also in heaven because the long summer holiday was the first time she'd had a chance to play house, tend her garden, listen to the Proms and explore the countryside with Partner, who grew in confidence every day. Often she picked blackberries so ripe and luscious in the hedgerows you could fill a bowl in ten minutes. But deep in the wood, the same berries were small, hard and green and would never reach fruition— like so many of her children, trapped by poverty. She vowed once again to start homework and breakfast clubs next term and campaign for a football pitch for Feral.

*   *   *

One muggy afternoon in August, she stood and gazed out of her bedroom window at the yellow shaven fields, the darkening olive-green woods and the gaudy butterflies, glutting themselves on the amethyst spears of 'my buddleia', she thought happily.

She had just been to court with Feral, who, refusing to admit how heartbroken he was at Paris's defection, had got hammered and totalled a stolen car. Bitterly ashamed of his dyslexia and that he could hardly read or write, he was

510

panicking how he could avoid utter humiliation next term without Paris to translate, explain and do his homework.

Even with Dora's frightfully disapproving mother Lady Belvedon on the bench, Janna's impassioned plea that it would be disastrous for Feral to miss the start of his GCSE course, and that she could vouch for his character, won over the other magistrates. When Feral got away with a suspended sentence, his relief was palpable. He clammed up, however, whenever Janna asked him about Paris or his family.

Taking off her rose-patterned suit, worn to charm the magistrates, Janna paused to glance in the mirror. Love seemed to have made her body curvier and softer. Last autumn's headmistress's bob had grown out, thank goodness; her red curls now nearly reached her nipples. If Hengist thought she was beautiful, maybe she was. He was not due till tomorrow, so she could veg out tonight and watch the four hours of *The Bill* that she'd taped.

'Bugger, bugger,' said a voice.

Returning to the window, Janna found her neighbour Lily, who'd been staying with friends in the Dordogne for a fortnight, forcing a mower through a hayfield of lawn.

'Get on, you utterly bloody thing,' Lily yelled as the mower stalled on a particularly shaggy corner, then hit a bone—probably Partner's, thought Janna guiltily—went into a furious clatter and stopped completely.

'Bugger you.' Lily kicked it several times to no effect. 'My bloody corns!' Then, frantically tugging a wire: 'Don't do this to me, I can't afford to get you mended.'

511

Next moment, Lily had collapsed on to a rickety garden bench and burst into terrible rasping sobs. Janna was appalled. Ramrod-straight, endlessly kind and merry, outwardly invincible, only occasionally grumbling about her arthritis, Lily seemed indomitable. It was like seeing Big Ben crumbling. Lily was such a good listener and had been such a comfort that Janna wanted to race downstairs, fling her arms round her and return some of the comfort, but felt Lily might feel embarrassed.

Partner, with no such reserve, shot downstairs and out into the garden through the gap in the fence. Dummying past an outraged General, he leapt on to his friend Lily's knee to lick away her tears.

Grabbing a bottle of white from the fridge, Janna followed more reflectively. Feral was flat broke and had nothing to keep him out of mischief. He'd always got on with Lily when the Wolf Pack came over on Saturday afternoons. Janna would get Lily's mower mended, and Feral could mow her lawn.

She found Lily drying her eyes with Partner's ears, her face ravaged by tears. It was sweet of Janna to suggest Feral, but she could honestly manage.

'Oh please, he's so sad about Paris, and he's desperately broke, you'd be doing him a favour.'

'I always liked Feral,' admitted Lily. 'He had such amazing ball control when he played football on my lawn. He never broke a flower.'

'Well, that's settled then. Let's open this bottle.'

'We mustn't forget to watch Christian Woodford's programme at six-thirty,' said Lily.

The Brigadier, who lived a few doors away, had evidently been asked by Rupert Campbell-Black to do a programme on Dunkirk.

'How exciting,' cried Janna. 'I'll just go and ring Feral.'

Lily's heart sank. She couldn't afford to have her mower mended, let alone pay Feral. Ever since she had been kicked out of her lovely riverside house Lily had existed in this damp, rented cottage on a hopelessly dwindling fixed income—with shares yielding one per cent.

Despite her outward insouciance, Lily was in despair. Although she adored her nephews and nieces, particularly Dora, their constant visits exhausted her physically and financially. She was reduced to selling silver and pictures every month to keep herself in drink and the faddy black and white General in chicken. Some days Lily herself existed on 'pussy's pieces', bought for General from the fishmonger and blackberries picked on walks.

There was another space on the drawing-room wall where she'd last week sold a little Sutherland drawing to pay some bills. Now she'd have to find extra cash to pay Feral and give him a good tea.

57

Feral looked as though he needed a good tea when he rolled up two days later. He wore a black baseball cap back to front, black loose jeans, a black T-shirt. Was he in mourning for Paris or did he think black suited him? Rangier than ever, he'd shot up three inches. His tawny brown eyes roved round the kitchen, checking in every corner for ways to escape.

It had been raining heavily. A few muddy gashes, a few roses clouted on the ankles, a clematis taken out altogether and a lot of bad language later, the lawn was mowed and the terrace swept. Lily gave Feral a pie made of potatoes, onions and cheese sauce, blackberry crumble and a glass of sloe gin. He had seconds of everything, as they discussed Arsenal and Larkminster Rovers' prospects for the coming season.

'Football makes me look forward to autumn,' said Lily, 'as foxhunting used to in the old days.'

The Premiership was due to start on Saturday and the joy of Arsenal winning, or despair at them losing, lasted Feral all week, until excitement about the next game kicked in. But it wouldn't be the same without Paris and the endless arguments they'd had about the relative merits of Emile Heskey or Thierry Henry.

'Paris loved Liverpool,' said Lily idly. 'How's he getting on with his new family?'

'Dunno.'

'You must miss him.'

Feral shrugged.

'How's Graffi?'

'His dad's out of work.'

There was a pause.

'You must meet my friend Brigadier Woodford, who lives four houses away. He might need someone to do odd jobs for him. Rupert Campbell-Black had him on television two nights ago; he was excellent, talking about Dunkirk. Did you come across Rupert's children Xav and Bianca when you went to Bagley?'

'Xav's a no-good nigger,' observed Feral. 'She and I did a dance routine in *Romeo and Juliet*.'

He was desperate to ask after Bianca who, since March, had tangoed through his dreams, but couldn't bring himself to. Instead, he volunteered the information that Randal Stancombe was looking for squatters. 'Pays four pounds an hour, puts them in to bring down the price of a house he wants to buy.'

Lily observed the swallows gathering on the telegraph wires. 'Perhaps I should apply.'

'Bit rough for a lady,' grinned Feral, helping himself to another spoonful of crumble.

Stiffly Lily got to her feet. Taking off her huge sapphire engagement ring and putting it on the draining board, she turned on the hot tap and added washing-up liquid.

'Haven't you got a dishwasher?'

'There's only me. Wouldn't want to risk my best china.'

General the cat appeared at the window. He landed with a thud then ferociously attacked a wooden leg of the kitchen table as the telephone rang. It was Dora. Bianca's friend, thought Feral longingly—as if Rupert Campbell-Anti-Black

515

would let me anywhere near his darling daughter. Fucking upper classes.

'Of course,' Lily was saying, 'no, bring Cadbury, that's fine, perhaps not Loofah as Feral's just mown my lawn most excellently. Yes, stay the night, we can watch *Midsomer Murders*.'

Putting the telephone down, Lily turned back to Feral, lines deepening on her no longer smiling face, utterly exhausted. Feral's tea had taken a lot out of her, and there wasn't any cheese pie or crumble left for Dora's supper. Then she glanced at the draining board. Her ring had gone. She was sure she'd left it there. She should never have put temptation in Feral's way. The great sapphire had been bought to match the blue of her eyes, by a husband she'd loved so much. She glanced at his faded photograph, smiling out at her, and wondered what to do. The sapphire had been like a safety net to keep from the door the wolf, but not the Wolf Pack.

Slowly, painfully, she opened the silver clasp of her red leather purse and with trembling, arthritic fingers gave Feral a tenner for mowing. Then, taking a basket, she went into the garden. It had been a wonderful year for plums; glowing ruby-red, they weighed down the trees like weeping willows. How often recently had she dined on bread and plum jam? Slowly she filled up the basket, swearing and sobbing as a sleepy wasp landed on her third finger where the sapphire had been. Back in the house, she found Feral puffing on a spliff and watching the sports news.

She held out the basket. 'Do you like plums?'

'Never had one.'

'Well, don't break those beautiful white teeth on

516

the stones.' Then, as Feral rolled his eyes: 'You might be able to sell them. I'll decant them into a cardboard box.'

'Fanks, man,' said Feral. With his first glimmer of a smile: 'I could sell them to Paris to put in his mouf, now he's gone all posh at Bagley.'

Lily laughed. Rootling around for an old Whiskas x 12 box, shaking out a spider, she filled it with plums. Handing them to Feral, she noticed the sapphire ring back on the draining board. Dizzy with relief, she had to fight back the tears. For a moment, their eyes met. Again Feral half smiled and shrugged. Then he handed Lily the spliff. Taking a giant puff, she practically burst her lungs.

'You need help wiv Dora's bed?' said Feral.

'You are kind. Actually it's already made up, a teenage friend stayed for a dance last week, only in bed an hour, so I'm afraid I made it up again.'

There was a pause.

'Would you like to come back next week? The grass still grows quickly at this time of year.'

'I'll fink about it,' said Feral.

He longed to feel welcome in an adult world. He needed people to talk to, to feel respect.

'Oh, OK,' he said.

*   *   *

As Brigadier Woodford, who was reading the lesson, drove Lily to Evensong in the next village, they spotted Feral. He was slumped by the side of the road with his Whiskas box, holding up a torn-off piece of cardboard, on which he had written 'Plumes for Sal'.

' "Bring me my white plume",' quipped the

Brigadier, slowing down. 'First-rate job you made of Lily's lawn. Well done,' he told Feral and although his garden was awash with plums, he bought a pound's worth. 'Can't resist Lily's plums.'

The collection could have a pound, instead of two, he decided as he drove on. He had skipped lunch at the Dog and Duck, so he could afford to ask Lily to have dinner with him on the way home.

'Your Dunkirk programme was such a triumph,' Lily told him.

'They did seem pleased.'

'With all those Second World War anniversaries coming up, I'm sure Rupert'll ask you to do some more.'

The Brigadier, who had been brought up to be self-deprecating, loved having someone to tell things to. Gratifying how many people at Evensong, even the parson, who was a notorious pacifist, made a point of saying how good he'd been.

'Rupert's going to pay me two hundred pounds,' he confided to Lily. 'Quite extraordinary for a ten-minute waffle. That's twelve hundred an hour.'

'Randal Stancombe will evidently pay us four pounds an hour for squatting.'

'Have to get a new hip before I tried any of that,' grinned the Brigadier.

By the time he'd levered himself out of the car on arrival at the Dog and Duck, to open Lily's door, she'd already clambered out. Good thing there was no shortage of single women in later life. If a husband came home these days, he would be far too crocked to leap into the wardrobe or pull on his clothes in a hurry. He'd had such wonderful escapades when he was young: wives of

518

commanding officers or even of a visiting general. He didn't think his wife Betsy had ever found out, but she'd looked sad sometimes. He'd made it up by nursing her to the end, although he'd often been rather irritable. Now he harboured a secret passion for Lily: so beautiful, so plucky. He suspected she was even broker than he was and wished he could help.

Although over eighty, the Brigadier was tall and upright, with a high colour which tanned quickly and thick hair, brushed back in two wings, in the same steel grey as his moustache.

Lily had refused his invitation to dinner at first because Dora was staying, so the Brigadier had invited them both to the Dog and Duck, where Dora admired the 'gorgeous springer spaniel' on the inn sign, and where it was sheltered enough to eat outside and admire an orange moon floating free of the darkening woods.

Dora, as usual, was brimming over with chat as she fed crisps to Cadbury and tucked into roast chicken, chips and peas.

'Only time to grab a sandwich at lunchtime,' she announced in her piercing voice. 'Patience and I have been getting Paris's room ready. He loves Liverpool, so we put posters of Owen, Gerrard and Emile Heskey on the walls and she's bought him a Liverpool shirt and a red Liverpool mug which says 'You're not drinkin' any more' on the bottom, and a lovely bookshelf and a tuck box with a key, so he can keep private things.

'He's so lucky,' went on Dora, dipping a chip in tomato ketchup. 'That room's got a terrific view of the stables and Patience has painted it a lovely warm corn colour. Ian's been so preoccupied letting the school to a bishops' conference, and getting fees out of parents like my mother who won't pay up, that Patience has been able to splurge. Fortunately, her aunt kicked the bucket and left her some money.'

The Brigadier, famished after no lunch, had nearly finished his shepherd's pie; Dora, getting behind, began feeding strips of chicken to Cadbury.

'Anyway,' she continued, 'Patience has also bought him a television, a radio, a laptop, a tape deck, a mobile and loads of uniform. Ian wanted her to buy it secondhand. Patience wasn't having any of it, so it's all new.'

'Eat up, Dora, darling,' chided Lily, 'it'll get cold.'

'I'll eat your chips if you like,' said the Brigadier, filling his and Lily's glasses with an excellent red.

'And he's got a double bed,' added Dora, aware the entire pub was now listening, 'so he can have women in, with a patchwork quilt. Patience put lots of Emerald and Sophy's old children's books in the bookshelf: *Babar* and *The Happy Prince*, which is what Patience wants Paris to be. I think he's more like Little Kay in *The Snow Queen*. We mustn't let his heart turn into a block of ice. Can I turn my fork over to eat my peas? It's quicker.'

The rising moon had grown paler.

'Not too cold?' asked the Brigadier.

'I'm fine. That was gorgeous. Thank you so much.' Dora shoved her knife and fork together. 'I'm truly full up.' She beamed at him. 'Well, I wouldn't mind some chocolate ice cream, if you insist.'

A second later, she was back to the subject of

Paris.

'I only hope he's very grateful because Ian and Patience have gone through so much to become foster parents—oodles of medical tests, and they've got to practise safe sex—sounds like a duet'—Dora pretended to play the piano on the table—'so that Patience doesn't get pregnant. She's a bit ancient for that, I would say.'

A woman at the next table choked on her quiche. Lily's eyes met the Brigadier's and, as they tried not to laugh, she attempted to steer Dora on to safer subjects.

'How many bishops has Ian let the school to?'

'Millions,' giggled Dora. 'The Bishop of Cotchester's sleeping in Cosmo's study. I hope he'll remember to water Cosmo's marijuana plants.'

58

Head boy at Rugby, a rugger blue with a second at Cambridge, commanding officer of a tank regiment, managing director of a highly successful Yorkshire engineering company, Ian Cartwright had had few setbacks in life until ousted by a boardroom coup staged by directors fed up with his brusque, despotic manner.

He then fell on desperately hard times, lost everything through foolish investment, descended into heavy drinking and nervous breakdown, only surviving on the money his staunch wife Patience earned working in a bar. The nightmare had ended two years ago, when Ian had landed the job as bursar of Bagley Hall, a Hengist appointment, which had been an unqualified success: the previous incumbent having cooked the books. Ian, who was utterly straight, industrious and excellent with figures, soon got the reputation of a man who could 'get things done', which was also a euphemism for being at everyone's beck and call.

Having been delivered from the hell of poverty, Ian was passionately grateful to his deliverer and in truth it was partly to impress Hengist that he had been keen to foster Paris.

Ian had also longed for a son with whom to discuss internationals, test matches and nineteenth-century poetry, who would look up to him, replenish his whisky, bring in logs and share manly tasks.

Although apprehensive, he was determined to do right by Paris and kept quoting *Timon of Athens*:

' 'Tis not enough to help the feeble up, But to support him after.'

Alas, Paris, already in explosive mood, arrived at the Cartwrights' at Ian's busiest time. Bills for school fees had been dispatched on the first day of the holidays and should have been paid—in theory—before the children set foot in school for the autumn term.

This had resulted in a flood of furious letters from parents outraged not only by the increased fees but at having to foot the bill for the demolition of Gafellyn Castle—letters which Hengist, having buggered off to Umbria, had left Ian to answer.

The majority of staff had swanned off on long holidays, leaving Ian to oversee the installation of new kitchens and damp courses and replace faulty windows in their houses and classrooms. No-Joke Joan rang every day from Lesbos to find out if Ian's maintenance men had unjammed the Tampax machine in Boudicca and whether he had looked at her suggestions for a second young women's boarding house.

Little Vicky Fairchild, on whom Ian had a crush, had already wheedled herself a charming flat overlooking the playing fields with a new en suite bathroom; whereupon all the young staff followed suit and wanted one too. In addition, it was Ian's duty in the holidays to let the school to bring in revenue. For the fifth year running, the Church of England had held their conference at Bagley, charming chaps who all wanted to play golf and ride Patience's horses, which ran away with them, which added to the pressure.

In the second half, the school had been taken

over by a group of Orthodox Jews, charming chaps too, a source of excellent jokes, but who as part of their religion insisted that their quarters should be plunged into darkness at ten o'clock. They had therefore wrenched out and mislaid most of the infrared lights that automatically came on in the passages as night fell.

Any conference involved a lot of tidying up for Ian's ground staff and maintenance men to prepare the school for the new term. Ian didn't mind, he relished hard work and found Hengist, who only raised hell if his expenses were curbed and the pitches were not mown, a dream boss. The job would have been perfect except for the endless bullying interference of Alex Bruce. Hell-bent on modernizing the school, Alex had insisted Ian learn to use a computer so he could do his own letters and figures and dispense with Jenny Winters, his kind, pretty and brilliantly efficient PA.

Ian was subsequently having a nightmare mastering the beastly machine, which seemed to have tripled his workload.

Normally, as bursar, after he had chased up the parents for payments and settled in the school, he and Patience would have taken their annual three-week holiday in the second half of September. This year, with all the expense of kitting out Paris, they couldn't afford to go.

In late August, when the Cartwrights finally got permission to foster, an exhausted, uptight Ian was hardly in the right mood to welcome and make allowances for Paris. Patience as a reaction became over-conciliatory and dithery, filling every silence with chat, until Ian put her down out of nerves.

Paris was equally uptight, at moving to both a

new home and a new school. He loved his new room. He loved his bathroom and, after the fight for often cold showers at Oaktree Court, luxuriated for hours reading in scented baths. He loved his laptop, tape deck and mobile, but since he'd fallen out with the Wolf Pack and Janna, he had no one to ring. The bliss of reading and writing in peace and being able to watch *Richard and Judy* or *Top of the Pops* to the end, without someone throwing a punch or snatching the remote, rather palled when you had all day in which to do it.

After the permanent din of the home where inmates shouted and screamed and were shoved in the quiet room, he found the repressed formality of the Cartwrights unnerving. Nadine had urged them to provide a stable environment with clear boundaries. Ian, tetchy and at full stretch, would return in the evening and order Paris around like an errand boy.

There was the disastrous occasion when Ian asked him to dig some potatoes, and Paris by mistake dug up all the precious half-grown artichokes. Or when Paris was ordered to collect the *Sunday Telegraph* from Bagley village and, settling down to read the football reports on a gravestone in Bagley churchyard on the way home, had crumpled and muddled up all the pages.

Ian, in addition, felt it was his duty to improve others. He started off on Paris's appearance. Sleeveless T-shirts were to be discouraged when they showed off a tattoo of the Eiffel Tower. Soon he was nagging Paris to remove his jewellery. As Paris's ear studs, plaited leather bracelet and necklace of wooden beads, threaded on to a bootlace, had all been presents from Feral, Paris had no intention of complying.

Mealtimes together were also a torment as Ian corrected Paris's pronunciation and table manners.

'It's beetroot, not bee-roo, Paris, and bu-er has a double "t" in the middle. Spoons go on the right and forks on the left and try not to hold your knife like a pencil.'

Patience's erratic time-keeping often meant Paris was summoned to lay the table in the middle of *EastEnders* or *Holby City*. Asparagus lost any initial charm when you were reproached for taking a knife and fork to it.

Even worse horrors occurred at breakfast: plunging your silver spoon into a cavern of phlegm because Patience had under-boiled your egg. It was also impossible to make conversation if your table manners and pronunciation were constantly criticized.

'Leave him alone,' pleaded Patience. 'You're making the poor boy self-conscious.'

'I'm only doing it so he doesn't get teased when he goes to Bagley.'

So Paris left his food and fell into silence. Plates brought to his room when Ian was away were found untouched and gathering flies.

For the first few days he sat with them in the evening, listening to the Proms, watching programmes on archaeological digs and wrecks being brought up from the bottom of the sea. One evening they borrowed and watched a tape of Brigadier Woodford's excellent programme on Dunkirk.

'Woodford lives near Lily Hamilton and Janna Curtis. Evidently he's an awfully nice chap,' observed Ian.

Paris felt the inevitable stab of anguish on hearing Janna's name. Patience felt reproachful. Both Hengist and Janna had promised to be around and help ease Paris's first weeks at Bagley but neither had been near the place, not even a telephone call.

Paris missed the Wolf Pack and Janna dreadfully. Patience couldn't stem his loneliness. She felt she was looking after someone's dog who pines constantly for his master. Trying to make Paris feel at home, she showed him family albums of her daughters Sophy and Emerald from when they were first adopted, through schooldays and eventually marriage and grandchildren.

'My life is recorded in social service files, not family albums,' said Paris bleakly.

'Not any more,' said Patience brightly. 'You'll be in our albums.'

Not if your poxy husband has his way, thought Paris.

The stingy bugger, furious that his wife had spent so much money on mobiles, laptops and new clothes for Paris, insisted Patience sew the name tapes on herself, rather than avail herself of a school service that only charged 50p a tape. Paris watched her pricking her big red fingers, straining her eyes as she threaded needles.

'At least you're not called something long like Orlando France-Lynch, or Xavier Campbell-Black. Bianca and Xavier are adopted,' bumbled on Patience.

'I know.'

'Bianca's such a happy little soul,' sighed Patience. 'Mind you'—she lowered her voice—'Sophy was always much happier and easier than

Emerald. Maybe it's younger children.'

To make Paris feel at home, Patience had asked Emerald down for the weekend—sadly Emerald's charming, larky husband Jonathan was in Berlin and unable to accompany her. And the baby Raymond, who might have broken the ice, was left in London with the nanny. Paris found Emerald as beadily bitchy as she was beautiful. She clearly hated seeing him ensconced in the spare room with Liverpool posters rather than her own paintings on the walls.

The evening was chilly, and Ian, showing off, had ordered Paris to fetch logs and coal for a fire. Paris, engrossed in *Great Expectations*, had told Ian to 'piss off' and been sent to his room.

A furious Emerald had followed him.

'How dare you cheek Daddy after all he's done for you, you horrible brat.'

'You could be horrid as a teenager,' protested Patience when Emerald returned downstairs.

'He's a yob,' said Emerald. 'He comes from the gutter and he'll go back there.'

Paris much preferred Emerald's plump, jolly sister, Sophy, Janna's friend, who was going to replace Vicky at Larks in the autumn term. But feeling Sophy might be spying or trying to heal the breach between himself and Janna, whose letters he had continued to tear up, he shut himself in his room whenever she dropped in.

Lying in the bath Paris watched a snail, which had climbed all the way up the wall of the house to escape the incessant rain, its trail glittering in the morning sun, its horns hitting the buffers of the gutter.

Like me, he thought, from the gutter to the
528

gutter.

*   *   *

Term approached. Paris grew more edgy and withdrawn as Bagley staff, back from their holidays, also popped in to check if their windows and sinks had been repaired and to register if he had two heads.

'You're a saint, Patience, adopting at your and Ian's age, and looking after the horses as well. You look exhausted. I hope you're getting paid. Of course he does have a free place.'

And Paris, who'd perfected the art of eavesdropping in care, lurking on stairs and doorways (which was the only way he could learn if he or his friends were being moved on), heard everything.

Watching Patience struggling across the yard with buckets and haynets, he longed to help, but didn't know how to offer.

He would never have survived without Dora, back from a turbulent week in Spain with her brother Dicky, her mother and one of her mother's admirers, a High Court judge.

'Although he was paying for all of us, Mummy didn't want to sleep with him so she insisted on sharing with me, which was so pants. He barged in one night plastered, forgetting I was there, so I whacked him with a black plastic bull.'

Dora's round face and her plump little legs and arms had caught the sun and, rather than plaiting it, she had pulled back her long, blond hair into a ponytail. She was still a tomboy, but as she rolled up with Cadbury and took up residence on his bed,

529

Paris reflected that she might one day have possibilities.

When he tried on his school suit for the first time, both Patience and Dora gasped as its dark severity set off to perfection his pale marble features and lean elegant body. Paris liked the slate grey overcoat. With shades on, he'd look like Feral's Uncle Harley.

'You look cool,' admitted Dora. She consulted the list. 'Two pairs of slip-on shoes. Try a pair on.'

'What am I going to slip on—a banana skin?'

'Are they comfortable?' asked Patience anxiously.

'Very. Change to have a pair that doesn't pinch or let in water.'

A din in the yard outside suggested a pupil had arrived early to drop off a horse. Patience disappeared to welcome them. Dora, who was cleaning tack, remained on Paris's bed, rather randomly applying saddle soap to Plover's bridle.

That tweed jacket must be a cast-off of Ian's, thought Paris. Christ, it was from Harrods, still with the label on, and those pale blue shirts were really cool. It was as though he was being kitted out by Wardrobe for a new play, but who knew if it would be a tragedy or a comedy?

'Let's see your duvets,' asked Dora.

'Thomas the Tank Engine and Beatrix Potter with Peter Rabbit cock-sucking a carrot,' grumbled Paris. 'I am going to get so much piss taken out of me.'

He was now skimming through the Bagley Code of Conduct with increasing alarm. There were pages of rules about not downloading porn.

'I wanted to download some stuff for Patience about Northcliffe'—Dora went very pink—'but when I logged into golden retriever, it was so

530

disgusting: women actually weeing on men. I don't understand the human race.'

Paris grinned and read on.

' "No one can leave the school without permission." How do they stop me?'

'Give you a detention, make you do hearty things like digging the garden and not watching television. The second time they cancel your leave-outs.'

'That'd be a relief, if Ian doesn't loosen up. "Once a week", he read, "all scholars must participate in an activity that involves serving others in the community." '

'Cosmo helps out at Larkminster Hospital,' said Dora. 'He's shagging one of the nurses.'

'Servicing others,' murmured Paris.

'Best way is to find a nice old biddy, weed her garden, then you get crumpets and cake for tea and to watch *Neighbours*. Feral's working for my aunt, Lily Hamilton, mowing her lawn. They get on really well. Janna fixed it up.'

'The happy highways where I went And cannot come again', thought Paris, wincing at the pain.

' "No hats to be worn inside",' he went on. 'That's crazy.'

'They're talking about woolly hats and baseball caps and you're not allowed jewellery.'

'I'm not taking mine off. "In cases of bullying, both victim and bully get counselling." ' Paris shivered. He'd heard a chilling rumour about the Pitbull Club in which older boys arranged fights between new boys and bet large sums of money on which one would first beat the other to a pulp.

'What the hell am I supposed to do in my free time?' he added in outrage. 'It says here, "Any scholar caught supplying drugs or having sex gets sacked." '

'Not always.' Dora went to Paris's basin to wash silver polish off Plover's bit. 'You're sacked if you're caught having sex with a girl. If it's a boy, you'd only get three hours' gardening.'

'How d'they work that out?'

'Boys don't get pregnant; it's meant to act as a detergent,' Dora went on helpfully.

'God, listen to this: "Swearing, spitting, chewing gum all incur five-pound penalties." This is a police state. What about smoking and drinking?'

'Fiver first time you're caught, then they double up.'

'What do they do with the money?'

'Goes to charity. Alex Bruce was hopping last term when brilliant Hengist sent the entire six and a half thousand to Greyhound Rescue. But as that tosser Boffin Brooks keeps saying'—Dora put her hands together sanctimoniously—'one only has to behave oneself.'

59

Determined to familiarize Paris with everything, Dora gave him a map and a tour of the school.

'Here's the gym, here's the music school, here's the sick bay. Most important, here's the tuck shop.'

Hengist had put him in Theo Graham's house, a two-storey neo-Gothic building covered in Virginia creeper, which was north-east of the Mansion with a view over the golf course.

'Here's your bedroom-cum-study,' went on Dora, leading him down a corridor. 'They're known as cells.'

The room was tiny—Paris could touch the walls with both hands—and contained a single bed, a desk for his books and laptop and a small cupboard and shelves for his clothes. The joint window was to be shared with the boy in the next cell.

'Who is it? Oh, Smart, he's a rugger bugger; hope he doesn't want the window open all the time. Next year you'll go upstairs to a bigger room of your own. I'll bring your Liverpool posters over later.

'This is Cosmo's cell.' She opened a door on the way out.

'Why's he got a room twice as big as anyone else?'

'Because he's Cosmo. Once he moves in his stuff it'll look like something out of the Arabian nights.

'This is Anatole's.' Giggling, Dora showed Paris the next cell. 'He's got a map of the world as his duvet cover and always sits on the United States because he loathes the Americans so much.'

And I've got Thomas the Tank Engine and Peter Rabbit, thought Paris. How could Patience?

'Oh look, there's Mummy's car outside,' said Dora as they wandered back to the stables.

Although Anthea Belvedon was wildly jealous of Dora's addiction to Paris and the Cartwrights, it freed her for assignations of her own. Today she had had lunch with Randal Stancombe, who was so attractive, and who hadn't a high opinion of Paris, who'd evidently tried to rape Jade on the field trip.

Having rolled up to collect Dora, Anthea was looking distastefully at the mess in Patience's kitchen (riding boots on the table, washing up still in the sink) while enquiring how Paris was getting on.

'Really well,' said Patience, terrified Paris might walk in.

'Emerald found him gauche and awfully tricky,' went on Anthea. 'Dora said you were awfully upset Paris never said a word of thanks about his lovely room. The working classes never know how to express gratitude, of course.'

'I wasn't upset,' squeaked Patience furiously. 'It's his right to have a nice room.'

'But such an expense: Sky, tape decks and computers—Dora says you emptied Dixons.'

'Mummy, I did not,' screamed Dora, who was standing appalled in the doorway.

Paris had bolted upstairs. Giving a sob, he hurled his precious Liverpool mug against the wall. Then he smashed a china dog, ripped the poster of Heskey off the wall and tipped over the bookshelf.

Hearing crashes, Patience lumbered upstairs, hammering on the door against which Paris had shoved a big armchair.

534

'Paris, listen.'

'Fuck off,' hissed Paris, grabbing his laptop.

'Anthea's a complete bitch; honestly, she's jealous because Dora loves being here and adores you. We don't expect you to say thank you for anything. We give you things because we love having you here.'

Oh God, it was coming out all wrong. But Paris put down his laptop.

'It'll be shepherd's pie and just you and me tonight; we can eat it in front of the telly.'

'So my crap table manners won't show. I don't want any supper.'

The window was open. Paris slid down the Virginia creeper and off across the yard.

It was only after ten-thirty, when Ian returned home, that Patience realized Paris had taken the car and just managed to stop Ian ringing the police.

'We'll lose him.'

'Bloody good riddance.'

When they went out looking for him they found the car undamaged behind a haystack.

Paris staggered in, plastered, at midnight.

'Go to bed at once, we'll discuss this in the morning,' shouted Ian.

*   *   *

Alex Bruce often rose at six to train for the school steeplechase and to spy on other masters, particularly Hengist's cronies, Artie Deverell and Theo Graham, who were both gay; Emlyn, who was engaged to Hengist's daughter Oriana (sort of); and, more recently, the brusque, dismissive Ian

535

Cartwright: all the King's men.

Hearing shouts from the Old Coach House, Alex broke his journey, jogging up the path, letting himself into the kitchen.

'Can I help?'

He found Dora Belvedon taking everything in, Patience by the Aga, looking miserable, and Ian, as boiling over with rage as Paris was icy with fury.

They all turned to Alex: not an attractive sight. A fringe like a false eyelash hung damply on his forehead, his drenched yellow T-shirt clung to his hollow chest, sweat parted the black hairs on his skinny thighs.

'Can I help?' he repeated.

'No,' snapped Ian.

'You OK, Paris Alvaston?'

'Fine, just fuck off.'

'Paris,' thundered Ian.

'If you'd started at Bagley, young man,' began Alex, 'you'd be fined five pounds for that. I will not allow foul language. I shall leave your foster parents to deal with you.'

'Lando France-Lynch owed the swear fund eight hundred and fifty pounds last term,' piped up Dora, taking croissants out of the Aga and throwing them on the kitchen table. 'Would you like one, Mr Bruce? You look as though you need feeding up.'

Paris went up to his room and slammed the door so hard all the china and glass crowded on the shelves below rattled and clinked. Ian shut himself away in the drawing room with his confounded computer.

Later, tipped off no doubt by Alex, Nadine the social worker popped in. 'Gather you're having a

536

problem with Paris, Patience.'

'I'm afraid my husband's working and Paris has just gone out. Would you like a cup of tea?'

'Thank you. You must open up.'

'We're fine, we love Paris.'

'Don't expect him to love you. When you foster a teenager at best you can expect to be a mentor or an authority figure.'

Did Nadine ever wear anything else but that funereal black, wondered Patience as she switched on the kettle. Getting a packet of chocolate biscuits out of the cupboard, she noticed mice had eaten a hole in one end, and hastily decanted the biscuits on to a plate.

'I know you want to rescue a young life and Paris longs for a family,' bleated Nadine. 'But your expectations are unrealistic. At an age when most adolescents are trying to escape from their parents and forge their own identity, you're going against the grain and trying to form ties. It's not easy.'

Then, seeing the tears spilling down Patience's tired red face: 'He's going to need a lot of counselling.'

*   *   *

It was nearly midnight. Paris still hadn't come home.

'Thank God he's boarding and'll be out of our hair by tomorrow,' exploded Ian. 'How dare he tell Alex Bruce to fuck off.'

Patience felt ashamed that momentarily she agreed with her husband. She felt bitterly let down that neither Hengist nor Janna had yet made contact. She turned out the horses and collapsed into bed.

It was a very warm, muggy night. Moths flying in through the window kept torching themselves on Ian's halogen lamp. Ian winced but there was no time to rescue them. It was after eleven and he was still wrestling with his infernal computer to provide Alex tomorrow with a list of parents who still hadn't paid up. As the whisky bottle emptied, he grew more clumsy. Scrumpled-up paper shared the threadbare Persian carpet with a snoring Northcliffe.

Ian glanced up at the photograph of himself in the Combined Services rugger team, strong muscular arms folded, hair and moustache still black and glossy, eyes clear and confident. He hadn't met Patience then. She was a good old girl, but she no longer stirred his loins, and tomorrow there would be no sweet Jenny Winters to sort out every problem and flash delightful pink flesh and thong as she bent over to pull out a file. On Radio 3, Rupert's older son, Marcus Campbell-Black, was playing a Mozart piano concerto so exquisitely it brought tears to Ian's eyes—a piece Mozart had evidently knocked off to pay bills. Would he had such talent.

Ian hadn't slept properly for weeks. How could he hold down the job of bursar if he wasn't on the ball? He was sixty-one, not twenty-six. He hadn't touched the pile of messages. Boudicca's Tampax machine was still jammed. But at least he'd reached the end of the list of the defaulting parents and tapped in Commander Wilkins, Spotty's father, who'd paid last year with a hogshead of brandy.

Lord Waterlane, Jack's father, had in the past

filled up the school deep freezes with venison and grouse, which made marvellous shepherd's pie. Anatole paid his own fees with roubles, Lubemir's father with a Pissarro which turned out to be a fake.

Having been destitute himself recently, Ian felt so sorry for the parents who worked all hours, forgoing cars and holidays and luxuries, to scrape the fees together, and for the grandparents who often paid them and who'd been equally strapped by pension scandals and the collapse of the stock market.

But he didn't feel sorry for Cosmo's mother, the great diva Dame Hermione, who, in lieu of a year's fees, had offered to give a recital to the school with Cosmo accompanying her.

'Normally, Ian, I never charge less than a hundred thousand pounds for a gig, so Bagley's getting a real bargain.'

Lando's parents seemed to be always broke too. Daisy, his mother, had offered to paint Sally Brett-Taylor for free last year. Nor did Amber and Junior's parents, both on high salaries, ever seem to have any money.

Anthea Belvedon, the prettiest little thing, played every trick in the book to avoid forking out since she was widowed two years ago. He'd have to summon her next week. He had a special Paisley emerald-green silk handkerchief, faintly flavoured with lavender, to mop up pretty mothers' tears. What a shame Mrs Walton had shacked up with Randal Stancombe, who'd paid Milly's fees this term. Comforting Mrs Walton had been an even more exquisite pleasure than glimpsing Jenny Winters's thong.

539

Bagley, overall, was in great financial shape. Since the geography field trip, the waiting list had doubled, as eager offspring pestered their parents to send them to such a fun palace. Hengist, routing the Education Secretary on *Question Time* last week, had brought another flood of applications. The school was booked solid till 2012. If only Hengist were as good at picking staff. How dare Alex Bruce steal Jenny Winters?

Thank God for that. Ian switched off the computer. But as he emptied the last drop of whisky into a mug entitled Master of the House, he noticed an envelope on the floor. Inside was a cheque signed by Boffin Brooks's frightful father Gordon for five thousand pounds. (Two thousand less than normal because of Boffin's scholarship.) Gordon always paid at the last moment to avoid both a two per cent penalty and losing interest.

Like most first-generation public-school parents, Sir Gordon Brooks clamoured for his kilo of flesh and would have gone berserk and straight to his good friend Alex Bruce if he'd been chased for non-payment, or if Ian had forgotten to put CBE (for services to export) on the receipt. Why didn't someone export Gordon?

Ian mopped his brow with his shirtsleeve in relief. But when he switched on the computer to delete Gordon's name, he couldn't find the file.

Drenched in sweat, heart pounding, blood swept into his brain in a tidal wave, trying to force its way out. Lightning jagged before his eyes. He was going to have a stroke. Nothing. He'd deleted the fucking thing—two whole days' work with his slow typing. He was far too drunk to type it out again.

'I can't go on.' Ian's head crashed into his

sweating hands. He'd get fired; they'd be destitute again. Snoring Northcliffe and Patience's horses would have to go.

He jumped, hearing a crash and rattle downstairs, and shoved the empty whisky bottle under the half-completed *Times* crossword. Hearing a step and a thump of a tail, he swung round. Paris trying to creep in had sent a walking stick flying.

'Where the hell have you been?'

The boy looked whiter than ever—a ghost postillion struck by lightning, haunting the Old Coach House.

'For a walk.'

'Too bloody late.'

Seeing despair rather than rage in Ian's bloodshot eyes, however, Paris asked if he were OK.

'No, I'm not, just wiped a bloody file,' mumbled Ian. 'Need it for Alex Bruce first thing.'

He banged his fist on the table. Everything jumped: the mug tipping over, spilling the last of the whisky on his written notes; *Times* crossword page fluttering down to reveal the empty bottle.

'I can't go on.' Picking up the keyboard, Ian was about to smash it.

Paris, rather encouraged by such loss of control, leapt forward. 'Cool it, for fuck's sake. Get up.' He tugged the keyboard from Ian. 'Lemme have a go.'

Sliding into Ian's seat, he went into MS-DOS and typed in the command to bring up the list of files.

'What's the name of the one you lost?'

' "Unpaid fees 2002 autumn".' Ian slumped against the wall. He didn't dare to hope. Oh, please God.

A blond moth fluttered on a suicide mission towards the lamp. Cupping his hands, Paris caught it. He got up and shoved it into the honeysuckle outside, before shutting the window. Returning to Ian's chair, he scrolled down.

'Reports, expulsions, health, recreations, staff performance, that looks in-eresting—or, as you would say, "intr'sting".' His eyes slid towards Ian. ' "Unpaid fees 2002 autumn." Got it.'

Ian gave a gasp of relief:

'Are you sure?'

'Quite,' said Paris, reinstating the file back on the computer in its original format. 'Do you need to change anything?' Then, scrolling down the list: 'There's that bitch Anthea Belvedon, Campbell-Black, Harefield, Lloyd-Foxe, Waterlane, always the rich buggers that don't pay up.'

'You shouldn't be reading that, it's confidential.'

'I have the shortest memory.'

'Can you delete Gordon Brooks, Boffin's father? He's paid.'

As Paris found the name, highlighted it and hit the delete button, his fingers made an even more exquisite sound than Marcus Campbell-Black.

'Let's print it out,' suggested Ian. 'I can add latecomers in biro. Thank God, Paris, you've saved my life, probably my job.'

Slumped on a moth-eaten sofa covered in a tartan rug, Ian looked utterly exhausted, his eyes red hollows, his cheeks and nose a maze of purple veins, the lines round his mouth like cracks in dry paths.

'Would you like a nightcap?' he asked, desperate for one himself.

Paris grinned. How could a face so shuttered and

542

cold one moment be so enchantingly warm, almost loving, the next?

'Thought caps weren't allowed to be worn indoors at Bagley.'

Getting the joke, Ian laughed.

'All those rules must seem a bit alarming. Have to have that jewellery off, I'm afraid. Wear it when you come back here for leave-outs.'

Ian rose unsteadily and wandered to the much depleted drinks cupboard, pouring a brandy and ginger for Paris and the rest of the brandy for himself, taking a great gulp.

'Thank you, Paris, so much.' Then, seeing the boy's eyes straying towards the crossword: 'Finish it if you like. Got stuck on a Tennyson quote. "Heavily hangs the broad . . .", nine letters, "over its grave in' the earth so chilly." '

'Sunflower,' murmured Paris.

'Of course, well done. "Heavily hangs the hollyhock, Heavily hangs the tiger-lily." Beautiful poem.'

Paris smirked. 'Any time, Ian. And if you have trouble with that computer, ring me or text me on my mobile and I'll whiz out of chemistry and sort it.'

'I suppose those wretched mobiles have their uses,' conceded Ian. 'Sorry, the last few weeks have been rough. All a bit nervous. Promise to telephone or pop into my office if there're any problems.'

'Thank you,' said Paris, feeling much happier.

*   *   *

When Ian looked at his computer next morning,

Paris had written, with some scarlet nail polish which Emerald had left in the bathroom, on the frame of the computer screen: 'To remind you to save it.'

60

Paris's first weeks at Bagley were hell. At Larks he'd bunked off any lesson he disliked and been free after three-thirty. Now he was flat out from the moment the bell fractured his skull at six-forty-five until lights out at ten, kept endlessly busy racing from chapel to lessons to games to prep and losing his way despite Dora's map. Used to being easily the cleverest pupil at Larks, he found himself woefully behind in most subjects and, with smaller classes, there was nowhere to hide. Nor had he dreamt rugby would be so brutal, but with Anatole and Lubemir in the scrum, he couldn't expect much else.

His rarity appeal had also gone. An arctic fox occasionally peeping out of the frozen tundra loses his mystery when he's caged in the zoo. Stripped of his lucky jewellery, disfigured by a savaging from the school barber and by his first spots ever (from existing on chocolate, rather than Patience's cooking), he had never felt less attractive. Ian's assault on his pronunciation and table manners had made him miserably self-conscious both in class and at mealtimes.

His first evening was a nightmare, with so many pupils rolling up in flash cars or helicopters with their glamorous parents yelling about mooring the yacht off Sardinia, or stalking in Scotland, or villas in Dubai where the jet-skiing had been out of this world.

Paris nearly died of embarrassment when Patience insisted on humping his stuff across the school into Theo's house, putting Thomas the Tank Engine on his duvet and braying 'hello' to all the other pupils.

'Theo's terrified of parents,' she whispered. 'Probably won't appear for hours. Now let's put up your posters.'

'I'm fine,' hissed Paris.

'Just want to settle you in. Where shall I put this fruit cake?'

'I'll sort it,' Paris almost shrieked. 'I'm OK, just go.'

The moment she left, he was frantically stripping off the duvet cover when his next-door neighbour, Smart, who already had a ginger moustache above his broad grin, wandered in, shouting, 'I'm Smart. Thomas the Tank Engine, fantastic, wish I'd thought of that. Where's the Fat Controller?'

So Paris left it on, and put up a poster of Tennyson between Michael Owen and Emile Heskey.

'Coming to supper?' asked Smart.

Paris wasn't hungry, but he needed an ally. In the dining room, the din was hideous, as they all yakked in their Sloaney way about polo in Sotogrande and the sailing lessons Daddy'd organized in Rock, or chatted to new conquests on their mobiles, or flagged up photographs of them. Paris noticed Xav, sitting alone, sullen and miserable, and felt a louse for avoiding his eye. He also realized he'd made enemies on the field trip. He'd never texted Jade or Amber after shagging them—not having a mobile at the time was no excuse. Boffin, twitchy at the prospect of being usurped by a cleverer boy, was reading the *New Scientist*. Cosmo was smiling his evil smile.

'Hengist really must install a runway, it takes such ages by chopper,' said a familiar bitchy voice.

It was Jade Stancombe, flaunting a butterscotch tan and a ravishing new short tortoiseshell-streaked haircut. Nicky Clarke had repaired the ravages of the sawn-off plait with something far more becoming to Jade's thin, predatory face. Mobile glued to her ear, chatting to some new admirer, she swung round, clocked Cosmo, exchanged a long eye-meet and, walking over, bent down and French kissed him for thirty seconds, sending a shiver through the room. Jade and Cosmo were an item again.

'Love your hair, Jade,' chorused everyone sycophantically.

'Brings out the latent homosexual in all of us,' murmured Cosmo. 'You obviously haven't been abused by the school barber, like our friend Paris.'

Everyone turned round and looked at Paris, who, not giving them time to hail or reject him, chucked down his napkin and, food untouched, stalked out.

'Don't go,' called Amber.

Resisting a temptation to bolt back to the Old Coach House, Paris returned to Theo's house where he found some post on his bed.

Seeing Janna's writing on a dove-grey envelope, Paris dropped it in the bin. Beneath was a parcel from Cosmo, containing a copy of *Tom Brown's Schooldays*. Inside Cosmo had written 'À bientôt, Flashman'.

Finally there was a letter from Sally Brett-Taylor. 'Good luck. Come and have tea with us very soon. Hope your years at Bagley are happy and rewarding.'

Like fuck, thought Paris.

' "The years like great black oxen tread the world," ' he declaimed. ' "And I am broken by their passing feet." '

'At this moment, you can't envisage a day let alone a week at Bagley being tolerable,' said a flat, rasping, mocking voice. 'I'm sorry I wasn't here to welcome you. I'm allergic to parents.'

'Lucky I don't have any.'

'Come and have a drink. Who are you next to? Oh, Smart. A misnomer actually. But he's good-hearted and an excellent rugger player.'

Months spent every summer in Greece and Italy poring over relics and ruins with never a drop of suntan oil had browned and creased Theo Graham's bald head and face like a conker soaked in vinegar. He had jug ears, jagged teeth and, like many schoolmasters, looked older than his sixty years, but his eyes were kind, shrewd and lively.

'This is my lair,' he said, leading Paris into his study, which reeked worse than a public bar of fags and booze, but which was almost entirely lined with literature, history and philosophy in the original Greek and Latin: ancient books with leather binding or faded dilapidated jackets. As well as a huge desk and an upright piano, the room was densely populated with busts of emperors and great thinkers and sculptures of gods, goddesses, heroes, nymphs, centaurs and caryatids, all poised to embark on some splendid orgy after dark. Paris's eyes were on stalks.

'I hear you're interested in learning Latin and Greek,' said Theo, rootling around under the papers on the desk to find a corkscrew. 'Well, you've come from the Old Coach House to an old coach's house,' and he smiled with great affection.

548

Adding to the chaos, a huge fluffy marmalade cat padded across the room and landed on the desk, sending half the contents flying.

'At least he's unearthed the corkscrew.' Theo pounced on it. 'His name is Hindsight, so we can all benefit from him.'

Having poured a large glass of red for Paris and an even larger whisky for himself, Theo settled a thunderously purring Hindsight on his knee and asked Paris what other subjects he was intending to take for GCSE. When Paris reeled off English, English lit., French, Spanish, history, geography, drama, business studies, science and maths, Theo heaved a sigh of relief.

'Thank God, none of those new subjects like leisure and tourism. How could one prefer a hotel to Homer?'

Paris took a slug of red and thought for a minute, then said, 'If I could have a night in the bridal suite with Bianca Campbell-Black, sir, I might prefer a hotel, but the *Iliad*'s one of the best books I've ever read.'

'Good,' said Theo happily, 'we should get along.'

Hengist had given a lot of thought to the right house for Paris. Biffo would have got drunk and probably pounced on him. The Bruces would have killed him with petty regulations and counselling. Artie Deverell, gentle, handsome, clever, tolerant, charming, adored by pupils and parents (particularly the latter, who invited him to stay in their villas in Tuscany and Provence for weeks on end), would have been ideal. But Deverell's was always hopelessly over-subscribed, which Graham's never was.

Theo, crotchety, very shy, dreadful with parents

and liable to take his hearing aid out on Speech Day, had a house with only a dozen boys. One to whom he was utterly devoted was Cosmo, who returned this devotion. Cosmo was clever and made Theo laugh. As one of the few people who could control Cosmo, Theo also believed that with parents like Dame Hermione and the evil, late Roberto Rannaldini, the boy was entitled to be a monster. Theo also took out his hearing aid when Cosmo and the Cosmonaughties were giving tongue.

If Cosmo started bullying Paris, deduced Hengist, Theo would pick up on it.

Theo drove Alex Bruce crackers calling his Chinese pupils 'Chinks', his Russians 'Little Commies' and banging any child if they were being particularly stupid on the head with an atlas of the ancient world.

Unlike Ian Cartwright he had refused to succumb to Alex's bullying and chucked his first laptop in the lake, continuing to tap away with two fingers on an ancient manual typewriter until Cosmo, terrified the only master who understood him would be eased out, taught him to use a computer.

Theo incurred disapproval because he smoked and drank too much.

'Why am I late?' he would ask his classes.

'Because you drank too much last night, sir,' they would chorus.

A typical holiday in the past would have been riding round Umbria on a donkey reading Plato's *Republic.* Now he took gentler vacations, occasionally grumbling about a bad back. In fact only he knew he had an inoperable tumour in his spine, which was why he drank so much: to ease the pain.

Apart from translating the plays of Euripides and now embarking on those of Sophocles, Theo looked after the classical library and school museum and was in charge of the archives, which chronicled the achievements of illustrious former pupils. Alex Bruce was desperate to scrap the museum and the library and replace them with an IT suite.

'Tradition is the enemy of progress,' he was fond of saying.

Alex was driven demented by Theo, but he was powerless to fire him because Theo got even the dimmest child through GCSE and, because of this and his wonderfully entertaining teaching, his lessons were always crowded out.

One of Bagley's favourite pastimes was watching Artie Deverell and Theo argue. For the duration of an entire cricket match they had been observed marching up and down the boundary waving their arms and shouting over whether Catullus had really been wiped out by love when he wrote his poems or merely portraying someone thus afflicted.

David Hawkley, headmaster of Fleetley, another great classical scholar, had dedicated his translation of Catullus to Theo and every Christmas sent him a litre of malt whisky. This irritated Hengist who longed to be admired by David Hawkley.

'Extraordinary, these new GCSEs,' Theo was now complaining to Paris. 'I gather they're thinking of linking RE and PE as one subject. The mind boggles until one remembers all those old jokes about when the high jump was first invented.'

'When was it?'

'When Jesus cleared the temple.'

Paris laughed.

'Or the first cricket match,' went on Theo, 'when Jesus stood up before the eleven and was bold—or bowled. Interesting that they're always described as schoolboy jokes, never schoolgirl.'

'If you'd been on a geography field trip with Joan Johnson, you'd understand,' said Paris.

*　　　*　　　*

At the same time that first evening as Paris was, to his amazement, really enjoying having a drink with Theo, Anthea Belvedon was delivering her son Dicky back to Alex Bruce's house. Here she sought out Poppet Bruce: 'Have you a mo?'

'Of course, Anthea. One of the reasons I'm nicknamed "Poppet" is because people are always "popping in" on me.' Poppet gave a soppy smile.

'My late husband nicknamed me "Hopey",' countered Anthea, 'because I always give people hope.'

After a minute on the importance of reminding Dicky to use his foot-rot cream because he'd infected Anthea's High Court judge on holiday, Anthea moved briskly on to Paris and the riches the Cartwrights had heaped on him:

'Would that I could do the same for my Dora and Dicky.'

'But I thought the Cartwrights were broke,' mused Poppet. 'I hope they're not spending Bagley money.'

'So do I.' Anthea sighed gustily. 'Surely a free place does not mean a free-for-all?'

'I'll have a discreet word with Alex.'

'You won't mention my name.'

'We haven't spoken,' said Poppet.

*   *   *

The upshot twenty-four hours later was a fired-up Patience barging into Alex's office brandishing bills and cheque stubs.

'How dare you accuse Ian of cooking the books? It's actionable. He's the most honest man in the world. He's been flat out through the summer holidays and we've given up our three-week holiday in France this year so we can be home to give Paris a proper start. You and your wife can bloody well apologize to him.'

'We do feel you're in danger of spoiling Paris Alvaston,' spluttered a discomfited Alex. 'His behaviour so far has been very challenging . . .'

Ian, in turn, was later apoplectic with Patience.

'How could you have shouted at Alex? I could have given him a perfectly reasonable explanation. Of course it looks odd you squandering so much on Paris. He could easily have worn a second-hand suit. How can I ask for a rise now?'

Dora, who suspected her mother of sneaking, had also spent too much money on Paris. She must sell some more stories.

Flipping through the papers in the library to assess her market on the first Saturday of term, she came across a piece about parents of truants being given gaol sentences.

If she bunked off for a week, would her utterly bloody mother go to prison? Although her awful old High Court judge boyfriend would probably get her off.

Dispirited, and unable to keep away, Dora wandered off to see Paris. A warm west wind was chasing chestnut leaves round the quad; green spiky husks were opening to drop gleaming brown conkers; the shaggy pelt of Virginia creeper flung round the Gothic turrets of Theo Graham's house was turning crimson.

She found Paris pretending to tackle a distressing amount of homework while listening to Liverpool against Everton on Radio Five, and expressing fury that he'd officially been given Xavier as a 'buddy' to show him the ropes. Talk about linking two social misfits.

Lucky Xav, thought Dora wistfully, but out loud said:

'It won't be so bad, you needn't see much of him after the first week and he might invite you to Penscombe. It's gorgeous. Fabulous horses and Rupert and Taggie are really lovely.'

'And Bianca's even lovelier,' said Paris bitchily. 'Only reason to brown-nose her lousy brother is to get a crack at her.'

Dora couldn't speak for the hurt, as though a huge wasp had plunged its sting deep into her heart, flooding poison through her veins. She knew Paris didn't adore her as she adored him, but he'd never mentioned Bianca, so she'd assumed he wasn't interested.

Seeing her stricken face, her blue eyes widening in bewilderment, Paris felt as though he'd kicked a puppy.

'Oh fuck off,' he snapped. 'You're getting on my tits.'

But as Dora stumbled out, tripping over a pile of

books, Paris was livid with himself. He liked Xav as well. Why did he have this urge to hurt and destroy people who were kind to him? He longed to explain to Patience, Dora, even Xav how sad and lonely he was and how sadness came out as anger, but the less you gave people the less they had to hurt you with.

Even Liverpool winning in the dying moments couldn't lift his spirits. On the hall table he found a parcel and a card saying: 'Dear Paris, good luck. Sorry this is late. Love Dora'.

Inside was a really cool Black Watch tartan duvet cover and two pillowcases.

Switching on his mobile, he dialled Dora's number.

'The person you are dialling knows you are calling,' said the message, 'and doesn't give a fuck.'

Meanwhile, on her way out, Dora passed Cosmo's king-sized cell. Glancing in, she saw it now accommodated a baby grand and, on the walls, a Picasso Blue Clown, oriental rugs, an antique gilt mirror and portraits of Cosmo's heroes: the Marquis de Sade, Wagner, Byron and his father, the late Roberto Rannaldini. On the king-sized bed covered with fur rugs lay a dark blue cushion embroidered with the words: 'It's hard to be humble and go to Bagley.'

Seated at the piano, Cosmo was playing and singing Mahler Lieder in a deep, hypnotic baritone of exceptional beauty. He was sporting a black overcoat with an astrakhan collar made famous by his late father, and which much became his night-dark eyes and sallow features.

Hearing a sob, he glanced round to find Dora's sweet plump face dissolving in misery.

'Dora, darling.' Pulling her inside, he shut the door and patted the bed.

'It's very cruel to have fur rugs.'

'I am very cruel. Now, whatever's the matter?' Cosmo stroked her blond hair and retied the blue ribbon on one of her plaits.

'I loathe my mother, I'm sure she shopped the Cartwrights to Poppet, implying they'd been using Bagley money kitting out Paris, whereas Patience has paid for everything out of some money her aunt left her.'

'Patience Carthorse,' drawled Cosmo. 'She ought to be pulling beer barrels round London.'

'She's lovely.'

'Not the word I had in mind. You must be blind and deaf.' Cosmo handed Dora a Bacardi and Coke from his fridge and relit his spliff. 'What else is the matter?'

'Paris is in love with Bianca.'

'And the rest.'

'He told me to fuck off. I gave him a new duvet cover today and earlier a video of *Macbeth*.'

'Young Alvaston needs sorting out,' said Cosmo thoughtfully. He had been reading in the *Observer* that Cherie Blair was offering to defend school bullies in court. What an admirable woman. His mission this term was to make Paris Alvaston's life hell and with Xav as his buddy ... what an opportunity to kick the shit out of both of them.

It was also high time he bedded Vicky Fairchild.

61

Vicky was not enjoying her first term at Bagley. The workload was appalling and there was no Sam Spink to fight her corner. After cajoling the lovely flat and bathroom out of Ian Cartwright, her charm objective wasn't working as well as she'd hoped. So many of the masters were gay or married and tied up with families. Piers, the head of her department, was rumoured to be having an affair with Rufus's wife, Sheena. Vicky and Jason had seen through each other long ago. Emlyn, easily the most attractive, and with a strange relationship with Oriana from which Vicky was sure he could be detached, was polite but cool, which exhausted the best heterosexual bachelors.

Hengist and Sally were kind, but Olympian and remote, like Jupiter and Juno, and hadn't invited her to a single dinner party.

There were enough boys in the school in love with her and girls, madly admiring, to feed her ego, but she wanted a husband or a steady partner to love and cherish.

Vicky found her thoughts straying rather too often to Cosmo Rannaldini, sexy little beast, with whom she had gone much too far on the field trip. Now he sat, staring at her, a wicked smile snaking round his full lips, unnerving her as she tried to initiate him and the rest of Middle Five B into *The Pardoner's Tale*. Anatole and Lubemir, meanwhile, were playing poker. Milly was painting her nails; Amber was writing to one of her numerous boyfriends; the Chinless Wanderers were studying the *Sun*, deciding which horses to back, except for Lando, lazy great beast, who was asleep.

'Can you tell me, Lando, what Chaucer is trying to say here?' she asked sharply.

Lando opened an eye. 'Can you tell me who the fuck Chaucer is?'

The class fell about.

'Don't use horrible language, Lando, that's another fiver for the swear box. And don't be so obtuse.'

Lando stretched out a large polo-stick-calloused hand for the Collins dictionary. 'What does "obtuse" mean?'

Vicky's lips tightened. She found the Middle Fifths very difficult and not nearly admiring enough—particularly Paris, who, as they had both come from Larks, should have supported her. His stroppy behaviour was becoming the talk of the staffroom with Hengist showing a curious reluctance to put the boot in.

Vicky showed no such reluctance when in the Middle Fifths' next English lesson, three days later, she asked them to describe a happy family experience in the holidays, using simile, metaphor, oxymoron and personification.

'Please, Miss Fairchild,' whispered Milly, 'Paris doesn't have a family.'

'Of course he does. He has the bursar and his wife, his new foster family,' said Vicky, so that everyone looked at Paris. 'You could write a most interesting essay on adjusting to your new placement, Paris, and how Bagley compares with Larks.'

' "Why, this is hell, nor am I out of it",' spat Paris.

'My mother,' piped up Amber, 'says placement is the most difficult part of a dinner party. She always forgets to do a seating plan, and is pissed by the time we get into the dining room. Why doesn't one learn important things like that in maths?'

'I hardly think Biffo'd be an expert,' said Milly. 'It's even worse if you're a single woman. If my mother asks Randal to dinner, is it coming on too strong to put him at the head of the table, or will he be miffed he's not on her right?'

'Don't be silly, Milly,' exploded Vicky.

'Silly Milly,' echoed Jade, sticking her tongue out at Milly.

'Write it as a play, Paris,' suggested Vicky, 'then we could all take parts.'

'Or as a poem,' quipped Cosmo. 'Living with the bursar could not be worser.'

'Shut it,' hissed Paris.

'Paris in fact is quite a poet,' went on Cosmo, dramatically whipping out a rainbow-coloured notebook. 'Listen to this epic about a snail,' which he proceeded to declaim in a camp Cockney accent:

' "O Snile, your gli-ering trile, leads from the gu-er up to anuvver gu-er on which to bang your 'orns." '

As Paris gave a howl of rage, uneasy laughter broke out round the room.

Milly put a hand on Paris's arm. 'Ignore him.'

'Here's another little gem,' continued Cosmo, turning the page, knowing instinctively that Vicky didn't like Paris. 'Here's what our new boy thinks of Bagley:

'Death is like a boarding school

559

From which you never come home
Where your name is carved on a
    gravestone
Rather than sewn inside your clothes.'

'Doesn't scan,' complained Boffin.

'You bastard,' whispered Paris, turning on Cosmo.

'I think it's rather good,' said Primrose Duddon with a shiver.

'I think it's very good,' came a voice from the back of the class.

It was Piers Fleming, head of English, who'd dropped in to listen to Vicky's class. 'May I?' He grabbed the rainbow-covered notebook and read both the snail poem and the death poem again, but in a normal and beautiful voice.

'The second one,' he went on, 'reminds me of Robert Frost describing a disused graveyard:

'The verses in it say and say:
"The ones who living come today
To read the stones and go away
Tomorrow dead will come to stay."

'It has the same icy hand on the heart. I'm going to put forward your poems for the school anthology,' he told Paris. 'We publish it every three years. You're probably too modest to submit your own stuff, so thank you, Cosmo, so much, for drawing it to my attention.'

Cosmo was hopping.

*   *   *

As the bell went and the Middle Fifths packed up, Piers very kindly suggested to Vicky she might fare better with one of the less demanding sets. If Piers and Vicky had seen the Middle Fifths at their next lesson, however, they might have changed their opinion, as the entire set listened enraptured to Theo Graham introducing some of their GCSE Latin texts.

'Poets were like rock stars around the first century AD,' he was now telling them as, hip hitched on to the side of a desk, he puffed away on a forbidden cigarette. 'Just as you lot might enliven an evening with a video or a takeaway or by hiring a stripagram for a party, the Romans sent out for a slave to read poetry.

'Some poets like Martial, who was charming and very witty, recited their own poems at dinner parties, but most of them were read by slaves. You didn't make money as a poet in those days, but people could sponsor you. Horace was earlier, of course, but he was such a good poet—we'll be looking at his stuff in a minute—that a rich Etruscan gave him a farm and a huge estate.'

'Just think if he'd liked your poems, Paris,' giggled Amber. Paris grinned and gave her a middle finger.

Lighting one cigarette from another, Theo shuffled down the row and lifted a lock of Amber's blond hair.

'You'd have been in trouble as a slave, miss, because Italians liked blondes, so lots of society ladies dyed their hair blond, and when it fell out, they shaved the heads of the blonde slaves and used the hair as a wig.

'That's probably why Pyrrha in our first poem

561

was considered such a beauty, Horace describes her as braiding her flaxen locks.'

'Paris would have cleaned up as a poet *and* a blond,' said Milly.

Feeling much happier, Paris came out of Theo's class slap into Poppet Bruce, who was always nagging him to drop in on her and Alex and pour out his soul. Now she wanted him to go public.

'Could you address our Talks Society next week? If a talk is too daunting, I could always interview you.' Paris raised a pale eyebrow. 'It would be such a broadening experience for our group to hear your views on your foster placement and being in care.'

The lad was certainly good-looking, decided Poppet, and the same age as their daughter, Charisma. She was very touched when Paris put a hand in his pocket and handed her a tenner.

'How kind, but you don't have to pay to join our little society.'

'No, it's for the two fines I'm about to get,' said Paris icily. 'You just want me to slag off Patience and Ian, to give you and Mr Fussy ammunition against them. So fuck off.' Then he spat at her feet, just falling short of her grubby sandalled toenails.

Poppet didn't miss a beat.

'I know you're hurting, Paris, and don't really mean it.'

'Hurt is a transitive verb,' snapped Paris, 'and I do.'

*   *   *

Despite half the staff competing to make him tell them if anything was wrong, Paris felt it was as

562

weak to admit terror as to display love and dependency. And so he waited for Cosmo. Whether it was a bomb in the tube or on Big Ben, the terrorists would strike sooner or later. He had already found a rubber snake in his bed and still kept hearing rumours about the notorious Pitbull Club.

*   *   *

It was after midnight on the second Saturday of term. Theo, after downing a bottle of whisky in his room, had passed out, his snores ripping open the night. Smart, in the next-door cell, had long since wanked himself to sleep over a photograph of Jade Stancombe. Paris could hear the Virginia creeper flapping limp hands against the window, floorboards creaking, Tarquin's ravishing strides, doors softly opening and closing. Just like Oaktree Court. Starting to shake, already drenched in sweat, he pulled Thomas the Tank Engine over his head. The chattering of his teeth would wake the dead.

Suddenly the duvet was wrenched off him and a torch brighter than the full moon shoved in his face.

'Get up, pretty boy.'

'Fuck off.'

'Get up,' repeated the voice.

In the dim light, he could make out a hooded figure, then groaned as the torch was rammed into his ribs.

'You're invited to the Pitbull Club. Move it.'

Paris froze, nearly shitting himself, heart crashing.

563

'Leave me alone,' he croaked, kicking out at another hooded figure that appeared on the right.

'Come on, Gay Paree.' He knew that voice. Next moment its owner had grabbed his hair, tugging him viciously to his feet.

'New boy's initiation. Let's see how brave you are,' mocked another slighter figure hovering behind.

The figure on the left jabbed him with the torch again. Paris moaned, then, reaching behind him, grabbed the knife from under his pillow. Leaping at the first figure, catching him off balance, pulling him against his own body, clamping him with his left hand, he put the knife against his throat.

The torch crashed to the floor.

The muscular, almost square body, left him in no doubt about the identity of the tormentor.

'Get out, unless you want your throat cut, Albanian pig.'

'Put him down,' ordered the larger of the figures on the right, who had a deep voice, and was moving in. Paris caught a waft of brandy.

'Don't come anywhere near me,' he spat, then, running the blade down Lubemir's cheek, split it open, drawing blood. 'I'm not just shaving him. Next time I'll cut deeper.' Kneeing Lubemir in the kidneys, he sent him crashing to the floor.

'Get him,' said the smaller figure on the right— with less conviction as, in the light from the fallen torch, Paris approached with knife poised.

'You don't scare me,' snarled Paris. 'I'll cut up the lot of you, and you'll lose more than your plait this time, Miss Stancombe.'

Jade gave a gasp, and fled, followed by Lubemir and Anatole.

564

Down in the cellar, the leader of the pack in his astrakhan coat was admiring his reflection as he snorted coke from a framed mirror lying on an ancient desk. His eyes were glittering but no less cruel.

Other figures stood round self-consciously, rather apprehensively, drinking from bottles or smoking.

Millbank, a new boy in blue-striped pyjamas, almost fainting in terror, was loosely tied to a chair. He had bitten his lip through trying not to cry. Despite the heat from the boilers, he shivered uncontrollably.

'Where's Paris?' snapped Cosmo.

'Won't come,' said Anatole.

'How pathetic is that. Three against one.'

'I'm not risking it,' said Lubemir, removing a blood-saturated handkerchief from his slashed cheek. 'He knows who we all are.'

'How?' Cosmo was hoovering up every last speck of cocaine.

'He listen,' said Anatole. 'How you think he's such a good mimic?'

'I'm going back to Boudicca,' bleated Jade. 'It was bloody scary.'

Cosmo grabbed her arm. 'You're not going anywhere.' Then: 'You can bugger off,' he told Millbank. 'You got off lightly, but don't breathe a word'—he jerked his head at Lubemir, who held the cigarette he'd just lit to Millbank's jumping cheek—'or we'll really sort you out. Understand?'

'Yes,' sobbed Millbank and fled.

Cosmo turned to the others.

'Are you honestly telling me three of you couldn't sort out that etiolated wimp?'

'He pulled a knife on us,' protested Lubemir.

'Oh dear,' sighed Cosmo, 'I do hope he didn't hold it like a pencil.'

62

Alex Bruce was incensed when Hengist gave any pupil who applied permission to go on the Countryside March. Far too many of the applicants had retakes the next day and would be exhausted and probably hungover.

'And is championing blood sports really part of our Bagley ethos?' asked Alex querulously.

'Damn right it is,' snapped Hengist. 'Bagley Beagles have been going for nearly a hundred years and'—he waved a hand in the direction of Badger's Retreat—'isn't that country worth saving?'

*   *   *

Patience asked Paris if he'd like to join her on the march.

'Rupert Campbell-Black, Ricky France-Lynch and Billy Lloyd-Foxe are all going. Rupert's taking his dogs. It should be a fun day out.'

Paris replied coldly that he didn't approve of blood sports.

'Alex and Poppet don't either,' said Patience with rare edge. 'It's not just blood sports, it's the whole tapestry and livelihood of the countryside, which this Government is hell-bent on destroying, totally undermining the poor farmers. If hunting goes, thousands of people will lose their jobs, and thousands and thousands more horses and hounds will be put down. People who make such a fuss about killing foxes don't give a stuff about the

567

horrors of factory farming or the dreadful transport of live animals.' Realizing she was shouting, Patience stopped in embarrassment.

'Still bloody cruel.' Paris stalked towards the door. 'Is Ian going?'

'No, he's dining with a supplier.'

'I'll dogsit,' said Paris as a peace offering.

Later he kicked himself when Dora told him that Xav and Bianca were also going, adding:

'Bianca's such an applause junkie, she can't resist crowds and photographers.'

Deliverance seemed at hand when Xav asked Paris to join them. Alas, social services stepped in. Paris couldn't join their party because Rupert hadn't been cleared by the Criminal Records Bureau.

'I can't imagine he ever would be,' said Alex nastily.

*   *   *

Boffin Brooks rose at six most mornings ostensibly to conjugate Latin verbs but in reality to spy on his housemates. Early on the Saturday before the Countryside March, he caught Xav in bed smoking a spliff and reading a porn mag. Noting the ecstasy with which Xav was inhaling, like a chief drawing on a peace pipe, Boffin launched into a sermon in his nasal whine:

'People smoke to look cool, Xavier, or because they're forced to by bullies or peer pressure.'

Boffin's spectacles enlarged his bulging eyes. Shaving his meagre ginger stubble, he had deheaded several spots, reducing his face to an erupting volcanic landscape. His full red lips were salivating at the prospect of reading that disgusting porn mag before he handed it over to Alex.

'I might be fractionally more lenient, Xavier, if you told me who sold you the stuff.'

'I'm not grassing up anyone, so piss off.' Inhaling deeply, Xav blew smoke rings at Boffin.

Boffin looked pained.

'It must be in your blood, Xavier. Colombia not only trains and supports the IRA and many other forms of terrorism, but also destroys billions of lives as the drug centre of the world.'

'Nice place for a weekend break.'

'Only place you won't be this weekend is the Countryside March. My only recourse is to report you to Mr Bruce,' at which point Xav launched himself at Boffin.

'You little idiot,' Hengist yelled at Xavier later in the morning. 'I know how you wanted to go on that march. Why on earth did you screw up? Drugs are not allowed and that's the second time Boffin's teeth have been knocked out in a year. How can I do anything but gate you? Your father will be devastated.'

My father couldn't give a stuff, thought Xav despairingly. He'll just regard it as another cock-up on my part.

*   *   *

My first leave-out and no one to look after me— thank God, thought Paris as Patience and Ian left the house.

He brushed Northcliffe, partly from self-interest to keep the dog's pale gold hair off his clothes; then he lit a fag and, pouring himself a glass of red, collapsed on the sofa in front of the television, where he was shortly joined by Northcliffe, who was not allowed up when Ian was around. Liverpool had won yesterday, so Paris flicked over to mock the Countryside March for a second and stayed to pray.

'There's Dora,' he shouted in excitement, shoving Northcliffe's face towards the screen as, dressed in jodhpurs and a hacking jacket, Dora marched proudly past chattering to Junior and the Hon. Jack, who were blatantly smoking and shouting to pretty girls among the mass of spectators lining the route.

They were followed by Isa Lovell, former champion jockey, now Rupert Campbell-Black's trainer, with his swarthy gypsy face, and by Rupert Campbell-Black himself, still the handsomest man in England, his eyes the colour of blue Smarties, his face expressionless as he ignored the cheers of the crowd. He was accompanied by half a dozen dogs: lurchers, terriers and Labradors, who kept stopping to fight each other and attack dogs in the crowd, until Rupert called them back.

Inside, Rupert was raging and desolate that Xav as part of the clan wasn't beside him. Instead, running to keep up, was Junior and Amber's father, Billy Lloyd-Foxe, laughing helplessly, grey curls astray, wearing a tweed coat with no buttons and an equally buttonless shirt, held together by his tie.

Reporting the march for the BBC, shouting over the tooting of hunting horns, Billy was giving an unashamedly biased commentary. 'This is the countryside fighting back, making its protest seen and heard, with the largest march London has ever seen.'

Even Paris couldn't restrain a cheer for the three couple of the Bagley Beagles, sterns waving like wheat in a high wind, and in their midst, a large grinning chocolate Labrador pausing to gobble up a discarded Cornish pasty.

'Cadbury,' shouted Paris. Even Northcliffe opened an eye.

In charge of the beagles, blowing their hunting horns, flicking their token whips, were Amber and Lando, glamorous in their teal-blue coats, breeches and black boots.

'I shagged that girl last summer,' said Paris, topping up his glass. He wished he could remember more about it.

And *look* at her: an utterly stunning blonde with the same cool face, blue eyes and ferociously determined mouth as Rupert. It must be his daughter Tabitha, the silver medallist, and that must be her husband Wolfgang who produced films, to whom Xav had promised to introduce Paris: 'So he can discover you.'

Close on their heels came a group who'd clearly had an excellent lunch. According to the commentator, they were former members of the England polo team. Except for Lando's father Ricky, who had a closed, carved, ascetic face and very high cheekbones, they all had handsome, flushed, expensive faces. Two of them, identical twins in their thirties, were holding lead reins attached to the wrists of a beautiful girl. Paris gasped. It was Bianca, inspiring as many cheers and wolf whistles as her father.

She had tied a scarlet bandanna round her dark ringlets and wore a flame-red wool shirt and dark blue breeches which clung to her impossibly supple and slender figure. Her lovely even complexion, the colour of strong tea, was faintly touched with colour. But neither twin could restrain her wonderful wildness. You could more easily have trapped a sunbeam as she skipped and danced, her laughing dark eyes making love to every man in the crowd.

Bloody hell. Paris refilled his glass. For, just behind Bianca and the twins, advancing fast, waving a 'Bring back Blair-Baiting' poster, his black curls flowing out from under his flat cap like Sir Lancelot, strode Cosmo.

'Fuck him,' said Paris, then his heart lifted as Patience came into view. 'There's your mistress,' he chided Northcliffe who was burying a Bonio in the camellia by the window.

Patience might resemble a scarecrow, but she looked so sweet and carefree as she laughed and gossiped to the Hon. Jack's father, David Waterlane and—my God—to Sally Brett-Taylor. It was brave of her to stick her neck out. All three of them were walking backwards now to watch and clap a piper who was leading a large contingent from Scotland, marching behind.

He could just imagine them: knights and ladies of the court, straight out of Tennyson, riding through medieval England on their great horses, a bobbing flotilla of white placards lit by the turning plane trees and Patience part of it. How dare Ian put her down so much? And what a tragedy for Xav not to be there.

I loathe what they stand for, he thought despairingly, but I long to be accepted by them. And Bianca was the only person who might get him over Janna, whom he still missed unbearably. He tried not to think of her. He hadn't glanced at the *Gazette* for weeks, nor been in touch with anyone from Larks. His mobile was dying from lack of use.

If only Janna were here with him now, discussing some poem, casually ruffling his hair. But if Sally was on the march, that satyr Hengist was probably now at Jubilee Cottage shagging her. Jesus, it crucified him. Paris was about to open another bottle when he realized Rupert was addressing the crowds in Whitehall. The clipped, arrogant, carrying voice hardly needed a microphone.

'We will not let a politically correct but morally corrupt Government dictate to us. We will fight to the death for what we believe in: England, freedom and the countryside.'

'What about Wales, Scotland and Northern Ireland?' reproached Sally Brett-Taylor, over the roar of approval.

'And of course the colonies,' grinned Rupert, chucking an empty hipflask to an adoring fan who rushed off to the nearest pub to refill it.

God, he's a cool bastard, thought Paris, and Xav was his only route to Bianca. Picking up the Cartwrights' telephone he rang Xav. 'Patience and Ian are out. Why don't you come over? Got any weed?'

'Some really strong skunk; it'll blow your mind.'

Happily Alex and Poppet had gone out and the deputy housemaster, Joe Meakin, who was new to the job and engrossed in the Sunday papers, was in charge.

'Can I nip over to the Old Coach House? Paris Alvaston's on his own and a bit down, adjusting to

573

a new school and all.'

'OK, don't be late,' said Mr Meakin, glad that Xavier had found a friend. The poor boy seemed so isolated.

'I'll sign myself out,' said Xav, and didn't.

Collecting the skunk, he put a pillow in his bed.

63

'Are you sure it's safe?' he asked Paris ten minutes later. 'If I'm busted again I'll get sacked.'

'Quite safe. Ian's out to dinner; Patience is on the march.'

Having finished the red, Paris handed Xav a glass of Ian's whisky and had one himself.

'Your dad made a good speech; I taped it. I understand now why you wanted to go.'

Xav's face sank into sullenness.

'They wouldn't want a black bastard like me around.'

'Don't talk crap, they all cheered Bianca. Have a look,' said Paris winding back the tape. He wanted to watch her again. 'And hurry up with that smoke. Ian's obviously been watering the whisky; it tastes like gnat's piss. Who are those dirty old men holding Bianca's lead reins?'

Xav looked up from the tobacco and the skunk which he was shredding into a king-sized Rizla.

'The Carlisle twins. Good blokes. The two in front are Bas Baddington and Drew Benedict, friends of my dad's who played polo for England. All terrific studs, who like to wind up Dad, who was the biggest stud of all, by chatting up Bianca. He goes ballistic,' Xav added wistfully. 'He hates people chatting up Mum too. Give me a slug of that Courvoisier; you're right about the whisky.' He emptied it into a nearby plant pot.

*   *   *

'You may not be the brain of Britain,' giggled Paris half an hour later, 'but you're a genius at rolling spliffs.'

Xav had obviously had plenty of practice, and he'd been right about the skunk: it blew their minds, putting them in a really mellow and expansive mood.

There wasn't anything on television and Patience and Ian had crap videos, so they put on a Marilyn Manson CD and, ignoring shouts of 'Turn it down' from all over the campus, they danced. Xav, rocking with the abandon that he drained glasses, was soon rolling another spliff.

After that they got the munchies. Paris remembered a shepherd's pie Patience had left in the fridge, which he put in the oven, and the remains of a boeuf bourguignon, which he fed to Northcliffe. He also found a nice bottle of white and a plate of smoked salmon sandwiches under clingfilm, which they wolfed down, dropping the crusts on the carpet.

Oh help! Paris noticed a cigarette burn on one of Emerald's poncy embroidered cushions and two more on the sofa. He'd sort it later. Drugs made him feel he could conquer anything, be the best guy Cameron Diaz had ever slept with, win the poetry prize, score five goals for Liverpool, have Little Cosmo pleading to be his best friend. Then you came down and descended into the abyss when you wanted to hurt and destroy anyone who loved you.

'Why were you in care?' asked Xav.

'My mum dumped me on the doorstep of a children's home in Alvaston and fucked off. They named me after the town. They reckoned I was about two, so they gave me a birthday on January the thirtieth. Makes me the water carrier—or wine carrier.' He filled Xav's glass with Pouilly-Fumé. 'Aquarians are supposed to be aloof and charismatic. I've worked on it ever since. What happened to you?'

Xav drew deeply on his spliff, eyes like black threads, face impassive, a Hiawatha with puppy fat.

'I was born with a squint and a birthmark, which, probably correctly, is the sign of the devil to the Colombian Indians. So they chucked me into the gutter to die. They shoot stray children along with dogs in Bogotá, so the place looks tidy when foreign leaders roll up. I was rescued by a nun who worked in an orphanage.' Xav's voice grew more bitter. 'Bianca was brought in as a baby when I was about twenty months. She came from a good family, strict Catholics, who forced Bianca's mother to give her up. Dad and Mum had placed an order for her and flown over from England; the nuns threw me in as a job lot. I know nothing about my parents. Bianca's posh but I'm a yob: I can tell that when I look in the mirror.'

Emptying the entire glass of wine, Xav choked. Paris bashed him on the back and said:

'You've got the poshest voice I've ever heard. Birthmark's gone, so's the squint.'

Xav glared glassily at Paris. 'Gets worse when I'm pissed.'

'D'you feel Indian or English?'

'Indian mostly. I love booze, drugs and fast horses. But I've got no stop button. Once I start I can't stop.'

'Your father can't mind that with horses.'

'My father is the most embarrassing person I've ever met. He doesn't give a shit. Wherever he goes

577

everyone gazes at him and Mum and Bianca, and sees how like film stars they are. Then they look at me, and think: Why's that ugly black bastard hanging round them?

'They used to spit at Mum when I was young,' continued Xav bitterly. 'They thought she'd been with a black man. They used to finger my hair and ask her if she ever washed it. I wash the fucking stuff every day. Boy, Mum got angry.' For a second, Xav's heavy face lifted. 'She used to yell at people. But no one ever asked Dad questions about me, because they're too scared of him. So he's never realized there was a problem.'

Xav was rolling a third joint, breaking cardboard off a cigarette packet for them to smoke through.

'Least you've got parents,' said Paris.

The bottle of white was empty. The only thing left seemed to be a bottle of medium-dry sherry. He filled up their glasses.

'Let's drink to yobbos.'

'Yobbos,' shouted Xav, draining his glass. 'Put on some more music.'

Putting on Limp Bizkit, turning up the volume, Paris opened the curtains on a sky full of stars and lit-up windows all over the campus.

'Hear that, you fuckers,' he yelled over the din. 'God stands up for bastards.' Then, as the chapel clock chimed eleven o'clock: 'I've got an idea how we can screw up Biffo's steeplechase.'

*   *   *

On balance, Ian felt the evening had been a success. He had lied to Patience. He hadn't been dining with a supplier, but with Poppet and Alex

Bruce, whom he'd taken to *Fidelio* in Bristol—on tickets admittedly given him by a supplier.

This had been to melt the distinct *froideur* which had grown between him and Alex since Patience's shouting match. As Alex wielded more power, Ian was increasingly edgy about losing his job. He knew Patience would disapprove of this move almost as much as Alex disapproved of her going on the march, so he had kept her in the dark.

Fidelio had been ravishing, with a Bagley old girl, Flora Seymour, singing Leonora quite magically. But although the opera was about liberation from tyranny, he didn't feel Poppet and Alex were fans of Beethoven—too militaristic perhaps.

'I prefer Eastern music,' admitted Poppet. 'Or early music on period instruments.'

Both Bruces had worn open-toed sandals and Alex, tieless, had displayed fearful short sleeves when he removed his jacket. They had certainly tucked into the smoked chicken, roast beef, avocado and spinach salad and apricot tart Ian had ordered for the interval, and between them downed the bottle of Beaune.

Ian, who couldn't drink because he'd agreed to drive them, couldn't stop thinking of that bottle of Pouilly-Fumé in the fridge at the Old Coach House.

On the way home, Poppet and Alex talked insufferably smugly about their daughter Charisma, who went to Searston Abbey.

'Of course she's G and T,' boasted Poppet, which turned out to be 'gifted and talented', rather than 'gin and tonic', and which made Ian long for a drink even more.

As they crossed the border into Larkshire, it was

579

still mild enough to have the windows open. Conversation moved on to the challenging behaviour of Paris.

'He's very troubled,' said Poppet firmly, 'and I'm afraid Janna Curtis gave him an inflated sense of his own ability.'

Ian didn't rise, saying they were finding Paris much easier and he seemed to be getting on well with Xavier.

'I'm not liking that,' mused Poppet. 'Xav is very troubled too. I blame Rupert. Xav gets a detention for challenging behaviour and instead of dropping everything to sort out his son, Rupert swans off on the Countryside March.'

'I asked Rupert to discuss Xav's special educational needs recently,' added Alex petulantly, 'and he said: "All Xav needs is a kick up the arse. He's a lazy little sod, like I was at school." '

In the dark, Ian suppressed a smile.

'Rupert of course is troubled,' sighed Poppet, 'and a very private person.'

Only because he runs like hell the moment you appear on the horizon, thought Ian.

Swinging the car in between the stone lions at the bottom of the school drive, Ian was surprised at the number of lights still on. Must be pupils revising for tomorrow's retakes. Someone was playing loud music. Through the trees he could see lights in the Old Coach House; perhaps Patience was home.

'I've got a nice bottle of Pouilly-Fumé and some sandwiches in the fridge,' he told the Bruces. 'It's a long time since supper.'

Paris, if up, could open the bottle for them and hand things round.

'Well, if you insist,' said Poppet.

580

'Christ,' whispered Paris, who'd been looking out of the window, 'Ian's home and he's brought Mr and Mrs Fussy.' Turning off Limp Bizkit, he chucked the remains of the spliff into the waste-paper basket.

Then he noticed more burns: in the 'Mother's Place is in the Wrong' cushion and on Ian's bridge table and on another of Emerald's cushions, shit, shit, shit. Paris turned the cushions over and shoved a pile of *Horse & Hounds* on the bridge table.

'Gather up the empties at once, man,' he begged, but, cross-eyed and giggling on the sofa, Xav was too far gone.

'Oh, for God's sake.' Paris scooped up at least four bottles and shoved them in Patience's little sewing cupboard, producing a chink and crash of glass, which indicated Ian was already secreting bottles there.

Paris was just trying to identify a smell of burning and shoving a swaying Xav out by the back door when they went slap into Ian, Alex and Poppet coming in through the garage.

'Mr and Mrs Fussy,' said a beaming Xav. 'Have you had a good evening?'

Seeing him momentarily handsome, showing excellent teeth and softened features, Alex thought for a moment Xav had turned into the egregious Feral Jackson. Then he caught sight of the shadow of a birthmark in the overhead light.

'Xavier Campbell-Black,' he thundered, 'why aren't you in bed?'

'Chill, man, I've been counselling Paris. I didn't realize it was so late.'

'You were ordered not to leave your house.'

'I got permission.'

'Something's burning,' said Poppet, fascinated to witness such chaos.

Wrenching open the oven, Ian found a blackened shepherd's pie. Opening the fridge, he discovered the bottle of Pouilly-Fumé and the sandwiches missing and, striding into the drawing room, found an utterly depleted drinks cupboard and took in the mess.

'Paris, come in here at once,' he bellowed.

Everyone unfortunately followed him, whereupon the waste-paper basket containing Paris's discarded spliff, not wanting to be left out, burst into flames.

'Fire, fire,' giggled Xav, emptying the last of the sherry over it, which turned the flame blue. 'Just like the Christmas pudding at home,' he added wistfully.

'We'll be forgetting that drink and sandwiches,' said Alex grimly, 'and take you straight home.' He seized Xav by the arm and turned to Paris. 'And I want you in my office before chapel tomorrow to explain yourself.'

Thank God, the burnt shepherd's pie had blotted out the smell of dope.

Giggling hysterically, Xav tripped over a side table, sending flying a 'World's Best Dad' mug and a Staffordshire dog, and fell flat on his face.

'For God's sake,' exploded Ian.

Xav was as unyielding as a bag of concrete as Paris lugged him to his feet. 'Getta grip,' he hissed. 'I'll help him out, sir.' Anything to escape from Ian's fury.

Outside, the peace of the soft September starlight was disturbed by a tantivy of horns and joyful off-key singing.

> 'The dusky night rides down the sky,
> And ushers in the morn;
> The hounds all join in glorious cry,
> The huntsman winds his horn.'

' "And a-hunting we will go, a-hunting we will go, a-hunting we will go," ' joined in Xav. Lunging forward he yelled, 'Taxi, taxi, take me to paradise,' as a lorry, driven by Patience, with Dora, Jack, Lando and Junior, and several beagles falling out of the windows, came roaring up the drive.

' "The dusky night rides down the sky, the huntsman . . ." ' began Patience. Screeching to a halt outside the Old Coach House and seeing Xav and Paris, she cried, 'Hello, boys, we've all had such a wonderful day.'

The Bruces, however, lurking in the shadows, felt otherwise, particularly when the beagles poured out of the back of the lorry after Joan's Burmese cat before relieving themselves all over the lawns and the flower beds. The calm of the night was disturbed again as Poppet Bruce's open-toed sandals encountered Northcliffe's regurgitated boeuf bourguignon.

Paris fled to bed, trying to blot out the sounds of Patience and Ian arguing furiously downstairs.

Oh hell, there was the main section of the *Sunday Times* on his bed all crumpled up by Northcliffe, which Ian hadn't read yet and would be crosser about than the booze. The paper lay open at a piece listing the advantages of boarding school which included 'the widening of horizons, the development of autonomy, and the relief from

583

tensions commonly built up in a nuclear family around adolescence'.

Paris buried his face in his pillow. 'I've been catapulted into a nuclear family,' he groaned, 'but I'm the bomb.'

64

As a result of the Countryside March, Bagley received excellent coverage. Many papers carried pictures of Amber, Lando and the beagle pack. The front page of the *Western Daily Press* showed Sally and Patience waving placards. Dora was ecstatic over Nigel Dempster's picture of herself and Cadbury. It would be so good for all her press contacts to be able to put a face to her name. There was however a bitchy piece in the *Scorpion* on the shortness of Rupert Campbell-Black's fuse. Was it due to lack of support from his two sons, Marcus, who was gay and allergic to horses, and his adopted son Xavier, who'd been gated by Bagley Hall (fees £22,000 a year) for undisclosed bad behaviour?

The star of the day was definitely Bianca, who, combining her mother's beauty and her father's ability to dazzle, was considered to be carrying the Campbell-Black torch. This did nothing for Xav's self-esteem, but his street cred rocketed when news leaked out via Dora and the *Evening Standard* that instead of marching, he and Paris had been busted for drunken trashing of the bursar's house.

This, according to the Bruces and a reproachful Nadine, would never have happened if Patience hadn't abandoned Paris so early in his foster placement to defend evil blood sports. Poppet promptly emailed the Cartwrights the telephone number of P.U.K.E., 'which stands for Prevention, Understanding, Knowledge, Education, a support group which takes a non-judgemental view of binge drinking'. 'Call them,' urged Poppet.

Patience put the email in the bin.

Paris and Xav were heavily fined and as punishment had to knock in endless posts and blue and brown flags for Sunday's steeplechase. This enabled them to earmark an outwardly impenetrable clump of rhododendrons and laurels about seventy-five yards from the start.

Xav had planned to invite Paris back to Penscombe that Sunday but the whole school was ordered to stay at Bagley to take part in the steeplechase or at least witness Alex Bruce achieve his personal best.

*　　*　　*

On a grey dank Sunday afternoon, with fog forecast, the Biffo Rudge Trophy for the first member of staff past the post and the Gordon Brooks Cup for the first pupil, donated by Boffin's father, glittered on a trestle table, reflecting the turning gold limes surrounding Mansion Lawn. Silver shields for the next five in both categories were stacked in a cardboard box.

The six-mile course itself was shaped like the frame of a tennis racquet. Contestants left Mansion Lawn, ran under General Bagley Arch, down the east side of the drive, past thick rhododendron clumps, turned left at the lion gates and continued in a big circle round the villages of Bagley, Wilmington and Sedgeley, turning left again at the lion gates, pounding up the west side of the drive under the arch to the tapes in front of the Mansion.

In chapel that morning, Biffo, nailbrush hair bristling even more fiercely, had sternly set out the rules:

'Students in the past have let down the school and themselves, straying into public houses, cafés and shops along the route. But your target is to be the first back here, where Gordon Brooks and I will be holding the tape. Occasionally pupils have taken short cuts, pretending they have completed the course. Wardens everywhere will be monitoring such transgressions. Any cheating or flouting of rules will be severely punished. Above all act on your own initiative. Don't let anything or anyone distract you from your goal.'

Despite this, all the pubs and shops along the route were staying open expecting excellent business. Janna, Lily and Brigadier Woodford had heaved deckchairs and several bottles and Melton Mowbray pork pies on to the Brigadier's flat roof to enjoy the spectacle.

As kick-off time approached, competitors gathered on Mansion lawn, chatting, shivering, running on the spot and jogging round in little circles.

The smart money for pupils was on Kippy Musgrave, a Lower Fifth beauty, already fleeter than a whippet from running away from lustful masters. Denzil Harper, the ultra-fit head of PE who ran marathons for the county, was favourite for the Rudge Cup, a rather stocky hare who had reckoned without Alex Bruce's tortoise, according to Boffin Brooks.

'I don't approve of gambling, sir, but I've put a whole week's pocket money on your being first past the tape.'

Boffin, his spectacles misting up in an orgy of toadyism, sporting long grey shorts which failed to disguise a bottom wider than his shoulders, breath reeking of breakfast kipper, was also determined to be in the first six.

Members of the first fifteen, including the glamorous captain, Tarquin Courtney, had perfected that rugby star walk, sticking out their chests, straightening their legs backward with each stride to make their thighs judder. Big bruisers, they outwardly treated the whole steeplechase as a joke but underneath, like Alex, they were hell-bent on winning.

Alex himself was in a trance. One must go inside oneself. Following Bianca's example, he had tied a red bandanna round his head; he was flexing his thigh muscles backwards as he swayed and hummed. Poppet, jogging on the spot in shorts and a purple vest, displaying Black Forests of armpit hair, was chopping up bananas for Alex and other runners from his house.

'We want Bruce students in the first six.'

Their G and T daughter Charisma was waiting along the route to ply Alex and Boffin with glucose tablets. Anxious to beat as many masters as possible, No-Joke Joan had, like Alex, been jogging round the campus for weeks.

'Have you seen her thighs?' asked Artie Deverell faintly. 'Like barons of beef.'

'Our Joan would be more interested in the baroness,' murmured back Theo, who was increasingly grateful for swigs from Ian Cartwright's hipflask. Patience, beside them, had gone purple with cold; Ian, looking bleak, had still not forgiven Paris, who hadn't been near the Old

Coach House since Sunday and whom he couldn't see anywhere. Probably too ashamed to show his face.

'I want ten pounds on Paris Alvaston for a win,' Dora, currently on three mobiles to various newspapers, told Lando who was keeping a book.

'Don't waste your money, he's two hundred to one.'

'I don't care.'

A chorus of wolf whistles greeted Vicky running out in a clinging pale pink fleece and pink pleated skirt, her hair in bunches.

'I am *so* nervous,' she told Poppet.

Alex detranced enough to say: 'Why not run behind me, little Vicky, until you get into your stride?'

She couldn't fail to be inspired by his tall good figure ahead of her.

' "Mark my footsteps, good my page!" ' mocked Cosmo, still in his astrakhan coat.

'Line up everyone,' shouted Biffo as the big hand of the chapel clock edged towards five to three.

In a long race with over three hundred runners, it didn't matter if everyone started at once, but Mansion Lawn was now entirely covered with competitors. The Mansion itself dozed in a shaft of sunlight which had broken through the clouds.

'Where the hell's Hengist?' muttered Biffo to Joan as he fingered the starting pistol. 'Why is he always deliberately insultingly late?'

'He looked over his shoulder For athletes at their games,' murmured Theo, noticing that Cosmo had at last tossed his astrakhan coat to Dora, and, oh dear, was sliding a thieving hand between Vicky's thighs. There was Smart, stubbing out a fag, but

589

where was Paris? Theo hoped he hadn't done a bunk. Hengist, who was keeping a paternal eye on the boy, had suggested Paris would benefit from a few hours' Latin and Greek coaching a week. Theo sighed. The temptation would be irresistible.

Ah, here at last was Hengist, flushed from a good lunch, laughing, joking, but in no hurry and making no apologies.

Biffo longed to turn the pistol on him.

'Get ready, everyone,' he bellowed. 'Two minutes to the off.'

Alex Bruce had been doing a quick interview with Radio Larkshire.

'Forgive me, the race awaits.'

'Of course, deputy headmaster.'

As Alex strode towards the start line, he passed Emlyn, who'd just enjoyed a long lunch at Hengist's.

'Why aren't you taking part?' he demanded.

'With stars like you, Alex?' Then, when Alex looked simply furious: 'Best of luck.'

Fifty yards down the drive, Paris and Xavier waited in their rhododendron hideout. Paris was watching the start through binoculars. 'One minute to three. Mr Fussy's crouching down with one knee bent, and the other stretched out like the Olympics. Now he's bowing his head. God, he's a twat. OK,' he whispered to Xav.

Crash went the starting pistol, which Paris and Xav had bought on the internet from Bristol last week.

Off set the runners, pounding down the drive, past the rhododendron clump, spilling out on to the roughly mown grass on the left, stepping up their speed to be first through the lion gates.

'Stop,' thundered Biffo, brandishing his unfired pistol, 'that was a false start. Stop the race,' he shouted into his walkie-talkie to Mr Meakin who, desperate to redeem himself after letting Xav out last weekend, rushed forward waving his arms: 'Stop, stop.'

But the leading runners and Tarquin Courtney, who thought Meakin was a wimp and had been ordered not to be distracted by anything, waved two fingers at him and pounded on.

A second later, another avalanche of runners including Vicky and Cosmo sent Meakin flying into a hawthorn bush.

'Blessed are the Meakin for they shall inherit the earth,' shouted Cosmo.

Not until a hundred and fifty or so pupils and masters, including Alex Bruce, had flowed out of the gates did Biffo manage to convince the wardens of the false start.

'Just like the National in nineteen ninety-three,' whinnied Jack Waterlane, who'd been planning to run off and see Kylie, 'except the front runners are halfway to Wilmington.'

Alex Bruce walked back to the Mansion, gibbering with rage, froth flying from his lips.

'Get everyone back. The race must be rerun.'

'Too late,' sighed Hengist. 'Unfair disadvantage to those who've run a mile already; they'll be exhausted.'

'I and many others have been training for months to achieve a pitch of fitness.'

'I know, Alex,' said Hengist sympathetically, 'it's too bad. I felt the same when I did my Achilles tendon just before the England–France game. Run it tomorrow.'

'The sixth form are off to CCF camp.'

'Then we'll have another steeplechase next term.'

'The weather is too unreliable.'

'Who fired that pistol?' spluttered an approaching Biffo.

'Better call a stewards' enquiry,' said Emlyn gravely.

Theo and Artie were having great difficulty keeping straight faces.

'Poor Mr Fussy,' said Patience, 'he was so keen to win.'

'What's going on,' whispered Xav from the dark of the bushes.

'Obviously a terrific row,' said Paris, who'd climbed a rhododendron bush to peer out. 'Biffo's gone purple and is waving his hands. Hengist is trying not to laugh. Poppet Bruce is jumping up and down, saying this is what she hates about competitive games. Her husband's more competitive than anyone.' Paris dropped back on the ground.

'It couldn't have gone better,' said Xav in ecstasy.

'Hush, here comes Boffin Brooks on a bike, we'd better stay put.'

*   *   *

Pedalling furiously, Boffin reached the back runners on the outskirts of Wilmington village.

'Stop, stop,' he yelled, riding straight through them. 'The race is being rerun, stop.'

'Fuck off, Boff,' said Junior, 'it's not the Tour de France.'

'Get off that bike, we were told not to cheat,' called out Lando, coming out of the Dog and Duck clutching four gin and tonics.

'Everyone's got to go back and start again,' panted Boffin.

'Oh, shut up,' grumbled Junior, 'you just want Mr Fussy to win. Throw him in the ditch, Anatole.'

'You're not allowed to drink spirits,' squealed Boffin.

'It's vater, you prat,' said Anatole, chucking Boffin and his bike into the stream that ran along the street.

Five minutes later, help was at hand. Joan had jumped into her British racing green MGB, which the girls in her house had nicknamed Van Dyke, and, hooting imperiously, had overtaken the front runners in Wilmington High Street. Just below a cheering Janna, Lily and Brigadier Woodford, she turned Van Dyke sideways to block the road where it narrowed, before going into the country. The red light of her great roaring face turned everyone back.

'The school buses are on their way to transport you back to the start,' she told them.

'If I have a heart attack,' said Cosmo in outrage, 'I shall get Cherie Booth to represent me.'

*   *   *

Back at Mansion Lawn Alex Bruce was still arguing with Hengist.

'This is a Bagley tradition we must not lose, headmaster.'

'You never stop saying tradition is the enemy of progress,' snapped Hengist, who for once felt outmanoeuvred.

'Someone fired that pistol,' said Biffo furiously. 'I

am absolutely determined to get to the bottom of—'

'Kippy Musgrave,' shouted a voice in the crowd to howls of mirth.

'Who said that?' roared Biffo.

Hengist bit his lip. Emlyn, Theo and Artie, standing on the Mansion steps, were openly laughing.

Xav and Paris were in heaven.

'We did it, we fucked the steeplechase.'

They were just about to slope off into the woods and chuck the starting pistol, wiped clean of fingerprints, into a bramble bush when, to their horror, runners came sulkily shuffling back.

'It's bloody unfair, I was in the lead.'

'Dotheboys Hall! I'm going to sue the school.'

'If any masters or boys have coronaries, Alex, I'll hold you personally responsible,' said an outraged Hengist, who'd planned to slope off to Jubilee Cottage. Now he'd be presenting cups at midnight.

Pretending he needed to collect a file, he retreated to his office to ring Janna.

'Sorry, darling, I was so longing to see you, but I can't make it.'

'Probably just as well, Lily and Brigadier Woodford are downstairs getting plastered. I do miss you. But it was terribly funny.'

'Wasn't it? Robot the Bruce is not amused. They'll be pounding past your door again in a few minutes.'

*   *   *

The sun had set, peeping out under a line of dark clouds like a light left on in the next room, as the weary winners, six of them bunched together, finally hobbled through the lion gates into the home straight. A hundred yards behind them, out of eyeshot, concealed by a bend in the road, came the second batch.

Just before the latter turned into the gates, a new willowy, white-blond competitor shot out of the rhododendrons, followed by a smaller, plumper, dark companion. Not having exerted themselves all afternoon, they were fresh enough to catch up with the front runners, and the white-blond boy in a glorious burst of speed began to overtake them.

Perched on the window seat in Hengist's study, peering through the gloom, Theo caught sight of Paris and yelled for the others.

'He's leading. God, he's going to do it, come on, Paris.'

The window seat nearly collapsed as Artie, Emlyn, Hengist, Patience, Ian and Elaine joined Theo, yelling their heads off as Paris passed a panting heaving Denzil and flung his breast against the tape. Xav coming in eleventh was just in the medals.

'Exactly like *Chariots of Fire*,' sighed Dora. She got out her calculator. 'I've made two thousand pounds.'

*   *   *

The joy in Ian's face was enough. Patience was crying openly as Paris accepted the Brooks Cup from an outraged and twitching Gordon Brooks.

'What a triumph, well done, Paris,' said Hengist, shaking him by the hand.

Paris was so overwhelmed by the reception he

595

forgot to scowl at his headmaster. Boffin Brooks and Alex, who were in the second batch and just missed medals, were absolutely livid.

'Never saw Paris Alvaston during the race,' panted Alex.

'Neither did I,' said Boffin.

'It was such a muddle, I'm surprised anyone saw anyone, particularly in the dusk,' said Hengist smoothly.

'I paced myself,' Paris, playing up for the cameras, told Venturer Television. 'Long before I came to Bagley, I perfected my technique running away from the police.'

'I'm convinced it was my counselling,' Vicky was telling everyone.

Back at the Old Coach House, Ian was so delighted he opened a bottle of champagne and shared it with Patience, Dora and Paris.

Perhaps they do like me after all, thought Paris.

Later Hengist rang Janna.

'Paris won; I hope you're pleased. He was so elated he forgot he loathed me. I think we're winning, darling.'

65

As Middle Five B shuffled towards history the following morning, Milly Walton rushed up and kissed Paris.

'Well done, terrific news, you deserve it.'

'Well done,' said Primrose Duddon, blushing scarlet.

'Well done,' said Jade, smiling at him for the first time that term.

'What you talking about?'

'Go and check the noticeboard.'

'Well done, Paris,' said Tarquin Courtney, captain of rugby and of athletics, who had passed his driving test and kept a Porsche in the car park. He knows my name, thought Paris in wonder. Then he went cold. Looking up at the noticeboard, he discovered that after his triumph in the steeplechase, he'd been selected for the athletics team against Fleetley on Saturday.

'This is the one Hengist always wants to win,' confided Tarquin. 'There's training this afternoon. We can sort out whether you're best at sprint or middle distance.'

Oh shit, thought Paris, particularly as next moment Ian charged out of the bursar's office and thumped him on the back.

'Well done, old boy. Patience and I thought we'd drive over to Fleetley to cheer you on. We'll take a picnic. If the weather's foul we can always eat it in the car.'

*   *   *

'What the hell am I going to do?' Paris asked Xav five minutes later.

'Aren't they always pushing steroids outside Larks? You could take some and test positive.'

'Don't be fucking stupid.'

Wandering off down the cloisters Paris went slap into Emlyn, to whom he'd spoken very little since the beginning of term. He wasn't in Emlyn's set for history, and Theo, unable to bear the thought of Paris's beautiful straight nose being broken, had so far managed to get him out of rugby. But Paris trusted Emlyn.

'Can I have a word, sir?'

Thirty seconds later he was in the safety of Emlyn's classroom. Stalin's poster smirked down from underneath his thatch of black moustache. I'll be shunted off to the Gulag any minute, thought Paris.

'I screwed up,' he told Emlyn flatly. 'I didn't win the steeplechase. I lurked in the bushes and slid into the back of the leaders.'

'I thought as much.' Emlyn dropped four Alka-Seltzers into a glass of water. Yesterday's lunch with Hengist had run into dinner.

Emlyn then got a pile of essays on Hitler out of his briefcase and started to mark the one on the top with a yellow pen entitled Afghanistan Airlines.

Bastard, thought Paris, as Emlyn put a thick red tick halfway down the margin.

'Sit down,' snapped Emlyn. 'Theo showed me that essay you wrote on the *Aeneid*. It was very good. Shame he encouraged you to wimp out of rugby. I suppose he sees you hurling discuses or driving chariots. If you come and play for my under-fifteen side, I'll get you out of athletics.'

'How?' asked Paris sulkily.

'As Hengist still runs this school, rugby takes precedence. It'd also please Ian. He'd go berserk if he knew you'd been cheating in the steeplechase and anything's better than the total humiliation of running next Saturday.'

Emlyn had reached the end of Cosmo's essay, and wrote: 'A+. You obviously identify with the Führer.'

'OK,' said Paris.

'If you play on my team'—Emlyn grimaced as he downed half the glass of Alka-Seltzer—'you must give one hundred per cent.'

Emlyn might not have been so co-operative if he hadn't yesterday morning received a telephone call from Janna, saying she was worried about Paris and could Emlyn keep an eye on him.

'Keep an eye on him yourself,' Emlyn had told her disapprovingly. 'How many times have you seen him this term?'

'I've been frantic,' replied a flustered Janna. 'We've got Ofsted any minute, and S and C are still refusing to give me any more money.'

So Emlyn said he'd see what he could do, adding, 'Let's have dinner and catch up and I'll tell you how to bamboozle Ofsted. I'll call you.'

*   *   *

As a fine former rugger player, Ian was thrilled, particularly when Emlyn gave Paris private coaching in the basics required of an all-rounder before his first game.

599

Tackling Emlyn, Paris felt like a flea trying to topple a charging rhino. Emlyn also gave him some videos of internationals to watch with Ian, but Paris still thought it was a strange, brutal, muddy game compared with football. And he already had pierced ears, without having them bitten through.

For the first game, Paris rolled up with hair tangled and unkempt, wearing shirt and shorts still muddy from his brief run in the steeplechase. Nor did he give a hundred per cent because he was terrified of getting hurt.

'If you play hard enough, you won't realize you're hurt till afterwards,' Emlyn assured him at half-time, and once the game was finished took him aside.

'Have you got a girlfriend, Paris?'

Paris went scarlet, kicked the grass and shook his head.

'I should think not, if you go round looking that scruffy. Don't think your hair's seen a brush since the beginning of term.'

'Such a fucking awful haircut'—Paris spat on the grass—'doesn't deserve one.'

The next game, Paris rolled up with his hair brushed, boots polished, clean shorts. The snow-white collar of his sea-blue and brown striped rugby shirt emphasized his deathly pallor. He was in a foul temper and soon into fights, quite prepared to thump and knee in the groin anyone of either side who bumped into him.

Emlyn kept up a stream of reproof: 'Don't hang on to the ball, don't tackle so high, those boots are to kick balls, not heads in. Rugby's not a free-for-all, it's a team game.'

He was about to send Paris off when the boy

scooped up the ball, sauntered towards the posts, kicked a perfect drop goal and raised a middle finger at the other players.

*   *   *

That evening Emlyn called Lando and Junior over to his flat for a beer. The two boys loved the big living room, which had a huge comfortable sofa, a massive television with Sky for all the sport, shelves crammed with books on rugby and history, and a view, once the leaves fell, of General Bagley and the Lime Walk.

Pictures included a few watercolours of Wales, photographs of rugby fifteens, portraits of Emlyn's heroes: J. P. R. Williams, Gareth Edwards and Cliff Morgan; and in a corner a group photo of himself, a giant towering over giants in the Welsh rugby team. The record shelves were dominated by opera and male voice choirs. On his desk were photographs of his late father, mother and sisters, and the exquisite Oriana, who seemed more distant than his father. If he didn't see her soon, his dick would fall off.

'Which one of you would like to take on Paris Alvaston?' he asked the boys.

'How?' asked Lando.

'In a fight.'

Both boys looked startled.

'We've got to break the ice around him somehow.'

'I will,' said Lando. 'I'm pissed off with the stroppy, arrogant little git.'

*   *   *

The following afternoon was cold, grey and dank with a vicious wind. The Colts were playing to the right of Badger's Retreat, separated from other games by a thick row of conifers.

Passing the Family Tree, seeing Oriana's initials on the trunk, Emlyn was overwhelmed with longing. She hadn't written for three weeks. Was she still in Afghanistan? If he flew out at Christmas, would she be too caught up with work to find time for him? His face hardened. It was a day to take no prisoners.

Within minutes of kick-off, Paris was landing punches, spitting and swearing. Groped too vigorously in a tackle, he turned on Spotty Wilkins, throwing him to the ground, fingers round his throat: 'Keep your fucking hands off me.'

Lando and Junior pulled him off.

Emlyn blew his whistle and formed the boys into a circle.

'I see you're spoiling for a fight, Paris.'

'I've had it with those fuckers.'

'Good,' said Emlyn coolly, 'Lando is only too happy to beat the shit out of you now.'

Lando stepped into the ring, long dark eyes for once alert, massive shoulders, scrum cap and gumshield giving him an inhuman look of Frankenstein's monster, body hard as teak, four inches taller and two stone heavier than Paris.

'Come on, wimp, I'm waiting.'

'This is worse than the Pitbull Club,' hissed Paris, turning on Emlyn. 'You'll get the sack for this.'

'I doubt it,' said Junior, trying to balance the ball on his curly head. 'It's your word against ours and there are lots of trees in the way. Go on, bury him,

Lando.'

Lando took a step towards an expressionless but inwardly quaking Paris. Emlyn was also quaking inside that he'd taken such a risk.

'You can either fight Lando,' he said quietly as Paris raised two trembling fists, 'or become one of the squad, and fight for them rather than against them. You're potentially a bloody good player, you've got the build, the eye and the short-term speed. We'd all be on your side.'

Paris glanced round the group; Junior, Jack, Anatole, Lubemir, Lando, Smartie, Spotty and the rest: all impassive, watchful, much stronger and bigger than him. Then he looked at Emlyn, an implacable giant, with the big smile for once wiped off his face. The pause seemed to go on for ever. He heard a whistle from a nearby pitch and the rumble and hoot of a distant train on which he could be off searching for his mother. But she had left him. Ian and Patience were his only hope. He held a shaking hand out towards Lando.

'OK,' he muttered. 'I've behaved like a twat, I'm sorry.'

'Well done.' Emlyn clapped a huge hand on his shoulder. 'That's the hardest thing you'll ever have to do in rugby.'

*   *   *

'The lads gave him a round of applause,' Emlyn told Janna over a bottle of red in the Dog and Duck that evening. 'They also gave him a lot of ball in the second half, and he played a blinder.'

'You took a hell of a gamble,' reproved Janna. 'Poor Paris could have been beaten to a pulp. You should have been fired.'

'I know.'

'How can you justify such bully-boy tactics?'

'I pray a lot.'

Miffed she wasn't more grateful, he asked her what was the matter.

'Bloody *Gazette* ran a libellous piece today saying: "In a county of too many schools, Larks would be a suitable case for closure." '

'They're only flying kites.'

'Not with Ofsted about to finish us off.'

Janna was also shocked by the change in Emlyn. The fat jester had gone; so had the double chin. His cheeks were hollowed and new lines of suffering formed trenches round his normally laughing mouth. No longer ruddy and bloated, he looked like Ulysses the wanderer returning from an endless and scarring war.

He was wearing too-loose chinos held up by a Welsh international rugby tie, a dark blue shirt and a much darned grey sleeveless pullover which Janna guessed had belonged to his father, about whom over more glasses of red he talked with great pain.

'Like John Mortimer in *A Voyage Around my Father*—that should be a set book—I just feel lonely now he's gone, and racked by lost opportunity. Why didn't I tell him I loved him more often? I betrayed him by going to Bagley—he could never understand it; and although Dad and Oriana were in the same camp, they never really got on. He couldn't comprehend anyone who'd been brought up with every advantage being so ungrateful.'

'How's your mum?' asked Janna.

604

'Crucified, bewildered, stoical. They'd been together forty years.'

Janna let him talk. It was a pleasure to watch him and to listen. Now the spare flesh had gone, he had such a strong fine face and, after a summer back in the valleys, his lovely lilting voice seemed deeper, with the Welsh open vowels more pronounced.

Oriana, it seemed, had provided little comfort when he'd flown out to see her in the summer holidays.

'She doesn't have the same relationship with her father.'

'But Hengist adores her,' said Janna unguardedly.

Fortunately Emlyn was too preoccupied to notice.

'Maybe, but she doesn't admire what he stands for. She can't understand how sad and guilty I feel. She's too taken up with the present, devastated at the plight of the Afghans. She's got a lead to Bin Laden, and plans to infiltrate herself into some Taliban spy ring. She could easily pass for a boy.'

'Oh poor Emlyn.' Janna topped up his glass.

'Sally and Hengist'—she felt her voice thickening—'must be out of their minds with worry.'

'I'm sure. But they keep themselves busy. Hengist has been at some conference in Geneva all week. He's expected back this evening.'

Janna was just smirking inwardly because she was going to see him tomorrow, when Emlyn added,

'Why have you fallen out with Paris?'

Janna's glass stopped on the way to her mouth. Careful, she told herself, Emlyn doesn't miss things.

'He was dangerously crazy about you. I always suspected he accepted that place at Bagley as the only possible escape route. He's giving Patience and Ian a really hard time. Trashed their place a few Sundays back, and although he seems to get on with Theo, he's been arguing and swearing and spitting at other teachers.'

'He was used to arguing and swearing and spitting at Larks. I bet you played up at school.'

'I was utterly angelic,' said Emlyn piously. 'I spent my entire school career as still as still'— briefly his face broke into a smile—'outside the headmaster's office.'

Janna laughed, but her mind was racing.

'Everything Paris loved has been taken away from him,' said Emlyn, his huge hands taking Janna's. 'He lost his mother; endless schools and care homes where he made friends; teachers; foster parents: all taken away. Oaktree Court, however much he loathed it, was familiar. His life's been like living in an airport. All the love and understanding you gave him, I guess he misconstrued it. It's hard for teachers. We have to be so careful not to inspire passion in kids who have had no love, and lead them on to yet another rejection.'

Not just in kids, thought Janna, removing her hands, which felt so comfortable in his.

'Let's get legless,' said Emlyn, about to get another bottle.

Janna shook her head: 'I've got Ofsted in a fortnight. Hengist calls it "Orfsted".'

God, what a slip.

Emlyn looked at her speculatively.

'What happened on the geography field trip?'

606

Suddenly he was much too big for their corner table, his eyes boring into her.

'I went to bed with a migraine.' At his look of scepticism, she insisted, 'I did truly. I was so tired; I nodded off and missed everything. You're always nodding off,' she added defensively.

'We're not talking about me. Paris was evidently good as gold until the last night. But he's so angry now. Did you turn him down?'

'I don't have to answer these questions,' said Janna furiously.

'Course you don't, lovely, but you're so instinctively warm and tactile. Perhaps he misinterpreted the maternal nature of your affections.'

'Now Paris has got a new school, I'm sure he'll settle down and find himself a nice lass.'

*   *   *

A few days later, Dora was lurking in the main hall, hoping to bump into Paris. She knew his timetable backwards. He was so preoccupied with learning rugby with Emlyn, he hardly noticed her. Late for English, because he'd been practising drop goals, he came hurtling through the yellow lime leaves carpeting Mansion Lawn.

'Shut your eyes,' she called out.

'If it's not seeing the new moon through glass, I'm not interested. Last time I wished for an A star for my Simon Armitage essay, effing Vicky only gave me a C plus.'

'Much better than that.' Seizing Paris by the arm, joltingly aware how he'd thickened out and muscled up since term began, Dora dragged him down the cloisters. 'Now you can look.'

The board was painted in dark blue gloss, like the board outside Larks. Here the gold lettering said 'Notices'. At Larks it said: 'Head Teacher: Janna Curtis'. Oh Christ, when would it stop hurting?

'You don't seem very pleased.

'What for? I'm late for English.'

'Here, stupid.' Dora pointed to a list of names.

In Emlyn's square, clear writing, Paris read, 'France-Lynch (Capt), Waterlane, Lloyd-Foxe, Smart, Rostov . . . Alvaston.' *ALVASTON!*

He couldn't speak; he shut his eyes as warmth flowed through him. He hadn't let Ian, Theo or Hengist down. He'd been picked to play for the Colts on Saturday. Even better, it was a needle match against St Jimmy's, who'd always sneered at Larks and hated Bagley even more. As the first, second and third fifteens would also be playing, the residual resentment between maintained and independent would come bubbling to the surface.

'How d'you feel about St Jimmy's being your first fixture?' asked Dora.

'Great!' Paris punched the air. 'Set a yob to catch a yob. I've always wanted to wipe the smirk off Baldie Hyde's face.'

'Ian and Patience will be *au dessus de la lune*,' said Dora, rushing off to ring the papers.

608

66

Saturday dawned meanly with the sun skulking like a conspirator behind charcoal-grey clouds, which provided the perfect backdrop for the gold leaves tumbling steadily out of the trees. Distant Pitch Four, where the Colts were playing, was hidden by a net curtain of mist. Despite this, a glamorous photograph of Paris as Romeo, sold to the *Express* by Dora, captioned 'Scrumpet' and announcing his rugby debut and desire to bury St Jimmy's, had attracted a sprinkling of press and a largish crowd.

'Only been playing a few weeks,' crowed Ian, who was watching with Patience, Artie Deverell and Theo, who in an old Prince of Wales check coat and a trilby on the back of his bald head looked like a bookie. Artie noticed with a stab of anguish how grey, now his Tuscany tan had faded, his friend looked in the open air. But Theo was in high spirits and getting stuck into Patience's bullshots. Five other boys from his little house, other than Paris, Anatole and Smart, were playing on various sides and only two from Alex Bruce's. Boffin Brooks, officious little shit, was one of the touch judges in the Colts game.

Then Theo growled: 'Here comes Rod Hyde, hubristic as ever,' as Rod, having travelled in the first coach singing revivalist hymns with his teams, strode about self-importantly, clapping leather-gloved hands on the shoulders of his 'men'—literally. They looked twice as old and hulking as their Bagley counterparts. Rod was wearing a new black leather coat, tightly belted, to show off his manly figure, and a new big black hat under the brim of which his eyes crinkled at the prettier mothers.

'Mr Hyde who never turns back into nice Dr Jekyll,' observed Theo sourly. 'Ah, here's little Vicky Fairchild with a pretty foot in both camps,' as Vicky, seductive in a long purple coat and a black fur hat, paused to kiss first Poppet and Alex and then Rod and Sheila Hyde.

'Isn't it thrilling Paris is playing?'

'I'm sure your counselling has helped,' said Poppet eagerly.

'I do feel I'm easing his passage,' smiled Vicky.

'The ambition of every Bagley master,' murmured Artie Deverell as the Colts ran on to the field.

'Come on, Bagley,' shouted Bianca and Dora.

'Go for it, Paris,' yelled Dora's brother Dicky. 'God, he looks shit scared. So would I be. Those St Jimmy Colts will never see fifteen again. Look at their moustaches and chest hair. They should have been made to produce their passports. Brute Stevens, their captain, is reputed to have a wife and three children,' he added as, locked together, the St Jimmy's scrum sent Bagley reeling backward.

'Hengist's little laboratory rat is going to be carved up,' said Cosmo approvingly as Paris fluffed three passes and holding on to the fourth was brought crashing down by Brute Stevens.

'That was high,' muttered the crowd. The referee took no notice.

Was it coincidence or had Brute Stevens been deliberately ordered to harass Paris, never Rod's favourite pupil? For the second time as Paris leapt for the ball in the line-out, Brute rammed a thumb down the pockets of Paris's shorts, nearly pulling them off. Around the ground, binoculars rose to a score of masters' eyes.

'Come on, St Jimmy's,' yelled the caring and concerned parents—hearties in Barbours or blazers with badges on their breast pockets, their wives in peaked caps or woolly hats, cheeks purpling against the cold, working up a good hate against Bagley. How dare any school have such splendid buildings, such an excess of land, such arrogant pupils and such a cavalier headmaster, who hadn't deigned to make an appearance so they could ignore him. Even the white goal posts and the helicopter pad said H for Hengist.

Sally Brett-Taylor, in a dark blue Puffa, navy-blue and gold Hermès scarf tied under the chin, her exquisite complexion unmarred by the elements, had reached Pitch Four, and was being fractionally more gracious to Sheila Hyde than she would be to the wife of the head of a major public school.

'How good of you to come. The chaps so love a crowd. No, Joan's taken the girls' hockey team to Westonbirt; she'll be so sorry to miss you. Hengist'll be out soon. He always feels personally responsible for all four matches. Oh, come on, Bagley. Come on, Colts. Emlyn's been working so hard on them. Well out, Paris. Well done, Smartie. Come on, Junior, come on. Oh, bad luck,' as the whistle went.

Hengist, who'd been in his study with Jupiter thrashing out New Reform's law-and-order policy, which could more profitably have been applied to the Bagley Colts, arrived to find Pitch Four in an uproar, St Jimmy's leading 28–7 and Emlyn in a

611

towering rage.

'We've done all the attacking and had ninety per cent of the ball,' he told Hengist, 'but the bloody bent ref from St Jimmy's is disallowing everything. He's given six penalties against us, none against St Jimmy's. If they knew how to kick straight, the score would be double. Boffin Brooks is touch judge, and can't see a fucking thing—or chooses not to.'

Rod Hyde meanwhile was leaping up and down, bellowing on his side: 'Well played, Wayne, well done, Kevin. Oh, good tackle, Brute. Come on, St Jimmy's,' clapping his great leather-gloved hands together like a walrus.

Bagley Colts, fast losing their tempers, were dramatically down to ten men, five—Junior, Lando, Smartie, Anatole and Spotty Wilkins—having been banished to the sin bin. The rest, like uncut stallions at Windsor Horse Show, were circling the ref.

'I was not orfside,' Jack was yelling, 'and that try was good. Can't you bloody well see?'

'Sin bin,' yelled back the ref.

As the roar of the crowd merged with the whirr of a helicopter, Rod was in ecstasy. Who were the yobbos and the bad sports now? Alex Bruce was also trying not to look smug. If that blockhead Emlyn Davies had introduced a few of Bruce's boys into the Colts, things would be very different. The Colts' moods were not improved at half-time as they sucked lemons and emptied water bottles to be told all the other Bagley sides were wiping the floor.

'High tackle,' yelled Ian Cartwright early on in the second half as Brute put a beefy arm round

Paris's neck, yanking him to the ground. 'Did you see that, Hengist?'

But no one had seen anything because Mrs Walton, utterly ravishing and smothered in blond furs, had just rolled up with Randal Stancombe to watch the Colts before taking Milly and Jade to Sardinia for the weekend.

I hope she's happy, thought Hengist as, smiling, he strode down the touchline to welcome them. He was wearing a fawn coat, his hair, always curlier in damp weather, falling over the dark brown velvet collar. St Jimmy mothers, turning as he passed, had to agree reluctantly that he looked even better in the flesh.

Randal was in joshing mood. 'With all your resources and expertise, Hengist, surely the Colts should be thrashing St Jimmy's.'

'Randal!' Rod Hyde strode up, pumping Stancombe's hand.

'You're doing too damn well, Rod.'

'We've been bringing on our young players,' said Rod smugly. 'Congratulations on that takeover, must have taken a lot of time and vision.'

'What takeover?' said Hengist, wrenching his eyes away from Mrs Walton.

He ought to know, thought Randal angrily.

'Both takeovers,' he replied lightly, putting an arm round Mrs Walton. 'Ruth's about to move in with me.'

'If you walk through a head hold your storm up high,' sang Dicky, who'd been drinking vodka in the rhododendrons with Xavier.

Revved up by Emlyn at half-time, the Bagley Colts fought back, and no one fought with more guts than Paris, battered by the terrible strength of

613

the opposition. Tries from Lando and Junior, one of them converted by Lubemir, followed by a stylish drop goal from Anatole, brought the score up to 28–22. Victory was at last within Bagley's reach.

The mist was coming down again; the light fading; the other games were over.

'Come on, Paris,' howled his fan club as he scooped up the ball. Escaping from a tangle of red, blue and brown jerseys and muddy shorts, he streaked down the pitch, pale hair flying, cheers in his ears. Seeing Brute Stevens pounding in like a mad bull from the right, he jinked to the left, bounding along the touchline, burying the ball triumphantly over the line at Boffin's feet.

'Disallow that if you dare, you sad bastard,' he panted, then, raising the ball triumphantly, waved it to the crowds to roars of applause.

In the closing seconds of the game, he had put Bagley almost level. Junior's conversion would clinch it. As photographers raced to get their pictures, Northcliffe broke free, bounding towards Paris, picking up a horse chestnut leaf as a prize. Paris could see Patience wiping her eyes, Ian joyfully brandishing his shooting stick, Theo waving his bookie's hat in the air and Dora and Bianca jumping up and down.

Jack and Anatole charged out of the sin bin to ruffle Paris's hair, and clap him on the back. 'Well done, man.'

Hengist sloped off to report the triumph to Janna.

But against all this din, the whistle kept on blowing and not for the end of the match. After a long consultation with Boffin, the ref was walking in Paris's direction.

'I'm afraid the pass was forward and your foot was in touch.'

Paris's muddy face contorted in fury.

'Do you actually know the fucking rules of the game?' he yelled. 'It was not forward and I was not in touch.'

'Don't argue with the ref, you posh bastard,' yelled Brute Stevens.

All the Colts were now shouting at the ref. From all round the ground came booing. Emlyn looked on stonily but impotently.

'I have never witnessed such appalling sportsmanship,' exploded Rod Hyde.

'Come on, we've still got two minutes,' pleaded Smartie.

Once again, Bagley stormed St Jimmy's' end. But tiredness and fury made them fumble.

'Come on, Paris,' he heard Bianca Campbell-Black screaming. Then the whistle blew long and plaintive, the train moving out of the station away from him, and it was over.

Rod Hyde had not been so happy since Margaret Thatcher was booted out of Downing Street. The maintained sector were proving themselves both intellectually and physically superior to the independents. He was already writing the piece in his head for *Education Guardian*. He was so proud of his students. 'Well done, well done.

'Bad luck,' he called out jovially to Emlyn. 'Several of our best players were off from injury. If we'd had our full side, you wouldn't have stood a chance.'

'Come and have tea in the common room,' Sally said hastily to Sheila Hyde.

'We were robbed,' a sobbing Dora was telling the *Mail on Sunday*.

Paris walked back, covered from top to toe in red-brown Larkshire mud, Northcliffe beside him.

'Beautiful, isn't he,' murmured Artie to Theo. 'And, God, he's brave.'

'Paris played a very gallant game,' insisted Ian.

'He did,' agreed Biffo grudgingly. 'There's no denying a first-rate public school can straighten out the most wayward lad.'

Through the twilight, he could see Paris stealthily approaching the little group round Rod Hyde and the ref who, relishing their moment of glory, were loath to leave the pitch.

'Read the fucking rule book next time,' hissed Paris and, smashing his fist into the face of the ref, sent him crashing to the ground.

There was a horrified pause, interrupted by a burst of cheering from the Bagley Colts.

'Hit him again, he's still moving,' yelled Lando as the ambulance hurtled across the pitch.

67

Hengist loved post-mortems after games. He and Emlyn would play back videos, pinpoint achievements, discuss tactics for next week. Emlyn always saw the cause, while others watched the effect. When everyone else was cheering a try, he could tell you fifteen seconds back what moves had created it. After it was over, he could recount the whole game. He believed if you could get boys to use their brains and think, they'd be much better players and enjoy the game so much more. The boys loved Emlyn for his deep commitment, his expertise, his dedication to transmit the skills he had learnt, his extreme seriousness beneath the jokey exterior.

There was no jokiness in his face that evening as he knocked on Hengist's door.

'Oh dear,' said Hengist a minute later. Throwing a log on the fire, he took a couple of cans of beer out of the fridge.

'I hope you don't mind, I told Paris to report to me up here,' said Emlyn.

Paris climbed the stairs. His neck felt dislocated by Brute's tackles; his knees locked together; his heart battered every bruised rib. Slower and slower he climbed, mocked on all sides by framed photographs of glorious former fifteens.

Inside Hengist's study, Elaine, reclining upside down on a dark green sofa, lifted her tail. Flames dancing and crackling in the red-tiled William Morris fireplace were a cheerful contrast to the bleak faces of the two men, huge shoulders against

617

the big bay window, through which Feral had once driven a golf ball. In the distance could be seen the orange glow of Larkminster.

'Shut the door,' snapped Emlyn.

Hengist retreated to his archbishop's chair, picking up a copy of Matthew Arnold's poems, which fell open at 'Rugby Chapel'.

Coldly, sadly descends
The autumn evening [read Hengist]. The field
Strewn with its dank yellow drifts
Of withered leaves, and the elms,
Fade into dimness apace,
Silent . . .

He must get on with his biography of Thomas and Matthew Arnold. Jupiter was so demanding. Hengist wondered if he really wanted to go into politics.

Emlyn, his normally genial face like granite, paced up and down for a moment, and then let loose his thunderbolt. How dare Paris let down his side, his house and his school and behave like a hooligan on the field.

'And you've let the independent system down, behaving like a yob in front of Rod Hyde, who you know will make political capital out of the whole thing.' Emlyn mimicked Rod for a second. ' "We could have told you he'd revert to type." '

After another two minutes of the same rant Hengist, who was a kind man, felt Emlyn was being too brutal. To lighten the mood, Elaine got to her feet and started running on the spot on the window seat, ripping the red Paisley upholstery with her long claws.

618

'I really feel—' murmured Hengist.

'With respect, headmaster, don't interfere,' snarled Emlyn, then turned on Paris again. 'You realize knocking out a ref is a criminal offence. He could suffer brain damage.'

'No brain to damage.'

'Don't be bloody cheeky,' howled Emlyn, 'just get out of my sight.'

'It's not a laughing matter,' said Hengist sternly, flipping over a page, he read:

Ah, love, let us be true
To one another! for the world, which seems
To lie before us like a land of dreams . . .

It was the same poem he had marked in Janna's copy. Poor Paris, he wondered, was he still hopelessly in love with her?

'Get out,' roared Emlyn.

Elaine shot under a sofa as Paris limped towards the door, shoulders hunched, the picture of desolation. He'd been so proud of being in the team; now he'd blown it. He'd let Bianca down too; he'd heard her screaming for him. Just as his desperately trembling hand reached for the polished brass doorknob, Emlyn drained his beer can and called after him.

'I also have to thank you.' Paris froze. 'If you hadn't knocked out that ref, I'd have been forced to do it myself.'

For a second Paris scowled round at him, then he smiled, slowly, infinitely sweetly. 'Brute Stevens accused me of being a "posh bastard", so I must be making some progress,' and he was gone.

'Christ, how can anyone resist that boy,' sighed

Hengist.

*   *   *

From then on Paris began to enjoy Bagley. He played regularly for the Colts. More importantly, Theo Graham began giving him four hours' Latin and Greek coaching a week.

As Theo devoted to him that gift of teaching, that insight into another mind, that patience and ability to inspire and ignite, Paris had his first real glimpse of the enchanted world of the classics and became not altogether of this world. He lost things, he drifted in late, he forgot to eat. He was in love.

Theo was battling to finish his translation of the seven existing plays of Sophocles. Knowing Paris to be confused about his identity, he gave him *Oedipus Rex*, one of the plays he had completed, to read.

'Not only the greatest play ever written,' he told Paris at their first session in his crowded study, 'it's also all about adoption and of the dire consequences of not telling a child it's adopted.

'As an abandoned child'—what Paris loved about Theo was that he never pussyfooted around a subject—'you must wonder if every man you meet is your father, or every woman you're attracted to is your mother.'

'Perhaps that's why I fancy Bianca,' said Paris dryly, 'who's so young she couldn't possibly be my mother.'

Theo himself had reached an age when he no longer expected reciprocated love, just something to look forward to and dream about at night to distract him from the often terrible pain in his

620

back.

The shadows under Paris's eyes were the pale mauve of harebells, his eyes the grey of overcast skies. He had the straight nose and pallor of an Elgin marble, which Theo would never give back to the Greeks.

Theo now had a second goal, not just to live long enough to complete his translation of Sophocles, but also to get Paris into Cambridge.

Continued in Volume 2